EXCERPT FRO

~

"KID, I'M NOT LETTING Grace go. End of story."

I bowed my head. "Then we all die together."

Detective Allen grunted and assisted Rosen in trussing me up, much as they had done Grace. They dragged me down the hallway, past the first holding room. I saw Grace through the small window and tried to smile at her. Our eyes met for a brief moment before the cops tossed me into my own cell.

"No one's going to die on my watch," Allen said. "We'll let the courts deal with you and Grace. I'll bet you get cut a break to testify against her, even. This is all going to work itself—"

A resounding crash thundered along the front of the station.

"Why don't you go see if that's something working itself out?" I asked smugly. I was a dead man and I knew it. May as well take a cheap shot at the know-it-all cop before the end.

GRACE UNDER FIRE

FROG JONES

ESTHER JONES

Impulsive Walrus

To Sue Bolich:
For all your advice, humor, excoriating edits, unfailing friendship, and one large tree, thank you. You are sorely missed.

GRACE

I HADN'T ACTUALLY EXPECTED to be crammed into a small corner underneath Seattle's Pier 57 pedestrian bypass with a plate of Smoked Halibut & Chips in one hand and an unruly fledgling spirit in the other.

I don't dress for stealth. I wore a loose blouse and skirt in bright red and blue, plus silver bangles. I even had an electric blue head scarf over my perfectly ordinary brown hair. In hindsight, my "hiding place" only qualified because I am such a tiny person in the first place. I could smell the food in the shops just above me and hear the long row of sidewalk vendors haggling with their customers, much too close for comfort.

My original idea consisted of a quick and delicious lunch at the Salmon Cooker before heading to the Grove headquarters for a little extra research. Gotta love compound rune sets. I'd just paid and started down the pier toward the water. Today the sky shone uncharacteristically bright for late August. I loved it. Then a black-scaled bipedal Visitor about six inches tall with long pointed ears streaked past my feet to steal a potato wedge from a tame, unsuspecting seagull standing only about a foot and a half in front of

—oh, eff me.

I scooped the spirit up on reflex, shoved him under the folds of my long blue jacket and made for the nearest hiding spot I could find. Which resulted in my current predicament, awkwardly crammed under the walkway. If anyone saw me with him, I would be well and truly screwed. I didn't think anyone would mistake him for a pet. His thick-lidded blue eyes took up half his face. They held no white at all. His ears resembled large varnished bat wings. He clutched my thumb and forefinger in his little hands, already squirming to get free.

The best thing would be to banish him as quickly as possible, but I had to find out where he came from first. If I was lucky, his presence here meant a small hole had developed in the Weave somewhere nearby. If I was unlucky, someone had summoned him here and then set him loose to run amok on purpose. I hunkered down a little farther under the boardwalk, listening to a multitude of tourists' footfalls clunking above.

"Do you and yours have business here? Were you invited?" I asked it. The tiny spirit looked at me curiously, cheeped, and stared intently at the plate in my other hand. Then back at me, then at the plate. This little guy appeared too young to have developed much sentience, or possibly only possessed animalistic intelligence to begin with. "You're no help." I sighed, grimacing.

As any first grader can recite, summoning is outlawed in the U.S., deemed to be the second greatest threat to homeland security after terrorism. President Herbert Hoover recognized its existence in 1930, then turned around and immediately outlawed it. Apparently, he blamed summoning practices for the Great Depression. A lot of natural disasters can be traced back to a sloppy, vindictive, or inexperienced summoner, but as far as I know the stock market crash isn't ours. Now, if he'd alleged that a summoner caused the Great Mississippi Flood of 1927—that's a whole other story.

Really, I suppose it doesn't matter which disaster got us outlawed, but it's always rubbed me the wrong way that the event used to outlaw our very existence is one time we *didn't* do anything at all.

Yep, don't mind me. Here I am, out in public, lots of curious tourists everywhere, and a baby Visitor in my lap. Perfect.

Even assuming I could get out of this without any kind of mishap, I would still get an earful back at Grove headquarters. This guy was small and weak enough—hell, he was non-verbal—that he couldn't really get up to any serious mischief, but your average citizen wouldn't know that. The little twerp could easily start a new tide of anti-summoner witch hunts if he kept running around out here. Plus, like babies anywhere, eventually there would be something bigger and probably pretty pissed off coming to find him.

Fortunately, since I had been on my way to do research at the Grove, I had thrown some extra summoning supplies into the bottom of my cavernous shoulder bag. I usually don't leave the house without a few basics, but it *is* essentially like walking around with a bag full of drug paraphernalia. I try not to have anything on me that would automatically get me detained by the police.

I put my plate down (out of the little guy's reach, to his total chagrin) and rummaged until I came up with a book about the size of a paperback novel, with a blank, nondescript black cover. At first glance, most normal people assume you are carrying around a pocket-Bible or a journal. The latter is a little closer to the truth; the little book serves both as a kind of passport and summoner ID in the Grove system. It essentially identified me, and my rank, to other summoners, and gave me the basic knowledge to deal with random visitors like this one. Specifically, it had an index of known Visitors, their home Weaves, and any relevant pacts. Since I didn't summon this scamp to begin with, I needed to look up the runes to his home Weave in order to send him home without hurting him. I could banish him outright in a jiffy, but it would hurt the little guy unnecessarily and I'd feel like a jackass. I doubted he'd come here on purpose. I fumbled through the book with my free hand while keeping a firm grip on my "little problem."

"Concentrate," I muttered to myself. Finally, I had the book open to what had to be the correct page indicating the runes to the little guy's home Weave. I showed it the page. "See! This is what you'll look like when you're older. At some point you *will* grow into those ears. Lucky you."

This summons would be tricky. Given his extreme youth, this spirit couldn't give me a name to ground the summoning on. He looked barely hatched. I'd have to try to tie him back to his own realm and then switch him with something from there.

Fortunately, the Visitor's pact with his realm allowed for an exchange of earth. Now the Sense we summoners use can't create new matter or energy. It just brings something from point A to point B. Which means if I summoned sand from halfway across the world, or even just across the city, I'd better be very sure about the runes I had just used to bring it to me. Otherwise I could end up accidentally causing a catastrophe even bigger than whatever I'd tried to prevent. Like, say, accidentally breaching a flood control for starters. Not that I'm admitting to anything; I'm only thirty-two years old. But still, you get my point.

If this little guy had just slipped through a hole in the Weave he might have caused an imbalance already, which would mean that pushing him back through by force might cause a bigger tear. Of course, so would mommy-dearest forcing her way through to find him. I didn't like my odds for getting caught by the Feds if I tried to smuggle him back to Grove headquarters either. And I wasn't keen on what would happen after that—life in prison as a drugged vegetable. Minimum.

Really, the whole anti-summoner law is just ridiculous. If every summoner in the world suddenly stopped using their talent all at once, there'd be a lot *more* things going bump in the night, not less.

Besides, it's not like anyone *chooses* to be a summoner. Either people are born with the innate ability to Sense—the ability to manipulate matter and energy, and through it the world around them —or they aren't. Now, the Sense by itself isn't very practical. Me, I only Sense things that are so close I'm almost touching them. That's where the blood and futhark runes come in. Which, given people's general squeamishness about blood, probably doesn't endear us to the world at large, either. Blood, any blood, acts as a medium for the Sense, allowing it to extend through the runes beyond the summoner's normal range. The runes give the Sense a target, or a roadmap about the summons' intended effect. The more complex the rune phrase, the more sophisticated the summons. All rune-based summons have to include a source, a destination, and an intended effect. The runes used to accomplish that depend on what the summoner is up to.

I blew a few errant tendrils of hair from my eyes, squeezed them shut, and tried to consider my options.

The little spirit suddenly started emitting high-pitched cheeps, struggling in my grasp. "Stop that," I snapped. "I'll get you back home as quickly as possible, but you need to stay quiet or we'll be in a world of hurt." I started to give him a gentle squeeze to indicate my displeasure, but a series of gloating cheeps from down by my left foot interrupted me. With a feeling of inevitability, I slowly pivoted to look. Sure enough, three more little spirit ankle biters, identical to the first, were feasting on my plate of halibut and chips. They looked at the little guy trapped in my fist with glee while they stuffed their faces as fast as their little hands would move. I could just hear the undertone of playground taunting. I swear one of them even licked his fingers and did a little swagger. My little guy gave one last aggrieved cheep and fixed a pouting glare on me that clearly communicated he considered this all my fault. What a day.

So now there were four little Visitors. I made an educated guess that it meant there were even more out there right now, running blithely around the waterfront stuffing their tiny faces. To do any good, I needed to use a summoning that cast a mystical net for all spirits of this type, caught them, sent them back to their own Weave, and accounted for any original imbalance. If I could do that, the Grove could send out a team to look for the tear this evening, and keep anything else from coming through until it could be mended. The summoning would have an auto-leveling system in case there wasn't an imbalance. Of course, without an imbalance the most likely explanation involved someone setting a mess of baby spirits loose in downtown Seattle for some unfathomable reason. Not a good sign.

No problem. This summoning was a piece of cake. A five-tier, alcoholic, mousse-filled, fondant frosted monstrosity of a cake. I drew in a deep breath and silently said a quick prayer that no tourists would take a wrong turn right this moment and discover my hiding place. Fortunately, these guys' weakness showed easily because it matched my own. They couldn't say no to delicious food.

I set my original offender down in the middle of the plate. All four of them were perfectly happy to sit there and chow down while I cut my finger. Using my blood, I drew the runes in a circle around them indicating that I wanted to summon all creatures matching these four from a—crap—ten-mile radius in any direction into the circle. With that done, I started on the second set of compound runes, which would trigger the next phase of the summoning after all the spirits had been summoned into the circle.

I could exchange earth of equal mass for each spirit to preserve balance and avoid further damage to the Weave, so that part came easily, but the potential of a prior hole and imbalance concerned me. I got down to some serious summoning calculus.

The farther away or the larger the object summoned, the more oomph your Sense has to exert to bring it back. You can mitigate how much juice you need with really complex and specific rune formations, which tends to be my favorite method of operation. I think of summoning as something akin to mathematical equations or chemical formulae. I put rune elements together that represent a specific solution or solid. My Sense doesn't carry much oomph, and I've studied my ass off to make up for it. I probably have the most extensive knowledge of rune combos of anyone in the Grove. Even if my Sense does fall sadly short of the norm.

This summoning would flow out, and for each spirit, if it found an imbalance, it would mend and strengthen the Weave. If I found any giant holes that couldn't be fixed immediately, I'd need to call for backup anyway, so I'd deal with that eventuality later.

To my great embarrassment, more than one person has called me a rune-prodigy for how quickly I appear to summon under pressure. What those people saw actually resulted from years and years of intense study. I've learned a multitude of possible rune combinations by heart. That perception also has help from the magnetic rune board I strap to my right arm. The runes are pre-drawn and raised from the tile so I can tell them by touch. I can usually line up the runes for all but the most complex summons in the space between breaths. Then I power them with blood and stretch my Sense through them like any other summoner. I don't know why no one else has thought of having a board like me. Or maybe they have, and it just doesn't come up. I didn't have the board today, since I'd planned on a day at the office. It's all a much more stressful and slow process when you need to draw each rune perfectly by hand.

I finished up my third tier of compound runes and focused my Sense to power the summons.

For a fraction of a second the ring filled as full as a Tokyo subway with little spirits all cheeping at me reproachfully, and then they all vanished, replaced by a pile of rocks about four feet tall in a rough pyramid in front of me. A few rolled down from the top of the pile as it settled. Well, that didn't bode well. If a small hole in the Weave existed, I couldn't feel it. So how the hell had all those little spirits gotten in?

I risked one last cleanup summoning to send all those rocks out to the bottom of the bay. Then I dusted my hands off and headed back to headquarters. Somehow I just didn't feel like eating fish anymore.

As I surfaced into the general throng, a familiar face ran up and sidled in next to me. She had blue eyes, red hair, and a temper to match. She was also the closest thing I had to a friend at the Grove headquarters.

"Hi, Amy," I said. "I have to get over to the office. It's been a hell of a day so far."

"If you know you have to get over to the office, where have you been? They've been looking for you all day. Since we were planning some research this afternoon, I thought I'd come out and see if you were lounging around the waterfront before heading in. Which you were!" she finished accusingly.

"Wait, what? The office is already looking for me? Those guys haven't been running around all day, have they? I'm pretty sure I took care of all of them, although we might need a cleanup team just to double-check."

She squinted at me suspiciously. "I seriously hope you didn't just call the Grove officials 'those guys' and act like you have this all under control. I really hate that they're sending you. No matter how good your ranking is, this is just stupid."

"Um, I think we have a miscommunication here. Let's start over. Why is the Grove looking for me?"

Amy opened her eyes wide and stared at me. "You really don't know?"

I shook my head. Her forehead wrinkled. Her lips turned down in a troubled frown. "I probably should let someone else tell you this, but it's not fair if you just walk in there without knowing, either. Rumor is, the Spokane Grove has some serious problems. The council is being annoyingly close-lipped about it, but it sounds like something targeted and took out a whole bunch of summoners, even the very powerful ones. Several people have been asked to take in and provide housing for the folks who brought the news—and they're barely more than kids. Probably just finished their apprenticeships."

My feet just decided to stop moving. "Are you sure? Do they know what did it?"

"No. And..."

"And?" I prompted impatiently.

"They've transferred you there."

Yep. Apparently Aisle 14 needed cleanup, and someone had just shoved the mop in my direction. It was turning out to be a bloody perfect day.

THE GROVE SECRETARY looked like someone had been kicking her favorite puppy all day. Her face lit up with relief when she saw me, as if I was just the person to save little Fido. She also buzzed me right through to the inner offices, which is never a good sign. I took it as a sure indication the director was already waiting, and not very happy about it. It didn't help my queasy stomach that the director's office served as the principal's office for the Grove—the only times you got called down were for kudos or smackin's.

I felt pretty sure they hadn't called me down to get a gold star.

I guessed someone had thrown me under a bus to save themselves. I wanted to get that person an I-really-loathe-you present. Something in line with ex-lax-laced brownies or a poison ivy plant. You know, something that just spoke to my appreciation.

It's not like I could avoid walking in there, either. The Groves were established precisely because the laws against summoning are so harsh—and so are punishments for acting outside the Grove rules. All summoners must register and report to their local Grove to pass evaluation. We are a pretty tight-knit bunch; we keep to ourselves and keep ourselves under control. The Grove Councils from different cities work together to keep summoner-caused accidents and vigilante summoners under tight rein.

My Grove headquarters (at least the part that isn't the library) is in a posh old hotel in downtown Seattle with the plush carpets your feet just sink into. Today it felt like I was walking through a swamp. I paused outside the polished mahogany door with its brass name plate that read, "Phineas Brandiole, Arboretum Director" to take a deep breath and compose my thoughts. As I raised my hand to knock, the door swung open, and I had to dodge to the side to keep from getting hit right between the eyes.

"You're late," a voice boomed inside.

I poked my head in the door and found the room full of people. Not only the director, but all the senior Grove officials. Perfect. I made my feet follow my head into the room, much as I'd have preferred not to.

"My apologies," I said. "I stepped out early this morning, and didn't realize you were trying to contact me. Nice to see you all. And, um, how can I help you?"

Director Brandiole motioned me to shut the door and take a seat in the one open chair. It was a red leather monstrosity with potted palms on either side, which made me feel even more like a sacrificial victim. I sat myself down gingerly and waited for someone to tell me exactly what was going on. The other three people in the room were all Grove bigwigs. The small office could barely hold all four of the people crammed in it; five if I included myself.

Mr. Brandiole cleared his throat and peered around the cramped room before turning to me. "You've probably heard we received news of grave import from our sister Grove in Spokane." He paused, waiting for confirmation.

"I heard rumors, but they were non-specific as to the exact nature of the news."

"Well, the official information isn't as complete as we would wish, either. What we know is this: as of twenty-four hours ago, something invaded Grove headquarters, killing all of the Spokane Grove council and nearly all their registered summoners during an all-Grove meeting." He waited for me to absorb the news, and I admit it, I was pole-axed. Not many things can actually take out a high-ranking summoner, let alone a whole group of them.

Annalisa Miller, Senior Grove historian, resumed the briefing. She wore a no-nonsense black pant suit that matched her plain features and tidy hair. "Currently there are one or two Spokane summoners who are only reported missing, as no body could be found, but it's likely they have also been killed. The few summoners who are confirmed living were either not present when the attack occurred, or were incredibly low-ranking. Only one or two are any better than neophytes—"

Unable to wait any longer, Mr. Brandiole interrupted. "The Grove Cooperative Council has asked that we send immediate emergency aid to the Spokane Grove headquarters to evaluate and eliminate any current threats." He paused and fixed me with a glower that made me want to squirm, but didn't seem to want to proceed.

"So where do I come into all this? Surely this is something that requires only the best of our summoners. Not to belittle myself, but I'm still firmly in the middle of the pack." I asked the question to make them spell it out, since I already had a nasty suspicion where this was headed. I was on the away team, and they were trying to pick out the folks who would be standing in front wearing a red shirt.

This time a thin balding man I vaguely recognized as the Grove Operations Coordinator spoke up. I scrambled to remember his name: something like Richard or Rickard? Anyway, his family name was Dewing.

"You may have noticed over the last few days we've had an increase in suspicious visitor activity in the Seattle area. There's been a lot of pressure on our Weave, which requires us to send a lot more summoners out for maintenance and cleanup just to keep the status quo."

"Now that you mention it, I did come across a bunch of mysterious little spirit hatchlings running loose down by the waterfront on the way in. I think I took care of them, but I'd recommend we send out a sweep-up team to check."

"You illustrate my point excellently, then. Incidents just like that are happening with troubling frequency, and while we're trying to pinpoint the cause of the instability, most of our manpower is already out repelling threats to Seattle. I can't pull a full team off any of the tasks they're currently assigned to."

Mr. Dewing cleared his throat. For the first time in his speech he came off as a little awkward. I took that to mean I wouldn't like what he said next.

"Our council has decided we must grant the Cooperative Council's request, but it's unlikely a large group would be effective at this point. Also, with the repeated Visitor incursions within city limits in the last few weeks, we have been advised against removing any of our current active teams from Seattle. In response to the concerns of all involved, we've selected you as our representative to go to Spokane and investigate the situation before we commit more resources."

That was *not* the explanation I'd expected. What about *my* concerns?

"Wait, hold on here. Let me make sure I understand what you're saying. You're sending me—*just* me—to fight something that has already taken out a whole Grove council with all its senior members present, and burned it all the way down so only the apprentices are left? No offense, but that sounds like a horrible idea."

Mr. Brandiole shifted in his chair and patted his large stomach. "You have been recommended to the council as someone who has a head on her shoulders and an adequate level of power," he intoned in that ponderous voice.

I noticed he didn't actually say I had "a *good* head on my shoulders" like you might expect, but I decided to give him the benefit of the doubt. My voice deserted me. I didn't *think* I acted like someone who loved to go on suicide missions. I thought of myself as more of a bookish type.

Ms. Miller apparently read my expression, and started back in more gently. "Assuming the situation is as described, anyone we send will be under intense scrutiny by the police as well as in a potentially dangerous environment. You have demonstrated in the past a very good mind for improvising. While the council has decided we politically cannot afford to decline the Spokane Grove's request for aid, we do not wish to put our members' lives in danger needlessly. Nor can we send someone who is already in a leadership role in this Grove, as the stakes are too high." She sugarcoated it pretty well, but Mr. Brandiole interrupted her again.

"We chose you because you are least likely to attract government attention, while still having the most summoning experience," he said bluntly.

You suck a little less than all the other people we considered, I translated silently. This guy didn't get the benefit of the doubt anymore, even if he did run the whole show. He was trying to get me killed!

"Assuming I take this suicide mission," I said just as bluntly, "what are you expecting one mid-range summoner to do? I'm trying to believe that you wouldn't send someone into a death trap just to appease your political obligations, but help me out here."

The whole room looked like they would like to strangle me for calling them on their bullshit. Why can't politicians anywhere just be on the up-and-up?

Little Ms. Miller threw up her hand in a calming gesture. "Your role will be to get to Spokane, assess the situation and submit a report to the council, who will then decide if any further action will be taken."

"If you accept the transfer, we expect you to put your affairs in order and leave for Spokane by tomorrow." Director Brandiole again. I decided I hated him, and if I lived through this, I'd move back to Kentucky. Also known as Moore family home territory. Go to the scene of a massacre with the perpetrator possibly still on the scene, and just...make a report. Yeah, right. Like anyone expected it to be that easy.

Mr. Brandiole, the rat-fink director, paused again as if expecting me to say something. I honestly couldn't think of anything which wouldn't literally send all the bridges in the vicinity up in smoke. An expression flashed over his face, barely more than a muscle tic, and I wondered if he could really be comfortable with telling someone they were expendable to their face. I hoped he had bad dreams tonight. I mean, what did he expect me to say?

"Yeah, I got this. No problem guys, easy peasy." No one could have been more shocked than me when those words actually came out of my mouth. There was still time to backpedal—I waited hopefully for the good and bad angels to pop up on my shoulders and tell me the right thing to do, but nothing happened.

My mouth didn't open itself back up to recant. I guessed that meant I would try to report on whatever big bad took out an entire Grove—while keeping out of the cops' way—and oh yeah, keeping anything else from out of town from popping through Spokane's Weave for a while. That shouldn't be too hard for one gal to do by herself, right?

Now that I'd agreed, the director seemed almost gleeful. Like I'd already solved some big problem for him, which from his view maybe I had.

Ms. Miller broke the awkward silence. "Once you send your first report, we will be better able to prioritize which areas are most in need of aid and reallocate summoners as needed."

That is, if you live long enough to report, I added for her pessimistically.

Well, if they were going to feed me to the wolves, I wanted to make sure I had all the artillery possible. "Fine. I've said I'll do it. I'll go and put my ass on the line for the Grove, but I have a list of tools I expect the Grove to provide me in return. Otherwise, no dice."

Total bluff; I'd still go, but I needed to see if I could get some concessions out of them to improve my odds of survival. Access to the heavy weapons might be useful.

Director Brandiole assessed me for a moment. "Understood. Leave your list with the secretary. We'll make sure you have it before you leave in the morning."

"Good enough." I stood up without waiting for other instructions and headed for the door. I stopped before exiting. "Catch you on the flip side." In hindsight, probably an ill-omened quote, but what can you do?

Oh, well. It's not like any of those fuddy-duddys would have watched that movie anyway.

ROBERT

THIS IS NOT the way these things are supposed to happen.

I mean, c'mon. Anyone who's ever seen any kind of movie *knows* the way romance is *supposed* to work. Nerdy-but-honest Boy meets popular-yet-unfulfilled Girl. Girl scorns Boy, even though she's secretly attracted to him, because to accept him she'd have to sacrifice some shallow edifice she clings to as an exterior symbol of her self-worth. Boy does some dramatic gesture (this can be anything from a complicated romantic gimmick to saving the world from killer robots, depending on the genre we're talking about). Girl finally accepts Boy as worth more than his appearance and allows herself to fall in love with him. Boy and Girl kiss. Music swells. Credits roll.

And that's it, really. Once Boy gets Girl, it's a happily-ever-after and we're done.

Wait...before you just stop listening to me, I'm not crazy. I know that movies are made by Hollywood big shots to make us feel good about ourselves. I get that the above story has been crafted over generations' worth of cinema, because there are more unpopular people in the world than popular people, and we like to identify with our hero (thereby spending cash on the movie). I get that the real world is different.

Hell, it's not like I went blind for years' worth of high school. I saw people all around me lighting themselves on fire to get the attention of their object of desire. This whole hormone thing was potent and I knew it; I'd seen people turn on friends they'd known for years in favor of their crush. I'd seen the smile, heard the giggles, taken passing note of the cheesy flowers and boxes of candy and cards. And I'd seen the tears, the heartbreak, even the overblown suicide threats that you were *almost* sure she wouldn't carry through.

Honestly, the whole thing had kind of nauseated me. I existed low enough on the social totem pole that I just lived with the assumption that all girls found me repulsive. Oh, sure, I'd go watch the boy-meets-girl movie and fantasize about being The Boy in all his awkward heroism, but deep down I knew that those fantasies were on roughly the same level as the fantasies I had when I got into my foster father's porn stash.

It's just that...it's just...for just a moment, it wasn't. It became real. I had it. I had the storybook 1980s-style cheesy romance.

I'm doing this out of order. I still get all emotional thinking about this. With both my parents dead since I turned thirteen, I'd been bounced around from foster home to foster home. Just the barest taste of someone giving a damn about Robert Lorents still throws me for a loop. I'll try to compose myself, and start at the beginning.

JEANELLE HARRIS WAS the classic popular-yet-unfulfilled Girl. She led the cheerleading squad, and she ran in "that" clique, the one everyone stood to the sides of the hallway for. Being a teenage boy, what I knew of Jeanelle involved more about her form than her substance. She was more than I could ever try talking to, but I knew her legs were long, soft, and unblemished. I would never have attempted to greet her in the hallways, but I knew her eyes were that brilliant color green that traps you inside and doesn't let go. She was...perfect, physically. Her flat stomach, her rounded, firm breasts, and her flowing sandy-blonde hair embodied everything that every boy my age ever thought about.

She was out of my league, and I knew it. I didn't try for her; I would never have had the nerve.

I did, however, have to speak to her. One of the oddities of high school is the amount of communication that has to occur between students in different activities.

I led the life of a band geek—certified and hardcore. My pimpled face never smiled more than when my lips were wrapped around the mouthpiece of my saxophone. Being a part of the band let me be good at something, and put me with a group of people who appreciated it. It wasn't as cool or glamorous as being a basketball star, but it was something, and I needed that.

Of course, pep band duties came hand-in-hand with being a band geek. To me, a high school basketball game was less about the sporting activity and more about a public performance. We played the same boring show every game, with "Mony Mony" and "Give Me Some Lovin' " blending into the theme song from *Magnum P.I.* and other various, cheap, peppy pieces that any freshman with a trumpet could blast out. Even so, we were still performing. In public. It forced people to acknowledge I existed, and that for a moment even my existence had some form of meaning. I think every teenager needs that. Besides, sometimes we could trot out our better stuff during halftime.

By my junior year, I had all the songs memorized. This is, of course, why I was the perfect patsy to be fingered when the time came for the band to coordinate with the cheerleaders on dance routines. As soon as the season started, our director appointed me the liaison, and I found myself alone in a classroom with Jeanelle, the cheerleader appointed to the same task.

At first we were all business. Jeanelle surprised me; she'd been doing her homework, in her own way. She'd been watching the band perform and checking out which songs had been the most crowd-pleasing. She wanted the cheerleaders to dance to the songs that the crowd liked the most. Actually, she kind of impressed me with that; it was a reasonable step. The problem was with the conclusions she drew. Looking pretty and dancing she could do; knowing music she could not.

"The crowd loves it when you guys do 'Moondance,' but it's too slow. Do a dance version of that song. Get rid of that slow beat and we've got a winner." She addressed me with all the haughtiness of a queen speaking to the boy who cleans the chamber pot.

"What? I thought I was here to talk to you about our playlist."

"You are. I want to add a faster 'Moondance' to the playlist." This was a command.

"A...faster 'Moondance.'" I was still in shock. I had admired this girl from afar for years now, and I had simply taken her perfection as an article of faith. What she so high-handedly told me to do, though, went against every band geek instinct I had finely honed from junior high on. In that moment, my illusions began to slip.

"Yeah, you know. Get rid of that slow beat, give it more of a pop rock feel, straighten the melody out a little bit..."

For those of you who have never heard Van Morrison's 'Moondance,' I suggest you give it a listen sometime. Once you do, you will know that what this angelic person before me proposed was *an abomination.*

"Not going to happen. Next?" I said it in my speaking-to-freshman-saxophone voice, that calm, cold voice of sure authority you *never* pull out in front of the beautiful cheerleader. Her eyes flew wide with shock. I had shot down her imperious commands without even thinking about what I'd done. I'm sure my face betrayed my shock almost as much as hers did.

"I'm here from the cheerleading squad, and we're supposed to work *together* on this." Her voice seethed with wounded pride. "You can't just decide something's a bad idea all on your own like that. 'Moondance' is your most popular song, and we need to dance to it. You can't just say 'no' and leave it at that."

I had crossed a line and we both knew it. I could have tried to persuade her earlier, tried to coax her away from her *hideous* idea and let her believe all the ideas "we" came up with were hers, so she could take pride in how well it turned out and in what an obedient little servant boy I had been. That was S.O.P. when dealing with this sort of thing: concede the field to the popular and hope that you could influence the direction a bit. I initiated a direct challenge to her authority on our totem pole, and in doing so I crossed the proverbial Rubicon. The only move I had left was boldness. I was cornered. So I did what any cornered beast does.

"And why do you think that the crowd likes 'Moondance' so much? Did you even stop to think about it? It's not like the song was one of the great icons of the early Seventies, or like anyone these days *cares* about a song from the early Seventies. You think any of these people go home, crack out the vinyl, and put them on some Van Morrison? Fuck no, they don't. So why do you think that song turns heads at a high school basketball game? It's *because* of the swing feel. We spend ninety-five percent of our time at a basketball game blasting fast on some pop-rock-dance piece. That's what's expected. People hear fast pop-rock-dance at a game and it's like..."

I hunted for an analogy. "You have a noisy fridge at home? My foster parents do. Thing is always making this loud, low-pitched hum. I don't notice it anymore because it's always *there*, you know? Same thing with fast-driving music at a game. It's always *there*. When the band shifts into a swing beat, though, and we take up 'Moondance,' the crowd notices because it's *different*. We take that beat away from it, then it's nothing the crowd cares about. No. We're not doing it. We're not going to water down our best song just so you and a couple of other girls can go dance to it. If you want a dance-pop song, we've got a whole list, but changing 'Moondance' to dance-pop isn't going to happen."

My face felt flushed. I was breathing hard as though I'd torn through the whole rant without taking a breath. By the end, my voice had risen almost to a yell. I knew this was it; my life as a teenager ended here. I had challenged one of the great pillars of our high school society. The tension thickened the air. The only thing I had going for me—a small thing, really—was that I was right about this. Jeanelle went quiet, staring at me with an unreadable expression.

I took a deep breath, and then exhaled. "Next," I said, struggling to keep that same authority in my voice.

She still didn't respond. Her face was inscrutable. It wasn't anger; I had expected anger. I had expected her to scream back, to make the thing a yelling match. Instead, she sat there staring into space. A couple of years later (or, more likely, thirty seconds, but perspective on time is a tricky thing in these situations), Jeanelle leveled those green eyes at mine and said, "Ok. That makes sense. So how do we use it?"

Not, I repeat, *not* the response I expected. Her voice held level, steady. The imperious tones were gone, replaced with a cold professionalism. It was progress.

"Umm...what do you mean?" I trod new territory here.

"Well, you said the crowd likes different stuff. I get it. But we need fast if we're going to do a dance routine to it. So how do we get both?"

She sounded like she wanted to have an actual discussion about this. She was trying to work as a team instead of issuing commands as any other cheerleader would do (based on the history of cheerleader-pep band relations).

It felt a little like blasphemy, but I didn't know how to act other than to, you know, go with it.

"Well, we can't slow down everything else. We have to do the fast peppy stuff for the teams. 'Moondance' only comes out at halftime when the players are in the locker rooms and we're not trying to pump them up."

"Right. I get that much. So we have to find a song different enough from your playlist, but fast enough to dance to."

"Fast enough to..."

An idea dawned. It was crazy; it had been forbidden by our band director for being "just not the kind of music that people wanted at a game." It wasn't pep band at all, but maybe...

"Follow me," I said, excitement beginning to pop through my head. "I think I have an idea."

~

THE BAND ROOM WAS EMPTY. I guided Jeanelle to a seat in the front row and went to our stack of demo CDs. I dug through the pep band stuff on top until I reached the gold below.

"You know that the pep band is the jazz band, right?"

"It is?" she asked with what sounded like genuine curiosity. "We have a jazz band?"

I rolled my eyes. I noted to myself that eye-rolling was a sign I was starting to become comfortable talking to this icon of our society. "Yes, we have a jazz band. See the trophy case? That's us. Same group, at least for basketball. Football, you want more volume; it's out of doors. Indoors, you want precision; the reverb from the gym walls will provide the volume." I found the CD I was looking for: "Giant Steps" by the Woody Herman Orchestra.

"We're not allowed to play our jazz band music at games," I said. "Ms. Erstwick thinks that the students wouldn't appreciate it because it's not pop. We can do 'Moondance' because it's Van Morrison, and we can pass it off as rock to the unsuspecting, but it's really a lounge jazz song."

"If you're not allowed to perform it at the game, why are we talking about it?"

I flashed her a smile. "Because if the *cheerleaders* request it, then Ms. Erstwick might be forced to give up the ghost."

She smiled back at this acknowledgment of her power.

And right there my young heart skipped a beat. Those eyes, those lips; she smiled because of me, and the beauty of it hit me as surely as a two-by-four to the face. I turned away quickly so she wouldn't see me blush and fumbled with the CD case.

"We need fast enough to dance to, but not dance-pop, right?" I asked as I slipped Woody's CD into the player. "Well, what if I went *faster* than dance-pop instead of slower? We can't take the speed down, but—"

The opening chords of "La Fiesta" began, a fast Latin jazz number that had won our rhythm section the "Outstanding Section" award at the regional Jazz Festival. Jeanelle's eyes went wide as she listened to the full big band kick in, a wall of sound moving twice the speed of any two-bit hack pep band arrangements. It wasn't built for a pep band; the precision and speed it took went far beyond what the arrangers for pep band contemplated.

The song played, all five minutes of it, with both of us just listening to it. My fingers twitched as though gripping my sax, an automated response to the music I had trained long, long hours to master. As the final chord punched the air, her round breasts heaved with her quickened breathing.

"You guys can play *that?*" she asked, her voice breaking ever so slightly with the excitement that had been building throughout the song.

"Well, we'll swap in our electric keyboard instead of the old-school Fender Rhodes for pep band purposes, but other than that, yes. The question is: Can you guys dance to it?"

Half her mouth curled up in the arrogant smile of a professional accepting a challenge. Our eyes locked, and in that moment we changed high school, ever so slightly.

I WAS right about Ms. Erstwick, really. The band had nagged her to use our good music during games, but she had stuck to tradition. She seemed pleased at how I'd end-run her stubbornness, and it struck me that maybe she really wanted to show off, too, and maybe there were people up the food chain from her, people who had taken the word of the holy cheerleaders over the band director's.

That was all faculty politics, though, and it didn't matter as far as I was concerned. We were playing "La Fiesta" at a game. Nothing else really mattered to me.

The resulting performance was spectacular. Usually cheerleaders dancing is pretty much just cheerleaders dancing; they fade into the background of a game as much as dance-pop, but "La Fiesta" drew a standing ovation from a crowd that, by rights, should have been at the concession stand refilling on soda, popcorn, and red ropes. As she stood there, her breasts rising and falling with the breath of her exertion, Jeanelle looked up at me standing in the bleachers with my instrument on my neck, and the smiles we gave each other sent a chill down my back and into...well, into other parts.

We collaborated several more times. Rarely does a pep band and a cheerleading squad get along, but in Jeanelle and I the feuding groups had found effective diplomats. I can't say that we became friends; all our discussions were strictly professional, but we did discard the remnants of the social hierarchy. We didn't know anything about our respective personal lives. We didn't acknowledge each other in the halls. But when we were working we respected each other, and it was effective for both of us.

IN MARCH, as we prepared for the State Tournament, Jeanelle came into the band room with tears running down her cheeks. I was not sure how to play this one. I knew nothing about her, really. But she looked to be in no shape to get any work done, and I was the only person in the room. I had to say something.

"Hey...um, you okay?" This was, at its root, a stupid question. She did not look okay at all. But it provided her the opportunity to pull herself together and lie to me. If she'd just told me yes, asked for a minute, shrugged me off...

"No...I jus...it's..." She could barely talk between her choking sobs. I felt at a loss; I didn't think anything *could* do this to her.

She gasped for breath and managed to choke out, "Duane dumped me."

Duane...who was Dua—oh, right. "Basketball Duane?" She choked up again. "Y-y-yes."

Duane Newman was the tall starting center of the basketball team. A junior like us, he rose to Varsity in the middle of his freshman year and he'd been starting since sophomore. He was a specimen of physical perfection. Of course he dated Jeanelle.

"He—he wanted to go out with some bitch from Central. Cindy. He's...oh God—he's been cheating on me ever since Winter Break." I felt bad for her and I wanted to help. Honestly, when a gorgeous girl breaks down like this in front of any teenage boy, the reaction is going to be similar.

"What can I do to help?" I asked, knowing there was nothing; I couldn't stop heartbreak, but I still wanted to do something to ease the pain. She shook her head as she sobbed, then she threw her arms around my neck and buried her face into my shoulder to cry. I didn't know what else to do, so I slowly wrapped my arms around her waist, shifted my hips so she wouldn't feel my awkwardly timed erection, and held her as she cried. As she composed herself, she raised her face to look at mine, and the hormones took over. I leaned down and gently pressed my lips to hers. Her hand moved up from my neck to hold the back of my head; her body melded toward mine.

ROLL CREDITS, right? Nerdy guy gets cheerleader. Happily ever after. See what I mean? It had all the makings of a Hollywood romance. Granted, more of a teenage romantic comedy than my preferred sci-fi/fantasy genres, but still. It fit the story that we are told since birth. It was perfect.

Yeah...

Well, it shared some characteristics, okay? I chose to overlook the differences. Her switch to me from Duane had been very sudden. The words *desperate* and *rebound* followed in our wake. I chose not to listen to them, and she at least did a very good job pretending to ignore it as well.

The rest of the year, and the summer, went by, predictable and wonderful. Stephen King once wrote that love is boring, and he was right; I don't need to tell you about all the secret meetings beneath stairwells or in the back seats of the late-eighties Volvo my trustee had allowed me to purchase as my first car. Alone, they're not important. As a whole, we were two hormone-filled teens doing what hormone-filled teens do best.

I fell in love. I threw myself into it completely, holding nothing back. You do that the first time. It's so innocent, so pure, and so consuming. I did all those things that had previously nauseated me: the flowers, the chocolate, the notes, the stuffed animals, the secret smiles—the works. I was in love, heady and wonderful and amazing.

THAT JUST ABOUT BRINGS US UP TO speed, really. There's one last bit to the story that explains what happens next.

The first day this school year, my heart raced to see her again—not that we'd been apart during the summer. In fact, we'd seen each other the day before, sharing kisses in the twilight. My heart always raced to see her, though. That's how hormones work when you're seventeen and in love with a gorgeous girl.

I saw her passing in the hall, and she smiled at me. It was like coming home to a warm fire, comfortable and soothing. I walked toward her to talk to her, and she walked past. I got a smile, a nod, and then a brush-off.

That confused me, but I assumed she was in a hurry to get somewhere. I didn't think much of it. It wasn't until lunch, when I saw her hand-in-hand with Duane, that I understood. She saw my jaw hitting the floor, broke hands with him and ran back my way.

"Rob!" she said, her voice chipper and full of the timbres of joy that I'd heard so many times. "Isn't it great? Duane broke up with Cindy the Central Slut, and he wants me back!"

Great? No. I did not think it was great.

"But—what about—" I couldn't even put the words together to ask. "I never could have gotten through this without you," she said. "You were there when I needed someone, and it helped me pull it together. But I don't need you to do that for me anymore, see? You can finally go find yourself a girlfriend instead of just being my crutch."

She said it with genuine caring in her voice, as though she really believed what she was saying. As though all I had been doing all along was helping her. Was that it? Was that all that we...?

I didn't think about it. Couldn't.

When Jeanelle broke down after Duane left her, she'd headed for the band room. I did the same. I cranked up "Things Ain't What They Used to Be," swung my sax around my neck, and tried to submerge my emotions in nothing more than vibrating air. It didn't work.

This is not the way these things are supposed to happen. Hollywood convinces us—No, that's not right. We convince ourselves there's a happily ever after in there somewhere. That once The Boy gets The Girl, the two of them last forever, blissful. Instead, The Girl ditched The Boy for The Old Asshole Boyfriend as soon as he opened his arms to her again, and The Boy found out that he had been nothing more than a substitute, a physical presence to help her deal with her heartache.

Jeanelle left me alone and wounded. Just keep that in mind; I could not think straight. Otherwise, I probably wouldn't have done what I did. Being lovesick and crazed is not an excuse...but I was hurt, and sometimes we just do stupid things when we're in that much pain.

GRACE

I'M NOT someone who enjoys "the open road," but I drove from Seattle to Spokane via I-90 and Snoqualmie pass. I know I passed some beautiful mountain views, but they were the last thing on my mind. I would have preferred flying, but with the trunk full of summoning aids I had strong-armed off the Grove director, the council wouldn't spring for a plane ticket, even though I assured them I could just summon them directly from the vault to my hotel room. They cited concerns about the wisdom of summoning next to the decimated headquarters, and I supposed that *might* be valid. But not really, since I planned to do some test-summoning as soon as I arrived, anyway. Whatever. I *had* managed to get access to a pretty hefty array of heavy weaponry.

The Grove had arranged for me to stay at the suites across from the mall. Apparently it was the closest hotel to the Spokane Grove headquarters, and therefore closer to the hotbed of action. I couldn't decide if I wanted to sleep *closer* to something which had already obliterated an entire Grove in no time at all, but at least the Seattle Grove agreed to pay the hotel bill.

My eyebrows rose in surprise when I passed the Spokane city limits before coming to my specified exit. The Grove headquarters was apparently in Spokane Valley, not Spokane proper, though like most metropolitan areas it really resembled one big urban kerfuffle. I pulled into the hotel parking lot about six p.m. on Thursday night.

The hotel itself nestled away from the street. Across the road the bulk of the Spokane Valley Mall complex sprawled, with several restaurants clustered close by. On the other side of the hotel ran the Spokane River. Beyond that there appeared to be some kind of industrial district tucked in behind the river, too. I could just see a water tower and the tip of a crane over one of the long buildings. According to the map I'd gotten from Seattle, the Grove headquarters would be just a bit south from here.

I checked in and chatted with the clerk about the local attractions. She handed me a brochure of local places of interest, which I pocketed. The uninspired title, "Spokane Vacations," didn't give me much hope for a fun read. I'd study it when I got up to the room, in case I needed to play tourist to cover my investigation later. She happily filled me in on the local news and gossip (of which the mass murder topped the list). Thanking her for the help, I grabbed more coffee, then lugged all my aptly named "miscellaneous luggage" upstairs.

The hotel room was a little small and plain, with cream colored walls, but perfect for my purposes. I stuffed the locked steamer trunk full of goodies under the coffee table and walked over by the entry way, double-checking that the table properly hid the trunk from view. Not that I was dumb enough to leave it unlocked with all my summoning stuff inside...but still. I left my suitcase by the bed and set the cooler on the luggage rack by the closet.

I kicked off my shoes and flopped on the bed briefly. *I should eat something.* Pulling a notepad out of my purse, I flipped through it until I found a fabulous all-American burger place I'd tried a few months back. For the last few years, I'd kept track of all the delicious places I'd eaten that offered takeout. When I felt a craving for that food, I summoned an order ticket, filled it out, and deftly slipped my Sense through the runes to shuffle it in with their other orders. After forty-five minutes or so, I deposited my money in their cash register and summoned my meal to me. It worked like a charm every time. I ate my ground sirloin burger with red onions and blue cheese as I finished settling in.

I stuck the "do not disturb" tag on the door knob and sat down to take some security measures. I faced an unknown threat. No one knew *exactly* what events had triggered the massacre. By summoning, I might announce my presence here to whatever had killed an entire room full of powerful people. I needed to take some precautions before I poked about trying to find it. I couldn't know how this thing killed all the summoners, but it seemed pretty obvious it didn't go around just indiscriminately killing folks. Otherwise, I assumed the string of deaths would have already spread outside the Grove headquarters.

Plus, getting slaughtered in my sleep would be especially mortifying. Not the way I wanted to go.

I sketched out a quick summoning that made the air denser around the perimeter of my room. I hoped if anything tried to come in, it would have to push its way through a compressed wall of air first. I then went around the room pushing little jingle bells (hurray for craft store bags-o-bells) into the barrier about every six inches. I bumped it with a fist to test it. It jiggled and they rang merrily. I don't recommend this alarm method if you're a heavy sleeper, but I just wanted something to delay the big bad long enough for me to wake up and make a fight-or-flight decision.

Now that my protective barrier stood sentinel, I decided to see if I couldn't tug on the Weave a little bit just to see its general state in this area. A rift of significant size would be obvious; I should at least be able to get a general direction.

The Seattle Grove had whole squads that backed each other up while testing and repairing the Weave. Anywhere the Weave weakened or tore, the chances of something nasty paying a visit went up exponentially. I only had me. This would take a lot more finesse than usual. Since I didn't want issue any invitations to something new, I broke into my trunk of goodies looking for the pair of copper bracelets with the rune chains laid out on them for testing and repairing the Weave. I clipped both bracelets on my right wrist so I'd be able to keep my left hand free to draw minor adjustments mid-summon.

Then I popped open the cooler and rummaged around in the ice until I came up with the plastic butcher container full of chicken blood. Asking for blood at the butcher shop can be less tricky than it sounds—specifically if the Grove happens to own most of the butcher shops like they do in Seattle. Even if you end up in a non-Grove shop, there are plenty of legitimate culinary uses for blood.

If the butcher is one of the suspicious types, I find that making fun of myself for liking "alternative cuisine," like blood pudding usually stops the awkward questions with a laugh.

Popping open the lid on the container, I rolled my wrists and dipped the runes directly in the container of chicken blood for maximum coverage. Then I focused my Sense on the Weave. The Weave is usually kind of springy and taut. It's the fabric that everything in the world is made of, and it's usually pretty resilient. The Weave here gave like a wet noodle under gentle pressure. Not good. Some of the stuff the Weave keeps out is harmless; the little guys from the other day were a nuisance, not evil. Other stuff it keeps out however, is evil on an apocalyptic level. If the Weave throughout the city had deteriorated, no wonder something nasty got through. The disrepair seemed out of place with the number of summoners who should have been in town up until the massacre. The thought nagged at me, and I filed it away for later.

I strengthened what I could in the area around me and narrowed the weakest vector down to a northern, maybe a little northwesterly direction. That's where I'd start poking around tomorrow after meeting my one Grove contact. I also needed to check out the remains of the local Grove headquarters. I unclipped the bracelets, carefully cleaned them, and then put them back in the locked trunk. For now I dragged myself to bed, fervently hoping I wouldn't wake to the sound of bells.

~

SINCE THE WEAVE was in such horrible repair, I put the bracelets back on when I met up with my only Grove contact, Matt Harper, for coffee the next morning. The runes were small. Someone would have to be really close before they could identify the bracelets as anything but normal accessories.

I headed for the door. As I put my hand on the cool metal of the knob, I had second thoughts and turned back. Shrugging my bag down from my shoulder, I pulled the trunk of summoning stuff out from under the coffee table. I put the "armory" of summoning tags Seattle had given me down at the bottom of the bag, then threw in my medallion belt. I also had a ring my mother gave me, fashioned to show a small acorn. Runes were stamped deeply into the old metal, so I couldn't just wear it openly. I ran my thumb over the small symbols before putting it in one of the outer pockets. It summoned one of my family's guardian spirits. If I needed it, I'd need it fast. I went to the cooler next and pulled out an insulated lunch bag full of small blood vials. That went into my cavernous shoulder bag too. As prepared as I could be for the day, I hung the Do Not Disturb sign on the door with slightly clammy hands and went to meet my contact.

We'd arranged to meet at a local coffee shop before I left Seattle. I told him I'd be the tiny dark-haired lady reading Dickens by the window. Upon arrival I glanced around to make sure I didn't see any muddy-haired, squat college boys already seated at any of the tables. His description of himself, not mine.

I ordered and settled in at a table. As promised, I sat reading, sipping my white chocolate peppermint mocha, until Matt showed up a few minutes later. He smiled and came over immediately, apologizing for being late. His hair looked more chestnut than muddy to me. As for stocky, well, everyone was taller than me. I noticed he had a pleasant, if grief-strained smile. He ordered coffee of his own before turning to ask me a question.

"Would you mind if we took our coffee outside? There's a park just a block from here with tables and things. I think it would be less crowded. I should have thought of it when we were talking before."

I peered around at the full tables surrounding us and agreed. We took our cups down to the park and picked a table well away from any other park-goers. Matt had a young, next-door-neighbor type face with an unfortunate case of acne. He couldn't have been older than twenty. When Annalisa Miller referred me to him, she indicated he went to one of the three or four colleges hereabouts, but I couldn't remember which one. I wanted to talk to him because he had been incredibly close to the massacre when it happened and walked out unharmed. That seemed pretty bloody lucky to be coincidence. It made me wonder what we were all missing.

"I'm going to get straight to it," I said. "Start at the beginning and just tell me what happened."

His hand gripped the espresso a little tighter. He seemed to prefer looking at it rather than at me. "I don't know how much help I'll be. My aunt is—er, was—pretty high up in Grove politics. She asked me to help out with refreshments in the afternoon, 'cause they were going to have a really big Grove meeting where they reelect officers and stuff. She expected pretty much everyone to show up." He glanced at me bashfully. "I'm actually more of a vanilla human than you usually get in a summoning family. I can't even bring fire to a candle unless I use a match. So I usually do behind-the-scenes prep stuff like making coffee. I'm not registered, so I don't vote. I helped in the kitchen down the hall from the main room refilling coffee urns all day. I was down there when I heard a really loud, sudden noise—like a bang—followed by the squeal of metal bending and more crashing." He stopped and took an audible swallow as he remembered. His hand holding the cup took on a visible tremor.

"Take your time," I said. "Anything you can tell me is helpful. I'm going to try to keep this thing from hurting anyone else."

He gave a jerky nod. "Sorry," he muttered. "I keep expecting the police to come drag me away because they've found a way to link me back to the crime scene somehow. And then I keep thinking if I was a proper summoner, maybe I could have done something other than run away."

He cleared his throat. "All of my family died in there. And now they're gone. I don't even know why. Or why I'm still alive when most of my friends are dead. I'm struggling to pay all my bills and stay at college, but what else am I going to do? I'm a total dud as a summoner, so it seems like a double insult to my parents if I drop out of regular college. Mom would hate it if I did that."

"I'm sorry, Matt. I'm sure no matter what you decide your mom would still be proud." I felt completely inadequate to deal with the situation. What the hell do you say to someone who just lost his whole family? He jerked his head slightly. I hoped I could interpret that as an acknowledgement. I gave him a moment to pull himself back together and then asked, "So after you heard the crashing, what happened?"

"At first I didn't realize something had attacked the Grove. I thought a car crashed into the side of the building or something else had collapsed. The kitchen has a small window. I tried it first. I didn't see a lot. Enough to know there wasn't a car accident out front. I heard more crashing and shouting from somewhere and realized the sounds came from *inside* the building. I went to the door of the kitchen and realized the people in the auditorium were fighting something."

Matt hung his head. "I don't know what I should have done. I could see flashes of light around the auditorium door at the end of the hallway. The most powerful summoners in the whole Grove were in there. I'm not a summoner myself. I thought if I went in, I would get in their way—cause someone to get hurt trying to protect me. So I just stood there, listening to the sounds of furniture and walls being torn apart. The yells and screams. I didn't really think the Grove *could* lose." Matt stared at his knees before continuing.

"But it started to get quieter, and I didn't see any more flashes of light. I snuck down to the auditorium. I didn't want to distract anyone if they were still fighting. By the time I got to the door, the sounds died out. I put my hand on the door to open it, but I got an awful feeling, and just stood there. I don't know how long I waited before I finally got up the nerve to push open the door."

Matt stopped and unclenched his hands from around his espresso, flattening his fingers against the table in a nervous gesture. If I could have gotten the information from anyone else, I would have told him to stop. Shutting away my empathy, I waited him continue.

"I can't even describe how horrible the inside of that auditorium looked. Our Grove had just over fifty members in attendance. Blood spatter washed up the walls, and in between the seats I could see body parts like arms and legs. Something had just gone through tearing people apart. I've never heard of any Visitor that could do that to a whole room full of summoners. I thought I'd seen gory stuff in movies before, but when you look at a lump of meat and realize that just a second ago it was a person, it really hits home. I closed the door because I thought I'd throw up. I managed not to. I turned and ran as fast as I could.

"I don't even remember leaving the building, but next thing I knew I was back on campus headed to my dorm. I've heard that some people have been reported missing, since their bodies weren't found among the dead, but it's hard for me to believe that anyone in that room made it out alive."

"I'm sorry," I said again. "I need to know. Can you think of anything else that happened? Did you hear anything like an explosion? Or any other noises besides the crashing? Feel anything strange? It may help me narrow down exactly what occurred."

"No, I didn't hear an explosion, although I noticed a big hole in the building afterward. I'm sorry I can't be more help," he added miserably.

I reached a hand over the table to grip his forearm in reassurance. "That's ok. You've been a great help. You take care of yourself, and I'll be in touch."

"What are you going to do now?"

"Well, I think I'm going to go check out Grove H.Q. That way I can get a feel for how stuff looks and take a look at that hole."

His eyes widened. "That place is crawling with police! What if you get arrested?"

I tossed him a wink. "I'll be careful. No worries." If only I were as confident as I sounded.

~

THE FORMER SPOKANE GROVE headquarters was encompassed by yellow crime scene tape and crawling with both uniformed cops and plainclothes detectives. It had been a little over forty-eight hours since the incident, but they were obviously still combing the place for evidence. *And "contraband,"* I added uncomfortably, thinking about the inevitable summoning things inside. I followed a side street and circled the building slowly in my Pontiac trying to look like someone who had missed a turnoff.

The Grove headquarters had been housed in a sprawling one-story building with brick on the bottom and wooden paneling further up. Large covered windows let light in, though right now all of them were cracked. The east corner of the building had been obliterated. It looked like the structure had been struck at high velocity—essentially shoved in by a large fist. Shards of broken wood, glass, and concrete were strewn about the parking lot as far as fifty yards away. Whatever hit the Grove had thrown two-by-fours and bricks as if they weighed no more than balsa wood.

From what I understood, the Spokane Grove covered this side of the state and part of northern Idaho, so the number of people who had died here boggled my mind. If this thing had attacked by working its way up the food chain, there was a chance they would have been able to defend themselves. Instead, it had taken out the powerful and the weak together in one go. Creepy. I hated to think like a conspiracy theorist, but I really hoped it wasn't some super-secret federally funded black op. I had no idea how the Seattle Grove would handle something like this, but I could bet they were putting together an emergency plan of some kind, just in case whatever happened here decided to go traveling.

I parked the Pontiac a few blocks away and began walking back toward the destroyed end of the building by an indirect route. If I could get a closer look at the hole, it might at least give me an idea whether this thing had entered from above or not. I didn't think the building could look worse, but as I walked closer the devastation took on an even more menacing dimension. The air itself felt miasmic and charged.

I checked to make sure no cops were looking my way, then ducked briskly under the tape and through the closest door. I stepped gingerly around the bloody footprints on the carpet, that were heading the way I'd just come. Some part of my brain noted that this plan bordered on really stupid, but I went ahead anyway.

I ducked into an alcove to avoid a detective, then continued down the hall toward the auditorium. The next door I stepped through accessed the kitchen Matt had told me about, with the urns tipped over and coffee grounds all over the floor. I moved carefully to avoid the coffee, as that would leave a whole different set of tracks I really didn't want to explain later. Police swarmed all over farther down the hall. There was no way I'd make it all the way into the auditorium without catching someone's attention. Dammit. For all the devastation reported in the auditorium, the rest of the building appeared surprisingly untouched. I didn't see any signs of fire or gunplay or anything like that.

Fine. I may as well not hang around here if I couldn't get any closer. I could test the Weave from somewhere close by a lot less dangerously than here. I'd just ducked back under the yellow tape and taken a few brisk steps down the block toward my car when the glint from a shiny, jagged piece of metal under a shrub caught my eye.

The thick shaving of metal, shaped like a lightning bolt, came off the ground easily, surprisingly light for its thickness. Its edges felt weirdly irregular, but it didn't look like it had been torn off a larger piece. I hefted it in my hand a couple times just to gauge the weight. To be that light, I guessed it must be aluminum. I gazed back at the building but couldn't see any metal that looked similar in the debris. I saw mostly ruins of glass, brick, wood, and rebar.

"Howdy."

I jumped and turned my head. A tall, grizzled man in a tweed suit with patches on the elbows crossed the street toward me, obviously looking to start a conversation. Had he seen me leaving the crime scene? I surreptitiously tipped the metal shaving from my hand into my shoulder bag.

"Hello."

"Didn't mean to startle you," he said apologetically, "but I couldn't help noticing you staring at the building over there. Did you know someone who worked there?"

"No. Why do you ask?" I hedged.

"My apologies. I didn't introduce myself." He held out a hand for me to shake. "I'm Detective Allen of the Spokane County Sheriff's office. You were just looking at the building so intently, I thought you might have had a relative or friend inside." I took his hand and gave it a good shake up and down. He gazed at me with eyes that were much too penetrating.

"Nice to meet you," I said. I decided go with honesty, up to a point. I hate keeping track of lies. "I'm Grace, and, um, no, I didn't know anyone there. I was actually just wandering around sightseeing. I'm from out of town, and all the crime tape caught my eye. That's a really impressive-looking hole."

"Huh," he grunted. "It's still under investigation. You been in town long?"

I shrugged. "Since yesterday."

"Odd place to start your sightseeing. Wouldn't downtown Spokane be better for catching the sights?"

"Not really. Someone told me about Valleyfest, and the Valley's also closer to Greenbluff. I'm hoping to drive out that way and get some peaches." Silently I thanked Sally the desk clerk at my hotel for that silly tourist brochure when I checked in.

"I think you're a little out of season for peaches. Any other plans while you're in town?"

"Just whatever catches my fancy, since I'm on vacation. Maybe some window shopping, et cetera."

"No family or business contacts in town?"

"No, sir. Just me."

"Hmm. Well, here's my card. If you come across something in your sightseeing you'd like to tell me, just give me a call. It's been a pleasure."

I waved goodbye as he jogged back across the street, then almost shit my pants as one of my rune bracelets caught the sun and glinted. I managed to choke back my swearing reflex. I had totally forgotten about those. Fortunately his eyes seemed to be already focused back on the crime scene.

"Well, shit," I said. I guess I still came off as suspicious.

It used every fiber of my willpower to walk slowly and casually back up the block to the Pontiac. I slid back in behind the wheel and let the car mosey down the roadway without burning rubber. My knuckles turned white on the steering wheel. I really don't like talking to cops. Especially cops who are looking for someone to pin a brand new mass homicide on. I made it one of my new goals to keep far, far away from—I double-checked his card—Detective Frank Allen. He did not seem like an acquaintance who would be good for my nascent ulcer.

I drove a couple blocks to the northwest of my hotel and pulled into a restaurant parking lot, closer to where I thought the rift would be. The sun cast the long shadows of late afternoon across the parking lot as I stepped into the restaurant. My meeting with Matt and scouting the crime scene had taken up most of the day.

The dining room had a homey feel that promised pastries baked on site. Technically, I should have been hungry, but I only tasted acid. My temples twinged. I ordered some coffee and pie and availed myself of the ladies room. The restroom was a two-stall in pale peach that didn't do well under the neon lights. I threw the bolt locking myself into the handicapped stall and rummaged through my bag to find a vial of blood. Using my left hand, I flipped it open, smeared the blood across the rune's etched surface on my right bracelets, and focused my Sense to activate the runes. The giant hole in the Weave loomed. It clearly worsened to the north, so at least I managed to triangulate its location. I'd also found the aluminum shaving at the crime scene. In fact, I had seen a giant aluminum plant sign on the north side of the river from my hotel. The day wasn't a total wash.

Now I needed to write my first report for the Seattle Grove about my findings.

I refocused my Sense and started repairing and strengthening the Weave around the restaurant. The Weave here gave easily under my Sense just like back at the hotel. It hadn't torn...yet, but this pervasive deterioration concerned me. I'd never seen anything like it. The local Weave was degrading unnaturally fast even given the deaths of its keepers. Two days shouldn't have been enough time for it to fall apart like this.

Beads of sweat formed on my brow from acute concentration as I worked the Weave. When I stopped, a tension headache started forming behind my eyes. Nothing like working complicated summons for an extended period of time with no backup.

I needed to get back to the hotel and sleep it off. The more complicated the summons, the more effort it requires to stretch your Sense through the runes. My arms felt sore and heavy like I'd just spent the day in heavy lifting. On a certain level, that was pretty true, I supposed, cracking a small smile. I wiped the bracelets clean with a piece of tissue and flushed it down the toilet.

I'd been in worse shape before, but I didn't want to push it without a really good reason while flying solo. I hadn't Sensed any other summoner activity in the Weave today; I'd bet on it staying quiet while I got some sleep. I just hoped no Visitors tested my gamble.

ROBERT

I KICKED my way through the back door of my foster parents' home with all the grace of a bison stampede.

"Whoa," said Francene, my foster mother *du jour*. "What's the matter?"

The problem with fosties is they've got really big hearts and grand ideals. Your basic foster parent who volunteers to take in a troubled teen isn't in it for the government paycheck; those folks take the infants, fill them with formula, and call it a day. No, if they're taking a teenager, they're trying to make the world a better place.

That means one of two things. They may be people who truly believe in doing good things for the sake of goodness. You know, the real hippy-dippy types who wear rose-colored glasses. If not that, then they are people who believe some religious entity has required them to do this thing, no matter what the burden. The former tend to get quickly abused by me; the latter tend to quickly abuse me. In the four years since my parents' death, I had been cycled through foster homes one after the other. Now I was on my...seventh? Eighth?

Eh. Who's counting, really?

Point is, either I came down hard on my fosties or they came down hard on me. Either way the relationships tended to be short.

The Rockfords were of the goody-two-shoes variety. They were, at heart, good people, and they did their best by me. They weren't religious, which I counted as a plus. They tried to take an active role in my life, though, as if Francene and Donald Rockford were actually my parents. They knew they were there to sub-in for parents, and parents were supposed to love their children, so they tried really, really hard to show me they loved me like parents.

Problem was, when someone acts like they have that kind of bond with you after knowing you for all of three weeks, it comes off as phony. I knew the Rockfords were trying their best, but I also knew they were faking it. If ever you want someone to ignore everything you say, convince them you're faking it. You become irrelevant pretty quickly.

"Nothing," I told Francene. I find single-word answers are the best policy with the goody-goody variety fosties. I tend to shoot for monosyllabic, actually; I'd been practically verbose this time.

"That doesn't look like nothing." That soft, pseudo-caring tone of voice grated on my ears. "You want to talk?"

Did I want to talk? No. I wanted to rip Duane's sternum out of his chest and force him to choke on it. I wanted Jeanelle to see she'd made a terrible mistake. I wanted to go upstairs and listen to some outdated Nineties goth-rock and fantasize about killing myself without actually taking myself seriously. I wanted to wallow. Francene would have undoubtedly tried to comfort me, but it would have been another hollow fostie trick. I'm sure the Fostie Handbook has a section about using the tragedies of your new pet teenager's life to form a connection.

"No," I said, wrapping all my tumultuous thoughts into one syllable.

Her face fell. Our eyes met for a second, and I saw that I had disappointed her. I'd caught that look on the fostie face before; she had seen an opportunity to improve on me, only to have me shut it down. But realistically, what could she expect?

Still, it was heartbreaking, and I'd had too many bridges burned today. I decided to go for a full sentence or two.

"Look," I said, quieter now. "Jeanelle broke up with me today. It sucks. I'm just going to go to my room and lie down."

"Oh, Robert, I'm sorry." She almost sounded like she meant it. It was too glib, though; she was trying to cover her joy that I had talked to her. I didn't want to deal with it. I had some sulking to do, and I needed to get on with it. I shook my head and started for the stairs. I got halfway to them before I heard her voice.

"Robert? I don't know if you care or not, but you got a package today. It's on the counter."

A package? Who would send me a package? I took a left into the kitchen and saw a box sitting on the counter, addressed to me. A glance at the return address was no help: Terry Linfarr, Attorney at Law. I actually did have an attorney for a bit when I was first taken into foster care, but I didn't think that was her name.

Nothing for it... I tore open the package and uncovered a stack of papers. Most of them were sloppy and handwritten, but on top was a letter addressed to me on official-looking letterhead from Mr. Linfarr.

Dear Mr. Robert Lorents:

This office deeply regrets your loss. We represent Mr. Lorents in the probate of his estate, of which I am executor.

Mr. Lorents? My father was four years dead, and his property already sat in a trust fund. What the hell was this?

Please find enclosed his personal effects, which he intended for you. Furthermore, please be advised that his real property is beginning the probate process, after which it will be held by this office in trust pending your eighteenth birthday. You should feel free to make use of it in the meantime. Thank you for your time, and please contact me with any questions you may have.

Terry Linfar

Attorney for the Estate of Herman Lorents

It wasn't until I read the text under Linfar's name that I realized what was going on. Crazy Uncle Herman was dead.

In my childhood, Uncle Herman stood out as one of the highlights. Looking back, he was actually a bit crazy. We didn't get to visit him much, but he always told the best stories and gave the best Christmas presents up in the mountains of North Idaho. He had a little log cabin setup, one room; he let us use it while he slept out under the stars with no blanket.

I didn't think you *could* kill Crazy Uncle Herman. I hadn't seen him since I went into foster care; the courts considered him unfit to parent me, even though he volunteered. He was a grizzled old woodsman.

For a full minute I sat there fighting the tears for Uncle Herman; I even managed to forget how upset Jeanelle had made me. I hadn't even thought about Herman for a couple of years. Mr. Linfar's polite letter managed to simultaneously remind me that someone out there genuinely cared for me, and then to inform me that he, too, was dead. Thanks, Terry.

I began flipping through the pages. They weren't organized, and they were mostly handwritten by Uncle Herman. A few pages down, I found this:

Dear Robert,

If your reading this, then I've finully met my end. If your less than thirty, then I bet it was wun hell of a show.

Anywayz, I've left you evarytheng, becuz your the last Lorents. It is sour, but thats how it goze sumtimes.

Herman

That didn't make any sense.

Not the meaning of the letter; that was really basic. Unnecessarily basic, really. But Herman had helped me learn to read. He liked the classics; I remembered the big old volume of Shakespeare he loved to read to me, even as a child.

Actually, looking back, no wonder I turned into a geek. Even my mountain man uncle taught me Shakespeare.

Point was, Herman led the life of an old mountain hermit, sure, but one who could read and write. This note...no, all of the documents, looked like they were written by a madman with a third-grade education. The old wise Shakespeare-reading hermit dude I remembered did not write like this.

"It is sour..." I remembered a trick Herman and I had used to pass notes. He'd told me the story of Benjamin Franklin's use of it the first time we had scribbled childish secrets to one another. They were mostly meaningless, but the fun lay in the fact that that my parents couldn't tell what Herman said to me.

I stood up from my seat on the bedroom floor and shot down the stairs to the kitchen. Francene was cooking something that smelled delicious. My stomach rumbled at me as I opened the fridge.

"No snacks!" barked my fostie mom. "I'm almost done with the meatloaf."

I ignored her, snatched the bottle of lemon juice from the fridge, and ran upstairs with it. I sprinkled a couple of drops onto the paper, then spread the acid out. As I did, a second message arose from beneath the first.

Dear Nephew,

Well done. I knew I was right to have confidence in you. You have a very solid mind with a great deal of potential.

If I'm truly gone, though, then I am sorry. The burden of this knowledge falls to you and not to me. I have done my best to train you without training you; now it falls on you to train yourself. What I am asking of you is dangerous in more ways than you know. If I could place this on a stranger, I would.

Contact the Grove at 14711 East Broadway; sign Petunia, countersign Magnolia. They should be able to Sense you from there.

I love you, and I believe in you. Good luck. Uncle Herman

I sat staring at the paper. The Grove, Sense... This was summoner talk. If I read his letter right, Herman had been a member of a Grove, an organization that did not legally exist.

I dug through the box. There were papers after papers, but towards the bottom I found an aged leather case. A lock held it secure, with six wheels of numbers. No combination presented itself. I tried each to the same number, but no luck. I tried my birthday, Herman's birthday, and some random number combinations. Flummoxed, I stared at the box, then slowly began turning the numbers. I spun a wheel until...well, until it felt right, really. There wasn't any outward sign, but "927556" felt *right.* Upon finding that final "6," the box clicked open.

Inside lay a pair of silver bracers with runes etched into them. They were old, and looked like the sort of thing you'd see on the History Channel or one of those fantasy movies my buddy Jake always watched. They held no rust—the case had done its job well—but the number of small nicks and scratches coating their surface showed they had been worn a great deal. The bracers were polished, beautiful, and horrible. Runes were the tools of the summoner; this confirmed it. Herman had practiced the dark arts.

History classes taught us about summoners; even before the practice was banned they had been evil. Summoning was punishable by a life sentence with a paralyzing IV in the arm, or even death in some situations. Urban myth told us the Groves were the Mafia of summoners: large, malevolent organizations bent on power and control. Everyone knew that summoners were dark, evil monsters who tried to enslave humanity. Just possessing these bracers could get me sent to prison for a good, long time. Power corrupts, and that made summoners the most corrupt, evil people to walk the earth.

And Herman had been one of them.

I went to my desk, a little student model in the corner, and pulled out a book of matches. I burned Herman's letter. Just possessing that thing was enough to get me thrown in prison, and I wanted none of it. The rest of the box I slid into my closet; the lemon juice I returned to the fridge without explanation. Crazy Uncle Herman was not only dead, but underneath that friendly, bearded face lay one of the most evil creatures in existence.

Francene served a delicious meatloaf that night. I ate it in silence, as I always did. Then I flung myself into bed and pretended I wasn't actually crying myself to sleep.

MY ALARM absolutely failed me the next morning by going off as scheduled. You'd think a device I had spent good money on would have the decency to fail when I needed it to. Instead, I wrapped my blanket around my head, rolled over, and tried to get just five more minutes of sleep.

No luck there. Donald, Francene's husband and my nominal foster father, poked his head in to yell at me. "C'mon, kiddo, get out of bed. You gotta get to school today."

Right. School. My uncle's treacherous secrets had pushed that impending embarrassment to the back of my mind. Donald's wake-up call brought it all back, and my personal tragedies swapped center-stage in my head.

Breakfast had been lovingly prepared by Francene: pancakes, bacon, eggs, etc. Cardboard in my mouth as I shoveled it all down. Afterward, I took my leave of the Rockfords with a nice, two-syllable "Later," then got in the Volvo, slamming the door shut.

I looked at the backseat of the Volvo for a moment. Just the other day Jeanelle and I had been back there. It had been wonderful, magical, awesome. If I thought about it hard enough, I could still smell her. Her perfume, her shampoo, and the more primal, exciting odors lingering underneath. Two days.

Before Duane.

I walked through the doors of the school like a convict going to the chair. Sure enough, as I rummaged through my locker, Jeanelle and Duane walked down the corridor, his arm negligently wrapped around her slender neck and his hand draped down the front of her chest, not quite on her breast, but close enough to display that he could and had.

Duane.

All I knew about Duane I knew from Jeanelle, admittedly a flawed narrator if ever I saw one. But I learned something about him then. He stared directly at me, winked, then spun with his star-of-the-basketball-team grace in front of Jeanelle and caught her up in the deepest, most passionate tongue-kiss ever attempted by teenagers in the middle of a school hallway.

I slammed the door to my locker shut, my books in hand. I would take the long way around to Biology, use a different floor of the school. Too late; the happy couple had passed me. Duane whispered something in her ear, then held back as she proceeded down the hall. I headed the other way. Not fast enough.

"Hey, band geek!" It was a rough whisper, but the hot stench of his breath told me his mouth hovered but inches from my ear. I didn't want this; no scene, no confrontation. I kept walking as though I didn't have a six-foot-six whipcord of a basketball star looming behind me. Duane kept up a steady, mocking chant in my ear as I walked.

"Hey, fucking hornblower. She thought about me, the whole time. You get that, right? You were just easy. She used you and threw you away like an old paper towel. You were out of your league, little boy. Just keep walking. Don't touch my little slut agai—"

I stopped, turned on my left heel, dropped my books, and punched him in the face.

"Don't call her a slut!" I screamed, defending the honor of someone who, until this very moment, I had been thinking of as a slut.

Stupid move. Stupid, angry move.

Duane had been waiting for it. My punch connected squarely, but it had all the force of overcooked spaghetti. It gave him the excuse he needed, though. His right fist plunged into my stomach and it felt like a ramrod. My breath left me. I started to double over. He grabbed the back of my head. His knee came up towards my face.

Then my world exploded into a cluster of stars, and it all went black.

I CAME to lying on my back in the school hallway, surrounded by my pointing classmates. I stood, doing what little I could to salvage some dignity, and left the building. I stopped by the grocery store for an ice pack and an extra-large bottle of lemon juice on the way home. Francene made a fuss over the shiner and asked me what had happened. I made up a lie. I had become good at doing that for shiners. I took the ice pack out in front of her to show her I was taking care of myself. Then I headed upstairs before she could ask me about the lemon juice.

Uncle Herman's box beckoned me to the closet. Power waited for me there, though it came at a cost. Had I been more stable, it would have sat there in the closet, collecting dust. Instead, I thought about nothing so much as my absolute need to avenge myself on Duane. I pulled the box from the closet and began to decode my Uncle's secrets.

The first several pages were listings of runes. I knew that summoners used runes, but I never really knew why. I kept flipping. There was a lot of stuff about something called the Weave. He had written a lot more on balancing of elements, runic formulations. It looked like more of Herman's crazy intellectual stuff. I didn't care. I needed the material about how to do very evil things to people you don't like; that was what summoners were supposed to be good at, after all.

Ah, here we were. Herman had a section labeled "Summoning in a Fight." Juicy. I sat down to read.

To begin with, using one's inborn Sense in combat is generally faster. Removing the need for runes and blood, one is able to adapt to any situation more readily. However, given the limited range the Sense affords us, generally some form of runework is required.

Always remember the basics of extra-Sensory summoning. The runes set the formula for the summons. In order to summon quickly, one needs to have runes pre-scribed, or the ability to scribe them in a rapid manner. I recommend both, but especially the pre-scribed runes, either on a tag or on some other piece of apparel. Having formulae ready in advance allows a summoner to use the longer, more controlled formulae. This allows for a more specific effect, without randomizing source material in the plane.

Okay, I understood maybe half of that. "Randomizing source material in the plane?" That sounded like gobbledygook. I did, however, look at the bracers. "Pre-scribed runes." It looked like I had that.

As for blood, there is some debate. While there is a school of thought that says one's runes should be pre-scribed on a blood-drawing device to power it with one's own blood for maximum power, I find that for most combat situations the blood of a small animal like a bird or squirrel is sufficient, and injuring oneself in a fight is never a good idea if it can be avoided. Keep blood in multiple, easy-access storage containers...

I remembered Herman's bota bottle, the one he never drank from. No wonder. I needed to use my own, though; I didn't have any squirrel's blood.

The hardest part about combat summoning is maintaining the concentration necessary for the Sense. In order to summon effectively, of course, one must maintain one's focus on the summons. However, in order to fight effectively, it is recommended that one focus on the fight. Thus, the art of combat summoning is the art of incorporating one's awareness of the fight into one's summoning focus...

That made theoretical sense, I guess. It seemed simple. What you needed to get into a summoner's fight was some runes, some blood, and focus. I could do that. I put down Herman's notes and picked up one of the bracers. I took out the Swiss Army knife my actual father had given me so long ago and sliced my left pinky finger with it. It hurt, but not too badly. I smeared the blood over the runes like they showed in the movies and stared at the bracer, trying to focus on it.

Focusing, by the way, is hard. As soon as I stared at the bracer and tried to think about nothing else, my mind immediately began cataloguing all the things I was supposed to be ignoring. The neighbor working on his car. A bird flapping outside the window. Jeanelle had left me. I kinda had to pee. I hated Duane. It sounded like Francene and Donald were watching TV downstairs.

I shook my head and tried a different approach. I fantasized about what I would do to Duane. I closed my eyes and envisioned me with these bracers strapped to my wrists. I said a magic phrase (they always say those in the movies, though it didn't look like you needed to from Herman's notes), and that oh-so-tough jock would ignite. I stood over him as his body became engulfed in my flames.

I focused on that, on my vengeance. I would take vengeance on Duane. The vision was perfect in my head. I could hear the fire crackling, I could feel the heat of it. The smoke filled my nostrils so heavily and thickly that it started to become hard to breathe, and I began to cough violently.

Which is how I realized that *my desk was on fire.*

Panic gripped me. I jumped away, tilting my desk chair to the floor and landing on the side of my face.

Smooth, Lorents.

Gathering myself, I yanked a pillow off my bed and used it to smother the flames. The smoke detector in the hallway went off. I ran to it and yanked the battery from it, but I knew I had been too slow. I sprinted back to the bracers, shoved them in my desk, and quickly lit about six of the incense sticks I had gotten from the mall a couple of weekends back.

I looked at my desk. The surface itself had survived with only a little charring. My math homework had turned into charcoal, and this one made "my dog ate it" look believable, but I hadn't permanently damaged anything.

"What's going on up there?" Donald called up the stairs.

"Nothing," I shouted back down. *Creative,* I thought to myself. *You just set off the fire alarm, the whole upstairs smells of smoke, and you tell him nothing. You may want to embellish this one.*

"I lit some incense to meditate with. It burned my math homework." There. Mix the truth into the lie; always made it smoother.

"Are you all right?" Donald asked, in order to maintain the facade that he cared.

"Yeah, fine. Gonna have to redo that math, but I'm good."

"Well, it sounds like you managed to punish yourself then. Be a little more careful. And air it out up there." He clomped away, and I began cleaning up. For all the fuss, though, I still smiled for the first time since Jeanelle dumped me.

I had homework to do, all right. Time to start memorizing runes.

ROBERT

OKAY, okay. It wasn't going to be a good idea to actually burn Duane alive.

To begin with, there would be a logistics issue. I mean, you can't just light someone on fire and walk away. There would be, at the least, cops involved. Everyone would be investigated, and I'd get nailed, hard. It's not like my motive hadn't been on display for all my fellow students to see.

Besides, it's one thing to fantasize about incinerating someone. It's another thing to actually *want* to go through with it. I had to seriously ask myself whether I would be capable of making someone suffer that much. Secretly, I had to admit to myself that I would not. As much as I wanted to act like the scary big shot, I also knew that was stupid. I'd seen the movies where the hero held the gun on the villain but didn't pull the trigger, and I knew you should never level the gun in the first place.

As I went through this thought process, it occurred to me I *had* just summoned fire, and I had apparently not turned completely evil. It appeared one didn't go evil all at once. The corruption that summoning leaves was, I decided, a slow burn. Good. I had time.

Killing Duane was out of the question. Herman's bracers looked like they were built to be some serious artillery, and that's not what I needed to deal with a high school basketball player. I needed something more embarrassing, less hideous. I turned back to Herman's notes, the lists of runes.

Who knew vengeance came with homework?

The rest of the week was spent keeping my head down at school during the day, and looking at runes at night. Herman had made some notes on how to string the runes together for a more specialized effect. By stringing two rune sets together, the second one became a kind of destination target. When I had rubbed Herman's bracer with blood, I'd hit one rune, "Kano," for "fire." If I wanted to learn to do this properly, I had to start stringing runes together.

Once I learned that, I knew what I could do. It was so simple. I carefully took the time to pre-scribe the runes I wanted to use.

"Wunjo" appeared to be the key there; Uncle Herman had been clear that I could limit the damage the summoning could do to a person by including the joy-rune in a rune set that started with "Mannaz," for humanity. It looked as though Uncle Herman had enough humanity left in him to construct these more humane figures of runes.

That gave me a little hope. I had already started down this path, but I didn't want to completely sell my soul. I didn't want to rule the world; I just wanted to make Duane pay. I couldn't do it in a fistfight, but Uncle Herman left me another way. I could use this knowledge, just this once. After that, I would burn Uncle Herman's box and walk away. I would do something silly with the power. Something painless. Something designed to humiliate, not to harm. Once I got him, I would be done with it.

I would retain my humanity, but come Monday I would have my revenge.

I put the tools of my anger away. Monday would come soon enough, but it was time for a weekend. Almost as if on cue, my cell phone (a little prepaid disposable number purchased by the fosties) rang, and the number came up as Jake. Good deal.

I'd met Jake when I first started at U-High, and we'd become fast friends. He played the trumpet, which is to say that he was outgoing and brash. Jake always acted coarse, rude, and (as a result) downright entertaining.

"Jake, what's up?"

"Hey, fucker, you want to hit the mall?"

Jake tended to refer to everyone he liked as a "fucker." I always wondered what he called people he didn't like; with Jake, though, that rarely came up.

"Um, ok. Better than hanging here with the fosties." "No shit, huh? How're the new ones?"

Jake had been there for the last pair; those had been more of the hard-line religious type. Those fosties and I had not gotten along, to say the least. Some of the bruises were still healing, and not just the emotional ones.

"Not bad. They're Category Ones, not Twos." Translation: They're well-meaning and naive, not religious and strict. Jake knew that code as well as I did.

"That's cool. Hey, I hear you finally managed to ditch your surplus baggage." Jake followed teenage male etiquette here; he really wanted to ask if I was okay, but he would never have shamed me by suggesting I wouldn't be.

"Yeah, I didn't need that bitch hanging around anymore." Sheer bravado on my part; of course I needed her. Just saying the phrase made me yearn to feel her flesh against mine again. Still, Jake had provided me the opportunity to preserve my teenage masculine pride, and I took it.

"Word, fucker. Let's hit the mall, check out some new asses, maybe catch a flick. Whaddya say?"

"Sure. I'm down. You want me to pick you up?" Jake still didn't have a car, and I had the Volvo.

"No, fucker, I'm just going to walk the four miles to the *yes I want you to pick me up, asshole.*"

"Ok, ok, I'll be by in a bit."

I hung up the phone and went about the business of combing my hair and rubbing on the cheap cologne I'd picked up. I always did this before going to the mall. The professed goal of going to the mall was to meet girls. It never actually happened, of course. Even so, the chance always remained that, this time, you might meet some girl you took a liking to or, more importantly, who took a liking to you. It never hurt to be prepared.

After my preening, I did a double-check to make sure all of Uncle Herman's notes were hidden. Looked good. I headed downstairs, told Francene I was off to the mall, then jumped into the Volvo and headed out. The clouds tried to overcast the day, but were not entirely successful, with the sun filtering through in bits and pieces. I drove to Jake's house trying to put Jeanelle, Duane and my impending vengeance out of my head. I instead tried to think about the font of possibility the mall represented.

It was hard to do.

Jake looked in fine form as he slid into the shotgun seat of the Volvo. His jeans were appropriately ripped, his black T-shirt read in white font "I am a bomb technician. If you see me running, try to keep up." He had perfectly ruffled his hair to appear as though he did not care about it while looking good.

"Hey, fucker, crank it up."

I turned up the music and we cruised our way to the Spokane Valley Mall.

THE MALL IS a strange place for a teenager. On the way there, it represents possibility: the chance to meet new people (read: girls) and to do any number of wonderfully entertaining activities (read: girls).

It never actually ends up that way. Invariably, you walk around the mall a couple of times, hit the arcade for a while, food court for lunch, and finally you go catch a movie. That's it, really. You leave the mall feeling like you had fun, but still slightly disappointed. You swear to yourself that next time, next time you will do all those things that you set out to do this time.

Rinse, repeat.

This Saturday was no different. We had made our laps, and there were some cute girls. As always, they were travelling in a pack; those were dangerous to approach. We browsed the music store for a bit instead of trying them, but we'd already illegally downloaded everything we wanted to listen to.

So I wasn't a model child. Hell, I had plans to sell at least a portion of my soul for petty teenage vengeance; illegally downloading music is tame by comparison.

I saw *them* during our stint at the food court. I had hit the Italian place for some baked ziti; Jake was all over some fish and chips. As we sat and ate, we talked about the school gossip, always being careful to avoid the topic of Jeanelle dumping me to go back to Duane.

Out of the corner of my eye, I saw a couple standing in line at the place with the lemonade and the funny uniforms. She had dark brown, almost black, hair, and a cute little pair of legs sticking out from a skirt her father would have called too high. At first, I didn't realize what I was seeing. I'd never actually met Cindy before, so I didn't know who the dark-haired girl in the backless halter-top could be until Duane turned around next to her.

Duane was with her, and she wasn't Jeanelle. I looked at the Central Slut, as Jeanelle had termed her. Given the way his hand cupped her ass, it looked like Duane hadn't actually broken it off with her; he simply wanted the double play.

I started to burn. Duane had destroyed my relationship with Jeanelle and he was leading her on again. Jeanelle had chosen this asshole over me because...why? Because he could play basketball. Because he had enough skill to take a ball and stick it through a ring. I loathed him.

Screw waiting for Monday.

Jake noticed my gaze, and must have seen my face go cold, because he turned to look over his shoulder. "Oh, snap," he said, sounding surprised. "Ain't that some serious shit."

I paid him little attention as he raised his cell phone to take a picture of the happy couple. I had flipped my napkin open and taken out my pen. I began tracing runes across the surface of the napkin.

"What. The. Fuck." The color drained from Jake's face as he watched me.

"Shut the fuck up, Jake."

"Dude, you have got to be fucking kidding me. Stop fucking around with that shit and throw it away before some mall cop actually thinks you're a summoner and pops you."

"Shut the fuck up, Jake. I need to focus here."

The runes continued to form on the napkin, drawing up the formula I'd practiced at home.

"No, dude. You can't...you don't know how to...what the fuck, man? What are you trying to do? You're going to get yourself arrested, you stupid fucker..."

I stopped listening to Jake as I ripped the scab from my pinky finger and pinched it a couple of times to get the blood out. His protests continued in a hushed, fast, urgent whisper, but I smeared the blood over the whole rune set in a line, and began to focus my hatred of Duane into the casting.

Jake had descended into a soft chant of "Oh shit oh shit oh shit" as he peered around for mall security and tried to block their view of my napkin. Jake's a good guy; he had my back even in a total panic.

I stared at Duane, boring through him with my eyes. I focused on his lower abdomen; I wanted to get at his colon. I felt the power building through me, and unleashed it in a surge of hatred and rage.

Duane's face was priceless. He felt it happening a split second before it did, and the effort he made to fight it showed across his smarmy mug. It was no good, though. I knew it wouldn't be.

I didn't expect the volume. Duane did not simply lose control of his bowels as I had originally planned. Instead, he became something of a fountain, blasting up and around his pants and spraying a good couple of feet behind him.

Too much. Too obvious. Too forceful. I hadn't meant for that to happen. That didn't look like an accident—it looked like a summoning. Not good.

Cindy jumped away from him, gagging. Duane took off running at his basketball player's sprint for the bathroom. The stench filled the food court. Mall cops began to converge as well as the janitorial staff. The word "summoner" started to float through the crowd. *Not* a word I wanted to hear.

On a plus note, Cindy stormed off without waiting for Duane.

Jake stared at me with a stunned expression on his face. I stood up amid the commotion, slipped my napkin into a nearby garbage can, and walked away toward the arcade.

Jake followed. "What the fuck was that, man? What did you just do?"

"Look, just shut the fuck up. You didn't see anything, ok? Duane must have eaten something funny, is all. Happens all the time."

"Bullshit," Jake said with finality. "I saw you drawing those symbols on the napkin. You rubbed blood on them. Robert, that's fucking summoning. That's drawing on the powers of the fucking darkness, and you used them for a fucking prank? That's some serious shit right there."

"Look, it's none of your fucking business. Duane had it coming and you know it. So shut the fuck up and be cool before you call attention to us. Be fucking cool, man. Calm down."

Jake still had a wild look about him as I dragged him to an old Mortal Kombat machine to contest our skills at pushing buttons in the correct rhythm against each other.

"It was kind of funny to see Duane's face," Jake said after our first round.

"Yeah. He looked like he was about to shit his pants," I said with a straight face.

Jake snorted. "You're right that he had it fucking comin'. That motherfucker did not play by the rules there."

"Can you fucking believe he still had Cindy? As if taking Jeanelle from me wasn't good enough; he just wants to have his cake and eat it too."

"No shit," said Jake. "Plus, it's not like you hurt him, right? A little embarrassment, but you didn't, like, crash the stock market or explode his heart or anything." Jake was still shaken, but he was trying to make the best of the situation. I appreciated that; it felt good to have him reach out his hand, confirm we were still friends even though I had just done something unspeakably evil.

"Yeah. I didn't really want to hurt him."

"Where'd you learn that shit, man? I mean, it's not like we have those runes in any of our school textbooks."

"It was a family thing. I'll show you next time you come over. Maybe you could even learn a couple."

Jake's eyes went wild again. "Nah." He tried to brush it off casually, but I could tell the notion deeply disturbed him. "I'll pass on that. Fuck, man, you've had your laugh, but you gotta lay off, too. Cops don't always just arrest summoners, you know."

I knew. I hoped that the amount of garbage in the food court would conceal the napkin with my blood on it, or else I had already screwed myself. But I also knew that I could not leave Duane alone until he had lost everything, including Jeanelle. Duane needed to be the laughingstock of our school, and Cindy didn't go to our school. So far, I felt all right. My soul could take one more summons.

Jake didn't need to know that.

"Yeah, man. I'm done with it; I just needed to get a little payback, that's all." I was lying, but he took it for truth because it comforted him to do so.

On the screen, his Scorpion thoroughly trounced my Reptile. I stepped away from the machine. "Hey, man, I think it's time to get clear of this place."

I knew that, with the size of show I'd made of it, the cops were going to want to investigate this one. I had gone from triggering a simple accident to triggering a felony investigation. My saving grace was that Duane had not seen me in the food court (mostly because we were beneath Duane's notice), and so my link to the "victim" of the summoning remained out of sight of the police. If Duane walked around the mall and saw me, though, I'd at least have to answer some questions. That would be bad enough. A search of my fostie home would end me. The fosties *thought* they were simply old papers from

Uncle Herman; they'd only seen pages that hadn't been rubbed with lemon juice. Once the cops went through the papers, though, the jig would be up.

"Yeah," said Jake. "You want to go catch a flick?"

That wasn't a bad suggestion. The movie theater would be dark, and it would effectively remove me from the mall for a couple of hours. It would also make my timing more normal, so as not to trigger any questions from the fosties.

"Sure. You know what's playing?"

"I dunno. Some cheeseball comedy, an action flick; you know, the usual."

"Let's head to the theater, then. We can decide on the way."

We stood away from the machine. As we did, the ground shook beneath our feet.

"You feel that?" I asked.

"Yeah." That panicked look was in Jake's eyes. "Is this your fault?"

"Nothing I did. Let's, um..."

Let's see, earthquakes. I tried to remember what you were supposed to do in an earthquake. I'd never actually been in one before. Spokane just does not get earthquakes. It's not like Los Angeles, or even Seattle. It just doesn't happen over here.

"Doorway?" suggested Jake.

"I guess." How fast were earthquakes supposed to be? This one was gaining power as time went on, the tremors becoming larger and faster.

The two of us went to the archway of the arcade, the closest thing to a doorway we could find. Throughout the mall, people were doing the same, or jumping under tables. A general panic ensued.

Then came the crash. It resonated from farther down the hall, and I couldn't see what made it. The single crash was followed by a scrabbling sound, like a dog digging up the back yard, amplified tenfold. The ground stopped shaking but the loud, rending noise of concrete and rebar being torn apart continued.

"What the fuck is that?" Jake asked.

I didn't have an answer for him. "I don't know. Look, Jake, you gotta believe me. I got nothing to do with this shit."

Jake nodded silently, but the color drained from his face. I couldn't fault him for that; my own knees were buckling at the sound.

And then the screaming started.

GRACE

I GOT UP EARLY on Saturday, slid behind the wheel of my car, and headed out to my new favorite local diner for a bite to eat and a cup of coffee. I'd repacked my bag with summoning supplies. I slid it to the far inside of the booth as I sat down, tucking it out of sight on the seat, and sat counting off what I had found out in my head.

Thing one: Matt had been down the hall from whatever took everyone out. It hadn't tried to get him, but had presumably fought off and defeated a large group of summoners. Even if I assumed some of them were crushed immediately when the outer wall gave in, that implied some serious fire power. Lastly, it had left by the time Matt worked up the courage to check. That meant something capable of moving with significant speed. It could be a flyer, or something similar that could get out without being easily seen. By Matt's own admission, he kind of checked out after he saw the carnage.

Thing two: The Spokane cops were keeping an eagle eye on the crime scene. Now that I'd already attracted attention once, I needed to be really careful not to catch their eye again as I did my investigation. Given the general deterioration of the Weave elsewhere, I really wanted to get up close and personal with the Weave at the crime scene. Who knows what I'd find out? It might at least give me a clue how something had managed to take out so many summoners at once. Not that I thought I would get a chance.

Thing three: There weren't any more summoners in town to talk to. Before leaving Seattle, the Council and I had tried to run down any leads on the few summoners listed as "missing persons." They'd all run into dead ends. We'd tried friends, families, bosses and co-workers. The council had acknowledged my report last night with a terse update that was really no update at all. As far as anyone knew, the whole Grove had died except for Matt and three apprentices in Seattle.

The waitress stopped by to take my order. I decided on coffee and a big Belgian waffle with spiced apples on top. What can I say? I think better after dessert. Anything covered in caramel, sugar, and whipped cream is definitely dessert, even when the restaurant tries to disguise it as breakfast.

The waffle's flavor burst over my tongue. Spicy, delicious, and warm, with the half-melted whipped cream over the top. I sat there letting the flavors linger in my mouth, nursing my coffee and staring out the window for a couple of hours as I racked my brain for what my next steps would be.

I sighed and rustled through my bag to dig out my wallet. I came out with the usual wad of crumpled receipts, and finally my slim black billfold. I've been told that I have manly taste in money holders, but I don't like clunky wallets. I have enough trouble digging through my bag without having to lift a brick out from its cavernous depths, thank you. Plus, I keep my magnetic rune tiles and paper rune tags at the bottom of my bag. I like the possibility of finding them without hefting the above-mentioned brick.

I paid the nice lady and went about stuffing all the crap back into my bag. The silver glint of aluminum nestled in the receipts caught my attention.

"Hey," I called before the waitress could leave.

"Yes?"

"What's the best way to get to the aluminum plant from here?"

"Why do you need to go there? I think that place is basically closed."

"Is it the only aluminum plant around here?"

"As far as I know."

"Yup, that's the one I want, then. Any ideas how I get there?"

She gave me a look that said I clearly must be a nut job.

I shrugged. "I take black and white photos of abandoned industrial sites as a hobby. You get really moody-looking photos. You'd be shocked how many people buy them." It was a weak excuse, but what the hell.

"I suppose that's not the weirdest thing I've ever heard of," she said, shaking her head. "But it's not too hard to find. If you go to the corner of Trent and Evergreen you can't miss it. The thing's massive. Just go north from here, then turn west when you hit Trent."

I thanked her and almost skipped out to the car. I had a date to keep with an abandoned aluminum plant.

THE DESERTED PLANT stretched like a big, hulking skeleton left to decay by the side of the road. The bulk of it seemed to stretch on for miles. Hundreds of large chimneys hung over the roof of the main building, so it resembled a forest of dark, pixelated mushrooms. A water tower which may have been white at some point still bore the faint letters "FINEST ALUMINUM." The restaurant lay to the south, lining the factory squarely up with the hole I'd felt in the Weave. I felt a prickle of anticipation on my skin. If the hole was here, I hoped the Visitor left some indication of its passing.

I drove down a little-used access road that felt like an accordion and found a gap in the old chain link and barbed wire fencing around the campus. I could have just summoned the fence past me, but if something here really thought summoners were yummy, I didn't want to risk catching its attention. From up close the building appeared even more ominous: all rust, broken windows and long-past glory days.

The air around the plant pressed my blouse and skirt against my skin with dry, prickly, and hot persistence. It seemed to settle down to the earth in an oppressive blanket of heat. The grass which had long ago turned brown and brittle rattled as I passed. I gave a half-hearted tug at one of the doors to see if it would open. No big shock when it didn't budge. I continued my hike around the campus, looking to see if I could spot any sign that someone had been in or out of one of the buildings recently. The scale of the plant really was epic. It looked like it could house a small town. I felt like an ant skittering around the edges of an old picnic which had long since dried out in the sun.

As I rounded the corner of the large building farthest from the main thoroughfare, I found a destroyed area of the plant. I'm not a big believer in coincidence. A portion of the wall bulged outward and there were pieces of debris and metal scattered over the desiccated ground in front.

"Ok," I muttered under my breath. "Come on, Grace Anne, it might be nothing, but this is what you expected. Don't freak out now. This is why you have your bag of tricks."

I gathered my suddenly skittish nerves and scrabbled through my bag. I drew out one of my sets of rune tags and strapped my portable rune board to my forearm. After a moment's debate, I unzipped one of the bag's side pockets and slipped the ornately carved acorn ring onto my right index finger. I grabbed the bag of blood vials next.

The vials I used for quick-draw summoning were one-sixth dram vials capped by stopper tops with an over-pocket clip just like a ballpoint pen. I got them from an online apothecary shop. I had no idea what normal people used them for, but they were really handy if you thought you were going into a situation where speed counts. I clipped as many little vials of blood to my purse strap as I could fit across my front. It served as my summoning equivalent of a bandolier. I approached the gaping hole in the wall and tried to peer into the gloom inside. The brightness of the noon sun made it difficult to see anything at all in there.

However, as my eyes adjusted to the dimness, I began to see shapes of large pieces of machinery farther into the building and the faint outlines of florescent lights hanging from the ceiling. The whole place reeked of must, dust and cobwebs, but the floor closest to the hole looked almost clean. I scanned the area, looking for movement. Some part of my brain noted that it was probably foolish to do this without even a hint of backup.

I didn't listen to it. Besides, if I did, what would I put in the report? "Found suspicious ruined factory. No further investigation necessary." That seemed both false and cowardly.

I rearranged the runes on my board by feel and summoned a flashlight before stepping gingerly into the darkness. I could feel grit or dirt on the floor underfoot. My footsteps crunched as I walked forward, but I still couldn't make out more than bulky shadows looming in the distance outside the range of my flashlight. I kept my eyes open for movement or anything which might explain the large hole in the wall. I glanced up and confirmed that all the damage seemed to go outward...meaning something or someone had broken out of here.

Creepily, I didn't see a corresponding hole going in. The perpetrator had probably come through the tear from a different Weave. But had it returned to its home Weave again? Goosebumps lifted on my arm.

Holding my breath, I took few more careful steps into the building, sweeping the flashlight in front of me. The dull glint of something on the floor just ahead caught my eye, beside a large compactor of some kind. I stepped over by the machine to bend down and pick it up. Sure enough, it turned out to be another irregular piece of metal, light and squiggly in shape. It closely resembled the one I'd picked up earlier. I bent down, aiming the flashlight under the machine to check for more.

Out of the corner of my eye I saw a large object fly over my head and crash down several feet beyond me. The darkness magnified it like a vast phantom; I could see movement more than form. But it was big. Really, really big. The room shuddered as it landed.

I jerked the flashlight in my left hand up as the floor rocked under my feet. My right arm flew out in an attempt to catch myself. My elbow collided with another machine in the darkness, flaring in pain. I gritted my teeth and stabilized myself against the first machine as a crack ran through the floor under my feet.

Something hissed at me with white fangs and red eyes glistening out of the inky darkness. On pure instinct, I jerked the beam of the flashlight up to get a better look.

It winced from the light. I had a split second to perceive a giant animal unlike any I'd seen before, looming at least five times bigger than me. Red and orange spikes covered its body, giving its torso a shape like a sea urchin on legs. Those legs ended with long crescent-shaped claws. Its head resembled something more like a raccoon, with pointed ears, a narrow snout and sharp teeth.

It screamed a challenge at me, displaying the curved teeth of a carnivore before leaping upward.

No way this thing could be anything but a Visitor, but hell if I knew what kind. I dodged underneath the machine. The Visitor crashed into it with force that reverberated along my skin as I crouched underneath.

Its jaws tore at the machine, trying to take large bites out of it. The metal creaked as it strained over my head. Large claws flashed out of the darkness and started rending the iron.

For something so large, the Visitor moved with mind-numbing smoothness and speed. Metal squealed as it started to give above me.

I tried to scoot toward the next machine on my knees, but my legs got caught up in the fabric of my skirt. I cursed. With one eye on the Visitor, I knotted my skirt up so the bulk of the fabric hung in a large lump at hip level.

It wouldn't win any fashion contests, but it freed my legs. I crouched low and half-crawled, half-frog-hopped to get under what I took to be a large super-duty conveyor belt.

The thick belt with its giant metal cross pieces had less clearance above the floor than the other machine. I had to crawl on hands and knees as I fled as fast as I could, keeping as much of me under the belt as possible. My hands left indentations in the dirt and grime. As I skittered back toward the hole, my knees swept over the prints. When I glanced back, I had left a snail trail in my wake.

I skimmed the room with my eyes, hoping I could use a cheap trick to kill the Visitor right here and now. I needed something handy to summon into his—I decided for no reason it must be a *he*—chest cavity. Hey, I'm allowed to be arbitrary. Point is, even if it didn't kill him, it should slow him down.

Dropping to my belly under the conveyor belt, I propped my weight on my elbows and brought the magnetic rune board on my right arm out in front of me. Feeling the raised runes on the tiles, I quickly strung the magnets together with my left hand, my fingers lining up the runes' familiar shapes. The feel of the runes was so ingrained in my fingers that I completed the rune phrase in the time it took for two breaths.

My hand whipped up to my purse strap and pulled a vial free, snapped it open with my thumb and splashed the contents across the runes on the board in one smooth movement. I focused my Sense, powering the runes.

The summons went off. A chunk of broken rebar bounced off the Visitor's chest and clanged off the concrete with heavy finality.

Damn.

The summons had rebounded. Naturally or unnaturally, this Visitor was warded against the summoner's quick and dirty assassination technique.

Any living thing is usually vulnerable to having something unceremoniously jammed into its innards. Not this guy. It could be an innate talent, or even a result of all the summoners it had already eaten. Either way, it was immune to my one get-out-of-jail-free card.

I swore. More sweat broke out on my forehead.

The Visitor let out a spine-chilling scream. The industrial conveyor belt I was hiding under began to rock. I watched in disbelief as the bolts holding it to the floor began to bend.

With an ear-splitting protest, the bolts came up, still covered in chunks of concrete. I scrambled under a different piece of machinery and positioned myself so I could see the thing. With a strange *woomph*-ing sound, the Visitor flung the conveyer belt so hard it rebounded off the far wall.

Effing hell.

I'd found the perp, all right. The air left my lungs in a giant rush, and I had to fight to get it back. My eyes refused to move off the cloud of dust billowing around the pulverized conveyor—even when I knew I should be looking around for the Visitor. The jumble of crumpled metal bits only loosely resembled the original machine.

Just a little telekinesis, Gracie, no biggie. You can do this.

Yeah, right.

If sanity ran in my family, no doubt I'd be mid-panic attack right now. As it was, I could feel adrenaline trying to push me into an instinctual response. Losing focus in battle can mean death for any combatant. For me, it would rob me of the Sense and guarantee it.

I made a conscious effort to bring myself back together. Forcing myself to breathe in deeply, I tasted the dust in the air, felt its dry sting against my nostrils. My hands clenched into fists. The familiar sensation of my fingernails digging into the center of my palms helped me re-center myself. I looked with renewed purpose at my surroundings. New Goal: Live long enough to indulge in a well-deserved rant to everyone back home. I only had *me* to make that happen.

The Visitor was outlined against the hole in the building, which made it difficult to make out any fine detail. I could tell he was easily twice as big as an elephant, with a short snout and fangs from earlier. It also had long, dangerous-looking spikes for a coat, and a monstrous, barbed, club-like tail. Not to mention those scything claws.

And, oh, yeah. It didn't take a genius to figure out he was hungry.

I braced myself for continued pursuit, but he didn't seem to realize where I had gone. He brought his huge club of a tail down and smashed it into a nearby compressor. The machine cracked and flew aside as if it were no more than a cheap, plastic toy. My stomach flipped. Okay, so much for my nascent Plan A: hide. So what should be Plan B?

The Visitor was still scrabbling in the debris for something. I squinted to make him out even as my fingers flew over my magnets, finding and moving the runes into a new chain. With the Visitor throwing around this much power, I needed a shield of air and force. I grabbed another vial from my purse strap and splashed it over the runes, my Sense powering the summons. The field sprang up around me on an extra surge of adrenaline. The Visitor's head snapped toward me. He padded over to the corner of the room closer to the hole in the wall. I watched as he deposited—more aluminum?—next to the wall closest to the hole now categorized in my head as "the desired escape route."

This Visitor liked shiny stuff, huh? At least that explained how aluminum had gotten to the crime scene. With the prize carefully placed on top of his glimmering pile of odds and ends, he paced back toward me with a predator's confidence.

"Don't you dare try to eat me!" I blustered. My fingers began finding the runes for earth and kinetic force almost before I thought it. I summoned all the large, jagged obsidian shards I could Sense with my hasty rune set and flung them toward the bristly raccoon-thing with all my might. If I could just get it to move, I might still have a chance to get out without having to fight it head-on.

The shards sped toward it, exactly on target. But before they reached the Visitor, they suddenly shattered against thin air. The multiplied shards whistled back at me at twice the speed. My improvised shield shuddered and shimmered with the impact of hundreds of obsidian flakes. I didn't think the summons had simply rebounded. Somehow the Visitor had caught it and turned it back on me. Only a few shards made it through the shield, but my face and arms were scored and stinging. *Fine*, I thought grimly. *Since it can catch and return projectiles, I'll just have to get more creative.*

The beast leaped, bringing my mortality into painful focus. My field of vision filled with its bulk—suspended in the air above me— but descending fast. My weakened shield wouldn't hold up to a full onslaught from this thing. In desperation, I summoned a puff of wind and soot, throwing the cloud into the Visitor's face and wrapping it around him. I dodged around the Visitor's shrouded thrashing. As soon as I cleared the reach of his claws, I ran toward the opening with all my might. *All you have to do, Grace,* I encouraged myself, *is get out of here and collapse this whole bloody building. I bet he won't like that. Those I-beams up there are good old World War II steel.*

I was maybe three feet from the exit when that giant tail swept across and raked the machinery behind me. It absolutely crushed the machine I'd been using as shelter. The building rocked with the force and I lost my footing.

I barely managed to tuck my head in and roll with the fall. I skidded across the floor, through the gritty filth, and (bless my luck), out into the welcome sunlight. I jumped up, disoriented. The world spun crazily. I poured all my concentration into standing and locating the spiny beast. It was almost on top of me.

All kinds of bits of broken machinery, rock, and aluminum hovered in front of it, held in some type of field. It pushed them toward me with breathtaking speed. I dropped flat on reflex. Frantically moving tiles on my rune board I slapped them into place one after another, removing all the supports from this section of the building. Then I hurled them down through the factory roof at high velocity. I managed to pull most of the building down on top of the creature. The rubble squealed and groaned as it crashed down, and then went silent.

I pulled myself together and limped across the big asphalt parking lot toward where I had left my car. My head pounded with the effort of pulling off such a large summons. I didn't remember twisting my ankle, but it ached like I had.

A traitorous piece of aluminum by my foot trembled, shook, and began slowly rising up off the ground.

"Oh shit." I glanced at the structure over my shoulder. More four-letter words sprang to my lips. The demolished part of the building, and several parts that weren't quite rubble yet, slowly lifted off the ground with the dignity of a soon-to-be catastrophe.

My stomach dropped down into the soles of my feet. "Great. That's just wonderful," I muttered. "This can't be good."

Behind my eyes, my head throbbed and a heavy blanket of weariness threatened to crash down as soon as my adrenaline rush faded. I shut my eyes and took a deep breath. Then I turned to face the factory. I refused to die today. As I watched, the rubble rose high enough for me to get a good, fully lit, eyeful of what I'd fought.

I faced a gargantuan Visitor that was surely a demon. Not surprising, given his hostile intent from the beginning. Although, even beneficial spirits can sometimes cause quite a ruckus by accident. But no, this Visitor was evil, and as such, he won the demon designation.

He even looked evil. Instead of fur, he had barbed red quills and orange stripes. He also had dark, beady red eyes and a giant, rocky, stalactite-like tail. The beast easily stretched thirty feet from end to end, with another fifteen feet in height and twenty feet of building debris held above his head ready to crush little ole me. His teeth and claws proved, sadly, as long, sharp, and deadly as I had guesstimated before. I strengthened my air shield again and tried to figure out how I was going to get out of this one.

Slapping blood on a tag, I summoned up a thick piece of sheet metal, positioning it in front of me to use as a shield as I threw a summons together on my rune board. Slowly I backed toward my car, whipping a blood vial from my bandolier. My head rang with the amount of power I'd expended. The beginnings of a killer headache rooted itself behind my left eye. I had no idea how long I'd be able to keep going; I'd never faced anything on this power level before.

In desperation, I flung blood across the summons on the acorn ring I wore and closed my eyes, concentrated on my summons, and hoped for the best as the metal crashed down on top of me.

When I opened my eyes, the branches of a mammoth, living redwood held me.

"You called, little sister?" The tree winked.

Giddy relief rushed through me as I stared up at its familiar weathered face. Redwood had been a Moore family guardian spirit for generations. Silently I thanked my mom for insisting I take the ring with Redwood's summons carved into it when I moved out to Seattle. Moms sometimes seem prescient. I'd argued that I could summon it by hand just as fast as using some old heirloom, but in this case, I don't think it would have been true. Granted, I still wasn't sure exactly how we'd get out of this, but at least someone I trusted stood with me.

"Why, yes, I did!" I hugged the tree's rough, stubbly bark. "Thank you, friend."

Tied to the ancient redwood forests, Redwood had been the very first tree I'd ever climbed. At the time, I thought everyone knew talking trees.

"We're not out of the woods yet," it rumbled, as if we were still playing some kind of childhood game.

I groaned inwardly at the pun. "Here he comes again."

Redwood buffeted the incoming missiles with a torrential gout of wind, sending most of the debris careening back to the ground. The demon-creature puffed up his quills, screaming defiance, and charged into the parking lot. The remains of the collapsed building jerked up off the ground with sudden violence.

The redwood brought up its winds again, but this time fewer of the projectiles veered off course. Several branches broke with a sound akin to thunder. I clutched desperately at Redwood's trunk and tried to avoid falling or getting hit by branches. The wind twisted suddenly and a miniature tornado struck the beast from the perfectly clear sky.

"Got 'em!" the tree thundered gleefully. "I don't go easy on those who hurt my friends." He set me down gently. "You go for help. I am hard to kill, but once it gets closer, I will not be able to protect you."

"Watch out! There are more things incoming!" I backed away hurriedly.

The demon seemed to decide it should take out Redwood first, his eyes focusing intently on the giant tree spirit as he charged forward, attempting to close the distance between them. The tree gusted its wind, trying to knock the demon off course. The demon bowed his head, forcing his way through them with little problem. Once he reached Redwood, he began thrashing his chitinous tail against the tree's trunk. Everywhere the tail struck made huge rents in the redwood's bark. The tree hit the demon with an even more violent tornado, but it didn't even seem to faze the thing.

I really needed to know what type of demon I was up against before I fought him again. I tore my gaze away and started to run toward the car, my ankle sending frissons of pain up my leg. That just marked me as the easier prey. The demon fired a blast of energy at me that knocked me to the ground, then pounced. At the last second a root shot up out of the ground, wrapped itself around the beast's hind legs and stopped him mere inches from me.

The demon launched itself upward to break the root. I lay there stunned and helpless. I couldn't make my body do anything. I watched the beast plunge toward me, my brain stuttering as though I were trapped in an evil dream. His red eyes smoldered with lethal intent.

He was so close I could feel his hot breath ruffle my clothes, tugging at the spots where scraped, bloody patches stuck to my skin.

Well, Gracie, this looks like it. Better luck in the afterlife.

I braced myself to be devoured...and nothing happened.

Power rolled through the Weave like a tsunami breaking on shore. The beast's quills stood on end until he resembled an evil, demented hedgehog. He almost seemed to grow with the wash of power. His head came up, pulling some scent from the air before he bounded away from me, focused on the source of the disturbance. He headed rapidly away from the aluminum plant, seemingly in line to arrive at my hotel. Not that I knew why, but that also meant he was headed toward a densely populated area. Four-letter words sprang to mind.

I managed to lever myself to my feet. The pressure behind my eyes throbbed warning, but I didn't have time to worry about it right now.

I spared a split second to look questioningly at Redwood, but it shook its leaves in response to my unspoken query. "I will not be quick enough to follow. I have taken too much damage. I will stay here and sleep. I can return to my Weave on my own."

It settled its roots into the parking lot and closed its eyes. The giant redwood looked out of place in the ruined parking lot, but in its dormant state, no one would be able to tell it was anything more than a big tree. I took another deep breath and started after the demon.

You don't have time to freaking die yet, Gracie. There are nice people out there who don't know they're counting on you. You're all they've got to keep this thing from absorbing all that power and becoming absolutely unstoppable. You have to go stop it, or the whole Spokane Grove will have died in vain. You're a superhero.

Really great pep talk, Grace. I almost believed me.

I vaulted myself into the air, hot on the beast's heels. My fingers busy with my rune board, I augmented my speed with a quick kinetic force summons and cushioned my landings with bubbles of air. I sped over the ground in long jumps, the arch of each leap just above the tall grass, the wind whipping at my skirts.

If that demon-beast landed among a bunch of people, it would undoubtedly cause all kinds of destruction—and probably more death. What I really wanted to do was turn around and walk away so I didn't have to deal with any of it. I knew enough to report to the council now. I could call it a day, but my conscience just wouldn't let me.

If I did nothing, I'd hate myself later.

Plus, I would bet solid money that it was intent on eating the source of that power surge. *Hell* if I was going to just let it take whatever that was, too. It was already insanely strong. So much so that I wasn't really sure I *could* stop it.

We bounded over the chain link fence around the aluminum plant's perimeter on the south side. The beast was not soaring as I had originally assumed, but using giant pouncing leaps at a high rate of speed. The max range on the leap seemed to be about fifty or sixty feet.

Beyond the fringe of grass outside the plant's fence, we came up on the Spokane River with frightening speed. Across the river, it was all developed area. The beast came to the river's edge and sniffed the air for a fraction of a second, then gathered its hind legs into a dynamic jump that cleared the water with ease. The feat did cause one or two automobiles crossing a nearby road to swerve in their lanes with shock.

So I was going to jump the river, too. Just peachy. My jaw clenched. If I continued to follow this demon into public, the government would make my life hell. Inconvenient didn't even begin to cover it. Then I peered ahead at the busy city. Not following it would be worse.

The river loomed wide, swift, and deep in front of me. If I missed the jump, I could land on the rocks or get swept under in the fast-moving current. I rearranged the tiles on my rune board and threw more blood across them, discarding the vial. I waited until the last possible second to throw myself up into the air, some part of me still denying I wanted to do this.

For a wild moment, I thought my reluctance had made me misjudge the jump after all and I would end up in the middle of the river. My arms wind-milling, I came down on the far side like a bowling ball that's been thrown too high, but my feet stayed under me. I kept running and took a second to reorient myself to the buildings on this side of the river.

I bit back more four-letter words. I knew where it was headed. My hotel would have been bad enough. It was steering right down into the Spokane Valley Mall, on a Saturday. The parking lot was crammed tighter than a can of sardines. Through the glass front and large windows, I could see stores full of people intent on where to find their next bargain or snack.

I couldn't think of any way to get ahead of it, or stop it, before it got there. Even with my augmented speed, I was too far behind. I would have needed to be a human cannon ball or grow jet engines or something. I actually considered the latter for a nanosecond, but decided I couldn't safely steal any active jet engines, and even if I did, I'd probably end up more like a seagull that had encountered one than a plane.

My primary focus narrowed to keeping that bright orange, spiky raccoon in front of me. I tried to ignore (somewhat unsuccessfully) that we were bounding along through the mall parking lot in front of God, the cops and everybody. We passed a small child whose mouth opened so wide he could have swallowed a goldfish bowl. My fingers danced over the raised runes on my board as I used every trick I could think of to pull the pedestrians in front of the mall away from the demon and keep them from getting under his claws but...I wasn't always fast enough.

This wasn't the kind of blood I needed on my hands. I hadn't been sent here for this at all. The Seattle Grove would have my butt for their afternoon tea. There was no way that busting into the mall with this thing wouldn't make the evening news. The public would think I had summoned it to kill them all. But somewhere in that mall was something it wanted, a power source I couldn't let it have.

"Grove politics be damned," I muttered to myself. "My name will just have to be shit."

I kept following.

Oh yeah, this was turning out to be a perfectly awesome assignment.

ROBERT

THEY SAY in high-stress situations the human body has two basic responses: fight or flight. Standing in front of the arcade listening to the crashing and the screams, I found that there's a third possible reaction.

Paralyzing fear.

With crowds of people blowing past me through the mall exit, with Jake screaming, "Come on, dude" and running back through the arcade to its own exit, I stood there and stared at the second floor of the Sears store. I knew something abnormal was happening. I knew I should be running with the herd of people. But I stood and stared, waiting to catch a glimpse of whatever was causing this panic. It came out of the top floor entryway of the Sears like a...

I got nothing. There was nothing I could compare it to. It was a horror, and I had never seen its like. I can't give you a comparison that would mean anything.

I used to read Ranger Rick when I was a kid: cute-little-raccoon-teaches-kids-about nature stuff. I loved it. I even forced my (real) mother to sew me a Ranger Rick costume for Halloween. I loved Ranger Rick.

Yeah, I was a nerd from the beginning.

Point is, this thing looked like Ranger Rick on a cocktail of steroids and PCP. It was huge, maybe thirty feet long and ten feet high. Bright reddish-orange quills covered its body. Those quills had impaled a good chunk of the Sears Men's Wear section and an "As Seen On TV" advertising sign. Its tail was this massive, chitinous mass twitching back and forth in the Sears, destroying what I could see of the bedding section and rupturing perfume bottles. The sweet, sticky smell wafted through the mall.

It stood above me, sniffing the air, and then it stared straight at me. Our eyes met; PCP Junkie Rick had a pair of burning, empty eyes. I shuddered but otherwise remained motionless. Some natural instinct grabbed me, held me, told me that if I didn't move, it couldn't see me.

This, by the way, is a stupid instinct. Never, ever listen to it; it gets you into trouble.

Rick jumped. It was more than just a jump; a cloud of air seemed to blast away from the floor as he did it, resonating with a deep-pitched *woomph*. He cleared the escalators between us, heading for the tile floor in front of me. My body finally let me move, ducking behind the entryway of the arcade.

I could feel the hot stench of Rick's breath as his jaws snapped inches from my face. He hit the tile and slid, slamming half his body into the arcade, leaving half in the mall hallway.

Right in front of the exit.

"Sonofabitch," I muttered to myself as I realized that I had gotten trapped in a mall with something out of a nightmare. Choose flight, folks.

That's when I first saw her. She came hurtling out of the bottom floor of the Sears like a crazed gypsy. She was short, far shorter than I, but in her mid-thirties-ish, I guessed. Her dark hair flowed back in this semi-ponytail, and her arms clattered with bangles. Her belt, a linked series of medallions, glittered as she ran. She had a bag slung over her right shoulder that had several vials on the strap; it looked like a cross between a chemistry set and a bandolier. Her right arm had some kind of weird rectangular buckler strapped to it. Her long, maroon skirts whipped in crazy patterns as she moved faster than any human I have ever seen.

Straight at Rick.

Rick stood up from his crash into the mall exit. He didn't notice her, his gaze fixated on the flashing lights within the arcade. Shiny things apparently fascinated him. Of course, giant raccoons apparently fascinated me.

The woman whipped a piece of paper out of her bag. As she took it out, I saw the runes. Runes on the paper, on the belt, on the bangles, and on the shield. Runes on her ring. Runes everywhere. I couldn't doubt it; this was a summoner. Not a dabbler like me, taking on a bit of taint for vengeance. I beheld the full-on evil.

I was about to watch a demon battle a devil.

"Run, you idiot!" she screamed at me as she slid past, her left foot sideways and her right leg bent low. She flicked one of the vials from her purse/bandolier onto the slip of paper in her hand, covering it and her hand in what could only be blood. She flung the paper into the air. I began to run, ducking behind the summoner as she focused on her spell.

I crossed the hall into the main section of the mall. I saw a chunk of lumpy, gray material pop out of the tag and impale itself on one of Rick's quills. The summoner wiped the blood from her hand onto one of her bangles and began to run at me.

Was she going to attack me next?

"I said RUN, dumbass!" She turned, sliding in next to me, and extended her bangled left arm toward Rick. I remembered Jake's shirt: "I am a bomb technician. If you see me running, try to keep up."

Rick's left side exploded, blowing up the entrance to the arcade and crashing it down on him. The shock wave tore through my body, half-deafening me. She'd done it! I looked up at her, afraid to know what she was going to do next, but she glanced at me with little more than contempt.

"Forthethirdandfinaltimebeforewebothdie, RUN!" she screamed at me with the intensity of someone who is absolutely convinced she has only managed to piss off a giant raccoon demon. I was sold.

I ran. Then I saw that she was running beside me. That was also probably not a good sign. Behind us, the roar of one giant, angry, possibly rabid raccoon beast started to crescendo; I assumed that meant it was getting closer, but I wasn't about to take the split second needed to look over my shoulder.

A couple of mall cops in white and black uniforms ran past us *at* Rick. They had their flashlights out, held in the club position. Up until now, I'd always thought of mall cops as being sort of laughable, but these were some brave, committed souls right here. I resolved never to mock them again.

Not that it was going to be an issue with these *specific* mall cops, of course.

I never did see what exactly happened to those two. They were heralded as heroes on the news for their brave action, and I can't dispute that. By the sounds of it, they delayed Rick for a couple of seconds. I'm not sure what would have happened to me without them, but I made it to the center area of the mall, the summoner hot on my heels. I sped through the central gallery as quickly as I could.

She did not. I had run a good fifty feet down the mall when I realized she had turned to face Rick down. There were four corners to the mall center, an intersection of sorts. A group of staffers wearing red shirts that read "Shop 'til you rock" were helping to herd people away out the far end of the mall. That insane little gypsy-looking lady slapped up two pieces of paper on each of two of the corners of the intersection, sprinkling blood on both. Then she stepped into my section of hallway and started playing with her buckler.

Only it wasn't a shield. I realized. She had a magnetic blackboard covered in magnets with pre-scribed runes and rune phrases. It reminded me of those cheesy refrigerator poetry kits, the ones that stick random words to your fridge and let you make meaningless sayings with them.

Except these were rune sets. She was slapping together a complicated spell, and she did it in seconds using this board. Okay, she was evil, but...a part of me (probably the same part that made me learn from Uncle Herman's notes) just thought she had style. Evil, corrupt, and out to control the earth, sure. But style.

Besides, only one of the two legendary evils in this mall had tried to eat me. I was going to root for the other one.

She splashed a little more blood on her rune-magnet buckler, thumbing the vial with the surety of someone for whom such an action was second nature. She held the board out toward Rick, who barreled down on her. A sheet of what appeared to be solid metal shot up between her and Rick. I heard a loud CLANG as ten tons of furious demonic raccoon slammed into what looked to be inch-thick steel.

I had to admit it. *That* impressed me on a Looney Toons level.

The steel wall managed to buy the people in the mall some time to try to get out, though I had no idea why a sworn enemy of humanity gave anything resembling a shit about those people. I stood and watched, fascinated by the raw power in front of me. I knew it was going to get me killed, but this beat any movie. The adrenaline crackled through my veins and I no longer cared about Jeanelle, or Duane, or anything. For the first time in a week, I felt alive.

The ceiling over the mall hallway rose two stories high, plus a cathedral-style skylight. Only ten or so seconds after the clang, I heard the now-familiar *woomph*, and Rick came sailing over the steel plate, making use of that high ceiling. In the blink of an eye the summoner was next to me, and we were running again.

I could hear her mumbling under her breath. At first I thought she was muttering some sort of a spell, but then I caught some of the words and I realized that she was cursing. Her wrath seemed to be directed at the "Grove Elders," whoever they were, as well as a "complete fucking idiot novice," which I feared was a reference to me.

"Umm...this isn't my fault?" I tried tentatively as we sprinted away from Rick. She glanced at me with disgust, dismissing that claim with a word.

"Bullshit."

Was it? I hadn't summoned this thing, I didn't want any of this to happen. I had no idea how it got here, but it *had* come straight at me. I didn't know what was going on, but I did know it had killed several people. Attached to a quill along with the men's wear was a bloody red shirt reading "Shop 'til you rock." Not everyone had made it out of the mall's center.

I put it from my mind. I didn't want that blood on my hands, so I chose to ignore her comment. Besides, it's not like I had a long time to think about it. Rick launched himself into the air again as we approached the far end of the mall.

"I have an idea," she said to me as we ran. "Up the escalator."

There was a second escalator at the end of the hallway, and by now it looked like the mall had been cleared of almost all bystanders. We sprinted up the escalator two moving steps at a time, and saw we'd made a mistake as soon as we made it to the top.

The second floor on this end of the mall held the daycare center. Inside, children huddled behind and under pieces of play equipment, some of them with parents who had made it here but no farther, some of them alone. The supervisors had stayed with their charges, much to their credit. Their eyes went wide as they took in my companion's outfit.

"Shit," the summoner said, looking at the children. "This way." We whipped to our right, around the front of the Macy's store. Rick was charging along the bottom floor, but he had already demonstrated that he didn't need an escalator to get up to us.

Another vial flicked out of the summoner's bandolier as she slapped another piece of paper in front of her. She hit it and another one of her bangles with some of the blood, then stood up and stared at Rick as he barreled toward us.

"Get ready to run again," she said under her breath to me. "In theory, this should work."

I was ready to run, al... Wait. What? My head whipped up toward my savior. "In theory?" I asked in a tremulous voice. She flashed me a crazed, toothy smile. We both heard the *woomph* of Rick taking to the air. Her left arm stretched out toward the monstrosity flying toward us, and suddenly I heard a second *woomph*.

Rick turned upside down as some invisible force hit him mid-air, sending him up over our heads and tail-over-teakettle into the Macy's. My new companion burst into what can only be described as an insane cackle as she slapped her left hand onto the slip of paper she'd posted and pulled a *freaking rocket-propelled grenade launcher* out of it. She spun with the motion of her draw, brought the RPG to her shoulder, and blasted Rick in his soft underbelly before he had the chance to stand.

Rick screamed in pain as the rocket hit him in what would appear to be the only point on his body without quills. Once the smoke cleared, I could see that his flesh was singed but not broken.

"What can kill this thing?" I demanded as the two of us broke into a run yet again, this time on the second-floor walkway. We headed back in the direction we had originally come.

"No idea," she said. "So far, I've tried rocks, a living tree, C4, a steel plate, and an RPG. So we can check those off the list. One sec."

Rick *woomphed* onto a bridge spanning the two walkways on the second floor of the mall, jumping from bridge to bridge. The summoner turned and hit him mid-air with another burst of force. He spun and landed on the bridge he'd just jumped off, then continued his pursuit. She turned around.

"He's learning," she said. "We need to complete the field."

"The field?"

"Never mind. Just jump."

"Jump?"

"Cut the broken-record act. We're going over the edge."

The first level lay about twenty feet below us. The food court was to our left, as well as a second-story exit to the mall. I gazed at that exit longingly as the lunatic I had followed here pulled me over the railing and into freefall.

She had pre-coated another slip of paper with a vial. As we fell, a pile of feathers sprang into being beneath us. We landed, not gracefully, in a poofy pile, on our backs. I saw a couple of red-shirted corpses and the steel plate, no longer flat, standing between the two corners.

She rolled out of the feathers toward the other two corners, grabbing papers out of her bag. She slapped one each on the two corners she had not used yet. Was she trying the plate trick again?

"A steel plate isn't going to do any more good this time," I called, as I heard the *woomph* on the other side of the first steel plate that told me Rick agreed.

"Just get out of there!"

I ran for the JC Penney's to the north, over the "Shop 'till you rock" display. She hit Rick with another blast of force, but he shrugged it off as he came in for a landing smack-dab in the middle of the mall. He turned toward the summoner, who fiddled with her magnets. He lunged at her, jaws open, as she smeared blood over her board.

She held her ground, but her chest rose and fell in rapid succession with her panting, and her knees buckled slightly.

I *felt* the power she expended. A rush pounded through my head like being in the middle of a waterfall. Her eyes stayed closed, and Rick's incisors got to within inches of her face before they just...disappeared. A hole opened up under him. He fell, scrabbling at the edge. I couldn't see how deep the hole went, but it was a perfect square, formed by the papers she had placed onto each of the columns. The summoner dropped to one knee, visibly exhausted now.

Rick, though, had other ideas. He braced himself against the corner of the hole and gathered himself for another one of his jumps. His blazingly empty eyes locked onto the summoner, and he leaped upward. This was it; she had run out of tricks. She knelt there, head bowed, eyes closed, unmoving. She waited, it seemed, for the inevitable end; she'd given up, and she'd given me up with her.

Steroid-rabid Rick was on his way up into the air when a column of dirt and rock roughly five hundred feet long crashed through the skylight. It took him in his back and plowed him like a pile driver down into the hole. The summoner's head lifted. She was smiling her huge, toothy, insane smile, as the column of dirt rushed past just feet from her face, driven by gravity down into its resting place. It crashed into the ground, burying Rick hundreds of feet below the earth.

When it finally came to rest with a billowing cloud of dust, the top of it was covered in shattered tile floor pieces that matched the mall;

she'd summoned the ground out from under Rick and set it to fall down on him from above. Then she'd stood there and gotten him to jump up at her just in time for him to get hit with it. Judging by the speed of the fall, it had to have been travelling at or near terminal velocity when it hit him, and he had been propelling himself upward into it. My mind teetered with the forces that came to bear in that kind of a collision. A small, guilty part of me wondered what it would be like to do that to Duane.

Like I said, she got points for style.

So why did she have a worried expression on her face?

"Let's go," she said, catching my wrist. She dragged me through the JC Penney's and out into the Saturday afternoon. Sirens were converging on the mall as we ran away from it.

I had gotten away from demonic Rick, but I had ended up with the thing that took him out. *She* might have been out of danger, but me?

My danger had just started.

GRACE

I GRABBED onto the kid and towed him out of the mall without the smallest hesitation. I didn't know how long that trick would keep the beast out of commission, but I bet it wouldn't be more than a few minutes at most.

"Do you have a car here?" I asked the teenager. He nodded, pointing down the row at a beat-up rust bucket. God knew if it could actually still accelerate, but I didn't really have time to be picky. I pushed us both toward it as quickly as possible.

If I was really, supremely lucky the combined force had knocked the demon out or dazed it, and we had a little leeway. I didn't expect it would take that thing long to dig itself out. Leaving the kid here would be tantamount to abandoning him to be eaten. Plus, judging by all the sirens I could hear in the distance, we didn't have more than a minute until they converged here. If one big bad didn't get him, the other one would.

I threw things that made me obviously a summoner back into my bag as fast as I could with my free hand while unclipping the vials of blood on the strap. My head felt like someone had hit it with a sledge hammer. I'd never done this much summoning in one day before. The adrenaline was still carrying me forward, but I would pay for abusing my Sense like this later.

I glanced sideways at my rescuee as I kept us moving. He was a tall, lanky boy, obviously still mid-growth spurt, and awkward because of it. I tried to wrap my head around the idea that he had caused that massive power surge in the Weave. Judging from the fight, he didn't know thing one about summoning. Hell, I didn't even know what he'd done to bring the beast down on him in the middle of the mall, anyway. Shoplifting? Trying to impress a girl with a "magic trick"?

I discarded those ideas. Couldn't be. Every time I started to do something in the mall, he stared at me like I just grown another head. He didn't look like he'd seen anyone summon before, not ever. If I hadn't felt the power myself, and seen the beast lock onto him, I would have said this kid came from totally, grade A, vanilla human stock.

Right now he looked every bit as young as he probably was, staring back at the destruction with a stunned expression on his face.

"Hey," I said to get his attention. "You realize you're in big trouble, right? As soon as that thing gets out, it's going to come after you."

"What?" he blurted.

"I dunno what you did, and right now it doesn't matter. But you definitely did something. Something with summoning. That demon knows you're here now, and all it wants is to have you for lunch. If you stay here it will, and it will take out anyone and anything between you and it to do it."

"Why not you?"

"Ah, well." I grinned at him. "It'd love to eat me too. But I'm not inclined to oblige."

We were at the doors of his car, so I stopped. "We're going to take your car, and we are going to get you far, far away from here. I'm pretty sure once we go past a certain point it won't be able to find you anymore."

"Pretty sure?" he asked tremulously.

"Pretty sure. More sure than if you stay here. I would say your chances of getting eaten if you stay are about ninety-nine percent. The other one percent is: you get picked up by the cops, they put you in prison for summoning that thing, and *then* you get eaten. We need to be on the road, stat. So we're taking your wheels. Give me your keys."

"No, I need to go check on Jake. He should be out here somewhere."

"No time. We have to leave NOW."

He looked like he'd really like to say or do something else entirely, but after a moment I got a sullen nod instead. My head throbbed.

Good enough. I'd take a sullen teenager over a dead one, any day.

WE PULLED out of the parking lot and headed down Indiana toward the interstate as the first police cars started pulling into the mall parking lot. I just hoped we had enough of a head start to keep the beast from picking up our scent, and that no one thought of putting up road blocks. So much for shopping in town anytime soon. I surmised that someone who'd been at the mall would be able to ID the small hippie chick summoner to the police sooner or later. I hoped for later...but if you haven't noticed, my luck hasn't been all that great lately.

I pulled onto I-90 headed east and began to breathe a little easier. The kid slumped in the passenger seat, watching the road flash past beyond the window. I had no idea where to take us at this point, but I didn't see a giant demon beast or flashing red and blue lights in the rearview mirror. No road blocks up ahead for as far as I could see. We might just squeak out of this thing and have a chance to regroup.

I needed to get a message to the Grove Elders. I would be in all kinds of hot water for this, and I would prefer they didn't hear about it first on the evening news. So much for a covert operation. On the other hand, I had gotten the kid out, and most of the mall occupants had gotten away on their own. Still, I couldn't think of any good repercussions from the kind of blatant display I'd been forced to make. The sooner I could warn everyone about that, and about how powerful this demon was, the better.

I glanced over at the kid as he peered out the window and realized I had just totally dragged him away from home. His parents were probably going to go nuts with worry, and I knew absolutely nothing about him except that the demon considered him prime snack food. I cleared my throat.

"So um, this is a bit late," I said, "but my name is Grace. Grace Moore." He shot me a glance that said he wasn't really sure he wanted to know my name.

"I'm a summoner from Seattle. Today was your lucky, lucky day, because if you'd tried to pull whatever stunt you just did two days ago, I wouldn't have been in town to save you." *And also my lucky day,* I thought. If that demon had eaten him and gained any more power, I doubted I'd be around to talk about it right now.

He didn't answer, so I tried again. "Although, there wouldn't usually be a monster like that around either, I suppose. My job is to try and figure out how to kill that thing." I tried to keep my voice friendly, in spite of the spike of pain that had taken up residence behind one eye.

"I'm Robert Lorents," he admitted warily.

"Nice to meet you." I flashed him what I hoped was an encouraging smile. I don't do that well with kids. He stared at me without saying anything for a minute, then appeared to make up his mind.

"Why was Rick after me?" His eyes dropped back down to his hands as he asked.

"Rick? Who the heck is Rick?" My brow wrinkled, trying to remember if I'd seen anyone by that name in the Spokane Grove's files. He saved me by clarifying.

"Ranger Rick. The giant raccoon."

I laughed, then cut if off as my ears rang. He had been a second away from losing his life, and he had time to think *that*? In spite of how big a liability he was undoubtedly going to be, and how crappy I felt from the extended summoning in the mall, I smiled.

"There are two types of Visitors. Spirits are neutral or beneficial

Visitors. Demons are malicious or harmful ones. Our pal Rick is a demon. From what I can tell, he eats summoners to absorb their power. Something you did made him think you would be tasty. What did you do?"

The kid grunted. I frowned in irritation. I really did not get kids. In my view, the joys of parenting, and especially teenage-hood, were overrated. Surely the fact that I had saved his bacon today counted for something. I pinched the bridge of my nose between my eyes, trying to ease my headache, and tried again.

"Ok, so why were you at the mall today?"

"Hangin' out."

Yeah, that was helpful. "Were you with friends?" My voice sharpened as I struggled to hang on to my frayed nerves and sorely abused patience.

"Jake. Who you made me run off and leave. He could be dead!"

"I'm sure he's much safer without you. Anybody else?" I forced the words out past the pounding in my skull.

He shot me a glare full of skepticism and mulishness. "No."

"Did you summon something to impress Jake?" I threw this scenario out more as an act of desperation than any hope of getting an affirmative. Something had to get to this kid eventually, right?

"What? No." His face relaxed in puzzlement. The question had genuinely shocked him out of his sullen mood for a moment. I pressed my advantage.

"Ok, but you did summon something, yes?" My voice had gained an obvious whine of exasperation. I cleared my throat.

Robert nodded. I took a deep breath.

"But it didn't turn out like you expected?" Goddammit, I *would* get information out of this kid, even if I had to pry at his monosyllabic answers all bloody day. Part of me started remembering an old text I'd seen with the runes for summoning thumbscrews…

"I didn't summon that thing." He stared at me. Great. We were back to stubborn and defiant.

"I didn't say you did. So your summons turned out just like you wanted, then?"

"Not really. It was just supposed to be a prank." Finally. An informative sentence.

"Tell you what. You tell me exactly what you were doing right before Rick showed up, and I'll be able to give you a better idea of *why* he showed up."

Exhausted, I rubbed a hand down my face and waited to see if he'd take me up on the offer. He did.

If only I'd known what I was asking beforehand. With that one innocent question, I got a sappy high school romance story and a tragic, sickeningly sweet, syrupy, overly emotional one at that. Just hearing it made my teeth hurt.

He obviously felt this girl's betrayal deeply, and I think it actually upset him more than almost being ended by an extra-planer being. However, as he got toward the end and crazy Uncle Herman's journals—along with his petty, wrong-minded, rash, and destructive summoning on a fellow human being, my irritation vanished. A sudden tide of hot anger flooded me, intensifying my headache and making my skin prickle. I took another deep breath. I suddenly foresaw a lot more breathing exercises in my future. Maybe I should take up meditation.

"How old are you, Robert?" I asked quietly.

"What? I'm seventeen."

"Summoning has the potential to be extremely harmful. What you did to Duane could have horrible repercussions. Do you know how summoning works?"

"You use blood and runes and focus to bring something to you. Whatever is specified in the runes is what you get, and you can use more runes to tell it not to hurt people or where to summon it to, right? I used Wanjo when I did it. Uncle Herman said that would keep it from harming people."

"That's not quite right. When you summon, you are moving something from one place to another. And you are using runes and blood and Sense to do it. Everything has balance. It's still not possible to create something out of nothing. That 'crap' you summoned into Duane had to come from somewhere. I can't think of anywhere that would be a good source...sewer treatment plant, porta-potties, septic tanks. Did you even specify human excrement?"

"No, I don't think so..."

"Horse manure, cow manure, dog poop, you get the picture?"

"It still didn't hurt him," he said grumpily.

"Regardless, revenge is a horrible reason to use summoning on someone. There is nothing as complex as a living body. Medical summoners train for years. Something like what you just did could have fatal consequences. Summoning is also not meant for vengeance or payback. It exists to keep balance in the world and maintain the Weave. Those who wield it must be sure to always do so responsibly."

"Yeah, sure, responsibility."

"What's that supposed to mean?" My voice sharpened with impatience.

"Like someone's going to tell *you* what to do." The kid actually rolled his eyes at me.

"You think nobody tells me what to do? I have bosses just like anyone else."

"You'd just pull out an RPG like earlier today."

I had never really understood why people pull over to the side of the road to yell at their kids before that moment, but as I brought the rust bucket to a stop on the shoulder it made perfect sense.

"Are you that dense?" I exploded. "Of course someone can tell me what to do. I am not the all-powerful *god* of summoning. I have four or five *tiers* of people who can tell me what to do, and a lot more people who are my colleagues and friends, even if they don't know I'm a summoner. The government may not have a good opinion of summoners, but in general we are doing our best to make the world a better place. And—keep—our—friends—safe." I jabbed my finger into his chest at each word. "Including trying to keep idiots like you from killing anyone else and keeping a whole army of things like Rick from invading and creating havoc over the entire world. I guess maybe you think that can be fixed by a grenade launcher? We barely made it out of there alive today. My friends and family die just as easily as yours. Sometimes more easily. You remember that."

"Sorry," Robert mumbled in a flat, teenage make-the-lecture-stop tone.

I took a big breath and tried to let my anger out. This boy was a babe in the woods, with no one to tell him better. I had to let it go for now. We needed to keep moving.

"We'll talk about it more later," I said, pulling the car back out into traffic. He huffed a breath out, crossed his arms over his chest and stared pointedly out the window. He didn't deign to answer, but by now I didn't really expect one. I noticed that the indicator for the gas tank pointed lower than I'd like. I started scanning the road signs for a gas station.

"To answer your original question," I said, forcibly choking down my ire. I'd just saved the punk. It would be counterproductive if I strangled him now. "Rick came after you because when you cast your summoning on Duane, you used a large quantity of power and very little focus. It rang the Weave like a gong. So you basically announced to it that you were in the vicinity, and also good eats. After the initial surge, it found you by the residue of the summoning that clings to you in the Weave. The longer you go without summoning, the weaker it gets, the less powerful it is, the harder it is to track. Make sense?"

"I guess so." He appeared to think about it for a moment. "So are you saying I am a really powerful summoner?"

"I am saying you have the *potential* to be a really powerful summoner."

"No. I don't want to be evil," he said softly.

I groaned. "There *is* no evil. Summoning itself is neither good nor evil. Much like any other tool, it becomes good or evil based on who is using it. Think about it like a knife. A knife is very useful, and can help you chop vegetables or cut twine, but it can also be used to kill someone. Summoning is like that, just more extreme."

He still didn't look convinced.

"Look, is there anything I can do to prove to you I'm not evil? Why the hell would you go with someone you thought was evil?" Intense curiosity filled me about that one.

"Well, you didn't try to eat me, plus you're a badass," he said. "I didn't want to piss you off."

I'm a badass? That was news to me. Actually, being called that felt nicer than it probably should have. Good to know that at least one almost-summoner appreciated me, even if it fell more on the fear and awe side than I would have liked.

"Listen. It probably doesn't mean much for me to just say it, but I'm not evil, and I'm not an angel either. I swooped in and saved you because that thing wanted to kill whatever had that much power so it could take it for itself. Each time it does that, it gets even harder to stop. I would have kept it from killing whoever cast that summons, even if it hadn't been you. I don't like that thing in my backyard, and I especially don't want it getting more powerful. I want to send it back where it came from, but I need more help than one novice who *supposes* I might be evil. So we're going to lay low for a bit while I do some research. And whether you like it or not, you're going to learn to control your power so you can defend yourself. Rick is not the only thing out there that's going to think you smell delicious. First, though, we need gas, so I'm taking this exit. If you know any campsites around here where we can hide out, that would be good."

Exhaustion pulled at me. If we didn't find a place, I'd have to pull off soon anyway. With everything I'd already been through today, I couldn't keep going on like this much longer.

Robert shrugged. I really did not get what went through his head at all. "I know a place," he said.

Well, Hallelujah. Assuming he wasn't pulling my leg, at least that solved one problem. Now if only someone else could do this call with the Grove director, life would be good. Oh, well. I picked up the pay receiver, deposited my coins, and prepared myself for some bitter medicine.

~

THE CALL with the Seattle Grove could have gone worse. They could have sent a disciplinary team to pick us up right then. They weren't *happy*, per se, that I had blown up the Spokane Valley Mall and taken off with an underage minor of unknown parentage. They reminded me that it was a very *bad time* to take an apprentice, and I reminded them that *right now* if Robert didn't get protection and training, then he made very good snack food. They agreed to lend me access to several basic summoners' books from the archive to begin his training, and commanded me to keep them posted on both fronts. I also asked Amy in a side phone call to look into the condition of the boy, Duane, from Robert's high school. The Grove didn't ask why Robert had been Rick's target, so I kind of omitted that part from my official report. Little white lie, give the kid a leg up, and if he turned into a bad seed later, I'm sure they'd have something else to hang him out to dry with.

All in all, I hung up the phone feeling as though I'd gotten off pretty light. Except...

"Robert, do you have anyone you want me to call? I can't tell them much, but I could let them know you're all right."

"No."

The kid's face made it plain I wouldn't get more of an answer. I pressed my lips together, but the kid suddenly seemed to remember something.

"Wait, let me call Jake."

I waited as he stepped into the phone booth, pointedly shut the door so I couldn't hear his conversation, and came back out.

"Anyone else?" I asked. "Your parents?"

"No."

"I'm sorry to hear that, but I guess that makes things easier. If you change your mind, let me know. Let's get out of here."

I couldn't help thinking that hanging out with me only slightly lengthened Robert's life expectancy. In the long run, there were actually good odds that being my apprentice might get him killed. I told myself that would *only* happen if I couldn't figure out demonic Rick. The winner takes all, Gracie.

ROBERT

UNCLE HERMAN'S cabin was just as I remembered it, which is to say small and dirty. He'd built the thing Abe Lincoln style, a box made from stacked logs with mud daubed in between. The walls of the cabin held his crazy mountain man accoutrements: the bear traps and skinning knives. He had one, single-wide bed with a goose down mattress (equaling the death of more geese than I care to think about). His chest stood at the foot of the bed.

He had hand-dug his well, complete with a hand pump. The outhouse out back would probably throw the health department into fits. As a child, a visit to Uncle Herman's had been a thing of wonder. He knew how to have fun, and it didn't involve video games or TV or really anything using electricity.

The fact of the matter is, there was something very real about Uncle Herman. I hate Thoreau, and I hate to quote him, but when I read the line "I went to the woods to live deliberately" in my junior year AP English class, I immediately thought of Herman. That man lived deliberately. You could tell he loved living every moment of his life, and the enthusiasm of a guy like that really rubs off on all of us.

Plus, he knew all the cool games in the woods.

Now I had brought Grace here. If I hadn't found out Herman did some summoning as well, I would never have defiled my memories of this place by bringing a summoner here. No matter what Grace said, I had seen the power she was capable of throwing around, and it was tremendous. I also knew that, with summoning, you didn't get that much power without throwing away your soul. I had escaped Rabid Rick, sure, but I had pulled up to this cabin in the custody of something much, much worse.

I had almost bought into what she said in the car, that there was no evil. She *had* worked pretty hard to save the people in the mall, after all. But then I figured it out. That thing wanted to eat summoners; it had come after me because I made a lot of noise, but it *also* came after Grace. Apparently it grew more powerful as it ate people. It was in Grace's interest, then, to stop it from eating people. In other words, Grace didn't save those people out of altruism; it was purely selfish.

Now she had brought me up to my childhood cabin, and she wanted to take my soul away as well. I'd already sold a small portion of it for what I did to Duane, but I deeply wanted to believe I was salvageable.

Grace settled herself down in front of Herman's old wood stove in one corner of the cabin. She stacked firewood in the stove, then wiped some of the excess blood from her sleeve onto one of her many bangles. A soft, cozy fire sprang to life.

"Um...it's, like, at least seventy degrees out. Do we really need to do that?" I asked.

"Need to? Nah, but I like it. You never get something like this in the city. It's cool."

I shook my head and walked outside to avoid the blistering heat. I settled myself down on the split-log bench in front of Herman's cabin and stared into the woods, remembering a simpler time.

"LOOK OUT AT IT, BOY." Uncle Herman said, pointing out at the forest sloping down and away from his little cabin. "What do you see?"

"Trees!" I shouted. I was six; when you're six, shouting the answer means you must be right.

Uncle Herman chuckled. "Yes, boy, there are trees. What else do you see?"

"Ummmm...stumps?"

"Yes, boy. There are stumps. What else?"

"I don't know. Lots of stuff." I was confused.

Uncle Herman took his arm from around me and pulled a piece of leather with some fur padding on it and a couple of straps hanging off it from inside his jacket; the same pocket he kept his pipe tobacco in. He covered my eyes with it. The fur felt soft against my eyelids as he strapped the blindfold around the back of my head.

"Now what do you see?"

"Nothing!" I laughed at his joke.

"Nothing, huh?" He took the blindfold off. "Let me try."

I giggled. This was a funny game. Then I caught the look on Uncle Herman's face. There's a thing that happens when you're a kid and you know an adult is serious. Maybe it's the tone of voice; maybe it's a facial expression, but whatever it was I knew in that moment that Crazy Uncle Herman was being entirely serious.

He placed the blindfold around his own head, fastening it firmly. "About twenty yards down the hill there's a stump," he said. "There's a broken branch that still has some needles on it lying over it. Just to the left is a big old Douglas fir, and it's bending down a little bit, into the slope of the mountain. Behind it is a larch, the grand tamarack, and its needles are just coming in with the new spring. The ground drops off shortly behind it, a rock face, and then there's a meadow."

I giggled. "How did you know that?"

He smiled at me. "I saw it. In here," he said, tapping the side of his head with his index finger. "When you know the land, boy, she will show you what you want to see. But you have to know her. Do you want to know the land?"

I nodded in that very serious way that only a child is capable of. "Good. Let's go introduce you." He took me by the hand and led me down. We got to the stump and he moved the branch off it. He wrapped his big, dirty, calloused hands around my sides, under my armpits, and lifted me up to the stump.

"This is Robert Lorents!" He shouted it down the slope, and the gentle breeze that had been blowing died as the land came to attention, listening. "He will be here to take care of you when I am gone! Know him, and allow him to know you!"

Crazy Uncle Herman got his name for a reason. I felt weird standing on that stump, being introduced to a clump of trees and grass. He took it so seriously, though, that I knew to keep my childish mouth shut and not say anything.

A LIGHT POPPING interrupted my reverie, followed by a scent I had never smelled in this place wafting into my nose. I poked my head back into the cabin.

"You hungry?" Grace asked. "I sent out for Chinese."

Lying on the narrow bed, on top of the hand-quilted blankets and underneath the hanging bear traps, lay a stack of folded white containers with pictures of pagodas on the side, sticking up from a rumpled, plastic bag.

"You sent out for Chinese? How..."

"There's this really great hole-in-the-wall called Ming's up next to Grove Headquarters in Seattle that does some of the best Szechuan out there. Here, try the chili prawns; they're to die for. Or because of. Depends on whether you can handle the spicy stuff." She held out one of the containers to me along with a pair of chopsticks in a paper wrapper.

I understood utilizing the forces of darkness to battle something like Rick. Up to that point, Grace at least had a solid reason for doing what she did. Sure, she'd thrown her eternal soul into the gutter, not to mention committed innumerable felonies, but she'd done it to save the lives of a whole bunch of people from a demonic raccoon. It was almost heroic, in a fall-on-the-grenade kind of way.

Or at least it would have been if she hadn't done it to save her own skin.

This, though? Grace had just committed a major felony, not to mention violated all the laws of nature, and she'd done it for a bit of decent Chinese. Well, judging by the smell, she'd done it for a bit of very, very good Chinese. Not the point, though.

Still...it didn't make the Chinese food evil, right?

I took the prawns and a container of rice. They were fresh, hot, spicy, and delicious, just as promised. Especially the spicy part. I glanced around for some liquid; Grace pulled a one-liter Pepsi out from under the bed. It was, of course, icy cold. The woman was scary, but my mouth was burning. I took the Pepsi and drank deep.

After my disturbingly out-of-context meal, I went back to the porch. There really wasn't a lot else to do, and I didn't want to be in the cabin with Grace if I could possibly avoid it. She had rather casually sacrificed a portion of her soul for chili prawns and a couple of Pepsis.

I remember once talking to Jake about Thai food. We loved the stuff, and in joking around with him I had claimed that I would sell my soul for a plate of decent Phad Thai. That joke didn't seem funny now.

I sat there on the porch, looking out at the twilight of what was at least the second worst day of my life, and cried a little for what I had lost. This place made me feel it more keenly. This was where Uncle Herman and I had parted ways.

AFTER MY INTRODUCTION to the land, any time I visited Uncle Herman, we would take hikes across his property and he would make me memorize everything.

"Know the land," he would say, and he meant it. After the hike he would test me, asking me where this pine was, or where a certain stump was. As the years went by, he wanted to know how many sprouts of clover were growing in a certain patch. I took it as a memory game, and I was always good at those. It was fun to try to guess what Uncle Herman would ask me about.

One day, when I was ten, we were seated on the bench. He looked at me and asked in that same voice, "What do you see?"

I gazed down the slope. "I see that the tamarack is losing its needles. About half are on the ground. The firs up the slope are coning; I can see it on the leaning Douglas."

He was smiling as he reached into his jacket and pulled out the old leather and fur blindfold. He placed it around my head the way he had on the first day. "What do you see now?" he asked, just as he had four years prior.

I laughed again. "Nothing."

"Look again. Look with the eye in your mind that knows the land." I sat there, very still, and tried to look with my mind. The wind was a gentle breeze in my face, but everything else seemed to hold perfectly still. Then I remembered. I remembered everything.

"I see that the clover patch behind the tamarack stand has been eaten by something. Judging by the pile of scat next to it, I'm going with deer. I see that the wind has broken some of the leaning Doug's branches off. The wood is still fresh underneath. I see that old stump in front of the firs has been colonized by ants; that rotted wood looks to make a good home for them. I see that marmots have taken up in the rock face. I see..."

"Well done, boy."

"But I'm not finished."

Uncle Herman chuckled at me. "Of course you're not. You never would be. But it's time to try something new."

"Something new?" I wasn't sure what Uncle Herman was going to suggest, but I knew it was going to be fun. Everything was fun with Uncle Herman.

"Run to the lodgepole pine at the far end of the meadow and back. Let's see how quickly you can do it."

"Just running? We do that in PE all the time." I had never known Uncle Herman to be so boring.

"Yup. Just running." His voice hid a smirk. I didn't know what he was up to, but it was Uncle Herman asking me. I obediently began to remove the blindfold.

"What are you doing? Leave that on."

"Leave it on? You want me to run through the woods blindfolded?"

"I want you to run through the woods using that eye in your mind that sees the land," he said. "I want you to be with the land and to feel her beneath you. You and the land are but separate parts of all of reality. Once you feel that, you will know how to move, because the land will move you."

I had memorized this landscape over years. Maybe I could do this. I stood up from the bench, and ran as fast as I could into the forest. About thirty feet in, I collided with a Douglas fir. I had known where it was; I had forgotten where *I* was.

Never sprint into a tree. It hurts. At least, it does until the unconsciousness kicks in.

After that, Uncle Herman and I drifted apart. I didn't trust him or his games anymore, and I wouldn't play them. I remember him telling my parents that he thought I was ready, but they didn't want to hear it. In the end, Crazy Uncle Herman was crazy. Running through the woods blindfolded. That was a good way to get yourself hurt.

I SAT on the bench outside Herman's cabin. It made sense to me, now. Uncle Herman had been a summoner; watching me feel that pain provoked a sadistic joy in him. No wonder he'd done it. And now, once again, I was here at this cabin with a summoner. I didn't even know what sort of pain to expect, but I knew it was coming.

And this time I deserved it. I had sunk just as low as Herman had. I had used the dark arts for vengeance. Pain would be my just reward.

A wild impulse seized me. I needed that pain, needed to be cleansed with it. I walked back into the cabin and rummaged around on the shelves until I found what I was looking for: the old leather and fur blindfold.

"What in the world is that old thing?" asked Grace. I didn't respond. What I was about to do was intensely personal. She wasn't allowed to have a part in it.

It had been years since I had memorized these woods, and even then I hadn't been able to do this. Undoubtedly, this was going to hurt. That was the point. I slung the blindfold over my eyes and took off toward the woods at a run.

As I ran, I called up my memory of the land. It was surprisingly fresh; I knew that I was running straight at a stump. Instead of tripping over it, I jumped, slamming my right foot down where I knew the top of the stump was, and leaped from it high into the air.

Behind that stump was the leaning Doug; I was very close to one of its branches, so I shot my hand out and swung down to the ground on its springy limb, being careful not to twist my ankle on the uneven ground below. From there, I dropped into a crouch and sprinted around the old tamarack to the rock face, knowing exactly where it was. I dropped to a slide in the soft grass before I got to it, then spun and grabbed the top with my hands as my torso shot over the side. I swung back in on the rock, then let go. I dropped for a foot and a half before my foot hit the ledge ten feet down. Once slowed like that, I could easily jump the other four feet into the meadow.

I remembered! Not only did I remember, but I could place myself in the memory. As I tagged the lodgepole pine at the end of the meadow and spun to sprint back, I could feel my knowledge of this land wrapping around me. My blindfold was irrelevant. In fact, I was seeing this land better through my memories than I could through my eyes. It was exhilarating.

When I got back to the cabin, I removed the blindfold only to see Grace standing in the doorway, leaning against it.

"That was impressive," she said, and it sounded as though she meant it. "Uncle Herman teach you how to do that?"

"Well, Uncle Herman used that trick to get me to hurt myself. I guess I showed him tonight."

"Why would your uncle want to hurt you?"

Now there was a question I did *not* want to answer. But she was looking at me with those honest eyes. Except for that one slip-up in the car, I had avoided insulting summoners. I definitely did not want to piss off someone who could pull an RPG out of a thin piece of paper. In that moment, though, her eyes were soft and her tone of voice expressed genuine concern that I didn't think she was capable of. So I took a deep breath and answered her question.

"He was a summoner. That's what you people do, isn't it? Hurt others for your own power?"

I don't know what I was expecting from Grace in that moment. Rage, anger...casual annihilation, maybe; I didn't know. But I can tell you that when she snorted, trying to keep herself from laughing, and failed by doubling over into a loud guffaw, I didn't see it coming.

She took a moment to compose herself. "Is that why you're avoiding me? I thought I told you. There is no taint. That's just propaganda, is all that is. Summoning doesn't make you evil any more than being a carpenter or a teacher or some such. It's a profession, not a religious choice."

"But why else would Uncle Herman try to hurt me like that?"

"Look at what you just did," she said, gesturing back towards the trees.

"What, the memory trick?"

"That wasn't a memory trick. I thought you said it'd been years since you were last here. Do you really think that every bush, plant, and rock is still in the same spot?"

I had to think about it. She was right, of course; it *had* been years since I'd made those observations. But I had also accurately called to mind everything here, as it was, tonight.

"I'm not positive, but I'm pretty sure he was training your Sense," she said.

"Sense?" Herman's notes had mentioned the word a couple of times, but I couldn't figure out what he meant.

"Look, summoning is the art of moving matter and energy in space, right? Well, the Sense is the psychic or mental or mystical or whatever ability that allows you to know where things are, and where you want them to be. Watch."

She grabbed an empty box of Chinese from inside the cabin,

holding it in her left hand. She closed her eyes, took a breath, and all of a sudden the box moved from her left hand into her right.

"That's impossible!" My face heated after pronouncing *that* priceless gem. I'd watched the woman drop a 500-foot pillar on a demonic raccoon, but moving an *empty box* I had decided was impossible. Brilliant.

"That's the Sense. If I'm holding it, and I'm moving it to a place where I'm holding it, then I know where it is and where it's going. That's really what the runes and the blood are for. The runes form a structure that seeks out locations; the blood powers them. Together, they guide your Sense out past your immediate body. That's what lets me do this." She dragged out her magnetic board and flopped some symbols around, then dropped a bit of blood onto it, and almost instantly there were two fortune cookies sitting on top of the board.

"Those cookies were back in the cabin, beyond the range of my Sense. I had to use the runes. But now that they're in range, I can put them wherever I want." The cookies disappeared from the magnetic board and reappeared on her shoulder.

"But when I want to send them out of my Sense, I need to use the runes again." She rearranged a couple of runes on her board, then re-wiped the blood. One of the two cookies vanished from her shoulder and ended up in my hand.

"It looks to me as though Herman was training your Sense. You've been training to be a summoner for years now without knowing it. How evil do you feel?"

That's a strange question to be asked, by the way. Do evil people ever think of themselves as being evil? I pondered that for a second before shaking my head. "So all that stuff about summoners being devil-worshippers and stuff?"

"Lies. Lies written into the history books to justify a governmental lockdown on power; it's been that way for millennia. Back in the day they had the Inquisition and the witch hunts. Now they have this." She peered at me and changed the subject. "You know, it looks to me as though your Sense gets out to, what? Twenty, thirty feet?"

"I really wasn't paying attention to how far out it goes."

"Look, between the amount of power you busted loose earlier, and the range of your Sense, you've got some serious oomph there, kid. And Spokane just lost most of its good summoners, including your uncle. Give me the winter to train you up right, and we just might be able to do something about it. I just need to take care of your raccoon friend first."

Huh.

I had a lot to think about. Grace was offering me a life of danger, excitement, and power. Did I want that? I wasn't sure. Even if summoners weren't evil, there was still a great deal of risk involved in being one. On the other hand, she had looked *really* badass in the mall. It was going to take some thought.

I opened up my fortune cookie. "Today will begin a new journey. Watch your feet."

Wow. The cookie nailed it.

GRACE

I JUST ABOUT SWALLOWED MY tongue when the kid strapped on that old ratty blindfold and the Weave changed around him as he started running. As I watched him dodge through the forest completely blind, using only his Sense, my breath caught in my chest and my arms broke out in gooseflesh. I'm sure my mouth hung open.

An old, master summoner might be able to extend his Sense in a similar fashion at the very end of his life, but he would have had decades of honing his Sense and his focus. I'd never met anyone among the Elders who would ever be able to Sense fast enough and far enough ahead to be able to dodge branches, trees, and boulders in the scant seconds required at a full run. This kid had some serious untapped talent.

And an amazing teacher at one time, even if somehow Herman had never gotten to the summoning itself. For all Robert's talk of summoners being evil incarnate, someone had taken a lot of care to make sure that one of the most basic, intrinsic tenants of summoning came to this kid as easily as breathing. Just who was this Crazy Uncle Herman, really? And if he'd been such an accomplished summoner, how the hell had Rick taken him out? A chill crept down the back of my neck.

The raccoon-demon scared the shit out of me. After all, I'd met him after he'd stolen the power from an entire Grove. It stood to reason one mid-grade summoner would have her hands full just trying to get away, but what about before that? Something about this massacre just didn't seem right. Occam's Razor advised I accept the answer that fit the most facts.

For now, I had to assume Rick got the jump on the Grove, killing and gaining power so rapidly that the others had no chance. It was a pretty depressing scenario.

Still, after Robert's feast with the Sense, I felt slightly more hopeful for the first time in days. He might be a whiny, confused teen, but he had all the makings to be a great force in the future—if only I could convince him that wielding his birthright did not automatically risk eternal damnation, etc.

I sank down on the log bench in front of the cabin, feeling a seed of pride begin to form in my chest about this kid. I had managed to rescue him, and even if he didn't know it himself, he represented the best hope this Grove had for a future in the long term. Watching the sunset gild the trees, I took a deep breath and let out a huge bubble of anxiety I hadn't even realized I held. First, though, he definitely needed more training in how to control his enormous potential.

Sitting there in the cooling evening breeze, I turned the fortune cookie over in my hands and thought back to my own childhood training.

AS A CHILD, I loved going to Grove Group. Obsessed over it, really. I didn't have any siblings, and I got to hang out with tons of other kids around my age. Plus, they were all summoners' kids, which didn't happen often. I'm sure the underlying rationale for putting the group together was much like any other kids' group—socializing, learning, that sort of thing. At the time, since the activities all had a summoner flavor to them, I thought of them as something like secret superhero lessons. The classes always took place in a new location, and the teachers rotated. The classes taught us valuable skills, but the instructors had unique methods compared to my average classroom teachers. Each session differed drastically from the last time by necessity. In hindsight, I'm sure they cycled locations and teachers to keep the classes from attracting attention from mundanes.

To six-year-old me, the classes moved to be awesome.

The kids were usually the same at each lesson. I keep in contact with one or two of them even though we've all moved on to different Groves.

On the day my silly superhero fantasies crashed, the teachers planned a treasure hunt with us. I'm surprised my over-the-top excitement didn't drive my mother right up the wall.

The goal of the treasure hunt differed from mundane ones. The instructors gave out points for identifying objects in the room with the Sense. The students stayed where they were, closed their eyes, and told the instructor what was in a specific box. The teachers placed boxes all over the room containing things of different sizes, shapes, and materials. The boxes made sure no one could cheat just by looking. The teachers ranked each box and labeled it with a number of points based on difficulty. The ones a single foot out were one point each, and it went up to as much as ten points at the far end.

As each kid found things, they would earn points; the more points you accumulated, the bigger prize you could get at the end of the day. I had my eye on an overstuffed unicorn plushy that looked incredibly soft but cost a ridiculous number of points. I was paired up with two other children, one chubby boy, younger than me, and one tall older girl in a black skirt and tights that made her look like an ostrich. I figured I had a pretty good chance of getting more points than either of them.

Our instructor, a soft-spoken, middle-aged woman with gentle hands and blue eyes, asked the boy to identify what was in the one-point box right behind him. He got it right, to his delight, and I thought, *Yep, piece of cake. That unicorn is mine!* She came to me next.

She started to ask me what was in a one-point box as well, but I interrupted her.

"I want to do a ten-point box! I can do it. Ask me about one of those."

She gazed at me a little reprovingly like she thought I was out of line but didn't want to call me out in front of the other two. "All right," she said. "Tell me what is in the blue box next to the coat rack on the way in."

I squeezed my eyes shut and concentrated. I could Sense the wooden floor under my feet and the dust motes in the air around me. I scrunched my eyes tighter and concentrated harder. I strained with all my being until my face heated with effort and my jaw ached with tension. The teacher cleared her throat. "Uh. Grace, let me come back to you. Make sure to focus on the box and concentrate, or else you won't be able to extend your Sense."

She moved on to the ostrich-girl, who got a five-point box with no problem and flashed a triumphant smile at me. Then back to the boy, who this time got a two-point box a little farther away than the first.

My turn again. "A five-point box. I can get a five-point box." So it went, with me insisting each time that I could get a four-point box, or a three-point box, and finally, a one-point box. By this time my bravado had worn thin and the other children thought I was playing some sort of obscure joke on the teacher. They complained loudly about the gimmick getting old. I stood there with my pent-up frustration and embarrassment, failing to identify what was in the one-point box.

The ostrich-girl squinted at me with disdain and said, "Just get one already."

My failures all piled up on me at once. In that moment she was the *enemy* even more than the stupid boxes full of stuff I couldn't see. So what if I could only fake being a superhero.

I wanted to hide. Somehow the next words out of my mouth came out the opposite of my deepest fears. "I don't need to Sense! You can't make me!"

I took off running, shoving everyone out of my way, scattering little mystery boxes in my wake.

I locked myself in the bathroom and got down to a really good cry fest, huddled up in the back of the stall farthest from the door. After an immeasurable time, my crying subsided to hiccupping tears and I heard a voice call through the stall door.

"Gracie? Are you in there? Won't you come out?"

For a moment I felt so ashamed I couldn't get myself to move. They had called my mom here because I'd failed. She would find out I didn't really belong with the Grove after all. Maybe I had been switched at birth or something.

"Gracie?"

I reluctantly stood up and unlocked the door, but went back to sit on the toilet rather than come out. Mom pushed the door open slowly. I saw the shape of her, exaggerated in shadow by the lights over the sinks. The silhouette of her loose slacks, her soft oversized blouse, and her hair swept up into a fishtail braid loomed over me for a moment. I wondered if she and Dad would disown me since my Sense was defective. Then the stall door opened and it was just my mom in her usual tan-colored slacks and peasant top.

Concern lined her face. She took one look at me and sighed. "Oh, sweetheart. Come here." She held her arms out.

Relief flooded over me in a rush. I flung myself into her arms and poured out all my frustrations, including my wild surmise that maybe, maybe she and Dad had another baby somewhere because obviously someone had gotten it mixed up with me.

She laughed when I got to that part. "No way! Not possible by any stretch of the imagination." She hugged me closer. "Your father and I may try to give you away occasionally, but you are one hundred percent ours. All the way down to the way you always bite off more you can chew."

I settled more securely into her arms and turned to gaze up at the curve of her chin as I complained, "But I can't Sense what's in the box! And all the other kids were doing it with no problem. Even kids who are younger than me. There *is* something wrong with me. Pretty soon

I won't be able to play any of the games, and I'll never ever be able to get enough points to win the unicorn for the rest of all time!" To her credit, my mother didn't even crack a smile when I pulled out the ultimate injustice.

Instead, she looked thoughtful. "Tell you what. I have some ideas about that. Let's try an experiment." She started rummaging through her bag, then paused and glanced up, grinning. "Close your eyes for a second." I closed my eyes.

She pulled something out of the bag and pressed it against my back. "See if you can Sense what I'm holding behind you."

"I already told you I can't do this game!" I pouted. "I don't have whatever lets you see it! It's broken."

"Try once more, just to please your crazy mom, ok? I promise I have an idea."

"Fine." I scrunched my eyes up one last time and pushed outward with my focus. This time I Sensed cold tile under my feet, Mom's arm still draped across my shoulders, and...

"I can see it! It's a green scarf with blue dots!"

My eyes snapped open and I spun to face her. "How did you do that? Why can I do it now?" I did an excited little hop dance.

"You did it, Gracie, not me. You do have a summoner's Sense, but for right now yours is very short range."

I stopped. "But I can train it, right? I can train it to go across the room?"

"To be honest, I'm not sure. It might be possible. But Gracie, even if your range doesn't get much bigger, you can still be a great summoner. If you want, you and I can check out a whole bunch of books from the Grove library, and tomorrow I can start teaching you how to read and combine runes to help you find things with your summoning that are farther out than you can see with your Sense. Would you like that?"

I nodded enthusiastically.

"All righty!" My mom laughed. "We'll show them all next Grove Group, eh, Gracie? Let's do our best." She winked at me. "To the library and home to your dad for dinner!"

My mom was as good as her word. We spent many nights studying old, dusty rune compilations after dinner to make up for my lack of Sense, a habit I still kept up even after I moved away. It all seemed like a very long time ago now.

I SIGHED. It didn't look like Robert would face the same challenges I had, but he would still need knowledge and discipline. That, I could give him. I'd been eight when I found out I wasn't quite your typical summoner. My disappointment from that day pained me a little, although in many ways I had turned a weakness into a strength. I'd studied runes desperately ever since, wanting to keep up with my contemporaries.

Oh yeah, there's a reason people think I'm a rune prodigy. I'm fast. I have to be. I've memorized more rune combinations than most people would believe possible. I'd call myself a genius of hardwork and necessity—not nature. Not that I go around advertising it. Sure, all those hours with my mom had paid off. In hindsight, after that incident she arranged my schedule so I attended events where runes were already in use. Any class that relied on runes made my inability to Sense much less noticeable. In layman speak, she used my handicap to essentially skip me ahead a grade.

I succeed so well in compensating with runes that to this day very few people know I can't do the most basic summon without them. The little trick I had shown Robert had only worked because I was already touching the fortune cookie.

I use runes as crutches to help me limp along within the constraints of my sadly myopic natural abilities. Robert needed to use runes for an entirely different reason: so he could harness his enormous potential and keep from just blasting his presence out to whatever happened to be able to Sense the Weave every time he released his will. That, and it should keep him from tearing the Weave asunder or blowing anything up. That would be good.

~

THE NEXT MORNING, I summoned myself a platter of herb and bacon quiches, a couple of scones, and a giant coffee from the 5th Avenue Cafe and Bakery. I absolutely love interesting places with "delivery." Next I piffed a note to Amy asking her to check out some books on runes for me from the Grove library and send me a note back with the books and whatever she could find out about the police situation in Spokane. Finally, I summoned index cards and a nice, thick, black pen from my apartment back home.

Robert gave me a quizzical look when I offered him the food but scarfed it down before going out to do whatever it is that teenage boys do in the middle of the woods on a sunny day. He still seemed a bit jumpy around me, and every time I used summoning it seemed like he wanted to crawl out of his skin. In other circumstances that might have been funny. Since I hoped to teach him how to use summoning himself, it became less funny and more disturbing.

I had grown up knowing my family were good people who happened to also be summoners. I didn't need anyone to tell me the government discriminated against us because that's just what people do when things scare them. Robert had no such support or background, so he had the worst possible view of summoners. On some level, he had to be scared of himself.

It was sad, but not without some merit. Completely untrained, he reminded me of a toddler with a machine gun. The machine gun wasn't evil, but someone should make sure he knew its dangers and couldn't hurt anyone with it.

I set to writing down the most common runes and their meanings. The front of the card had the symbol and the back its standard uses. After a little internal debate, I split inverted runes on to their own card and marked one corner so I would know which way pointed up without having to check the back each time. Once I had the rune-meaning flash cards, I diagrammed out the most common rune conjunctions and made them into their own set of flash cards, complete with usages on the back. To really do more, I would need the books I had requested from Amy.

I scrawled another note asking her to hurry it up already and piffed it over. The sun sat high in the western sky, pointing at a time little past midday; I figured Robert should be headed back fairly soon. At least I knew I hadn't scared him off completely, because his beat-up old rust bucket was still parked in front of the cabin. I grimaced. Whoever took care of him would probably have reported it and him missing. I bet whoever it was actually cared about him more than he thought. He could be kind of a standoffish, prickly kid, but still.

I heard a low thrumming in the air and turned around to find the books from Amy sitting on the floor along with a note. I'd asked for encyclopedias and descriptive essays on spirits and creatures from outside the Weave. The last one she sent turned out to be a basic rune usage manual and dictionary. I had found it particularly useful when I was younger. I read the note first.

Wow, you have really created a mess over there. It's all over the news that some summoner tried to kill a mall full of people with a demon familiar in Spokane. The media is making it seem like this may just be the first attack in a terrorist campaign. When you get back I really want to know what happened. I'm sure you've already sent the Grove headquarters your report so I won't bug you about it right now.

Crap. I hadn't done my official report. I would do that next. Joy.

I did find reports of a boy from the mall who might be Duane. He's in the Spokane Valley Hospital in serious condition and all the news outlets are saying the summoner "hexed" him with blood poisoning before destroying the mall. Kid of about 16-17, apparently fine before the attack and now is seriously ill. Could that have anything to do with you needing beginner-level rune primers, and suddenly showing up with a big nasty in a populated area? I am dying to know exactly what is going on over there, but I'll bet you twenty bucks the queen of "I'll never take an apprentice" just picked one up on the cheap. Heh. Well, anyway, good luck. Let me know if you need anything else.

I sat back and thought about what I had just learned. I'd been hoping that somehow Robert had gotten off lucky, but summoning on the human body is notoriously complicated and tricky. His crude attempt at revenge had sent this Duane kid to the hospital. That sealed it. He needed to start learning how to wield his power today, even if I had to drag him through it kicking and screaming.

Next I wrote the official report to Grove headquarters, line by painful line, and outlined the state of Spokane Grove headquarters, the police effort, the incident at the aluminum plant, and finally the incident at the mall which culminated in the kidnapping of a minor and holing up in the woods. I outlined my plan for the next few days: researching demon Rick and regrouping once I found information on his abilities and weaknesses. I scrawled my signature at the bottom and sent it off before I could succumb to the urge to try and rewrite it to make it sound better. I judged it impossible to make that string of events sound good.

Writing the report honed my anxiety. I could feel the hairs on the back of my neck refusing to lie back down. I sighed and rubbed my shoulder. *You really need a hobby, Grace. Or a vacation.* I gave good advice. Maybe I would actually listen to myself later.

The cabin had a homey, lived-in feel. As I sat with my back against the surface of the logs facing inward, I almost felt as if it were still waiting for its owner to come home. The bookshelves on the far wall caught my eye, and I wandered over. Uncle Herman seemed very well-read for a mountain man. The shelves held the collected works of William Shakespeare, Walt Whitman, Emmanuel Kant, and Lawrence Kohlberg to start, plus several essays and novels from authors I didn't recognize. I took the Kohlberg and went to sit outside in the sunshine while I waited for Robert.

HE DIDN'T CREST the hill outside the cabin until the sun was almost on the horizon line. I'd "ordered out" again, but this time went for Greek food full of feta, tzatziki, and amfissa olives along with the meat and leafy vegetables. I still sat on the bench outside the cabin with my back propped against the outer wall.

"Welcome back." I gestured at the food. "Grab some grub."

He grunted a totally unintelligible reply, but he did take some of the food. I waited until he finished chewing. "I made you some study aides today. You can start learning all the runes and how to combine them." I reached into my pocket and pulled out the index cards.

He took them and stared at them for a second. "Really? You made me flash cards? What do you think I am, a six-year-old?"

"As far as your summoning goes, yes! You have no control and you just go firing off power willy-nilly. Summoning is the delicate art of moving a specific thing from point A to point B. *You* are picking up everything in your vicinity and cramming it down on point B. That's a good way to unintentionally cause really bad catastrophes."

The kid glared at me defiantly. I knew I absolutely wouldn't like what came out of his mouth next.

"That's not fair. You know I didn't know anything about Rick, and it totally wouldn't have been a problem without him there. I didn't try to hurt anyone. My summoning was just fine. I was just unlucky 'cause he was there eating summoners like *you*. You can't blame the mall thing on me. That's just stupid. And I have Uncle Herman's journals, so there's no way I need your stupid flash cards." He glowered at me and kicked a rock out into the grass for emphasis.

I tried to take a firm grip on my temper but I could feel it pulling away from me.

"Right now, your summoning sucks. A six-year-old could do better. You don't understand how to combine runes to make sure the only thing that happens is the effect you intended. Your summoning is like buying a really big mystery bag from the grocery store that turns out to have rotten tomatoes inside." Yep, I definitely lost my temper. And his next words just sent any shred of control I had left up in smoke.

"You're lying!" He threw the index cards on the ground next to the bench and crossed his arms over his chest like that finished the conversation. Oh hell no, it didn't.

"Fine," I ground out. "I'll show you then." I whipped out my rune board, set the summoning in a white heat of fury, and dropped my Pontiac six inches from his toes. "Get in, we're going on a field trip."

His eyes got as big as the moon just peeking up over the trees, but at least he didn't give me any lip as he slid quietly into the passenger seat. A victory of sorts for me, I guess.

ROBERT

YEAH, yeah, I was being a little silly about this whole thing. But come on! Flash cards? Learning to be a summoner was starting to look a lot like school and a lot less like badass stuff. She was right; it wasn't evil, but *boring*. We're talking about a profession that lets you, for instance, fight a giant raccoon monster in the middle of a mall and win. The idea that the same profession could involve a new set of homework seemed silly.

After all, I'd already proven I could summon stuff. I thought I'd be doing more of *that*, not this rune-memorization. I understood runes were important, kinda. I just wanted more lab work, less book time.

I didn't need any more bloody homework.

This was what I thought as I sat quietly in the passenger seat of the Pontiac, with Grace staring ahead at the road. I also remembered Luke Skywalker making roughly the same complaint to Yoda, but I was too embarrassed to admit it.

That trip passed mostly in awkward silence. Grace kept her head pointed forward, an unreadable expression on her face. I couldn't run, so I tried to change the subject.

"Is going back to Spokane really a good idea?" I asked tentatively. "I mean, isn't Rick there waiting to eat us?"

"Oh, probably." Grace sounded like she was acknowledging the possibility of rain tonight, not a fight to the death with a demon raccoon. Points for style, but it didn't make me feel any better.

"All right...and aren't the cops still looking for us?"

"Yup," she said, again in that flat tone.

"So why are we going back?"

This struck me—all things considered—as a fair question, but she simply snorted at me and said, "Because you need to learn a lesson."

That...was ominous. Grace had a pretty big reason not to feed me to Rick, but I didn't think she had any qualms about getting me arrested by the cops. I distinctly didn't want to "learn a lesson" in the system. That was a phrase reserved for the most dire of foster parent conversations. When fosties said it was time for you to learn a lesson, they were either going to throw down a beating or call the cops.

If Grace wanted to throw me a beating, she could have done it at Uncle Herman's cabin. That left the cops. I sighed and pondered my fate.

WE PULLED up at the visitor's center for the Valley Hospital. "The hospital?" I asked Grace, but she kept her poker face on as she got out of the car. I had no choice; I had to follow her.

That too-sterile smell of the hospital hit me like a wall of memory. The last time I'd smelled that, I'd been watching my parents die. That's not actually true; they were dead before they got to the hospital, but there were a great many of the customary last-ditch attempts—paddles, tubes, needles and such. On paper, and in my heart, they died when the doctor said "Call it. 2:38." After that, there was no hope. I'd sat in the hallway of the ER where I probably wasn't supposed to be and choked in rough gasps of the sterilized air before a nurse swept me away from the corpses of my parents.

Coming back to that smell was unpleasant. Grace, however, was cold-faced about it, and didn't seem to notice as I paused, my eyes growing wet. I shook my head, trying to bring myself around.

"What are we doing here?" I asked.

Again I got a stoic non-response. Grace blew past the information desk and went straight to the elevator, punched the key for the third floor and let the door close. Hospital elevators have no chintzy music in them, but I expected it in an elevator, so I tried humming as we ascended. Grace snapped me a look of fire and rage; I stopped.

After the doors opened, Grace made her way to the ladies' room. I waited outside as she did her business. Grace's business, as it turned out, consisted of summoning a couple of bouquets of flowers. I did not see that coming.

"Flowers?" Seeing Grace with a bouquet was like seeing Charlie Manson with a Teletubby doll.

"They're customary for visitation in a hospital. No reason to be rude." Visitation? Who were we—

All thought immediately ended on rounding the corner and seeing Jeanelle weeping in the hallway. She had her back to the wall in a crouch as though she had been leaning against it and slid downward. Her delicate arms were braced across the top of her knees. Her head rested on them and she shook with the kind of racking sobs I knew all too well. It still had an effect on me.

I spun to give Grace a shocked look. "You brought me here for *Jeanelle?* Why? Just to screw with my head? I don't get it."

Jeanelle's head lifted from her knees, She leveled those gorgeous, wet eyes of hers at me.

"Ohmygod, Robert," she said, getting to her feet. "I'm just so..."

She flung her arms around my neck and buried her face in my chest. My body enjoyed the sensation thoroughly. The body of a teenage boy is, however, *deeply* stupid. I kept my head up and did not hug her back. I'd been down this road; it had sucked, and in spite of my growing erection I wanted nothing more to do with it.

Grace...started laughing, and I'm pretty sure it was at my expense.

"Oh, God!" my Jedi Master choked out as she gained control over that cackling giggle of hers. "Now I get it, I think. Oh, that's priceless. You two are just..." She lost it again.

Both Jeanelle and I stared at her, steely-eyed and offended. "I'm sorry, I'm sorry," Grace said after a bit, breathing deeply. "I just wasn't expecting that one. Good to know I can still be surprised."

A head poked out from one of the doors nearby. It had dark hair, definitely young. When her face turned toward the three of us, I pegged it instantly. Cindy.

"What's going on out here?" asked the Central Slut, and her eyes locked with Jeanelle's. "Oh, you're still here? I thought you'd gotten the message by now. Let me repeat it, since I didn't make myself clear. Stay. Away. From. My. Man. You. Worthless. Cunt." The last words snapped like a whip hitting ice. I felt a little bad for Jeanelle, but that was kind of a side dish to my Schadenfreude. I can't lie; her pain gave me a little, cruel, petty happy.

I had the grace not to crack a smile.

I also had *the* Grace, who burst out laughing again. "Oh wow; who needs the soaps?" she chortled, slamming her fist into the wall. I tried to keep a straight face, but it's hard to do when someone is laughing *that hard*.

"Bitch, you got a problem?" Cindy snapped in that high-pitched teenage-queen voice. I half-expected Grace to turn on her; I even had some image of Grace getting violent, which would not be anything approaching good here. I didn't have to worry; Cindy's arrogance only made Grace laugh harder.

"Oh...oh, my God. It's like a living stereotype. It's too good. Quick, tell me if I don't show some respect, you'll give me a smackin'."

Cindy looked like she had been about to say just that. She paused with Grace still sniggering at her, unsure what to do. She fell back on her default, "Bitch, get out of my face." Her arm came up, flicking at the wrist in a negligent gesture of dismissal.

Suddenly, faster than I could track, Grace was less than an inch from Cindy's face. "I need to take Robert in there," she said in a calm, authoritative voice. "You and your little friend here are going to leave us all alone while I do." Calling Jeanelle her "little friend" was probably inaccurate, but I didn't want to bring that up.

Cindy was not about to let this one go. Some other female had challenged her authority, and clearly Cindy was used to being the alpha. I was so focused on their staring contest I didn't notice that Jeanelle had unwrapped herself from around me and taken up a position cowering behind me until I heard her soft voice.

"Robert, the news said you were kidnapped by a summoner. Everyone figured you were going to be sacrificed or something."

"Yeah... I wasn't exactly kidnapped. More like rescued. And she hasn't sacrificed me yet."

"Robert... Is that woman—"

Fortunately, I didn't have to deal with the next question, because Cindy decided it was time to bluster again.

"Bitch, talk to the hand," she said, trying to fling her palm into Grace's face. I winced. This was going to get nasty. I did not envy Cindy.

Grace produced a pair of handcuffs. Whether she summoned them or simply carried handcuffs around with her I still don't know, and don't want to. She snapped one cuff around Cindy's wrist and the other to the handicapped railing down one side of the hall. Cindy jerked back, but too late.

"You crazy fucking—"

I saw Grace's hand on a bangle, knew that something was happening, and suddenly Cindy went quiet. She still looked like she was screaming at Grace, but no noise came out of her mouth. Her face went from enraged to frightened as she dealt with her sudden muteness, then her head reared back and she let loose with what could only have been an attempt at a full-volume scream.

Nothing came of it.

Well, something came of it. Just not sound. Grace flicked her wrist around to a new section of bangle, tapped it with a bleeding finger, and an invisible force bitch-slapped Cindy without laying a hand on her. It wasn't a lot of force, but it was artfully done.

"Now," pronounced Grace in a measured, steely tone, "you stay here like a good little girl while Robert and I go visit the patient. Yell for anyone, do anything to draw interest to yourself, and you make it to the top of my list of people to do unspeakable things to. Are we clear?"

Cindy nodded.

Behind me, Jeanelle squeaked in fear.

"Robert, come," said Grace. There really wasn't an option at that point. I obeyed.

I KNEW it was going to be Duane. No other patient would have both Cindy and Jeanelle as visitors. He did not look good. The hospital had hooked him up to several machines with a lot of graphs I didn't understand. An IV ran into his wrist and several different bags of medicine dripped their way into him. His face was pale and gaunt, a shadow of the basketball star who had threatened me in the hallway only a week ago. He wasn't conscious; I didn't know if he was just asleep or in a coma. Point is, he looked like hell.

"So... Duane's in the hospital. Sucks to be him, I guess. I'm not going to lie; I never really liked this guy. Why am I bringing him flowers now?" I asked as Grace arranged the two bouquets on the table next to his unconscious head.

"Because you put him here. The flowers should be in the nature of an apology."

"What do you mean I put him here? I didn't lay a finger on him, and I certainly didn't give him whatever he has right now. Sure, I played a joke on him—made him crap his pants—but you don't end up looking like this by crapping your pants."

"How did you make him do that?" she asked. Her voice was quiet, but firm. Her eyes narrowed, then locked onto mine, boring into me.

"I summoned some feces from somewhere else into his butt, is all."

"And how did you make sure that none of the material you summoned went outside his colon and into his bloodstream?"

"Well, for starters, I threw the Wunjo rune into the inscription."

"And that alone protected him?"

"Well, I thought so. Uncle Herman's notes said it was a good idea to—"

"A good idea, yes, but did they say the use of the Wunjo *ensured* that no harm would come?" Her questions were coming harder now. Faster. I scrambled to justify myself.

"No, I guess not, but I figured—"

"You figured? Based on what other training? Based on what summoning experience did you make this calculation?"

She was right, of course. Not that I could admit it. "Well, none, but—"

"None. Let me tell you something, Robert. Not even I summon things into or out of the body of someone I don't want to kill. I'm no doctor, but I don't need to be one to tell you that introducing even a small amount of raw feces directly into someone's bloodstream can cause a pretty nasty infection very, very quickly. That's what's happened to Duane here. Unless you were *trying* to kill him in one of the most painful ways you could have imagined, you missed your target by a mile. There are, by the way, medical summoners, but they're few and far between. To become Grove-certified to perform a medical summoning, the first thing you have to do is get yourself licensed to practice medicine just like any other doctor. Only then can you *start* your apprenticeship in medical summoning. The level of training it takes to add or remove things from a body *without killing someone* is one of the most intense training regimens the Grove puts people through, and you tried it with no training at all. Duane here is dying. The antibiotics they have him on will fight some of the infection and slow the process. It won't stop it, though; he is going to die if I can't get one of those medical summoners out here. I'm not sure what all is in there, but he's headed downhill."

As Grace explained in that cold tone what I had done, I began to sink slowly into depression, and then panic. "Well, why don't you get one here, then? I mean, I didn't want to kill him, and you know people who can fix it. So let's fix it already."

"Didn't I just tell you that a Healer is one of the rarest types of summoners? Were you listening? We *don't* put them at risk, and right now we're in a combat zone. That raccoon demon you call Rick is out there somewhere, waiting to eat any and all summoners he can find. Healing takes a significant amount of power and concentration; if I don't get that monster cleared out, I can't risk bringing a Healer in. I can't get Rick cleared out until I have you trained, because otherwise Rick eats you and gets powerful enough to kill us all. Duane is not my problem; he's yours. His blood isn't on my hands; it's on yours. If you don't want that, the only thing to do is help me get rid of Rick once and for all."

I thought about that. I had put Duane into this position, and I didn't want to be a murderer. The fact was, I didn't know what the hell I was doing. I apparently knew just enough to get people killed, and that wasn't good enough.

"How long do you think we have?"

A weak voice came from the door. "The doctors said he might have a month at most." My head, and Grace's, whipped up to see Jeanelle, her body half-blocked by the doorframe. "Are you... Can you actually help him?" She sounded so lost.

"Oh, sweetheart." Sweetheart? Where the hell had *this* Grace come from? This woman could turn emotions on a dime and give you ten cents change. She glided over to Jeanelle, wrapping her up in those long, floppy sleeves. "I can, but it depends on Robert here. If Robert works hard, we can save him. If Robert doesn't *listen* to me—" She punctuated "listen" with a shift out of her gooey voice onto the edge of a razor blade. "—then Duane is going to die. It's all up to him, sweetheart."

That was just...cruel. Jeanelle gazed at me with those green eyes of hers, eyes that begged me to save the boy she'd ditched me for. And I had to do it. "He'll be fine," I said gruffly, hoping I could hide the nervous tremor in my voice. "I'll make sure of it."

"Good," pronounced Grace with a "that's-that" finality. "Now, let's get out of here."

I nodded. Grace and I swept past Jeanelle into the hall. "You could have just told me," I said to her under my breath.

"You bitch!" cried Cindy as we walked by. I peered over my shoulder before glancing at Grace. She kept walking.

"I wasn't sure that you would believe me. Easier just to bring you here."

It took me a moment to trace the conversation back to where I had left it. Upon reflection, she had a fair point. It hurt to admit it, though.

"Yeah." I murmured, almost in a whisper.

The elevator doors opened on us, and we stepped through. As they closed, Grace sighed and rubbed the blood on her bangle over to another, covering a new rune set. The handcuffs appeared in Grace's hand, and she tucked them away under her blouse.

We rode the rest of the way to the lobby in silence, each in our own thoughts.

When the door dinged open, there stood three men in beige sheriff's uniforms, weapons drawn and pointed at us. Grace's eyes flicked up to a camera in the corner of the elevator, then she shook her head. The man in the center held forth a badge along with his gun, and he had a smile on his face as though he had just hit the lottery.

"Ah, yes. Well-timed. Ms. Moore, I believe. You would, of course, be under arrest."

GRACE

WHEN THE ELEVATOR doors hissed open on our little welcoming committee I had a moment of wishing I were someone else. Someone more mundane and less likely to get herself into messes like this.

"Hands up, please."

So much for thinking we could drop in and out of the hospital without attracting attention. I really should have stopped relying on my luck by now. Clearly, the fates were conducting some kind of vendetta against me.

Augmenting our speed and running away tempted me, but wouldn't work. Rick would be on us like white on rice. Fighting our way out had too many ethical considerations *plus* Rick, so that only left option three: lie, bluff, and hope they let us walk away before things got ugly.

I put my hands up and wiggled my fingers at the officers. "I'm sorry, but I think you must have gotten me mixed up with someone else. I don't know what you think I've done, but I promise I'm not the type of person you need to hold guns on."

I started to step out of the elevator so the doors would close and protect Robert from gunfire if it came to that. The cops raised their weapons and stepped back. "Oh, don't shoot!" I gasped, freezing my movement right outside the doors. "I'm just a tad bit claustrophobic, so I couldn't stand it in there a second longer. I'll be right here until you can figure out what the mix-up is."

The other cops looked at the big guy in the middle as he spoke up.

I labeled him "the boss." His name tag read "Captain M. Carlenos." "There is no mix-up, ma'am. We have confirmation you were at the scene of several crimes. If you're Grace Moore, I'm to take you in for questioning."

My eyes widened in shock.

"Never!" I exclaimed, as I mentally gave him points for not beating around the bush. I'd *really* like to know how he came by my full name. Not that any possible explanation boded well for me. Time to brazen it out, Gracie.

"What crimes? When?" I waited for the elevator doors to close, then cursed Robert for holding them open. I hoped he wouldn't do anything stupid this time. Fortunately, the cops' attention still seemed to be focused on me.

Carlenos kept his granite-like poker face. "Lady, I'm sure you have been the cause of more crimes than I can count. We know you're a summoner because we have surveillance footage."

He fished around in his pocket with one hand and pulled out a folded piece of paper, keeping the gun in his other hand trained on me the whole time. "If this isn't you, you must have a twin in town who shares your bad fashion sense, and that just ain't likely."

The paper was a grainy black-and-white security photo of me crouched low in front of the destroyed "Shop 'till you rock" stage, with the start of a large slab of metal beginning to materialize from the mall floor. Perfect. You try to save a few people, and no one shows any appreciation.

I feigned shock and pointed a finger at the photo. "How?? That's freakish. How can that person look like me! She stole my face! That's not possible! That summoner framed me! She—she's a doppelganger!" I shot an accusing glare at the boss. "Why don't they warn you that summoners can steal your face? Why aren't the police doing anything about it? Sir, I want you to make this woman—" I punctuated my words with my pointing index finger "—stop impersonating me this moment and maligning my character! And my fashion sense isn't that bad!"

At this point, the bluster and divert blame tactic was a long shot, but still worth a try.

Summoners had such a bogeyman reputation that the captain actually shifted his feet slightly and started to look a little doubtful. "I'm sorry, ma'am. Even if it isn't you in the photograph, I have to detain you for questioning until that can be confirmed by my superiors."

I wasn't about to lose the small opening he'd given me. "Do you detain every citizen who looks like they might be someone you saw in a grainy, nasty, black-and-white photo? Isn't someone supposed to be investigating and confirming these things?"

"I have been."

The voice came from my left. I craned my neck to look. Detective Allen stood by the doors into the lobby in the same crumpled tweed suit he'd been wearing when I met him over by Grove headquarters. "I also have a warrant for your arrest right here."

He held it out so I could see it before pretending to study it himself. "I had to disturb the judge at dinner and he wasn't very pleased. I think the ink on his signature may be still drying. You're under arrest for crimes against the State. Miss Grace Anne Moore, it is my pleasure to read you your rights."

I didn't turn to look at Robert, but I could feel his eyes burning into the back of my skull. I'd just rubbed his face in how his vindictive teenage blunder was going to kill someone. I'd promised to help him fix it as long as he finally listened to me and we took care of Rick. Now that chance of salvation was dwindling...and he got to see firsthand how unfriendly law enforcement was to those accused of summoning.

Our options were rather limited. He wouldn't be able to learn without me, and I wouldn't be able to defeat Rick by myself. If they searched my person pursuant to arrest, this would all be over in a heartbeat. I had enough summoning aides on me to confirm my profession. I couldn't find any good solutions to get us out of this, so I went for a bad one. A bad one, but one where we might still have a chance of saving Duane, and the city.

I dropped my hands, covering my face. "Why does everyone believe I'm a summoner? I don't understand." My conscience screamed at me about using my power on public servants who were just trying to do their jobs and keep the city safe. I ignored it.

With my hands on my face, I summoned a tag from the purse against my side into each hand.

Relief flooded me that I had the tags within the range of my Sense at all.

I brought my teeth down on my lip decisively to get the blood for the summons, then rubbed my face in my hands as part of my faux crying. I hated with every breath that my actions were fulfilling the stereotype of the deceitful summoner.

I summoned and released a wall of wind in front of me to force the deputies back and to the left. The lobby doors blew open. One of the window panes popped out whole, shattering on the asphalt. I followed up quickly with a giant sheet of inch-thick bulletproof glass which I anchored in the floor and positioned between the deputies and us, cutting them off into one part of the lobby.

Robert stood frozen in the door to the elevator, his hand holding the doors open like an idiot. I ran for the exit, motioning him to follow. As soon as we were clear of the door I summoned a chunk of concrete the size of the entryway. It would take the police a while to get that cleared out of the way.

We busted out into the parking lot, which contained a veritable forest of police uniforms and flashing lights. I had time to think nasty four-letter words before something hit my shoulder, seizing up all my muscles. The world turned black.

WHEN I CAME TO, my shoulder was still sore, but surprisingly, I didn't see any blood anywhere. It felt like I had something closer to a burn. I was, however, trussed up like a Thanksgiving turkey. I don't know who came up with the summoner restraints, but they are a true crazy-suit. My hands were cuffed behind me, with each hand in its own leather mitten. Likewise, my ankles were cuffed together, and my shoes also had "anti-summoning" covers over them. I didn't look forward to finding out what happened when I had to pee.

Someone must have been watching for me to wake up, because just a few minutes after I regained consciousness, they moved me to an interrogation room. In another situation it would have been humorous —they were so afraid of removing any of my "restraints" that they carried me suspended between two officers as if I were a small child. If I wasn't such a freak with the Sense, I would have been able to summon their guns right out of their holsters even with these restraints. I could still probably get rid of the turkey suit without too much effort, but currently I thought that would probably just lead to me getting knocked out again. So I waited. I hadn't seen Robert in any of the cells we passed, so I hoped he hadn't done anything wildly idiotic.

They deposited me in a grungy wooden chair in front of a Formica table. The small whitewashed room had mirrors along one wall. I'd watched all the cop shows, so I just grinned at my reflection: my little gift to creep them out and bolster my morale. I should really learn better impulse control.

A few moments later, Detective Allen and another gentleman in a much crisper, shiny gray suit stepped into the room. Apparently they were both going to ask me questions. Oh, joy. With any luck, they might have information on this situation that I didn't have. The trick lay in getting them to tell it to me.

The man in the gray suit was of indeterminate age, with the smooth face of a politician, blue eyes and brownish hair beginning to thin on top. Allen introduced him as the Eastern Washington Federal summoning liaison.

Next to him, Frank looked like what he was: a slightly rustic man who took his job seriously, had lost all his hair a long time ago, didn't care about fashion at all, and earnestly pursued what he believed to be justice. He acted like he'd rather catch a crook than bathe. Sadly, he believed I was that crook. They both sat down across the table from me. Just like in all the cheesy detective movies, a bright light blinked on above me.

I squinted up. "Really, guys? Is that necessary? What is the big spotlight supposed to accomplish anyway? It's never really made sense to me. I'll have to remember to tell people about this when they talk about getting their 'moment in the spotlight'."

Gray Suit glowered at me. "We ask the questions here. If you don't want things to go badly for you, you'll sit there and be quiet unless you're telling us what we want to know."

"Yes, sir, roger, sir."

I swear the temperature in the room dropped ten degrees. Apparently that was still too flip. The two cops let silence fill the room for a few minutes. Finally, Frank spoke up.

"We can already prove you're a summoner. You made sure that all of us eye-witnessed your summoning at the hospital, in addition to the other evidence we have. So I'm going to start out with the easy questions. What took place at Grove headquarters on September sixth?"

"I don't know. I wasn't in Spokane on the sixth."

"Where were you?"

"At home in Seattle."

"Do you have anyone to confirm that?"

"You can call my hotel; I checked in on the eighth. And I have grocery receipts from Seattle before the trip."

"Hmm. We'll check it out. Why were you at the scene of the crime on the ninth?"

"I'm sorry, what?"

"Why did I see you at Grove headquarters on the ninth?"

"I do remember seeing you on the ninth, but I wasn't at Grove headquarters."

"All right, why did I see you in the vicinity of Grove Headquarters on the ninth?"

"I went sightseeing that day. I saw a destroyed building with a lot of flashy lights, so I got curious."

"Why would a summoner like you be curious about police activities unless you're involved somehow?"

"Is your normal citizen who slows to look at a traffic accident also a suspect? 'Cause that's what it feels like you're saying there."

"But your normal citizen who slows to look at the wreck doesn't pick up a piece of the debris either. You did, didn't you?"

"I picked up a piece of metal sitting in the bushes by the sidewalk. I found it all the way down the block, but you already knew that. It's not a piece of the building, and you didn't want it. If you think it has import now, you're welcome to it."

"But you agree the destroyed building was the Grove headquarters?"

"Well, that's what you keep telling me. I'm sure you must have good reasons for thinking so."

"So why go to the mall?"

I smiled slowly. That silly tourist pamphlet was going to save my ass again.

"I like the mini-golf and Nordstrom's coffee. They have one of those windmill holes, so I get my exercise. If you go there before lunch on a weekday, it's usually pretty quiet so you can just sit around and have coffee in peace, but they have fantastic air conditioning. Almost nowhere on the west side has air conditioning."

"There is no mini-golf at the Valley Mall."

"Really? They have it at Northtown."

"Let me narrow it down. Why go to the Spokane Valley Mall on the tenth?"

"Well, rumor has it that they had a "Shop 'til you rock" contest going on for a five hundred-dollar shopping spree. I don't really get those types of contests, though."

"So, why would you summon something to attack the Spokane Valley Mall on that day?"

"Oh, I didn't."

134

"How would you know there was a contest if you hadn't been there?"

"They had fliers for it at my hotel, since it's really close by. I guess it was supposed to be a tourist attraction. Personally, I always find being trapped in the audience for karaoke or amateur dancing to be excruciating rather than fun."

Frank sighed. "Look, we know the Seattle Grove sent you here as some kind of lone gunman, and we have footage that puts you and the summoned monster in the mall on the tenth, as well as the forensic and crime scene data. The same summoned monster tore up the Spokane Grove headquarters. What I can't put together is why the Seattle Grove decimated the Spokane Grove and made such a public hit on two snot-nosed kids. The Lorents kid has been in the foster care system forever, and the other kid's family is so squeaky clean, he can't have connections to a Grove at all. Why the hit on them? And why come back? If you answer my questions now, it will go much easier for you in the future."

"I'd love to answer your questions, Detective, but I have no idea what to say. Those sound like some wild conjectures right there."

Frank opened up a manila folder. "I had Seattle PD send this over. Grace Anne Moore, resides Seattle, Washington. Family has strong Grove ties, began taking Grove assignments in 1998; no arrests or charges filed, but under continuing investigation due to suspicious activities. It would help me out here if you just cut the crap."

He skewered me with a brooding glare. I guessed he wanted me to say something, but it didn't really feel like the right time for another of my flip comments. Ah hell, what else did I have at the moment? Like I'd confirm any of that.

"My, that file certainly *sounds dangerous*." I laughed. "Careful. Those conspiracy-theory cooties may be contagious." I leaned over the table and smiled at him mischievously.

Gray Suit shifted in impatience or irritation. Frank slapped his hand down on the file hard enough to get me to scoot back and raise my eyebrows. I'd been right: totally not the right time for a flip comment. Frank's face closed and threw down shutters. He'd had a poker face before; now it was a blank wall.

"Let me put the timeline together for you." His barely contained voice suggested his temper hung by a thread. Not that you could tell by looking at his face. Oops.

"The Spokane Grove gets taken out professionally and thoroughly on September sixth, but something goes wrong. On September eighth, the Seattle Grove just coincidentally sends you to Spokane to do 'sightseeing.' On September ninth, I see you near the scene looking for something. I don't know if you found it or not, but on the tenth, you carry out the biggest hit on a public place that I've ever heard of. What I don't know is what the Seattle Grove hoped to accomplish by taking out the Spokane Grove in such a public display, and why you didn't leave immediately after that and the Valley Mall incident. But I will find out. It would be much better for you if you just fill in the holes for me now."

Well, hurray, bonus. Not only had I managed to thoroughly piss off this detective for minimal new knowledge, I had an open investigation on me back home. Not the information I had been fishing for, but...good to know, I guess. If they didn't have Robert pegged as a summoner, there was a good possibility they thought him just a regular civilian who'd got caught up in this somehow. I hoped so —it meant I just had to get myself out of here. And it was a good time to find out exactly how much dirt Detective Allen had on me.

"Look, I already told you that I didn't even arrive in Spokane until the eighth."

"And you don't have anyone to back that up," Frank's skepticism showed plainly in his voice. "Why were you at the hospital today?"

"Just paying a visit."

"To the boy you gave blood poisoning? Were you trying to finish the job or just scare the other boy into participating in some kind of sick ritual? You even gave the boy's girlfriend funeral flowers."

"I have no idea what you're talking about. It is, however, customary to bring flowers when visiting the hospital."

"It isn't customary to handcuff people at hospitals, however."

"Are they having problems with people doing that now? How peculiar. Is it the doctors or visitors? 'Cause I've heard that some patients can get really unruly. But if it's the doctors and nurses together, well, I thought that only happened in X-rated videos."

Frank stood up and shook his head sadly. "We're done here. Maybe you'll be more willing to talk to the interrogators at the county jail tomorrow. I've heard they have much more... *persuasive* methods." He walked over to the door and called for an escort to take me back to the holding cell. Well, I guess that told me something. The Spokane County sheriffs thought the Seattle Grove had conducted some kind of elaborate ritual to do...something epically bad.

Spokane wouldn't be hospitable to bringing in more summoners for a long while. Thanks to Detective Allen and Rick, I now had two reasons I couldn't bring in a medical summoner or ask for back-up. Frank had obviously tipped off the Seattle cops that he thought some kind of massive hit was going on. They would be waiting to snap up any more people Seattle sent this way.

That left just me against a giant rift in the Weave, the Sheriff's office, an out-of-control demon and an accidental blood poisoning. Robert was out there somewhere now, too, like a catastrophe waiting to happen.

I doubted enough plans existed in the world to cover all those contingencies, but I figured I'd better start trying. No sweat, Grace; you're a summoner, figure of legends and scare-er of small children. Nothing could be simpler. Yeah, right. It would be easier to believe myself if I was sitting somewhere other than in a fishbowl holding cell, complete with an open-topped toilet and no way to actually pee without asking for help. On the upside, I didn't have any cellmates. They could have put me in with someone dangerous.

ROBERT

STRONG ARMS SEIZED me from behind as I watched the tazer drop Grace like a sack of wet potatoes. I struggled, knowing it was futile but needing to get away, to escape. I couldn't see who held me but I knew this was it. I was a terrorist. The cops had me. I was going down.

A voice slipped softly into my ear. "It's all right, kid. It's over. I've got you."

Wait... What?

That didn't make any sense. I stopped struggling as they began to affix some kind of weird restraint device to Grace's hands and feet. Unconscious, she didn't look like a bastion of power. She looked like any other unconscious person: helpless. The uniformed cops put her into the car, and the guy holding me relaxed his grip. I turned to face him.

"Are you ok?" he asked me.

Was I okay? Really? That was the question he had for me? Not, "Are you now or have you ever been an agent of supernatural evil?" The realization began to dawn on me that he thought I was a *victim* here and not a collaborator. Being a victim was very, very easy; it's how to get what you want out of foster parents who try to give a damn about you. I had a chance to get away from this with the rest of my life intact. I had to take it.

I flicked my hand up to wipe my eye, glanced at him, and gave him my best make-the-fosties-feel-sorry-for-your-woeful-state face as I nodded.

"Good," he said. "I don't know what she did to you, but let's get you taken care of. We can talk later; for now, let's get you home. Your foster parents have been worried sick about you. I'm Detective Frank Allen, by the way." He held out his hand and I took it. I made sure to keep my grip soft, reinforcing my weakness.

Time to play for some information. I threw that victim warble into my voice as I asked, "You know who I am?"

He chuckled. "Robert, after that woman kidnapped you out of the Spokane Valley Mall, we've been tearing the whole county apart looking for you. I've got AMBER alerts out as far as Montana and California. Your face has been broadcast on the local news channels. Hell, give me another week and I'd have put you on the milk jugs."

So... I wasn't an apprentice summoner, learning the dark arts at the foot of my evil master. I was the poor boy who had been kidnapped by an evil summoner, for use in some unknown-but-surely-dire ritual. I let a tear well in my eye, sniffled, and said, "I just want to go home."

He nodded and led me to his unmarked Suburban. I climbed into the passenger seat. The ride to the fosties passed in what, to Detective Allen, must have seemed like peaceful silence.

FRANCENE MET me at the door and embraced me in a deep hug to satisfy her maternal self-delusion. In the eye-line of Detective Allen, I submitted to her choked sobs and tight clutch. She released me and Allen beat a retreat away from the door; he was letting us have "our moment."

Then there was hot chocolate. What is it, exactly, about hot chocolate? Is it really that comforting a drink? Because any time fosties want you to feel at home, they make you a cup of it. I took it and offered a series of monosyllabic responses to Francene's insipid questions about how awful that must have been. The fact that I was sitting at the kitchen table drinking the hot chocolate proved to Francene what a great pseudo-parent she was. I didn't really have to put a lot of effort into the conversation.

Meanwhile, my head spun. Without Grace, I could go on with my life. The cops weren't on to me. The giant raccoon from hell really only showed up when I tried to use my power. The fact was, I could walk away from all of this. I could go back to my normal life. I could just be the nerdy kid with the saxophone. God, it was tempting.

I walked upstairs to my room and removed my instrument from its case. It had been days since I'd practiced, and that was never good. I was sure my embouchure was already starting to weaken. I draped the padded strap around my neck and pulled the horn from its case. The grease on the cork of the neck had dried, so I applied a new layer before slipping the mouthpiece on. The brass of the instrument was cool to the touch; my fingers found their way home to the plastic pseudo-ivory that lined the keys.

I inhaled and began to riff off the D blues scale. Yeah, improvising some blues isn't really practice, but what I really needed was to think. A nice blues riff will let you do that; it clears your head and lets you see where you stand.

The fact was, I could never live with myself if I let things go down this way. If I tried to get back to my life, Duane was as good as dead. Grace would spend the rest of her life incarcerated, assuming they didn't just kill her. I might be able to avoid the notice of Rick the summoner-eating raccoon, but he would still be out there. As my ring finger and the pinky on my left hand flicked from A flat to A and back again, I knew I couldn't let things stand.

I gave myself this one bit of time. It wasn't practice; it was saying goodbye. Whatever happened, I wouldn't be in this house again. This, I thought, could be my last session with this horn. No more Jake or jazz band. My saxophone dropped low, wailing the loss of a mundane life. As I jammed my way up to a climactic high D, releasing all my fingers save my left thumb and slamming the palm of my left hand into one of the three levers next to it, I stared at what that life entailed. I stood in a borrowed foster room, playing a borrowed horn. I lived a borrowed life anyway. *Enough,* said my sax, dropping back to mid-octave. My course was set, and it was mine. I let the horn fall from my lips, cleaned it and replaced it in the case, carefully, with the respect its sacred nature demanded.

Then I pulled out Herman's box. I didn't really know what I'd need, but I figured pure force and fire were going to be the best ways to get the job done. I hadn't yet studied Grace's flash cards. No matter. These bracers were a piece of armor; surely most of these runes were combat effective. I just needed to look them up. I smiled, knowing that Grace was going to chastise me for this one even if it did save her ass.

I turned my thoughts to blood. For something that every single person on the earth has over a gallon of, blood's awfully hard to come up with in a pinch. I didn't want to use my own for this; I didn't really want to open up a vein before a fight, but it's not like I wanted to bleed out the fosties' dog either.

Side trip, then; I'd need to stop by the butcher's.

I grabbed my keys and went out for my... Shit. My car was still at Uncle Herman's place. I had no idea how Grace had done her summon-the-car trick, but I was pretty sure I couldn't duplicate it without blowing my car up or something. No, it was time to resort to the teenager's classic backup: the ten-speed. I threw my supplies into my backpack, dusted off my old bike helmet, and mounted up.

I huffed my way down Sprague to the butcher's shop. I could only imagine there would be suspicion involved in buying just blood, and I felt awkward simply asking for a container. Instead, I ended up buying two New York Strip steaks, a sirloin roast, and oh-could-you-throw-in-a-quart-of-cow's-blood. The butcher handed me my order without fanfare. Maybe I was overcompensating; I didn't know. No time to think about it though, because I had to get to the Valley station before they moved Grace.

At least I had dinner figured out. She'd like that.

Here's where I figured I had a bit of an advantage. Fact of the matter is, you don't grow up bounced from foster home to foster home without spending some time inside the local police department. I knew they'd hold Grace in the Valley, question her there. They might even keep her overnight. But by tomorrow, she'd get whisked off to the county jail and I'd have lost my shot. I also knew that they'd keep her in one of the two cells toward the back of the place. If I went in through the front door, I'd have all the cops in the Valley between me and Grace.

If I went in through the back, maybe I'd have a chance.

The Valley station is actually very easy to get to. From the back, I could still hear the traffic on Sprague Avenue. I didn't know which of the two cells they were holding Grace in, and it's not like I had blueprints or anything. I was going on a rough guess. I pulled into the back and glanced up at the security camera staring at me. Right; the clock was ticking.

I got out of the car and pulled my sleeves up, revealing Uncle Herman's bracers. I looked to a rune on my left bracer, one of the physical force ones. I smeared some of the cow's blood from the styrofoam cup on it, then closed my eyes, took a deep breath, and concentrated.

I heard a crash, the sound of squealing brakes and crumpling metal. It shocked me, but I didn't have time. I suddenly had control of several thousand pounds of kinetic force, which I sent toward the back wall of the station.

The Spokane Valley Station blew inward with a loud cracking sound, and I stepped through into the hall to catch my bearings.

I'd missed the hallway for the interrogation room. Instead, I found myself in a corridor unfamiliar to me; this must be one of the places they didn't bring detainees. Crap. So much for my advantage.

The captain from the hospital poked his head out of a room, shouted in surprise when he saw me, and ducked back in. I had to decide quickly; I charged him, rubbing the blood on the bracer as I did. I sent out a blast of force, hitting the captain in the chest and throwing him back against the wall.

Oops. Too much. I dashed toward him, hoping to find him alive. To my relief, he was, though dazed. I handcuffed him with his own cuffs, behind the back, and handcuffed the chain of *those* cuffs to the big-ass filing cabinet in the room.

Okay, I was committed now. I'd just directly attacked a cop with supernatural powers, and I'd done it on video. I was in all the way. *No more hesitations. You're a summoner. Do it.*

I took the radio off the cop's desk and clipped it to my belt. It lit up with chatter; the car crash out front had served as a great distraction and somewhat covered the noise of my break-in. The captain I had just disabled was coming around; I flashed the rune-and-blood covered bracers in front of his eyes.

"Captain, can you hear me?" I asked, in my most menacing tone.

At least I tried to. Stupid puberty kicked in, and my voice squeaked on *hear.* So much for that. It didn't seem to matter; the cop nodded quietly, then started to talk to me.

"Look, I don't... I have a wife, a couple of kids. That's them, in the picture over on—"

"Oh shut it. Look, I don't want to kill anyone here. There's been enough of that as it is." I squinted at his nametag. "I'm sorry, Captain Carlenos. Is that Mexican? You don't look Mexican."

"Ummm... Spanish, actually. My grandpa came from Seville. Hey, you're related to Herman Lorents, aren't you?"

"His nephew."

"Frank owes me a beer."

I wasn't sure what that meant, so I shifted the conversation to the more immediate situation. "Look, you've got a friend of mine in detention here, and I really need to get to her. I've done something a little dramatic—"

"A little dramatic? You've just assaulted a law enforcement officer, and you've committed a burglary to do it."

"Well, yeah. That, too. But actually, what I've done is a lot worse."

Captain Carlenos' face blanched as he tried to imagine something a lot worse.

"Anyway, I need to get to the detention cells and get my friend out before we all die. She's probably the only one who can stop us from getting killed right now." I tried to keep a calm, level tone to my voice. It felt like I did, but you never quite know. Looking back, I'm pretty sure that if I heard myself, it would have been fast, rushed and anxious.

I had just endangered everyone here. Rick was probably barreling his way through the Spokane Valley right now, having been given the "Nummy-Treat-Here" signal. If I didn't get Grace free of those bonds quickly, I would have to fight Rick myself.

And I didn't kid myself; that wouldn't end well.

Captain Carlenos choked a little, then softly said, "Out the door, right at the end of the hall. There's a couple of holding cells. Your friend is in one of those."

"Thanks, Captain. Oh, if you call out, I'll burn you alive." A hollow threat, but he didn't need to know that. I winked at him and stepped into the hallway.

There were two men at the end; one of them in uniform, one not. Both were holding shotguns, which they leveled at me. Shit; I dove back into Captain Carlenos's room as they discharged them.

"Trouble?" asked Captain Carlenos sardonically. I decided right there that I liked the good captain. He had encountered something he believed to be the soul of evil and gotten trounced by it. He had been intimidated not thirty seconds ago. To go from that to mockery while still cuffed to a filing cabinet, I found to be very good form. I flashed him a grin.

"Yeah, well, looks like you've got a couple of buddies here."

"Hey, you're the away team."

"I guess. Let's see...is that body armor?" I asked, though it obviously was. I was a little skinny for the bulletproof vest built for Carlenos's barrel chest, but it was better than nothing. The black vest with the bright white POLICE lettering across the front hung loosely on me as I slipped it over my shoulders. Carlenos chuckled.

"What?" I asked.

He didn't have time to tell me. His compatriots took the opportunity to move to opposite sides of the door to his office. I closed my eyes and reached out with my Sense; they were standing with their backs to the wall on either side of the door.

Well and good. The wall consisted of drywall and two-by-fours, which splintered easily as a blast of force from my left hand blew through the wall and took down Mr. Plainclothes. The other deputy began to round the door frame, lifting his shotgun in my direction. I ran to stand next to Carlenos; he checked his fire. The deputy advanced on me, trying to get between me and the captain so he could get a clean shot. I fumbled with the bracer, hoping for another blast of force. My hand slipped on the wet blood. *Good enough*, I figured, then concentrated on the summons.

A flat sheet of solid stone, maybe ten feet by ten feet and about one foot wide, sprang up between the deputy and me, balanced precariously on its end. The deputy must have been startled, because he fired his shotgun into the stone sheet. It didn't punch its way through to my side, but the wall began to fall my way.

I used another burst of force to tip it back at the deputy, pinning him. It wouldn't hold long, but I didn't need it to. I slammed my foot into the rock, hearing an "oomph!" from underneath it as I jumped over and sprinted down the hallway.

Hot damn! I was doing good! I cuffed Plainclothes as he lay on the ground. He appeared worse off than Carlenos; some of the wood had splintered into him and cut him up pretty bad. No time to worry about that, though. I had to find Grace.

As I rounded the corner, I caught a blur of motion. I tried to jump back and compose myself, but the man who had been hiding there brought a small, black object up in an arc, slipping it under my arm past the loose-fitting armor. He slammed the taser's bare nodes into my side. My muscles spasmed and I dropped to the ground, face down, in pain. Quickly he dropped his knee into my spine, placing the taser firmly against the nape of my neck.

"Hands out," he commanded.

I pegged the voice. Detective Allen. I had no choice. I complied.

"Good. Rosen, get these things off him." The deputy I had hit with the rock wall limped over to me, pulling Uncle Herman's bracers off me.

"Goddammit, kid. I thought you were the victim, not an accomplice. Why'd you have to go and do this?"

"I—need—Grace," I coughed out. The pressure of his knee on my back made it hard to breath.

"Grace? Seems like she's the one that got you into this mess. Why do you need a mass murderer like her?"

"Not—a murderer. Only—hope—now." Rosen snorted at this, but Detective Allen's voice remained level.

"Kid, you're a juvenile, but you're old enough to get tried as an adult." His voice had turned soft, encouraging. I recognized the tone immediately; it matched the fosties' pseudo-caring. "I may be able to get the State to go light on you because of brainwashing or some such, but you have to talk to me."

He stood me up, handcuffing me. I took a deep breath and shook my head. "None of that matters, now. We're all going to die if you don't let Grace go."

"Robert, you know I can't do that. Hell, she's one of the worst criminals of the century here in Spokane. She's killed more people—"

"She hasn't killed anyone! She's...a good person."

He sighed. "No, boy. She's the worst kind of evil there is, and she's corrupted you. I just pray that the system manages to straighten you back out. Waste of a good life, if you ask me."

That's when the ground started shaking. "Detective Allen, do you feel that?" I asked.

I saw Rosen out of the corner of my eye, looking about nervously.

He leveled his gun at me. "What are you doing?"

"Nothing. But that's a big, nasty thing that likes to eat summoners, and I'm not any good at concealing my power when I use it. I've seen Rick get hit with an RPG and it barely fazed him. I don't think your taser's going to do much good. There's only one person in here that can deal with him, and it isn't me or you."

"Kid, I'm not letting Grace go. End of story."

I bowed my head. "Then we all die together."

Detective Allen grunted and assisted Rosen in trussing me up, much as they had done Grace. They dragged me down the hallway, past the first holding room. I saw Grace through the small window and tried to smile at her. Our eyes met for a brief moment before the cops tossed me into my own cell.

"No one's going to die on my watch," Allen said. "We'll let the courts deal with you and Grace. I'll bet you get cut a break to testify against her, even. This is all going to work itself—"

A resounding crash thundered along the front of the station.

"Why don't you go see if that's something working itself out?" I asked smugly. I was a dead man and I knew it. May as well take a cheap shot at the know-it-all cop before the end.

GRACE

I SAT IN MY CRAMPED, dirty holding cell envisioning my escape plan on the blank wall opposite me. Suddenly, summoning magic started pounding against the Weave fast and heavy. It resembled the summoning equivalent of someone playing the drum solo from "Sing Sing Sing" in a small room with thin walls. If I'd had free hands, I would have face palmed. Only one person I knew possessed the power and the naiveté to set off a cacophony like that.

Well, on the bright side, at least I knew the police didn't have Robert in custody.

An alarm started wailing. Blue emergency lights flashed on above the cell doors opposite mine.

On the down side, judging from the loud crashing and swearing from somewhere down the hall, and the fact that my guard had just gotten a transmission on his radio and run out of the room, that oversight wasn't likely to last much longer. The ground shook; metal caved in with a thunderous clap somewhere fairly close by.

As expected, after a while the alarm cut off along with the emergency lights. I didn't have to wait much longer before a couple of deputies walked down the hallway past my holding cell with a hangdog Robert between them in his own mummy bag. Our eyes met for a fraction of a second. His were apologetic and hopeful. Mine probably appeared surprised and a little touched.

The brat had actually tried to free me. I admitted to myself that this jail break, despite the ill-advised and crazy plan he'd come up with, made me a little warm and fuzzy. The kid's heart was in the right place, even if he was clumsy as hell.

I remembered how awkward I'd been before learning the runes, and found myself admiring his gumption. When I was learning, I didn't have to worry about blasting my essence into the Weave. I just didn't have enough juice for it to be a problem. I was a precision summoner by both nature and necessity. He'd failed to get me out, but he had ensured we would have one hell of a distraction. The kid wasn't stupid, but damn, he could be reckless.

My lips curved up in a stupid, devil-may-care smile. Well, I supposed we were going to do this, then. I just hoped I could keep most of the deputies away from harm. I didn't even kid myself that I'd be able to keep them all safe. I'd do my best. The deputies popped open the holding cell next to mine and plopped Robert into it. They provided two hall guards with their guns out, ready to shoot and ask questions later if we moved. Nice.

A crash came from the front of the station. I knew with ninety-nine percent certainty that it meant Rick had begun to force his way in. He wouldn't have been that far behind Robert's fireworks. From the cacophony, it sounded like Rick was having a field day tearing up the front of the building.

I considered warning our guards to get everyone out, but decided the miniscule chance of one of them believing me was heavily outweighed by the high probability of a twitchy trigger finger. An evacuation would have been their best move, but they surely wouldn't take my word for it.

I quickly ran through the most likely scenarios for the next couple of minutes in my mind, focusing my will to be ready for action as soon as an opportunity presented itself. Somewhere in the back of my brain, lounging on a sunny beach with a mojito sounded better and better. A little bead of nervous sweat trailed down my back under the clumsy turkey suit.

The sound of glass breaking, coupled with metal squealing and gunshots, echoed in from the front. The shouting started up again, at a higher intensity level than before. The alarm and flashing blue emergency lights came back next. I braced all my muscles against the leather restraints and waited. It couldn't have been more than thirty seconds at most, but for me, time crawled like a glacier before the crashing, shooting, shouting and occasional screams began to work their way closer.

One of the guards hefted his gun nervously and shot an accusing look at me. "Is this another one of your friends coming to break you out?" His weapon swung toward me.

"Sadly, no." I shook my head and looked at the guard somberly, then took the chance that since he'd asked, he might listen. "That thing is none of our doing. But it is extremely dangerous to everyone here, including Robert and me. You may wish to evacuate the building if you still can."

The deputy gave me an incredulous look and got back on his radio. I couldn't make out the words over the crackle of the radio, but his pistol never wavered from my direction.

"I already told them that," Robert's voice called. "They won't believe it."

The sounds of fighting came much closer; if the guards didn't go check it out soon, I would have to take action with those guns still trained on me and hope for the best. *Not* acting would get us all just as dead as getting shot.

The guard received some kind of transmission on the radio, swore, and walked over to the other guard. After a whispered conference, they jogged down the hallway past the holding cells to look out the fishbowl window in the heavy door.

With their attention finally elsewhere, I reached my Sense into the restraints and threw the whole mummified turkey suit into a heap on the floor next to me. We were incredibly lucky that Spokane Valley Station was apparently not outfitted to deal with summoners. The guns made things awkward, but not impossible. Now if they'd started me or Robert on the drugs, we'd truly have been severely handicapped, possibly even comatose. I didn't know why they'd held off administering them, but I wasn't going to look a gift horse in the mouth.

Bringing my thumb to my lips, I bit down and began tracing a summoning for my things in the station. I needed my bag and my rune board at the very least. The bag came to me easily, but the rune board had been stored in some other evidence locker; it took me several precious seconds of fine-tuning my formula before it came to me. I strapped my trusty board to my arm, slung the bag over my shoulder, and double-checked that the guards were still preoccupied. I quickly lined up the necessary runes on the board, ran my still-bleeding thumb over them, and sent the heavy door to my cell up to the roof. The sound of it disappearing whispered softer than a ripple of wind.

I peeked my head around the corner of the cell. The guards had opened the heavy retaining door at the end of the holding cells and were rushing through with their weapons still drawn. Neither of them looked at me; their attention was riveted on something outside. I didn't have to think hard to guess what.

The door closed behind them with a resounding bang that nicely hid the sound of my footfalls running down the hall toward Robert. Another alarm started somewhere and the lights went out for a moment before the backup generator kicked on. The lights came back on, dimmer than before.

"Took you long enough," Robert had the gall to quip when I dashed up.

"Shush, you. Since when was this a good diversionary tactic?" My fingers flew over the rune board and my thumb smeared the blood. Robert's door vanished.

"Since I failed at being able to get you out myself." He gave a lopsided and apologetic grin. "I thought we would be long gone by now."

"Cocky, boy." I dropped his restraints on the floor beside him.

"Keep up with me and try not to get any police killed. Or yourself, I guess. If we live through this, I'll be sure to hug you, before I smack you upside the head for doing something so stupid. Did you bring anything with you?"

"Just Uncle Herman's bracers. The police took them away from me and put them somewhere, though."

I shut my eyes and concentrated as my hands flew over the rune combinations. His bracers were on a desk out front still waiting to be cataloged as evidence. I vanished them out of plain sight, confident that no one was likely to notice their absence with a giant slavering raccoon tearing apart the station. I handed them back to Robert.

"I'm glad you didn't lose a keepsake from your uncle. Put them back on, but only use them if you have to. I want to bust out of here as quickly as possible. With any luck we can either stop Rick long enough that he loses interest, or lure him somewhere else to stop him. If I give you this sign—" I flashed him two fingers raised in a "V" for victory as the red button signal "—I need you to back me up by blasting Rick with those things and getting his attention."

We were in a time-sensitive, life or death situation, and he still found time to roll his eyes at me. "That's the best sign you can come up with?" His whole body conveyed teenage disdain. "Can't you think of anything less, well...lame?"

"Shove it. It's easy and I won't have to think about it. I'll take speed and ease over coolness any day."

I ripped the evidence tag off my bag and tossed him a couple of the blood flasks before clipping more to its strap for my use. I sketched out a rune set on the board, powered it, and placed my hands on his shoulders as I began to summon raw Kevlar from the jackets in the storage lockers to wrap around the fibers in his clothing.

"Hey! What's with the touching all of a sudden? That's creepy."

I glared at him. "I'm reinforcing your clothes so they're more likely to stop a bullet if we get shot at. Still, better drop flat if you see someone firing at you, ok?"

He had the grace to blush. "Yeah, sure," he mumbled. "Thanks."

I did the same to my own clothes before stepping up to the door out of the holding cells. "You'd better be ready for this, 'cause here we go. I probably don't need to say this, but whatever you do, don't let Rick corner you."

Robert gave a brisk nod that didn't match his expression. I opened the door.

THE SCENE on the other side gave new meaning to total mayhem. Rick had crushed the whole front of the building coming in, leaving a trail of broken glass, concrete, wires, and miscellaneous police stuff. He crouched with one giant clawed foot on a turned-over, dented desk with its contents spread around him in a paper explosion. His chitinous tail hovered over his head, just waiting to crash down on anyone unwary enough to step close.

The deputies were all in a line facing the giant demon, their backs to us. The room roared with the fire of semi-automatic weapons leveled at Rick, but most of the bullets fell to the ground before even reaching him. Those few that did make it bounced off his spiky hide without causing damage. Fortunately, none of the ricochets hit the deputies.

It also meant Rick was facing us. I swear his black rubbery lips twitched up over his fangs in a brief smile when we appeared. A chill wormed its way down my spine.

He launched himself toward us, smashing through ceiling tiles and overhead lights in the process. I threw Robert and myself forward through the rain of glass and sparks. We landed prone in a currently unoccupied corner of the room. Robert fetched up sprawled out in front of me.

My feet pointed back toward Rick. I propped myself up on my elbows, grabbed a vial and opened it with my right hand. Swiping blood across the runes on my left bracelet, I pivoted my weight onto my right elbow as I felt the familiar heaviness of the throwing axe arrive in my left hand. Twisting my body so all my weight rested on my right side and I could see behind me, I extended my left arm in an arc, releasing the axe at the top of the swing. It hurtled toward Rick's unprotected belly.

It looked right on target but I couldn't wait to make sure. I rolled up to my knees and spun to face Rick. In my peripheral vision, I could see Robert jumping to his feet behind me.

Instead of dodging or using kinetic force to deflect the axe like I expected, Rick made a very un-raccoon-like movement with one of his forelegs and batted it away, embedding it in the door by the holding cells. He didn't even cut his paw. Rick threw back his head in what could only be called an eerie laugh.

The deputies in the room used the opportunity I had created to fall back and regroup toward the ruined front of the station. That suited me just fine. As long as they didn't decide to shoot me or Robert, I would prefer they stayed out of the way. I thought I saw Detective Allen talking to the captain toward the front of the line.

"Try to evacuate if you can!" I called to them. "I'll attempt to keep it busy here. It shouldn't be interested in any of you. I believe it will only harm people who get in its way."

I didn't wait to see if any of them actually listened to me. Robert and I kept running. Debris from the desks threatened to trip us up. Blooding another of my bangles, I blasted it out of the way with a gust of wind stolen from over the South Pacific. For a moment the station smelled bizarrely like salt and pineapples, but our path cleared of detritus. At this point in time, I counted that as a small victory.

Rick started gathering himself for another leap. Robert and I dodged to the middle of the room behind a large support pillar and a little green fern in a glazed ceramic pot. A hooting noise that still sounded creepily like laughter drifted around the police station.

What the hell was going on here? He was acting less like a beast than before. The Rick from the fight at the aluminum plant and the mall acted on instinct only. This Rick could only be described as evilly gleeful. The flashing lights from the alarm system didn't faze him at all.

The chill that had been creeping down my back intensified,

sending a shudder after it. Could there possibly be two of them? God, I hoped not. No way could I fend off two Ricks at once.

The floor shook but I didn't hear crashing anywhere near our pillar. I peeked around it. Rick had disappeared from the back of the station. He wasn't near us... With dread, I peered into the only other part of the station where he could be.

Rick was sitting in the middle of the deputies at the front of the station. They hadn't evacuated, but I hadn't really expected that they would heed advice from someone who had just broken out of one of their own holding cells. It went totally against their job description.

It would also have made my life *so* much easier, but of course luck never smiled on me that way. I braced myself for Rick to start thrashing and killing cops, since they were in his way, and tried to think of anything I could possibly throw at him to lure him over here with minimal collateral damage.

A round canister on the floor behind the pillar caught my eye. I picked it up and grinned. Maybe I could do something with this. I slid it into the pocket of my skirt, motioned Robert to stay put, and stepped out from behind the pillar. I arranged the runes in a summons I had never had the need for and probably would never need again.

"Hey, Rick!" I yelled. "I have something that might interest you, but you have to come here to get it!"

I finished my summons, sending a shower of shimmering stage confetti down. It caught on the air current and swirled around me, flashing in glittering abandon. If this was the Rick I knew, this should definitely get him over here, and then I'd plan what came next.

Instead, the hooting laughter filled the station again, and Rick actually *spoke.* I almost swallowed some of the confetti.

"Whuft! No doubt that is just the type of display guaranteed to get my minion's attention, but unfortunately for you, he is not home today." Not-Rick's lips twitched upward in a truly terrifying smile as he spoke. His voice echoed in the room, jovial, almost paternal, and it sent sick shivers all the way from my scalp to my elbows. "You have been much more troublesome than I expected, Grace Anne Moore. I had no idea you would be able to push me into needing to appear here. These nice constables would like to lock you up so you never see the light of day, and yet you still try to lure my pet away from them. Humans are so...humorous. Always trying to save those who do not give them any respect back."

Not-Rick's eyes narrowed, and he stared at me with a weird gleam in his eyes. If I'd been facing a human, I'd have called it a crazed expression, but his whole face was alien. I couldn't be sure.

The muscles around his snout twitched. "Do you really wish to save these humans, summoner?"

"I would not stand by and watch people die if I can help it," I answered guardedly. It's *always* a bad idea to bargain with an unknown Visitor. So this was Rick's boss, huh? All in all, I preferred the beast that killed on instinct rather than its master, who seemed to be killing based on some kind of cold calculation.

"There is but one thing you need to do, then. Give yourself and the boy to me, and I will let all of these puny humans go. They are no use to me. I promise your sacrifice will be well rewarded."

One of the deputies started to move. Boss Rick barked out, "Do not think to move! If any of you beige men try something, I will make it very painful for this one."

I heard a sudden groan and saw that Rick had a paw curled loosely around a man in a brown suit who already had one of Rick's spines sticking out of his right shoulder. Detective Allen. Of course it would be his gun arm that Rick injured. Otherwise, from that angle, he might actually be able to shoot Boss Rick in the eye. Probably wouldn't take him down, but you never knew.

"Whuft! It would be a shame to start with this one," Boss Rick went on. "What will you do, Grace? You cannot think to defeat me with only yourself and a worthless, sniveling boy with no real talent. He doesn't even know how to wipe the snot off his own face. It baffles me why you insist on saving him from me."

Predictably, I heard "Hey!" from behind the pillar. In typical, hot-headed teenager fashion, Robert started to run forward; I grabbed him by the back of the shirt. As it turns out, there is more than one use for super-strengthened cloth. His momentum arrested, Robert sat down hard next to me. I leaned over on the pretense of pulling him back to his feet.

"He's baiting you, dummy. Wait for the signal, ok? We can still do this."

I straightened up. "And what guarantees do we have from you that you will leave this area and not come back?"

"Oh, you don't. However, you two are the last juicy morsels of any worth in the Spokane area. I suppose I will wander on after this, and you will have saved these people you seem to like so much."

Call me paranoid, but something just didn't add up here. Rick had held Robert and me against the ropes in every confrontation, and yet somehow, something wasn't going to his boss's satisfaction. He'd possessed Rick and come out to see us himself. That meant that somehow, our presence in Spokane threw a wrench into his plans. Given that, there was nothing to do but keep trying to be a pain in the ass any way I could think how. Not that it changed much. I still needed to get Frank and all the other cops out of harm's way.

I stepped forward a few paces. "Ok, let's say we take you up on your deal. You have to let the officers go first. If you do that, I'm willing to believe you."

"I will let them all go, except for this one. He stays as my surety for your cooperation."

"Done, then. Let the other men go."

"Everyone except the man in the brown suit may leave."

The deputies looked at Allen. He looked intently at me for a fraction of a moment, then said, "Do it. Everyone clear out. There's nothing more to do here until we receive more backup."

The deputies stumbled out of the building into the parking lot. I could hear sirens approaching. The city contracted with the county for police services, and I didn't think enough time had gone by for it to be the State Patrol. We stood in the Valley's only cop station. Which meant that whatever those emergency vehicles turned out to be, I didn't think they'd be able to help much. That left me, Robert, Detective Allen, and Boss Rick.

"Ok, then. Robert, stay behind me in case he tries anything tricksy."

I started slowly forward with Robert right behind me. Resting my hand on my purse and concentrating my Sense, I pulled a tag from my bag and hid it against my palm. I had to give the kid points for not throwing a fit, since it looked like I was offering us up to be kibble.

About eleven feet from Rick, which was much closer than I would *prefer* to be, and just out of reach of his tail (I hoped), I stopped, motioning Robert to stop, too. I dropped to one knee in what I hoped Rick would assume to be obeisance. Its lips curled upward creepily and its eyes gleamed with triumph.

"I have two questions." I held my fingers up in a "V" to illustrate. "The first is—"

Robert, bless him, immediately picked up on the signal. I whipped blood off my purse strap and slapped it into the waiting tag barely a nanosecond before I felt Robert let loose a veritable wall of kinetic force. It careened through the Weave above me. A round area of floor just under the detective disappeared. I broke his fall with hay that a farmer on the outskirts of town would be very perturbed not to find tomorrow morning.

The force Robert unleashed activated the demon's telekinesis. Rick deflected a good portion instinctively, destroying more of the ceiling, but as I'd hoped, he couldn't deflect and keep his attention on the detective. The force was enough to push Rick back from the hole by a good six feet.

I kipped up and used some of Robert's leftover kinetic force humming in the air to augment my running speed as I used my Sense to pull the canister from my pocket into my hand. I let the whole can of pepper spray loose in Rick's face before his telekinesis could come back up. He scrabbled at his eyes, howling.

For good measure I summoned quick-hardening cement from a nearby construction company and dumped it over him. I didn't think it would hold him, but it should keep him out of commission long enough for us and the deputies to clear out. Rearranging the tiles on my rune board, I summoned a portable ladder for Frank, securing it at the top of the hole.

"Please hurry, Detective. You have a minute at most to rejoin your deputies and evacuate before Rick breaks through that cement. I expect it to try to follow Robert and me when we leave. As long as you stay out of its way, it shouldn't hurt any more of your people. Come on!"

I motioned for Robert to follow. We jogged out the shattered front of the police station into the parking lot. I took a quick scan of the situation. It looked like the cops present were still picking themselves up or cautiously peering over the debris looking for Rick. No one tried to stop us.

Still more emergency personnel, fire trucks and ambulances, had responded to a large pileup of cars on Sprague in front of the station. EMTs were helping the wounded on both scenes. I suppose the wreck provided another distraction from us, but I couldn't approve. I really needed to have a talk with Robert about the mechanics of summoning. The pileup seemed a little *too* coincidental.

In an unblocked part of the parking lot I summoned the Pontiac for the second time that day. We piled in and high-tailed it away from the scene. So far Rick had only hurt mundanes when we were present. I had to believe that trend would continue. We couldn't do any more if we stayed here. I doubted the cops would leave anything up to chance if we got arrested again. We could expect to be unconscious until the Feds came and picked us up. There wouldn't be a second jail break.

Ye gods. Once again we had just managed to stay alive by the skin of our teeth. Out there somewhere beyond the Weave we were thwarting a demon at...what? Now if I could figure that out, I'd be a genius.

ROBERT

I SAT in the forest outside Uncle Herman's shack and breathed in the crisp mountain air. Two weeks had gone by since Grace and I had retreated here. Fall had definitely started to make its presence known in the North Idaho woods. The air tasted cool and clean. Around me, my Sense extended, taking in everything it could. I felt—no, I *became* —the trees, the animals, the colony of ants in an old rotting stump, and the wind itself.

The Sense is a heady experience, really. Grace had told me it probably seemed more so for me than others, given the range of my Sense, but I can only tell you it was an experience that could be called transcendental. It mimicked the kind of out-of-body experience I got when I busted into a serious Paul Gonzales-style saxophone solo. It was at once peaceful and yet filled with activity. I felt each second as it passed and tried to make the most of it. I focused on my training, joining myself to the world and the Weave around me. By being it, I could control it.

AFTER WE DROVE AWAY from a giant raccoon amidst a scene of destruction for the second time, I had mixed feelings. After all, my plan had worked. Or, at least, the contingency section of my plan had. I hadn't managed to be the big badass hero, but Grace and I were free and headed back to the cabin. Mission accomplished.

Except...I had also managed to get a couple of cops hurt in the process. I may not have harmed them personally, but I had brought Rick down on the station knowing full well what that meant. With Duane, I had accidentally endangered a life. With the police, I had intentionally endangered them. It weighed on me. I was no longer innocent; I had indirectly caused injury to several men who were only trying to do their job. I felt *almost* certain that it had been the right thing to do, but even so I couldn't let it go. I reminded myself to check the news and see how Captain Carlenos and Detective Allen had fared. Granted, Uncle Herman's cabin was secluded enough to not *get* either television or the internet, but I was pretty sure I could get Grace to summon a paper.

My training began in earnest during that car ride; I think Grace tried to distract me from the repercussions of what I had done. "What is summoning?" she asked. This, of course seemed a silly question coming from a master summoner, but she had that bent to her mouth that suggested it was a trick question. I knew I would be wrong as I said it, but I had nothing else. Besides, my weariness dragged on me, so I didn't want to take the time to ponder.

"It's making stuff appear," I said. "Or sending something somewhere else, I guess. Depends on what you want to do."

"Where does this stuff come from?"

"Ummm...I'm not sure, really. Somewhere?" I had never thought about this part being important.

"Very true. You've just hit on your major problem. The reason we summoners are so despised is because, long ago, many of us didn't think about where it comes from. We just did it. That's dangerous stuff, right there."

"How dangerous?"

"Well, let's say that what you need is hot water. You pack a bunch

161

of energy into summoning hot water, but you ignore where it's coming from. You slam energy out into the Weave, and the hottest water in range of your summons responds and appears." Grace proposed this hypothetical situation innocuously. I knew she had set a trap for me, but I couldn't avoid falling into it.

"Well, it seems you got the hot water you wanted. What's wrong with that?

"What's *wrong* with it is that the last time a summoner did that he was a couple miles outside Chernobyl. Didn't work out well for the summoner, either; he got bathed in irradiated steam from the cooling core of one of the reactors. Killed him pretty quick, I hear. Not quick enough to miss the excruciating pain stage, though. Didn't work out well for the entire city of Prypiat, either."

"Wow... Ok, I guess that makes sense." It did, too; I may be bullheaded, but I certainly didn't want to create large-scale disasters.

"I say this because it would appear you opened up the back of that station using raw kinetic force."

"Yeah," I said proudly. "I used...this rune here." I pointed to the rune on my bracers.

"One rune." Grace said flatly. "And did you, say, hear anything as you did that? Something along the lines of...a car crash?"

I had. I hadn't really thought much about it at the time, but there *had* been the sound of crashing metal as I blew in the back wall of the police station. "I did, actually. I was concentrating on other things, but now that you mention it..."

She whipped her voice at me, fire under steel. "Those things you were concentrating on caused that crash." She laid into me, flailing me with her voice. "You used raw kinetic force. You pulled that force from one of the cars on Sprague. It went from thirty-five miles an hour to nothing in a split second, with no brakes and, more importantly, no warning to the guy behind it. You pulled that force away from the car, and you put it into the wall. You paid no attention to where your force came from; *you just used force.* Think about that, because when we get back you're going to learn to control the source of your summoning. Then, *maybe*, you won't be a walking disaster."

My head began to pound as she railed at me. I leaned back in the car seat. A wave of exhaustion hit me. I closed my eyes and took a deep breath.

"Ah, it's finally catching up to you, I see?"

I mumbled something incoherent. I didn't want to talk to this nagging woman anymore; I'd been yelled at enough. I'd saved her; couldn't she just be happy with that?

"The sloppier you are with your power, the more it hits you. You were wild and uncontrolled back there; that's the second reasoning summoning the way you did is a bad idea."

"You did all kinds of summoning back there; if it feels like this afterward, why aren't you worn out?"

"Oh, I am. I'm just better at dealing with it than you."

KINETIC FORCE. I chuckled as I thought about it, sitting in the forest. I reached out with my Sense and took the kinetic force of the wind, changing its direction, swirling it around. If it was in range of my Sense, and I concentrated on it, I could make the wind dance. I cracked a half smile as I concentrated the wind's force to a fine point. I chiseled the words "Robert wuz here" into the side of a pine thirty feet above ground. If this place was ever logged off, someone would be confused.

Summoning is the art of moving something from point A to point B, and as long as both A and B are in range of your Sense, you don't need a lot of help doing it. I realized that now. Frankly, I enjoyed using my Sense; it felt...peaceful. When I extended my Sense, I just felt calm.

"SUMMONING IS LITTLE MORE than a manipulation of the Weave." Grace said with *that's-that* finality. We were sitting on the bench outside Herman's cabin, looking at his little patch of land and eating catfish, chicken, and ribs I'm pretty sure Grace had simply summoned straight from some soul food restaurant, though she just gave me a grin when I asked.

"Rrriiiiiight." I did my best to imitate Bill Cosby in his Noah routine. "What's the Weave?"

Grace rolled her eyes. "It's...everything. It's the thing that holds this world together. It's also the thing that holds this world separate. Here. Maybe a visual demonstration." She scratched out a couple of runes, smeared some blood over them, and a massive pile of tangled yarn showed up on the ground in front of the bench.

"Imagine this snarl of yarn as...well, as the raw material for everything." Grace scribbled down more runes on a pad of yellow paper as we talked. "Physicists are still trying to get down to it; string theory is about as close as they've come, but they're almost right. At its base level, all things are made out of the same stuff. Matter, energy; it's all the same, and it's all made out of...well, for purposes of this discussion, out of yarn."

"Ok."

"Well, our world is nothing more than the yarn woven together. It takes the chaos of all of this, and...it makes something out of it."

Grace pulled the piece of paper off the pad and smeared it; the entire paper was coated with runes. Suddenly, some of the yarn rearranged itself into what I immediately recognized as a hacky sack. The back of my mind noted that this seemed an extreme amount of work for a hacky sack, but I tried to pay attention to the lecture.

"So the Weave holds our world together," Grace went on. "It also holds it apart from the rest of the chaos out there."

"And when we summon, we move the threads around?"

Grace smiled, snapped her fingers, and pointed at me. "Give the boy a gold star. Summoning is about using one's Sense to change those threads."

"But my Sense is really, really short-range. Are you saying I can't pull anything in from outside of fifty feet?" Growing visions of my Jedi-like power shattered.

"Robert, you have one of the longest Senses I have seen in any summoner. The advantage that's going to give you is really remarkable. My own Sense doesn't actually extend past what I'm physically touching. It's the runes that channel our Sense. Runes form a framework for the Sense to run through. The blood highlights that framework by giving it life. Using the runes and the blood, we give our Sense a conduit to reach out in the Weave to wherever we need."

A conduit. I'd been using the runes as a talisman, not a conduit. "So, we're going to do two things over the course of the next couple of weeks," she said. "You've already been trained on using your Sense to...well, to sense. Now we're going to teach you to use it alone to move things within it. And, yes, we're going to spend every night studying runes until your eyes bleed. Once you know how to put a rune phrase together, you're going to be able to use that Sense of yours to do some amazing work. Here, we need some fresh blood anyway. Bring up your Sense."

I closed my eyes and focused, slipping into the Sense. Grace scribbled out some runes on the back of a box that, up until recently, had contained some very nice fried catfish. As I Sensed, she brought up hers. I could feel her do it, a slight aura of power surrounding her. It wasn't much.

Then, for a split second, it seemed to funnel into the flimsy cardboard box. The runes on the box filled with Grace's Sense, which had left her entirely. It came back, and with it came a styrofoam cup with a plastic lid. Grace set it down on the bench, then ducked into the cabin.

"You see," she said from inside, "the runes provide a pathway. Your Sense travels through the runes and back, and carries with it whatever you send it for. Or with. Or both."

She began wiping out her small glass vials and refilling them using a funnel from her bag. "The trick is getting your Sense through the runes." She cracked a smile. "You're going to have to work on your control. And your rune formulas. We have a lot to do and it's not going to be very fun. For you, anyway."

I raised one of my eyebrows at her. She laughed.

AND SO I sat in the forest chiseling my name into trees. I filled a squirrel's nest with pine nuts when it wasn't looking. It turned around, saw a nest full of food, and stared at it in bewilderment. I chuckled. There were several ripe huckleberries still on a bush thirty feet away; I took them one by one off the bush and popped them a couple of inches above my mouth, letting them fall in and fill my mouth with their juicy goodness.

An arrow came speeding toward me. I took its kinetic force and applied it in a reverse direction. It flew away, spinning nock over point until it hit the ground. I ate another berry. They were delicious.

I stood and walked back toward the cabin, keeping my Sense drawn about me. As I went, I felt an owl asleep in its den. I felt a rabbit go completely still, hoping I didn't see it. The coming bullet wouldn't hit anything, so I did nothing to it. The moisture in the air rose, and I felt the first raindrops come down. I used them to refill my water bottle; the water was sweet and cool, and my head stayed dry.

A massive boulder hurtled toward me. I simply transported it to my other side, letting it continue its journey into a cliff without me. Then I plucked some late-blooming sunflowers directly into my hand, forming them into a bouquet which I impishly presented to Grace with a toothy smile. She took them from me.

"Yup. I think you've got the hang of it. Now let's test your runes." Gulp.

LATER THAT NIGHT, Grace and I sat across the small, wooden table from each other. Our eyes narrowed and a hush settled about the room like a silken sheet. Her hands traced a pattern back and forth on the small board in front of her. I braced myself, wondering what form of attack she would open with. She outmatched me and I knew it, but she had challenged me to this fight. I knew I had no choice but to accept.

The first move was hers. I waited. Her hand rose up. Here it came. "Ha!" Her fingers flew across her rune tiles, laying out an intricate combination of seven runes as she launched her first attack. "There. Let's see...that's an Inguz rune, a double-double, and of course there's the bingo for using all seven tiles. I think that gives me...two hundred fourteen points. Suck it down, buddy."

This was not even remotely close to fair. "Look, if this were actually Scrabble, I could go to the dictionary or something. For all I know you're just throwing down tiles and claiming they're phrases."

I received an arched eyebrow for this.

"Well, how am I supposed to know that phrase does anything? It's not like I've had time to memorize all of them." I grasped for a defense here. Or at least to stall my turn. Anything to do that, really.

Grace rolled her eyes dramatically, dipped under the table and came up with a vial of blood, which she wiped on the modified Scrabble tiles. A split second later she ended up with a pre-plated slice of a caramel-topped cheesecake, complete with fork.

"Only one slice?" I asked, miffed she would not *only* challenge me to such a lopsided game, but would also eat a delicious treat like that in front of me to rub it in.

"Look at the runes. If I wanted to summon a whole cheesecake, I would have Fehu where that Eihwaz is. I wish I'd had that, by the way; I could have racked up more points. Alas, I didn't draw a Fehu tile, so I settle for eating this cheesecake in front of you." She settled back in her chair, dessert plate in her hand and a smug smile on her face.

Some people get wise old Asian men when they go to the wilderness to train. Me, I got the gloating gourmand. Fabulous.

"Enough whining. Time for your move."

Argh. Let's see... If I crossed that Eihwaz rune with my Gebo, Wunjo, and Hagalaz, I should be able to summon an umbrella; the gift of the end of hail that brings joy. Worth a crack, anyway. I laid them out.

"Let's see... Eihwaz, Gebo, Hagalaz, and Wunjo. Where's your source?"

Crap. I had forgotten her lecture. I had to specify not just the *what* but the where as well. I looked at my tiles and grinned. This was an easy one, and better points. I placed the Othila rune at the head of it.

"Nice. Homeland. So you're going to summon an umbrella from your house?"

"Umm...yeah?" I'd challenged her on her cheesecake and received the mockery of watching her eat it. I should have known she'd challenge me on this.

"Ok, then. Do it." She leaned across the table, extending her bangle-clad arm, vial of blood in hand. I had no choice; I smeared my five-tile set with it. Then I settled myself down, closed my eyes, and began to slip into my Sense. Gradually, the tranquility that comes with being one with everything settled about me. I made sure to note the location of all the rune tiles; that might come in handy.

The runes I had smeared with blood lit up like a beacon to my Sense. They echoed with the power I projected, calling attention to themselves. I focused on them, and on the fly resting on the wall behind me, and on the coyote outside that thought he smelled something interesting coming from the wood shack but knew it was a scary place, and on the grass slowly dying outside, and on the...

Right. Perhaps "focus" isn't the best word.

But some portion of me settled around the rune-phrase, and I tried to slip through it. I couldn't; the part of me aware of the runes was merely a part of the whole, and the whole thought about the three spiders in the rafters busily spinning webs and the slow decay of the mud caulking the northern wall of the cabin and the crackling fire in the stove consuming its...

I couldn't stop being those things just to be this rune. I tried, but I couldn't. My Sense wouldn't let me.

I had used runes before, though, and I knew something Grace hadn't said: you don't have to slip your Sense through them to use them. I sent raw power at the rune, concentrating on the umbrella. Sure enough, an umbrella appeared in my hand. So what if I hadn't ended up with the one from my house...it was still an umbrella.

Grace's face looked like red-hot steel.

"Out of curiosity," she whipped at me, her voice cracking with sudden anger "Do you think I don't know when you do that?"

"Do what?" The last resort of the foster child: deny everything.

"I'm willing to bet that's not the right umbrella. And the reason I'm willing to make that bet, mister, is because of the way you acquired it. You didn't slip your Sense through the Weave; you broadcast your desire to the whole Weave and waited for the closest approximation to show up. That umbrella isn't from your house. It's most likely from the house of our nearest neighbor, and you have just committed not only summoning, but theft to boot."

She took a breath, calmed, and slowed her speech. There was no more joking around about Scrabble points; Grace had moved into a dead sort of seriousness. She spoke slowly, deliberately.

"Robert, we have to break you of this habit. Summoners who do things this way are the ones that give us a bad name, and we don't tolerate them. The Grove will...take steps...against anyone they believe is abusing their summoning. Remember all the evil things you used to think about summoners? Start thinking them about summoners *who do this.*"

"Steps?" I definitely wanted some clarification there.

"Assassination-type steps," Grace whispered. "Right now, you're my apprentice. Apprentices have the leeway to do this *once*, so that their master can have this very conversation with them. From here on out, the Grove will have you killed if you do it again. Worse, they may very well take me out, too, for failing to instruct you properly. Weave-beating is absolutely the most serious crime any of us can do. So *don't do it again.* From now on, slip your Sense through the runes; don't use the runes to beat the crap out of the Weave."

"But..." I whined. I really don't want to call it that, but that's what I did. This was an absolute being handed down to me, and a good student would have accepted it. I, however, couldn't help protesting. "My Sense won't go into the runes. I can't make it. I've tried and I've tried, and I keep thinking about other things."

"Try harder. And in the meantime, don't take your failure out on the Weave. Otherwise, you'll get both of us killed."

GRACE

NOW THAT I'D resigned Robert to the flashcards, and hovered over him enough to be sure he'd started on his way to understanding summoning mechanics and memorizing the runes, I had time for a little research into Rick and his mysterious puppet master. I had one or two books with me I could still check, but I scrawled out a note to Amy asking for the more in-depth bestiaries, any encyclopedias of spirits with full profiles, and anything she could find with an emphasis on spirits who specialized in possessions.

Then I wrote a quick-but-thorough report to Grove headquarters about Rick and the latest developments, and sent that off for review as well, with my recommendation that backup not be dispatched at this time. I also requested that as soon as I could report safe conditions, a medical summoner be dispatched to Valley Medical for Duane. I summoned his medical charts for no more than a few seconds every day to make sure he still breathed. He needed help fast. I just had to hope he would hold out until Robert could keep his promise. Either way, I needed to come up with some kind of plan to take this demon out ASAP.

I even went and asked Robert if it was all right to summon the rest of Uncle Herman's notes so I could look at them. He looked up from the rune flashcards and scowled at me for interrupting his concentration. It was all right with him as long as the cops hadn't confiscated them yet. Not likely. I'd actually moved them to one of the Grove's safe houses as soon as he told me he'd just shoved them under his bed. I hadn't had time to think about them since.

The kid was right; the cops would be all over his foster parents' house. I felt bad for them, since I doubted the foster parent training would have prepared them for this type of intense scrutiny from the police. I summoned the notes but put them aside for the moment. I scoured my family's Grove book and the books I'd brought with me, trying to find a reference to anything that sounded like Rick. I scrutinized every demon, but none of the descriptions stood out to me as being relevant. Hmm. No response from Amy yet, so I pulled down Uncle Herman's notes and started going through them. They didn't seem to be in any particular order, so I just started reading the first one that caught my eye.

Manipulating the Weave and its Relation to Sense

The widely accepted view of the Weave states that it is the membrane between worlds that keeps different dimensions or "worlds" from colliding. It also states that at certain points it can weaken or develop holes based on how closely the other dimensions press upon this one. This is a very limiting view of the Weave.

While the Weave does serve as a barrier between realities and must be maintained to ensure the security of this plane, its barrier function is but one of many purposes that the Weave serves.

By much experimentation (the notes and formulae from which are attached as an appendix), I have found the Weave also serves the following major functions:

The medium through which the Sense operates

The conduit through which the power for summonings is allowed to rearrange matter

A temporary door between dimensions

He continued with laying out "Lesser properties of the Weave and their uses," but I scanned down past the rest until I came to his elaborate formulae, which were marked out with very deliberate pen strokes, and the footnotes. At first it looked like absolute gibberish to me. He didn't use *any* simple runes. All the runes in the summoning were already compounded rune sets, which would usually be their own formula, chained together to work with the previous one. I used complex rune sets all the time, but this seemed complicated to the point of absurdity.

When taken individually, though, nothing indicated the underlying rune clauses wouldn't work. The whole summons worked on such a ludicrously gargantuan scale. I couldn't say whether it would or wouldn't produce the intended effect. However, even if I assumed Uncle Herman's certifiable genius, and not insanity, you also would need an inhuman amount of focus and intent for it to go off correctly.

I sat there, going over the formulae for about the tenth time. Abruptly, I felt the familiar prickle of Amy's Sense as she stretched it through a rune summoning. The things I had requested from her appeared on the table, along with a note.

Hey, I hope you and the kid are doing ok. They had bulletins all over the news that two confirmed summoners had destroyed the Spokane Valley Police Station while breaking out. Not to put you out or anything, but your mug shot was not your best likeness. Looked like you'd just put your finger in a light socket or something. They must have caught you mid-summon? Tsk, tsk. The grove bigwigs aren't too happy about all the publicity either, but they have their hands full with other things at the moment, so I don't think there are any plans to cut off their support...

I grimaced.

...or anything like that. Be sure to keep your head down. I'm not sure how many more disasters they'll be able to take.

I grabbed all the reference books from the library that I could. Some of the ones that I would have loved to get for you were already checked out.

You didn't ask for food but I know you are always starving, and I bet that kid isn't much better, judging by the school photo they showed on the news. I got you a surprise, which should be pretty easy to eat even if you guys are hiding under a rock somewhere!

Take care, Amy

She had tied a grocery bag over two rectangular Styrofoam takeout boxes on top of the books. A light, spicy aroma wafted up. My mouth watered. I opened them up to find kefta-stuffed flat bread and babouche. Hurray for Moroccan food.

I decided I'd better call Robert before my bad intentions got the best of me and I ate it all myself. For the first time ever he didn't even look twice before digging in. I found myself strangely pleased by that. I picked up the first reference book and started to peruse it for a mention of Rick or a Demon known for controlling other Visitors as I munched on a babouche.

"Hey," Robert asked after a minute. "How come you eat such weird foods all the time? Don't you ever, like, eat American food?"

I considered that. "I just like really good food," I said finally. "I don't consciously set out to avoid 'American food.' I love a spicy apple or pumpkin pie, and there is something extremely satisfying about a sirloin burger with a thick wedge of sharp cheddar, thin sliced red onions, and dill pickles smothered in barbeque sauce on a potato roll. But whatever it is, it has to be *delicious*. I don't really go for cheap food that only tastes like salt. And really, why should I? I don't have to make myself eat stuff that doesn't taste good, when I can make food from any restaurant in the world that will take my money appear on my dining table. It's even better than delivery, and one of the best perks of being a summoner."

"You are such a total foodie." Robert sighed and stuffed the rest of the kefta in his mouth, grabbed a handful of babouche and headed back outside. I settled in for a long night of reading.

I WANTED to pull my hair out. The kefta and babouche were long gone, and I had found no mention of anything that sounded like Rick or his spooky boss in any of the books Amy had sent me.

Robert had stumbled back in a few hours ago and bunked down in the narrow little bed at the back of the cabin. His light, regular snoring marked the passage of time better than a clock.

My gaze fell on Uncle Herman's notes and his references to the Visitant Pacts. As a rule, I hated using them. Any time you mess with calling spirits who aren't tied to your family, it is easy to get in trouble. Making a pact with a new spirit is very rare and tricky—and only partly because you have to run into an unbound spirit to begin with. There are family guardian spirits who may or may not be helpful, but that is a bit different, since the spirit has to sign up for that in the first place. Even they can be occasionally tetchy with their descendants.

Still, given the total lack of help from my usual resources, it might be the last way to get information on these guys.

I didn't have to like it, though, and I wouldn't do it without sleep. I stood up and stretched. I'd been pouring over books for hours.

I opened the door and shut it gently behind me so I wouldn't wake up Robert. The moon hung high in the sky, and a light layer of frost coated the grass. The late night autumn chill hung in the clear air. A glow came from the cabin's one window, and a small spiral of tangy wood smoke drifted from the chimney. Uncle Herman had chosen this spot well. From here, you couldn't see the city's lights or ambient glow. It gave the illusion that I stood in a different, simpler age. I hugged that thought to me shamelessly as I gazed at the multitude of clustered stars never visible in the city. No one can look at the true night sky on a clear night and not feel wonder. Don't get me wrong. I love convenience, but there is something primal about the night sky in the middle of the woods.

On impulse I walked down the drive from the cabin and drew out the summons for Redwood. No hurry today. I didn't need the ring.

It greeted me with a sleepy murmur. The rents in its bark were healing well. Soon it would be recovered enough to return to its Weave. It would need some time to recoup its energies there, but no permanent harm had been done. I ran a hand over its bark and sighed.

"I'm glad you are well, friend. I thought you might prefer to heal here." I climbed up in its branches as I'd been done more times than I could count.

"It is good to be back in a forest," Redwood rumbled. "The earth is rich here."

"I'm glad. You are welcome to rest here before you go back to your Weave. Just don't go wandering off in front of people."

"You won't be able to see the tree for the forest," Redwood quipped, and I laughed. "But honestly, I will go home soon. I have responsibilities there, too."

I nodded. "Thank you, friend. I've asked a lot of you recently." I patted its rough bark and leaned back against its weathered trunk. We watched the stars together in silence. A low hoot sounded from somewhere nearby.

Startled, I realized I'd nodded off.

An owl blinked at me from a nearby branch. Redwood winked.

Smiling, I wished the tree good night and headed back into the cabin. Redwood's large, bulky shadow remained, a reassuring presence along the drive.

A bit chilled, I popped the trunk of the Pontiac and grabbed an extra blanket before curling back up at the table. I fell asleep reading the Encyclopedia of Visitors.

THE NEXT DAY dawned bright and sunny, but I woke up with a crick in my neck and a puddle of drool on the table under my cheek. Not an auspicious beginning. I wandered outside and watched Robert at his training until I awoke fully. Redwood had already vacated the spot by the drive. It must have headed back to its home Weave. I heaved a sigh of regret, but it was a valid call. No doubt it would be more comfortable at home.

Robert's memory of the individual runes was already improving at a steady pace. Rune work couldn't be called his forte yet, but he had a good grasp of the basics. He struggled with powering the runes for some reason I still couldn't figure out, though. Given his huge Sense, he possessed the potential to pull just about anything he wanted out of the Weave. Whatever held him back from exerting that potential through runes was something new.

Robert's attempt to break me out of jail had both shocked me and forced me to see him in a slightly different way. I didn't agree with his attitude, which frequently sucked. He also had the unfortunate tendency to say just the wrong thing at exactly the right time to send my patience up in smoke. Despite all that, at the jail and in the days since, I'd started to see that underneath it all glimmered the makings of a good and courageous kid. The jail break had taken a lot of daring, and put him in a lot of danger.

I would trust my instincts on this one. He needed a real mentor and a support system, whether he wanted them or not. I'd never had an apprentice. Correction: I'd never wanted an apprentice. Sometimes it's best to just bow to the inevitable while you can still haggle for the best terms.

I waited for him to pause. "Why don't you take a break for a bit? I have something here I want to show you."

We sat down on the bench outside the cabin. I brought out my little black Grove book. "You might have already picked this up on your own, but this is called a Grove book. Every summoner has one."

I flipped it open. "The reason for that is because it lays out the rules of the Grove, specific ritual summons, and also any spirits that your Grove has made pacts with. For example, the Seattle Grove spirits' names are here, starting with Kikisolbu, the Fremont Troll, Orcinus, etc. Then on the next page are family spirits. Family spirits are special, because they have bound themselves to the well-being of your ancestors and their descendants. They can be ancestors themselves, or it may be a spirit that bound itself to a family in exchange for certain protections or benefits. Calling on spirits isn't like the other summoning we do, where you are just moving an object from point A to point B. Spirits have their own agendas. If you don't deal with them carefully, they can also be very harmful. That said, they can also be very powerful allies. Either way, they should be treated with great caution. Sometimes opinions on harmful and beneficial results can be surprisingly subjective, especially if the thing evaluating the outcome is not human to begin with. There are exceptions, of course."

"So what do all these warnings have to do with me?" Robert asked. "Why would I need to know all this at all? I don't even have one of those books."

Forcing down my nerves, I took a cleansing breath and forced myself to look him dead in the eyes while I said something that made me feel intensely awkward, and couldn't have been any less weird for him. "Since your relatives are no longer living, and I haven't seen a Grove Book among your uncle's things, I don't know if the Lorents have their own family spirits. It may be that they have hidden their family records away somewhere. They could suddenly pop up, or they might just be gone.

"I-I guess, what I am saying, is... I am officially acknowledging you as my student and opening up my family records to you. I've asked my family for a Grove book for you. It will have notes from all the generations of Moore summoners, and a lot of information about other Groves' spirits and families. I want them to add the Spokane Grove information to it, so it won't be here for a while. It will have an area for you to make notes for your descendants or student or whatever, too."

I don't know who looked more shocked at my little announcement, him or me. I hadn't meant to reveal this yet. His mouth opened but no sound came out. I couldn't tell from looking at him if he seemed happy or just kind of freaked out. His face whitened, so he felt something, I'm sure. His expression didn't give away any clues.

I held a hand up. "Don't worry about it too much. I just wanted you to know, if something bad happens to me and you get stuck on your own again, I've made arrangements for you at the Grove and with my family. If you don't have your book yet, just grab mine, contact Amy at the Seattle Grove, and she'll take care of you. I wrote the runes you'll need to contact her on the back of the last page. I didn't want to take the chance that you would get marked as a rogue summoner by both sides. That would make your life a *real* circus."

I winked at him to lighten those words, even though they were absolutely true. The Grove took regulating and finding unregistered summoners very seriously.

He gave me a sullen poker face that told me nothing about whether he'd actually contact Amy if something did happen. I sighed. I'd done what I could. I doubted continuing to talk at him would have any effect.

"Enough of that. I actually came out here because I'm going to summon one of my family spirits to ask for advice, and I wanted to introduce you. I probably won't have another opportunity to do so any time soon. Even family spirits are generally something I don't mess with unless I'm in a really difficult situation. Out of all the Moore family spirits this guy is probably the safest and my favorite. He'll play by the rules, but he's still a badass, so don't be rude."

Robert rolled his eyes. Deciding to pick my battles, I settled for shooting him an irritated look and flipped to the right page in the Grove Book. "So here are all the Moore family spirits." I showed him the page and pointed to a specific rune set. "This is who we'll be summoning. It's possible you've even heard of him, since he is an ancestral guardian spirit, and was a *little* famous in his time. Sir John Moore? Created light infantry, orchestrated the British retreat to Corunna?"

Robert just looked bored. Damn. I'd hoped to spark his interest with this particular ancestor. I squashed my disappointment.

"No? Ah, well, he died young. Even some of the history books skip him over. He's every inch a soldier's soldier; crafty, innovative and just a bit nuts. Which is why we're gonna find out if he's picked up any rumors that might be useful to us."

"So how do we summon this badass ancestor of yours?" Robert looked a little green around the gills. Considering that just a few weeks ago he'd thought summoners innately evil, just the fact that he'd asked the question spoke volumes.

"We're going to use runes, just like any other summons." I gave

Robert a reassuring smile and pretended not to hear his exaggerated groan. "The only difference is, this time we are going to use the runes to punch through the Weave into a different world to pull out the entity that we want. However, since we are taking something—some*one* in this case—out of their own home Weave, we have to temporarily exchange mass from our Weave to plug the hole their absence creates. Does that make sense?"

"Not at all."

I shot a look at him, expecting to find him giving me lip. Instead his expression showed honest confusion. I tried again.

"We've already shown that when we summon something, we don't create it. It has to have a source."

Robert nodded.

"Now we're reaching into a neighboring Weave, and we're bringing in something that didn't exist in this Weave before. And in the source Weave, we're leaving a hole from whatever we grabbed for our summons. In order to keep the balance in this and the other Weave stable, the Visitant Pacts set up a counter-exchange. Since this is your very first time with spirit summoning, you're fine to just watch. I just want to introduce you."

I started to put the runes together on my magnetic board.

"W-wait!" Robert spluttered. "Are you just going to summon him out here? Won't he look like—like a ghost or something?"

I laughed, guessing that Robert envisioned a wailing apparition like something out of Dickens. "Ghosts are highly overrated. Some spirits may change their appearance to conform to our myths about ghosts, but a lot look just like you or me. If they do look strange, they'll look like something totally crazy. Like our friend Rick."

I gave him a reassuring smile. "I think Uncle John will like it out here. I'd be shocked if the opportunity to summon him in surroundings like this comes up again anytime soon. I remember once I summoned him to one of those one-stall bathrooms with a locking door. He was totally scandalized that a female relative would summon him to a privy and then tell him he couldn't leave." I chuckled at the memory of Uncle John's stiffly disapproving face. Robert just raised an eyebrow.

"He's super old-fashioned, ok? Just...never mind."

"I didn't say anything," Robert protested innocently.

I felt a smile curl my lips. "You didn't need to. No smart-alecky stuff while he's here. He may be family, but in this case he's the grumpy grandparent with a big cane who loves to smack people with it."

"Literally?" Robert sounded shocked.

"No, of course not. Metaphorically. Do you really want to be here for this? 'Cause on second thought, maybe I don't have to introduce you yet." I quirked an eyebrow at him, daring him to back out.

"Well, first you say he's cool, but then you say he's a cantankerous old fart with a stick. I was confused." Robert crossed his arms over his chest and glowered at me. I couldn't tell if he meant it. Probably not? Ah well.

"All I am trying to say is: summoning spirits, any spirit, even if you've done it a hundred times before, is dangerous. So don't let your guard down, because you'll get in trouble."

"Why didn't you just say that to begin with?" His voice brimmed with teenage impatience.

I leveled a mock glare at him. "Are you ready now? Can I continue?" I stuck a hand on my hip and waited.

"Don't let me stop you. You're the one carrying on about how dangerous this is—"

I intensified my glare. He cleared his throat. "Ok, yes, by all means, Ms. Grace. Continue to summon. I will wait here meekly and be polite to your cantankerous dead relative."

With exaggerated care he repositioned himself a bit further away from me on the bench. Really, this kid was such a wiseass. I gave him a final look to indicate I was not amused (although, secretly I was), double-checked what I had already laid out, and finalized the summons on my rune board.

I powered the runes. A wind that didn't stir the pine branches suddenly blew past us. A gentleman with a mop of brown hair and a narrowish face with a long nose, clad in a red British military jacket and the traditional white pants, stood before us. He had been a soldier in life, and he continued to be one in death.

Robert's mouth dropped open. I couldn't quite suppress a chuckle. He obviously hadn't been expecting Uncle John to look so substantial after all.

Uncle John took a moment to look around him. "Why, this is quite splendid. I don't know why you can't take pains to call me to places like this all the time, Niece. The ambiance here is much improved from your usual cramped habits." He placed his hands on his hips, took a deep breath, and rolled his shoulders, obviously taking the opportunity to enjoy the open air.

"Good day, Uncle. Thank you for coming to my aid."

"Ah, well, I get bored anyway. There is never any good excitement in the afterlife, you know. Just gossip. Although, they have opened a pub in Glasgow in my honor, did you know? Quite a classy establishment. I've taken to haunting it on principle, just so it can be authentic. They even have a Baker rifle over the door."

He appeared to notice Robert for the first time. "Here, now! Did you finally go and whelp? Doesn't look a thing like you. Your husband must be powerfully ugly."

Robert jerked upright, his mouth curling into a familiar scowl. I stepped in hurriedly. "Uncle, this is my student, not my child. His family has died, and so I am asking that the Moores adopt him as one of ours."

"I say, I knew no man would be ballsy enough to take you." He winked at Robert. I wanted to sink through the ground; I should have seen this coming. "Every time I see her, she's always in the middle of some kind of bedlam."

Robert shot me a wide-eyed look. I could almost see him thinking, *This* is the spirit I'm supposed to be afraid of?

He coughed and tried rather unsuccessfully to hide his snickering behind a hand wiping at his mouth.

Uncle John gave me a jovial pat on the back, using way more force than necessary. It almost knocked off my feet. I staggered before regaining my balance. He grinned at me unrepentantly. "This one's always finding trouble. Though I suppose I shouldn't throw stones at the lass. Being in the thick of things is a Moore trait through and through. At least you don't bore me, Niece. What's your name, lad?"

Robert dropped his hand from his mouth and stood up straight. "Robert Lorents, sir. Nice to meet you."

Sir John paused for a moment. I had a sudden horrible fear that he would refuse. "Well, Robert Lorents, I am very pleased to make your acquaintance. As my niece has asked me to accept you as one of the family, please consider yourself another of my nephews and call me when you have need." He held out his hand. Robert shook it with obvious nervousness.

"So, Niece, as much as I enjoy the view, I would guess you have some other business with me? Although a sedate afternoon with you would not be so bad once and a while, I am expecting, as usual, you have some impending and immediate catastrophe for which you desire my aid?"

"Ah, yes, Uncle. This area is being terrorized by a large, orange beast that hunts summoners. It's covered in spikes, has red eyes and a large club-like tail, and in general looks somewhat like a giant, spiky, demonic raccoon. It also appears to have telekinesis and/or some control of kinetic force, and as it kills summoners, it gains power from them. I haven't been able to find references to anything like this in my research. Can you think of anything that might fit that description? We have narrowly escaped from it several times, and I would dearly love to know if it has any weaknesses."

"Hmm, a beast that consumes summoners, controls momentum, and is covered in spikes. I have heard rumor of several beasts who consume summoners to gain power, but usually they are easily defeated and not very intelligent."

"I believe this one to be of beast intelligence, but also to be under the control of something else, acting on the instructions it receives. Recently, it seems to understand tactics and strategy and even spoke to me, but before that, it appeared to only act on instinct. I think we have irritated whatever is controlling the demon enough to force possession of it, but I have no idea why."

"If it's under control of something else, then a number of malevolent demons could be responsible. But I think the beast itself is probably a Cornuprocyon. Its form is very much as you say, and the Weave it originates from has many beasts that control some small portion of power, and hunt and consume each other to gain more. Much like our carnivores live off flesh here, those beasts live off the flesh but also the inherent power in the blood of their prey. However, a Cornuprocyon is very territorial and unlikely to stray far from its den, so for it to be here is indicative, as you say, of someone else using the beast to his own purpose. When it spoke, what did it say?"

"It said it would spare the mundanes and leave this area if I would surrender Robert and myself to it to be eaten."

"Hmm, it seems I have heard a rumor of something like this before, but I cannot place it. Did it explicitly *say* it meant to eat you if you surrendered?"

I thought for a moment. "No. Now that you mention it, it just demanded I give Robert and myself to it, in exchange for the lives of the people we were protecting."

"It may be that this spirit is using the beast to weed out summoners it doesn't believe to be useful before trying to capture the summoners left behind for some other purpose."

"I don't know, Uncle. It has been trying awfully hard to kill us."

"The thing behind this beast may be using it to kill and gather power, yes, but there are also other uses for live summoners, if you are going to break the Visitant Pacts. Have you ever heard of a homunculus?"

I shook my head.

"It was a practice before the Pacts, of spirits using humans, usually summoners, as 'little power sources'. They would hook them into a ritual and use them as fuel for it, like steam moves a locomotive or fire moves a bullet. Except, they were binding humans to do it. Be very careful of this demon. It sounds to me as if it is plotting some major coup in this Weave."

"Thank you for your concern. We are being very careful. Does the Cornuprocyon have any other weaknesses we can exploit?"

"Unfortunately, I have given you what I know of it. It does not travel far; it grows more powerful with the consumption of the summoner's humors; and it is liable to act on instinct. I have never heard of a sentient one, nor one as powerful as you are describing. You may try asking some of the local spirits if it has been here before."

Well, that was just peachy. Rick was a badass, the spirit behind him was probably a super-badass, and I was going to have to summon some unknown spirits to double-check if he might be a frequent flyer.

At least the weather was decent.

"Thank you, Uncle. I appreciate you sharing your knowledge. Your help is invaluable as always. I'll be sure to contact some of the local spirits." I smiled warmly at Uncle John. He saluted snappily.

"Be careful," he warned me, his voice light but serious. "Not all spirits are as genial company as myself." He gave me a nod and tossed a final wink to Robert before disappearing. One second he stood under the trees as solidly as Robert or myself, and the next he vanished like he'd never stood there in the first place. A pang of sadness tightened my chest. Talking to Sir John always reminded me how much I missed my family. I blew a long breath out and turned to Robert.

"Well, I'd better find some Spokane spirits to talk to. While I do that, I want you to go in the cabin and study those new rune combinations I gave you last night."

"Why? I want to watch." Robert frowned at me.

"I don't know the spirits I'm about to summon. If things go south, the spirits could get hostile fast. They aren't bound to me; they're bound to the Spokane Grove. All those people are dead. If they decide to honor their pacts, we're good. If they don't, well, who knows what they'll do. It's too dangerous. I'd love backup, but in this situation, you're not even close to being that yet. Go prove to me you can learn to use the runes, and we'll see about you helping next time."

"I can do a lot without using runes." Robert's fists clenched. He glowered at me in obvious frustration.

"And there's a lot you can't do without them," I countered firmly. "Go."

～

I DECIDED to summon the local earth spirits, since earth spirits are usually slow of thought and slow to anger. Robert hunched over the flashcards in the cabin, plainly discontented, but I'd be negligent if I exposed such a new summoner to possibly hostile Visitors. Summoning unknown spirits could go wrong in all sorts of unpredictable ways. If only for my concentration, I needed Robert well out of the way.

I sketched out the new summons. The spirits, when they appeared, were a lot smaller than expected, and actually kind of looked like stick bugs I'd once seen at the zoo.

"Welcome. I have summoned you, the Loess, according to the Visitant Pacts of 1612, and your pact with the Spokane Grove. I ask your aid, and vow I mean you no harm."

The voice that responded boomed around me, surprisingly deep given their small bodies. "Yes, daughter of blood. We hear you, and honor the pacts. What do you wish this day?"

"A beast kills the other daughters and sons of blood in this valley. I seek to find if this spirit has been here before."

"It has and it has not been."

"My apologies. I do not understand. Are you confirming the Conuprocyon has come here before?"

"That one has not."

"So the spirit possessing the Cornuprocyon has been?"

"To the west that one came, and the sons and daughters of blood cried out. Too slow, too ponderous, to aid. Through the years, daughter of blood, it still reverberates in the Weave."

"Do you know that spirit's name? Where can I find it?"

"That one is thunder in the sky. It is not of us, and we name it not. Storm and lightning it harsh times brings. It the beast rides and shackles with blood of the earth."

That was clear as mud.

"Has it captured sons or daughters of blood before?"

"Daughter of blood, it rains tears in our fields and cracks the womb asunder. Withers the stem."

"I'm sorry. I still don't understand. It has?"

"We have said all. The daughter of blood should listen and force lightning through to beyond. Daughter of blood, call lightning to earth to aid."

And with that they blinked out, leaving me with more questions than I had even known existed. Call lightning to earth? Were they saying to strike the beast with lightning? Could I really believe that's what they meant?

All right. I believed that could be arranged, and it might just work, if I had understood the little bugs correctly. That was a *big* if. Time to go rope in some slave labor in the form of the newest honorary Moore. This time, we needed to go big or go home, and that seemed just Robert's style.

ROBERT

I COULDN'T TELL if Grace was making sense.

"I think I know how to fry Rick," she said. "The Loess are telling me to hit him with lightning. It makes sense, actually; Rick has a lot of defense against kinetic force, so we're going to hit him with an entirely different form of energy."

"And he's not just going to absorb it?"

"The only thing we've seen him absorb has been Sense energy. If we keep it in the realm of the physical, we should be all right. Of course, lightning would be a heck of a thing to arrange. I thought maybe we'd use hydroelectric instead."

"You mean, like, dams?" I tried to put this puzzle together.

"I mean the power generators at dams, yeah. It's the Pacific Northwest. We've got hydroelectric everywhere. Time to start using it."

"So...you want to take a giant raccoon monster—"

"Cornuprocyon."

"Cornuprocyon, right. You want to summon the power from a hydroelectric plant into it."

"Not into. I tried that first off. Something is warding him." She considered for a moment. "Actually, I want to use the plant itself; channeling that much raw juice would probably hurt like hell, but moving some wires around wouldn't be too hard. We get Rick to the dam, and we fry him. Problem solved."

"Oh, well, that's much better then. We'll just take a big-ass, spiky, club-tailed, telekinetic raccoon and—"

"Cornuprocyon. Let's keep our terms straight."

I sighed. "Fine, fine. We'll just take a big-ass, spiky, club-tailed, telekinetic *Cornuprocyon* and we'll put him on a leash, get him to walk with us over to Grand Coulee, and then move some wires. That'll work great."

"A leash?" Grace looked amused. "We're not going to need a leash. We can bring Rick wherever we need him. We've got bait."

I did not like the way she said that. The twinkle in her eye as she stared at me *especially* did not like. "I thought you said doing that would eventually get me killed."

"It could. But in this case, not doing it stands a better chance of getting you killed, so I'm going to give you the green light for one big, noisy summons. Bang the dinner bell for him; he'll come running."

Oh good. I had permission to be bait. Wasn't that lovely?

"I banged the gong from up here and got nothing from him. The Columbia's farther away from Rick than this. How would I get his attention all the way out there?

"Bah! You lack imagination. The Columbia isn't the only river around, just the biggest. Hell, there's a dam in downtown Spokane, isn't there? Riverfront Park?"

"You want to fight Rick in Riverfront Park?" My eyebrows rose. That sounded like a good way to kill a whole *bunch* of people, especially since Rick had apparently picked up the habit of taking hostages. The power plant at Riverfront Park sat smack-dab in the middle of downtown Spokane. "Even if we fought at night, we'd endanger thousands, maybe more."

Grace shook her head. "Well...no. Too many bystanders. But there's gotta be other dams on that river. You're from around here, take a second. Where's a good place to get some power?"

Come to think of it, I did remember one set of fosties taking me for a "family picnic." The trouble with family bonding activities like picnics is you don't really want to bond with your fosties. They're going to be done with you within a year, so why bother? A picnic always just seemed like a really good way to have mediocre food, bugs, and forced, awkward conversation.

That time, though, they had taken me to some park over across the border in Post Falls, Idaho. I remembered it because, even though it was a city park, it offered some trails that I could wander in order to get away from the cloying, hovering presence of my then-foster parents. I had enjoyed said trails, and actually spent a great deal of time staring...

...at the dam. Post Falls took its name from a series of waterfalls in the river, and the Falls Park had as its centerpiece an impressive dam sitting atop the falls, elevating the water level above them. I had stood at the observation point and watched the river run through the canyon below.

"Post Falls," I told Grace. "There's another dam in Post Falls."

"Well," she said. "Let's go take a look."

FALLS PARK IS ACTUALLY A RELATIVELY idyllic location. Back in the day, I guess some guy named Post had a big old lumber mill that used the falls to power his saws. He built a log dam across the top of the falls to give himself an added boost, and thus the Post Falls dam came into the world.

The Park is where he built his mill. The old mill pond has been converted; it's where you bring kids to feed ducks now. A series of bridges and culverts divert the mill race through the park, giving it a lot of water features. At some point, someone thought making water spray straight up looked kinda cool, so there's a fountain in the lower mill pond. It's a nice park, really, as parks go.

We weren't interested in the park, though. We went south through it to the river, where the dam itself awaited us. It was late

September, so the water barely crested the top of the spill gates. The dam itself made an "L" shape, with the corner of the "L" pointing upstream. On the long side, eight small spill gates lifted up and down like the portcullis of a castle. One large gate formed the short side of the "L," looking like it spun inward rather than lifting straight up.

The gates were only about ten feet high, but they rested atop the natural falls, which fell deep into a canyon below. The gates were closed because of the low water level, and so the trickle running through the falls left most of the rock exposed: great crags rubbed smooth by centuries of water erosion. Several logs were jammed into them at weird angles, left where the last buffet of water had placed them. It hit me, all in all, as a majestic, awe-inspiring sight.

"Pretty," said Grace, but her voice stayed flat. "Breathtaking. Really. Where's the power?"

I looked again. She was right! There were spill gates here, elevating the water level behind the dam, but nothing in the way of high-voltage lines running from the dam. It made no sense. Why build a dam if you don't want power?

Maybe this wasn't the place after all. I looked up at the observation point; the trail led along the top of the canyon wall as the canyon got deeper below it. At the top of the hill, some genius with a flair for harnessing the suicidal impulse in people had built an observation platform overlooking the canyon. I headed for it. Grace followed me.

I don't know what I expected to see from the observation post. I just remembered liking the view from up there. The canyon curved, and from up on the post you could see the dam upstream, the water rushing through the narrow canyon below and opening up under the...bridge. A bridge! I began to rush up to the post.

There it was. A beautiful, arched, concrete structure spanned the canyon just as it started to widen out. Above the bridge, high voltage power lines ran across the river.

"Ahhhh," I heard behind me. Grace's voice began to show some excitement. "That looks more like it. I bet this dam only exists to funnel the water through another dam. That's not the other side of the river over there on that side of the canyon—it's an island. Let's go see if we can get across that bridge."

The bridge, however, was closed; a barbed wire fence stretched across the near end of it.

"A power plant alone on an island where the public is specifically prohibited from going," purred Grace. "Robert, I believe you have found us the perfect location to have a good old-fashioned showdown. We'll come back late tonight and set up. In the meantime —know anywhere good around here to eat?"

GRACE HAD this amazing ability to suss out the most delicious restaurant in any given location and go there. How it is that she can eat like she does and stay as skinny as she does is beyond me. We ended up at the White House Grill, this little Mediterranean place in Post Falls. I had some pasta, hot with garlic but delicious. Amazing food was, I guessed, one of the side benefits to being Grace's apprentice.

When the waiter came back with her receipt, Grace politely asked if they did takeout, and whether she could order over the phone. When he said yes, she removed a small notebook from the folds of her draped robes and began making notations in it.

I believe this is the highest form of compliment Grace can give a restaurant. Frankly, her obsession with food confounded me. On the other hand, I really love the saxophone, and I think that confused her. When it comes down to it, I guess all of us have these little weirdnesses. They may be different, but it's comforting to know that you're not the only weird person out there. I watched in silence as Grace performed her ritual of inscribing the White House Grill into her notebook. When she looked up, things got serious again.

"We going back?"

"Yup."

I smelled the reek of garlic on her breath and pointedly passed her one of the mints on the little tray left behind by our waitress. She took it without comment and placed it in her mouth, then looked at me straight in the eye.

"You ready for this, kiddo?"

No. I badly wanted to say no. I *wanted* to just get in the car and drive away, leave this city behind me. I *wanted* to break my promise to Jeanelle and leave Duane to die; he meant nothing to me. I *wanted* to let Rick run loose in the Spokane Valley until someone finally brought in some power big enough to deal with him. Maybe the Seattle Grove could. Maybe the U.S. military. The point was, why should my life mean so much less than the other lives that would be lost. Why me?

I hadn't thought about it until she asked, but I wasn't ready. I didn't want to do this. I closed my eyes, hung my head. Fear of tonight suddenly surged through me, and a tear ran from my eye down my cheek. (Not that I cried. As a card-carrying teenage boy, I don't do that. No idea where that tear came from.) I shook my head, too overwhelmed to talk.

A memory caught in the back of my head. I heard the old, cracking voice of Uncle Herman, looking out over the land with me. "Boy, there's those of us that do, and those of us that have done to. I want you to be a doer, you hear me? You get out there, you live your life, and you hold your head high."

I wasn't ready. But it didn't mean I intended to bail. I'd do it anyway. I wiped the tear from my eye and lifted my reckless grin across the table.

"Nope," I said flippantly. "Let's do this." Grace smiled.

GETTING past the fence was simple. Grace started to summon a cutting torch but I beat her to it, extending my Sense and manipulating the lock to pop open.

"Showoff," she complained, and we walked over the concrete span. Grace's deduction turned out to be right; an island lay on the far side of the bridge. In fact, it looked to be one of two separate islands, with a third small, southern channel of water. This northern island, though, was the one we wanted. The center channel had the power plant; an entirely separate dam lay across the river. Judging by the power lines, this dam housed the generators creating the power to run Post Falls. After a quarter mile or so the road from the bridge forked. One ran southwest to what looked like some sort of a storage area. The other ran half a mile southeast to the power station. The station itself hid us from view of Falls Park behind a large hill.

"Perfect," said Grace. "Oh, this will do nicely."

She began moving magnets around on the little board strapped to her arm, then blooded and activated the summons. Eight suspicious-looking circles appeared next to each other. Each one spanned a little over a foot wide and resembled a large can of tuna. A small, conical device was attached to the top of each one, large side down.

"Ok." Grace got down to business. "We're going to want to be really careful with these; they're active."

"Active? What are they?"

"This is a TM-62M."

I waited in silence, staring at Grace until she clarified. "A Russian antitank mine. I summoned them out of the fields in central Africa. Down there, they're just going to hurt someone."

"Whoa, what?" I backed away from the discs. "These things were activated, left in the ground, and *then* you summoned them?"

"Yup." She beamed. "That way, Farmer Mgobwe doesn't run over them with a couple of oxen and blow himself sky-high some day. Most humane thing, really."

"Yeah...except we now have eight armed bombs with us. What are we going to do with these besides get ourselves killed?" I knew I was signing up for a suicide mission here, but it didn't seem right to commit suicide *before* the fight.

"We? I did the work of getting them here. *You're* going to use that fabulous Sense of yours to mine the stretch of road leading up to the power plant. I don't think these will kill the Cornuprocyon, but they might weaken it before we have to fight, and every little bit counts. Just use your Sense to gently move them and place them. No big jarring. In theory, it should take at least one hundred fifty kilos' pressure to set these off, but I have no idea how long they've been in the ground or how stable they are, so be careful."

Oh, lovely. I knew the odds of living through tonight weren't spectacular to begin with, but it felt like they'd just decreased a little bit. Still, I brought up my Sense and began slipping the mines along the ground.

The goal here was to summon them so they were exactly *on* the ground, not above it. That way, I could make sure that any sensors on the mines felt no vibration at all. I took one mine, stepped fifty feet in front of it, summoned it fifty feet in front of me, and then walked beyond it. Once I had the mine at the proper location, I summoned enough dirt out of the ground to bury the mine, then summoned the thing into the hole. I finished by summoning some of that same dirt over the top of it to disguise it. I didn't actually know why I disguised the mines. I doubted Rick would know the difference.

Still, they were landmines, so I covered them. That's what one *does* with landmines.

I managed to get them all summoned into the ground with a thin layer of gravel over them without blowing myself up. It took a couple hours of delicate work, but I was alive at the end of it, so yay for me.

Grace came down off the hill to the north of the road; I guessed that she had made some form of preparation up there but I didn't know what. When I asked, she just flashed me that toothy grin of hers. It looked like I was going to find out the hard way. We re-chained and locked the gate with a lock of Grace's choosing, the better to prevent someone else from finding those mines before Rick.

Our preparations were done. We had only one thing left to do.

"Ok," Grace said. "Looks like we've got our hook. Time for our bait to go do some wriggling."

I chuckled. It wasn't that I thought anything was funny, really. I laughed because the time for crying had passed. I knew I was going to die; that much was almost certain, but I had pushed past the fear that comes with that. The smile growing on my face came from the wild place in all of us that exists on the other side of fear. Grinning like a madman, I strode to the concrete span connecting this island to the normal, human life I had left behind.

I STOOD AT THE BRIDGEHEAD, listening to the water run underneath. Up the canyon, a set of huge floodlights lit the river and the spectacular sight of the falls, but here the moonlight reigned. The stars were out and the moon shone down bright and full. It was a crisp night, on the edge of being cold but not quite there. It felt peaceful, for now.

Time to ring the dinner bell. I needed to summon something using runes; something harmless, something that the lack thereof wouldn't injure anyone. I knew just the thing. I reached into the bag of rune tiles I'd brought with me and carefully laid out a sequence on the ground. Out of my shirt pocket I drew a mini-MP3 player with my playlist loaded up on it. I clipped it to my collar and placed the ear buds in my ears.

The familiar base line of *La Fiesta* began, the fast-driving beat that had drawn Jeanelle and me together. This song was, in many ways, responsible for my standing in this place at this time. I didn't know whether to credit it or blame it. I did know, however, that the Woody Herman Orchestra still had the power to remove me from myself and send me on a ride. First came the piano solo, soft-fast and soothing Fender Rhodes-style action, and then the piccolo joined in with its complex trills.

I waited for the horns; I knew they were coming next. The trumpets began blasting. My eyes flew open. I smeared blood over the runes in front of me and hammered my Sense at them, pulling through them, drawing my power through the Weave from every direction, sending out the claxon call of my presence to all those who could sense it. Through the runes, the object of my desire traveled to me.

The energy drink I had summoned appeared in my right hand. I smiled at the successful misuse of my power. *Safe and useful,* I thought.

The first saxophone solo began as I cracked the top and began to drink.

Then I stood there, Latin jazz and caffeine pounding through me, my Sense pounding into the Weave, and waited for my opponent to arrive. It wasn't going to be long.

GRACE

I PREPARED for action on top of the hill beside the power generator. I wore my usual outfit of peasant top and skirt, or 'demented gypsy togs' as Robert had so flatteringly called them earlier in the day. He wanted to know why I never wore practical clothes like jeans. I told him if we lived, maybe someday I'd have time to actually answer that. In teenager fashion, he immediately lost interest.

From where I stood I could see the road Robert would run up to lure the Cornuprocyon to the power plant. The moon shone shockingly bright, casting the scrub bushes along the roadway with a silvery, peaceful sheen. Street lamps punctuated the road on either side every twenty feet or so. I only wished my nerves matched the scenery. Robert's tall figure, made small by distance, stood at the edge of the bridge below me, but I could feel when he pounded his will into the Weave. The power crashed and reverberated all around me, ringing the dinner bell with style.

Between the moon and the sporadic street lights I had a perfect view of the road as it curved along the hill toward the power plant. The distance from Robert's starting point to the plant spanned about seven hundred and twenty feet, or two football fields.

He'd assured me he'd have no problem sprinting that far while keeping his Sense up. He still struggled with runes, so he'd have to rely on his Sense. Not totally convinced, I'd had him demonstrate for me by sprinting the distance with his Sense up before we planted the traps. He'd pulled it off. I'd comforted myself that I'd be here to cover his back if anything went wrong.

Something appeared in Robert's hand but I couldn't tell what from this far away. His movement gave it away as he cracked the pull tab on the drink and threw it back, gulping it down in a fluid motion. I suppose a caffeine boost was a fair call. He tossed the empty can to the side, and then we both stood tensed and waiting for Rick to show.

I'd had plenty of time earlier today to doubt the validity of my plan. I should have done more research; I could have summoned more spirits to question, etc. The time for those doubts and preparation had passed long ago. *Now* was all about focus, getting the job done, and taking out a menace. I felt horrible that Robert would face Rick down there and not me, but I couldn't pack enough punch to guarantee the Cornuprocyon would stay on me. To get Robert, the raccoon-demon wouldn't even think about veering off-course.

As we waited, my nerves wound so tight I thought I might choke on my own breath. The Cornuprocyon appeared right on cue, bounding in from the west over the bridge, making a beeline for Robert. He raised his hand almost negligently, and a twenty-foot wall of indigenous black rock shot up between him and the demon. The Cornuprocyon skidded to a halt, swerved around it, and picked up momentum again. Relief and pride hit me in a giddy rush. Some part of me had worried Robert wouldn't pull it off, that I'd asked something of him he wouldn't be able to do, but was too proud to admit. I truly believed now. We *would* do this.

The kid spun on his heel and sprinted up the road like he had lettered in track instead of band. The street lights along the old access road outlined his fleeing figure against the night. He looked so small. I snapped off a quick summons, threw some giant nails I'd twisted into X-shaped caltrops down in Rick's path, and said a quick prayer to all my ancestors.

The Cornuprocyon snapped at Robert's legs. His teeth came so close I winced. I had sent Robert down there as bait, but I was not prepared to see him die. I knew that might turn out to be a pipe dream, but I would use all my power to keep Robert ahead of the Cornuprocyon.

Robert's immense Sense allowed this plan to work, since he essentially had a three hundred and sixty degree view of everything around him, but he couldn't do it forever. The strain of keeping his Sense extended and tracking so many things at once had to be immense. Time for some help.

I blooded my rune board and threw an oil slick under Rick's claws, unbalancing him. He fell heavily onto his side but recovered quickly. He levered his paws underneath him and filled the night air with the familiar *woomph* of his telekinetic leap.

It brought him close in behind Robert, who was only about five yards ahead. Robert put on an extra burst of speed as Rick tried to swipe him with his left forepaw. Biting my lip, I lined up my magnets and threw up a force shield protecting Robert just as the beast hit the first TM-62M anti-tank mine. It flung Rick up into the air along with a storm of rock and dirt. Those mines were meant to punch through armored vehicles, and I wagered they would punch a good way through Rick's exoskeleton if we could get just a few good hits off.

Rick came down in a rain of debris on a steep slope to the right of the roadway. He hit it rolling, scrabbling to regain his footing. The shifting earth and rock didn't provide good footholds. He ended up sprawled at the foot of the slope next to the river.

He stood up, shaking off the explosion, and bounded back up to the road, immediately intent on pursuing Robert. He passed under one of the tall lamps next to the maintenance access. If I squinted, I could just make out several large cuts and tears on his legs from the mine. I whipped out another of the Seattle Grove's munitions tags and dropped a big ole dose of industrial thermite on Rick's head, plastering it down his back. I blooded the runes and summoned enough magnesium and fire to light all of it at once. Rick screamed, bucking around blind trying to shake it off. He set off the next antitank mine instead. The thermite dripped onto the ground in glowing pools and burned little divots in the old asphalt of the road. Some road crew would hate me in the morning.

Robert used the time to lengthen the distance between himself and Rick, racing down the side of the road well clear of the mines. I threw down some trees and boulders in the Cornuprocyon's path, trying to herd him toward the next mine as a preemptive strike. Rick finally shook thermite out of his eyes, leaving a big, bubbled scorch mark on his head between his pointed ears and a layer of scorched hide on his back. He took off with less speed than before, vaulting over my roadblock. He hit the next land mine dead on. The blast jammed him back into the barrier. He hit it centermost, cracking the trees and rolling the inner boulders off the road. Rick growled, staggering to his feet. The skin on his legs and underbelly dripped blood from multiple ruptures. Without our previous run-ins with Rick I would have been shocked he could still stand. Despite all this damage, I had only managed to slow him down slightly. Rick gathered himself and shot after Robert.

I kept out of site in the brush at the top of the hill as much as possible. Rick bounded after Robert like he didn't even realize I existed. I wanted to keep it that way. It didn't hurt that Robert used his Sense to create spikes and rifts in the roadway, herding the Cornuprocyon toward the mines. As I watched, Rick veered away from a rock spike Robert threw alongside him, and plowed straight into another land mine.

I blooded a bangle halfway up my arm and summoned Hyctea, an owl spirit about twice the size of a condor. Her wings stretched twenty-two feet wingtip to wingtip. She perched on my shoulder, her claws pricking through the fabric of my blouse. Her weight almost unbalanced me. I shuffled my feet to avoid being tipped over. Her head bobbed, and she nuzzled my neck with her feathered crown.

"It's good to see you," I told her. "I need your help harassing that demon there and keeping my apprentice safe. Can you help me with that?"

The owl gave a low hoot and flapped her powerful wings, sweeping herself back up into the sky. The wind from her flight buffeted me, blowing my hair into a tangle and belling my long skirts out behind me. I pushed my hair out of my eyes. My hand trembled with too much adrenaline. I steadied it by force of will. I could shake after this ended.

Hyctea circled high above Robert and the Cornuprocyon for a few moments, unseen by either of them. Suddenly, she let out a blood-curdling screech and dove at Rick, clawing at the Cornuprocyon's glowing, red eyes. Rick blasted out kinetic force, flattening several small trees along the road and shattering some rocks off the hillside.

Out in front, Robert caught the edge of the tempest and staggered, almost losing his footing. Hyctea swerved to avoid the blast before swooping back in with her claws extended. The giant bird latched her talons into the leathery hide on Rick's snout, savagely ripping at the Cornuprocyon's head with her beak. Rick shook his head viciously, but Hyctea dug her talons in more firmly. She flapped her great wings for balance, fueling storm winds of her own.

Rick brought his massive tail down over his own head, forcing Hyctea to let go or be crushed. The owl attempted to fly out of range but Rick caught her in a blast of kinetic force that bashed her against the cliff face. Hyctea gave one last flap of her powerful wings and lay stunned by the roadside.

Robert used the distraction to erupt a line of jagged rock from the ground behind him as he ran, forcing the Cornuprocyon to land in the only clear area behind him.

It worked like a charm. The Cornuprocyon hit another mine dead-on with his forelegs and less-protected underbelly. The shock ripped through the road, but incredibly, the nearby street lamp stayed on. A large chunk of Rick's underside and spiky exoskeleton flew off and embedded itself in the shoulder of roadway.

I started to give a gleeful little whoop, but the gaping wound started scabbing over almost immediately, filling back in. As I watched, tiny spikes grew back with disturbing vigor. As he passed under each new street light, the rents in the skin on his legs visibly mended as well. It reminded me of those old flip books, except instead of just watching him run, I watched him heal. The Cornuprocyon let out a spine-chilling scream. Except for the initial jolt, the mine did not stop him or even slow him down.

Well, crap.

I had no idea how Rick had done that. Clearly we hadn't done enough damage to him at the mall or the police station to trigger this ability. I swallowed the sudden lump of fear in my throat. Rick jumped, and hit the next mine. It blasted off some more of his exoskeleton. That immediately started re-growing, too. Not good news.

My fingers flew over my magnetic board, dousing him with sulphuric acid in an effort to slow the regeneration. As he ran past the next street light, smoke rose off his back but the healing continued. When he hit the next mine, part of his chitinous skin flew off and actually caught fire. I put it down as an almost-victory.

In the flickering light from that fire I realized Rick had slowly begun gaining on Robert. There were still three mines and a good hundred feet for Robert to run before they reached the transformer station. All that summoning of rock and throwing things at Rick had slowed Robert down. I bit off a swear word and racked my brain for what to do next.

I threw a hasty barricade made of boulders from the cliff wall and a few fallen trees in the Cornuprocyon's face. Rick blasted it to smithereens with his kinetic force. It didn't slow him down more than half a second, but it *did* give Robert a chance to put a little more distance between them and narrow Rick's available run path.

As the Cornuprocyon triggered his kinetic ability again, I removed a large chunk of the road in front of him, then dropped it on him as he leaped to avoid the gaping hole. It pinned him to the ground for a few more precious moments as Robert sped ever closer to the power station.

I love that trick.

The kinetic force the Cornuprocyon used to rip his way out from under the chunk of road exploded upward. The ground shook under my feet; the pine trees shivered and swayed in the moon's light. The street lamps along the road finally blinked out. Thankfully, the power station and the parking lot around it still glowed with lights. It seemed unlikely that Rick would manage to knock out the power plant itself, but if he did, we were screwed.

The big block of asphalt and rock rushed toward Robert's fleeing figure. I tried to slap together a summons to knock it aside, but it cannoned toward Robert faster than my hands could move.

Robert never stopped running. The hunk of road flew so close I felt certain he'd be crushed. Without looking back he flicked out a hand and made a gesture with his wrist. The menace flew off course and bounded down the ravine to land in the river below. *Damn, I wish I had his Sense.*

We had managed to piss the Cornuprocyon off to a royal degree, but not noticeably taken down its power level. Nothing says, "You've pulled shit duty" like an irate, crazed, unstoppable raccoon beast trying to rip your head off with several tons of earth and asphalt.

Robert finally ran close enough that I could see his crazed expression in the lights of the parking lot. It seemed to say, "I'm still alive? Really?" His arms and legs were pumping faster than I ever would have imagined possible for a skinny, geeky kid. I doubted Robert played sports. Still, he'd almost made it to the generators. Totally impressed, I summoned a few more boulders to be a pain in Rick's ass.

I waited for the Cornuprocyon's next leap and summoned a violent gust of wind and sharp bits of earth into its face. I quickly followed that with a roundhouse baseball swing using a full-grown tree. Rick deflected the tree a fraction of a second before it made contact, sending it spinning.

Robert ran through the last of the mines, avoiding the flame and shrapnel behind him with deft adjustments, guided by his Sense. He changed his trajectory slightly after each one to drag the Cornuprocyon through the worst of the effects. Even with the damage he took, Rick seemed unimpressed.

The Cornuprocyon had activated his telekinesis to keep the explosions from reaching him. I used the small lag to blood my last tag and summon a deluge of ignited copper thermite on top of him.

One of the advantages to spending as much time reading books as I had is that you learn obscure information. Copper thermite doesn't burn as hot as regular thermite, but its advantage lies in creating a significant amount of molten copper during its rapid reaction. The thermite ignited with a bright burst of light, and the molten copper poured down over Rick. It gilded him like a giant spiky hood ornament. The copper splayed out around him and created a rather artistic-looking pedestal. The Cornuprocyon howled with rage and pain and stopped advancing while it thrashed and tried to shake the molten copper off.

I had not been expecting that (but should have). I cringed, thinking it would splash the kid, but Robert picked the flying copper out of the air with his Sense and pooled it on the ground in front of him, near the transformers. Turns out I should have been worried about me; a stray glob of it streaked in my direction. I couldn't dodge fast enough. It plastered itself over my left shoulder. I managed to deflect it using my Sense or it would have singed me down to the bone. Even so, I got a nasty burn before I could peel it away.

Even after dropping molten metal on him Rick didn't notice me, only Robert still sprinting up the hill toward me with all he had. He was panting, his legs and lungs laboring. He'd almost made it to where I needed him to set off the grand finale. In a few seconds he'd be in position.

The Cornuprocyon, resembling a shiny, metallic pincushion, charged up the hill to the transformer station, bellowing its rage and pain. With Rick just outside the transformers, I triggered the last trap. The earth under his feet opened up, revealing a deep slough of soupy clay and mud underneath. The Cornuprocyon flailed as it tried to scramble out of the pit. No use; I had cut the opening wide, and Rick sank up to his chest in the glop. Tomorrow I would make sure that the clay disappeared and the City of Post Falls would be able to use its transformer station. Tonight, I wanted this thing to be as conductive as I could possibly make it.

Running down the slope to the power generator, I hit the Cornuprocyon with a blast of snow and arctic wind to make sure the copper and mud would stick, hoping it would make it more difficult for Rick to get out. The beast hissed defiance and turned aside some of the snow, but the temperature shift did what I wanted. The Cornuprocyon started to have trouble moving under all the mud and its hardened copper jacket. It was now or never; if I left Rick alone too long, he would figure out how to use his telekinesis to blast his way out.

Fingers flying over my runes, I jammed all the power lines from the transformers into the Cornuprocyon's shiny copper-plated back. A cloak of electricity and sparks enveloped the raccoon-demon. The lights in the park and surrounding neighborhoods blinked out. The night seemed to press against me, untouchable outside the snapping spears of electricity in front of me. Around the beast, the night shone with the intensity of a small sun. The mud bubbled and snapped, the air smelled thickly of ozone, and the Cornuprocyon snarled. The night abruptly looked pitch black to my dazzled eyes.

All of a sudden, Robert yelled, "Watch out!" and blasted me aside with a frenetic burst of energy. I rolled, banging my injured shoulder on the ground. Stars danced in front of my eyes, and my breath left me in a rush. I swore and struggled to find my feet, weaving slightly. Robert ran over and grabbed my right elbow, helping me up. The spot where I had been standing was smashed to smithereens. A few orange spikes were embedded in the earth, bits of copper still clinging to them. Rick had unleashed a massive surge of kinetic energy, exploding the clay and copper off him in all directions.

The electricity lines I had been holding jumped and wove like drunken acrobats. Copper and clay lay strewn all over the power station. Rick clawed his way out of the pit, shedding the last bits of copper and goo. It didn't seem fazed by the fifteen megawatts I had pumped through it at all. In fact, it looked invigorated.

The Cornuprocyon crouched over the pit, its eyes fixed on Robert, ready to pounce. Crap. Okay, so this hadn't worked; that meant I had no idea what the earth spirits had been getting at. And now we were good and truly effed. I hoped Robert had another good sprint in him.

"Time for Plan B!" I yelled, my hearing nearly gone from all the explosions.

"What's Plan B?" he yelled back. I blooded another bangle, trying to distract Rick with a flashy firework, but the beast's attention riveted on Robert again. Apparently Rick wasn't all that interested in kibble when steak was available.

"Get the hell out of here, then come up with a new plan." I threw out yet another roadblock in front of the Cornuprocyon as we backed away.

"Next time, we may want to equip Plan B with simple little things like an escape route. I'm just saying!"

"Noted. Less talking, more running."

If we lived for a next time, I'd listen to whatever the squirt wanted, since it seemed like none of my plans lately turned out as expected.

Who knew a demon raccoon could take fifteen megawatts for breakfast? Rick ate it and came back for second helpings. Turns out, you *do* learn something new every day.

ROBERT

OH. Shit.

Panting with the effort of the run, I watched as Rick took the electricity we had fed him, swelling and expanding with the power of it. Our moment of triumph was gone; we had screwed up. Grace's little bug spirits had just flat-out missed the boat on this one.

We were hosed.

I don't know if you've ever had a near-death experience, but I can tell you, nothing—*nothing*—makes you feel more alive than almost dying. When I cleared that mud pit I knew I'd made it, and I exulted. We had done it. Except, of course, that what *we had done* simply compounded the problem. The "feeling alive" part looked to be quickly coming to a close.

Now we were alone, on an island, with Super Rick. Rick Plus. As though the original weren't bad enough, now we had the "New and Improved" version. This was going to suck beyond the telling of it.

I didn't even hear Grace talking to me. Something about Plan B? I knew I was being flip, but my mind was churning on our impending doom. I tuned my consciousness back in as Grace said, "Less talking, more running."

"Ok. So run."

"Screw that!" my mentor snapped. "You run. I'll hold him as long as I can."

Grace wasn't going to be able to defend against Rick and we both knew it. She had offered to make a heroic last stand, which was admirable, but I hoped to come up with something brilliant.

Then I *did* come up with something. It wasn't brilliant, more rash and suicidal. It was the dumbest thing I could think of, but it fell into the so-crazy-it-just-might-work category.

"Oh, I'm gonna run. But I'm pretty sure that since I'm the tasty treat, he's going to follow me. So get out of here and cover me as I go. I have something which slightly resembles a plan."

Grace raised her arm as though she were about to say something, but I turned my head away. This was crazy. *Come on, Lorents*, my fight-or-flight systems screamed at me. *Get the hell out of here*. The fact of the matter is, the human psyche simply wasn't built to handle this.

Instead, I faced Rick, slipping back into my Sense. Its tranquility comforted me; my impending death became simply one more fact in the vast array of things around me. Those things included Grace, who cussed loudly and turned to run up the hill north of me. The Cornuprocyon leveled his masked-fur face at me and blew the hot stench of his breath around me.

"Ok," I said. "I guess we're going to do this."

Rick extended his snout, opening his mouth wide to consume me. I leaped back, tying the power lines through his mouth with my Sense as I did so. He lunged forward, my makeshift bridle only holding him back for a moment. Just enough time for me to evade his snapping bite. He growled. I knew what came next. I felt his primal anger, his hunger; it was a part of him, and I was a part of him as well. This beast wanted me more than anything else.

I leveled my gaze at him. "Come and get it," I said, in the cool voice of the Sense-calm. He reared back, cutting loose a blast of kinetic force, slamming it at me like a loaded freight train. I grabbed it with my Sense, wrapping it around myself in a circle, then in a straight line back at *him*. He felt it coming, saw what I did, and tried to exert more force as a counter.

That's when I felt it. The Cornuprocyon wasn't a summoner. He wasn't bringing this force in from some outside source; he generated it. He created kinetic force outside his body as easily as lifting a finger. For him, it was just another muscle. I had him, then. He couldn't remove or deflect the force I'd steered in his direction. Instead, he generated a counter-force.

My catch and turn of his force had been too slow; I'd given him time to recover. I felt it as he started, his defenses coming up, an equal force acting against mine.

So I pulled that counter-force out from under his control, added it to my own, then hit him with the force of *two* freight trains.

He wasn't ready for it, and it took him right in the ribs between forelegs and rear. He slid to the side, crashing into the wall of the power station. The cracking of reinforced concrete split the air. He yowled in pain.

I flashed him a grin. "Oh come on, you spiky bastard. I've been bullied all my life, and you're not even in the top five."

That was sheer bravado, of course. Rick definitely outranked Jeremy Martin from the first grade, but I wasn't going to tell him that. I chuckled as I faced down the giant raccoon. The prospect of victory rushed into me, replacing my weariness with a mad light-headedness. My heart began to race again, my palms started to sweat. I had closed in; I had him. I grinned with triumph.

Mistake. While I was gloating, the focus of the Sense slipped from me.

Rick's massive club of a tail slammed into my left side, blindsiding me and hurling me back. I bounced down the road, skidded to a stop, and curled into the fetal position.

Rick had nailed my rib cage good; it felt like I had a couple of broken bones in there. Breathing hurt—a lot. I uncurled in time to see the tail slamming down at me from above, and rolled to my left to avoid it. Lances of pain stabbed into me as my weight carried me over my broken ribs, but I was alive.

I staggered up from prone to all fours and adjusted my blurred eyes. I tried to slip into the Sense but the pain pulled me out. Finding that place of concentration is tough when you've just had your ribs broken and there's a thirty-foot raccoon charging you. Seeing weakness in his prey, Rick came in for the kill. I leaned back, kneeling in the dirt. I had taken my shot and blown it. I took one, last, deep breath and leaned my head back for a final glimpse of the stars.

A loud chattering erupted from the hillside. I jerked out of my pre-death reverie to see a stream of small flashes coming from the side of the hill above. Muzzle flashes? Somewhere up there, Grace cut loose with some kind of machine gun. Rick and I both stopped our battle to assess this new threat.

With Rick still on pause, I struggled to my feet, reeling. This wasn't over.

The storm of bullets cut through Rick's kinetic defenses. Bullets began to pile up around the two of us, and only some of them still retained their original shape. It looked as though he had problems generating force quickly enough to counter a steady stream of projectiles.

His armor, though, looked to be a different story. As cool as the machine gun was, it couldn't punch through Rick's layers of chitin. It chipped some of his spines, irritating him, but it had about the same effect as walking into a hailstorm. One of the most lethal pieces of person-sized equipment in the armed forces, and to Rick it ranked as obnoxious, not dangerous. He turned his face up the hill, preparing to go for Grace.

It gave me a chance to breathe, to focus again. The hit from his tail had knocked my mini-MP3 player out of my ear; I found the earbud cords and reinserted them, changing the track to Van Morrison's version of good old *Moondance*.

I looked up. The full moon still glowed in the sky, smiling down on me. It was, as the man says, a marvelous night for a moon dance.

I pushed my pain aside, feeling the loose, swing rhythm as it convinced me this was nothing more than a date that would be followed by martinis. Mind you, I didn't know what a martini really was, but I knew you had them while listening to lounge music.

The music carried me back into the Sense. I resolved to stay there.

Grace fired the bullets: I funneled them into a single stream, using their force to redirect them to one point on his armor. Rick sensed what I was doing and tried to block, but he was still too slow. I bored through his armor and into his back with the bullets, opening a bloody hole.

Rick turned on me, his tail lashing. He blasted out another gout of force; I stole it from him, hit him with it again. My knees weakened with the effort of it, but I gritted my teeth through the exhaustion and pain.

His force blast wouldn't work on me as long as I could keep this up, but I needed to get him away from Grace. Rick charged toward me, angered by my bitchslap. He kept his head low and his claws gripped the ground to drive his massive bulk forward. I pushed myself to run in front of him. My lungs all but exploded with the effort of it. A thirty-foot raccoon beast is a *hell* of a motivator, though. I ran on, pulling him toward my trap.

From above, weapons of destruction rained down on Rick; I wasn't sure exactly what Grace was doing, but I knew she kept the fire on him, hot and steady. There were bullets. There were explosions. At one point it looked like there were spears. It may have slowed him a bit; I'm not certain. Rick rammed out more force at me; I used it to accelerate my way back along the road like a sail uses the wind. I burst toward the bridge, raising rocks and felling trees behind me to buy myself time. Rick bulled his way through, blasting the obstacles out of his path. I was hoping he'd get tired; I certainly was.

The bridge. Decision time. If I crossed, I ran the risk of being blown into the gorge. I wasn't sure I could save myself if that happened. Van Morrison sang in my ear, reminding me the night was magic. He'd gotten that much right. If I didn't want to cross the bridge, and I didn't want to stay on the road, only one option remained.

I stuck my left leg out into a slide, jockeyed a hard corner and pointed myself parallel to the magnificent rock wall that formed the canyon. Below me ran the cold, shallow waters of the Spokane River. On the chain link fence preventing me from entering the canyon, the moonlight showed me a little sign with a stick figure swimmer crossed out in the middle of a circle, no-smoking style. It read: STAY OUT. STAY ALIVE.

In this particular case, I figured the sign had it wrong.

I launched myself forward, using my Sense to find footing too narrow to hold Rick, a skinny path down to water level. Downstream, the canyon widened, but upstream toward the dam the walls were sheer.

Upstream it was. As the wall became vertical, I used my Sense to grab rocks from the shallow water below, stacked them in front of me, then jumped to them.

Behind me, I heard a loud scrabbling as Rick tried to corner as hard as I had. Like an idiot, I turned to look. My foot slipped on my next platform, sending me into the shallow water. I stuck my head up, spluttering.

Rick looked over the cliff wall at me from downstream, growled low, and began running parallel to the top of the cliff, toward me. I heard something that sounded like a rocket slam into his far side, but the cliff stopped me from seeing the light show. The amount of power I'd been throwing around was taking its toll, and breathing alone was a struggle. I couldn't keep this fight up. Eventually, the Sense would slip from me, and I'd be just a normal teenage boy. Shortly thereafter, I'd be dinner for one big, angry raccoon. Not yet, though. I stood up in the calf-deep water and began my run toward the dam.

Above me atop the cliff, Rick slammed his tail into the cliff wall, breaking it into large boulders which plunged down toward me. I used my Sense to fend them off. He did it again. This could only last so long, and it could only end one way.

All of a sudden, thunder filled the canyon. I have no idea what Grace hit him with, but it was easily her biggest shot yet. It blindsided him as he stood atop the cliff, taking him in the right side, the far side, hurling him into the air, over me.

I didn't dare to hope anymore, so I wasn't disappointed when Rick blasted out his force too far away from me to be able to do anything to it. He leaped off nothing to rebound to the opposite canyon wall, then landed on its rock face with all four clawed feet, silhouetted against the moonlight. He looked at me across the rushing water.

Stop staring, I told myself. *Run.*

I continued upstream. Rick bounded back and forth between the canyon walls above me, his fast zigzag pattern easily keeping up with my slow, straight-line gasping. The canyon narrowed enough as it descended to the water's edge to prevent Rick from diving. Had he dropped, I could have collapsed the cliff wall on him, but instead he seemed content to bounce about above me, throwing rocks down.

So much for Plan B; was there a Plan C? My mind raced to find one. And I was running out of canyon.

I exited the narrow part into the bowl beneath the dam. The falls and the spill-gates loomed above me, a path that would lead me upward, where Rick could get to me. Still, I had no choice. Plan C was going to come down to whether I could make this climb or whether I got eaten in the process. I began angling my steps upward, finding the rough footholds that allowed me to ascend.

In the open area of the bowl, Rick sprang at me, fanged mouth ready for the kill. I paused, focused, gritted my teeth with the effort, and stole a portion of the energy fueling his jump. I didn't get enough to slam him again, but it *was* enough to propel me onto one of the bare rocks in the middle of the falls, snugly situated in the crook of the "L" formed by the dam.

Rick hadn't anticipated the loss of momentum, and his landing on the far wall was less than graceful. He slipped, scrabbling for purchase, giving me the second I needed to breathe deep and prepare myself for his next, inevitable move. I looked at the top of the dam, glowing in the moonlight; it was about twenty feet up and twenty feet to the south. This rock had been a big target; my next one was going to take a little more precision.

My breath seared my chest as I slowly exhaled. Rick gained his footing, turned and snarled at me. I bent my knees, prepared to jump. For a moment, our eyes locked, and I swear the corner of his fanged mouth bent into a smile. Somewhere on the far side of him I heard Grace cut loose with another burst of weaponry, but it was too late.

Rick sprang from the wall toward where I stood stranded on a rock in the middle of a waterfall.

Once again, I slipped a fraction of his force out from under him and leaped, running. I looked at the dam, flailing my arms in the middle of my jump, and realized with a sinking heart that I hadn't been able to steal *enough* force. Instead of landing atop the dam, I was going to undershoot and smack into the middle of the long spill gate.

This would be followed, of course, by a fall to my death.

I was saved, of all things, by the hunger of my beastly pursuant. Rick had anticipated the lack of force this time, had landed square, and had already bunched his muscles. As he jumped, I reached out with my tattered Sense, grabbing as much of his force as I could.

Screw precision; I'd take a water landing over hitting the rocks below me.

The force I snagged from Rick launched me upward, coming down *almost* perfectly on the top of the long spill gate forming the bottom of the "L" that was the North Dam. My right foot solidly impacted the walkway. Then it rolled under me. Pain shot up from my ankle to join the pain in my chest, and I fell stumbling into the railway.

I collapsed to my knees as I saw the rising maw of Rick coming up to meet me.

Reaching down with the last of my Sense, I felt the inner workings of the dam and used the pressure of the back-built water behind it to pop the crank holding the spillgate closed. Rick got a mouthful of pressurized river for dinner instead of me.

The gate spun loosely, freed from its man-made shackles. Water pounded down the falls. The river took the Cornuprocyon midair, at his most vulnerable. It gripped him by the top of his head, throwing him back toward the logs and rocks below. The small piles of rock I had used to make my way here were washed away. My whole path of ascent drowned in seconds.

I began to really respect that STAY OUT, STAY ALIVE sign. It had a point.

I didn't have enough concentration left to affect Rick's fall. The narrow crevasses between boulders in the falls held him, though. I saw a couple of bursts of water as he tried to blast the deluge away from him, but the water he blew away was replaced as soon as he did. The river flowing from above was shooting through a narrow spillway, and Rick scrabbled against the rock simply to find room to breathe.

It wasn't going to hold him. Nothing ever held him, it seemed. But it would do to get Grace and me out of here, let us recuperate, try again. I forced myself to my feet, using the railing of the dam to hobble my way north to the car. I threw a look over my shoulder. Grace had gained the ridge and seen my trick with the dam. I waved my hand toward the car, but couldn't see or hear a response.

When a hang glider burst onto the scene, its straps already fastened around my mentor, I figured she'd gotten the message.

The sudden appearance of the hang glider, in perfect position, let me know I still had a long way to go as a summoner. Even in my wounded, bedraggled state, I took a moment to appreciate the sheer artistry of that summons. Then I began my own painful trek back to the car.

I beat Grace to the car and had it started before she got in. She gave me a look of displeasure that I was in the driver's seat of her car, but I pretended not to notice as I pulled out of the Falls Park parking lot and headed toward the freeway.

As we hit the on-ramp, my stomach twisted at the sight in my rearview mirror. We sped up to the freeway, but I knew we weren't getting away clean this time.

"Grace? I don't mean to alarm you, but I think we're being followed."

I was hurt, tired, and about to die. I didn't have time for originality.

GRACE

THE MOONLIGHT OUTLINED Rick's massive, jagged silhouette pulling itself up from the river canyon, heading toward the interstate with sickening speed. It looked like a giant section of log was still stuck in his spiky back. Rick resembled an escapee from a demented carousel.

I couldn't see if the log was embedded on his quills or if it had actually managed to penetrate that damned exoskeleton. I could only hope for the latter. Maybe it would give us some kind of edge in this thrice damned night.

"Keep your eyes on the road!" I told Robert. "We won't be able to do anything if we get into a wreck. I'll watch Rick."

I loosened my seat belt and flipped around to face backward in the seat with my burn well out of the way of the shoulder strap. The scenery flashed by in a blur of yellow grass silvered by the moon, street lamps, and scrubby black pines.

I raised my right hand to wipe sweat out of my eyes and realized it was shaking. I hoped that wasn't the first signs of shock setting in. I didn't have time to fall apart. I glanced at Robert, but he hadn't seemed to notice. Good.

The car slalomed around a curve as the interstate turned left to follow the river. My head rapped against the passenger window and left a smudge on the glass. I gripped the door, desperate for more stability, and wrenched my bad shoulder. For a moment, Rick and the moon disappeared and the car flooded full of stars. I fought with everything I had to keep a handle on my senses.

Hold it together, Grace. You can do this. With excruciating concentration, I brought the car, the moon, and the evil porcupine-raccoon thing back into focus.

In the quickly shortening distance, a very large, very angry demon beast shed big fat drops of the Spokane River as it sprang to run parallel with the oncoming traffic.

Robert pushed the accelerator down; the engine of my Pontiac whined in protest. I fumbled with the window control but the muscles in my burned shoulder cramped up, making my movements clumsier than usual. Once I had worked it down all the way, I stuck my head and shoulders out of the window to get a better view, unobscured by the ceiling or sides of the car.

A large semi-truck with square yellow headlights cruised in the far oncoming lane about six car lengths behind our dark red Pontiac. Rick landed beside it with an audible impact, obviously scaring the shit out of the driver, because the truck swerved and started to jackknife. I swore.

We'd planned our showdown for late at night because fewer people would be awake in the vicinity of the dam, but there were still quite a few cars on the interstate. If that truck jackknifed, there was going to be a nasty pileup. I gritted my teeth, forced my fingers to move the correct runes into position and pushed out a summons. My head pounded.

Robert shot me a wild look when our car suddenly cannoned forward, propelled by momentum stolen from the semi. He swerved into the next lane, narrowly avoiding careening into the red taillights of the car in front of us.

The semi's engine suddenly regained freeway speed, snapping the trailer back in line with the cab. The cars behind it passed with no problem, although they all slowed to look at Rick when they should have been speeding up. Gotta love the innate, voyeur instinct in humans that makes us all stop and gawk when we should be running. Luckily for them, Rick's entire being was fixated on our little maroon car and the meat snack it contained.

"I thought you said we wouldn't be able to help anyone if we got in a wreck! What gives?" Robert screamed at me. We sped like a cruise missile down the interstate with Robert fighting to bring the car back under control as the excess momentum burned off. Rick chased us along the median, paying no attention to the other vehicles.

Oh hell. His clawed hind leg came perilously close to crushing one of the gawkers. My fingers blazed over my magnets, finding the runes I needed. I summoned fire from all the cars behind Rick and stalled their engines, throwing down lit road flares behind them to warn any other vehicles. That cleared the immediate area of bystanders, and would delay any other cars traveling this direction. In front of us, there were only two sets of tail lights. That would be easier. So far the oncoming lanes were clear. I wished I could believe they would stay that way.

I grimaced at Robert. "Sorry. I'll try to give you a warning next time. I prevented Rick from creating a massive wreck behind us." I returned my attention to Rick.

"More warning would be awesome." Robert snapped off the last word abruptly, re-focusing his attention on keeping the car on the road.

"Noted."

My fingers danced across the summoning board in a blur, feeling out the runes I needed. I blooded them and pushed my overused Sense to power yet another summons. Right before the next off-ramp, steam suddenly billowed out from under the hood of both cars in front of us. They pulled off at the exit. I didn't need to imagine their swearing as we whizzed past.

We rocketed down the interstate at a ridiculous speed, but I figured any cop who tried to pull us over had bigger problems. I totally didn't trust Rick *not* to take out bystanders for spite if we failed to keep him busy.

The Cornuprocyon gathered itself for another upsurge as we pulled away. With a giant accumulation of kinetic energy, it bounded up, passing high over our car in a bristly flash of sharp orange spikes briefly outlined by the street lights. It overshot our car.

For a moment, I thought it had misjudged how far to jump with its new souped-up strength. I took a potshot at its underside with a strategically positioned stick of dynamite just on principle. Not surprisingly, it didn't do much except further impair my hearing. Still, worth a shot.

The Cornuprocyon landed on the Mcguire Road overpass crossing the interstate, and I realized my mistake. He turned to face us, eyes glowing red and teeth gleaming out of the darkness. The stupid log still protruded from his back, accentuating the illusion of a bizarre, evil, reverse raccoon-on-a-stick. He crouched, waiting for us to pass underneath. It didn't take much to guess he planned to bring his claws or tail down and rip us apart.

I had a fraction of a second to make a snap decision before our car would be opened like a can of sardines. I did the first thing that popped into my head.

I summoned one of those giant, cordless parachutes meant for kiddy activities and threw it right in Rick's face, hoping to blind him. With luck, the silk would get caught on his spines and his movement would be hampered for the fractions of a second it would take us to floor the accelerator and get under the overpass. I like to think that if I'd had more than a fraction of a second to make a plan, I would have foreseen what happened next.

I'd miscalculated because the plan required that I throw something with lots of air resistance at his *face*. He could see it coming with plenty of time to deflect it back at us with a blast of energy.

Suddenly, our car was shrouded in the parachute. We were headed toward an overpass with ugly cement supports braced against the road, with Rick poised above to knock us aside like a ball trying to go through the windmill at a mini-golf green. I ducked back into the car, figuring this was a bad time to be hanging out the window.

"Grace!" Robert screamed as the car fishtailed. "What the heck? Help!"

I took some of the careening force from the out–of-control Pontiac; not enough to slow us down completely, but enough to rend a huge hole in the parachute and summon a gust of wind to peel it away from the car. In hindsight, the parachute turned out to be one of those ideas that seems-like-genius—right up until it tries to kill you before anything else can.

The parachute did mask the car just enough to mess up the Cornuprocyon's aim. He botched his strike to latch on to the car, so when his tail landed with crushing strength, it ripped off the bumper and possibly part of the trunk, but didn't crush the passenger area. The car bucked up and down wildly under the force. Robert grunted in pain. A second later, the parachute parted and freed up the windshield—just in time for Robert to keep us from completely smashing into the rightmost overpass support. The right rearview mirror brushed against it.

Yellow sparks and the ear-shattering squeal of grinding metal erupted down the right side of the car. The mirror flew off behind us down the interstate. We didn't *really* need that one anyway.

Robert wrenched the steering wheel to the left. We lurched back into the true lane of travel. I didn't need Robert's strained face and quirked eyebrows to tell me I was seriously off my game tonight.

Come on, Grace, you can do better than this. I took a deep breath. The Cornuprocyon gained on us, ready for his next gambit. He ripped up a pine tree from the roadside with a blast of force and flung it at the car from the side, trying to knock us off the road.

This time, I summoned a triangular concrete barrier about five feet tall. The tree smashed up against it. The barrier started to skid toward the car, but slowly enough that we were able to squeak by. Splinters and pine needles rained down on the Pontiac's roof.

I braced myself for the next bout, but the Cornuprocyon veered off-course. At first, I couldn't understand why. Then I realized that whatever controlled Rick hadn't been able to fight off the irresistible temptation of the flashing Post Falls Outlet Mall sign. Rick gave an almost playful swipe as he went by, bringing the whole sign crashing to the ground. It took out a good chunk of the parking lot. He gave it one final smash with his tail for good measure before his eyes snapped back on target. He vaulted onto the highway and after our vehicle.

Robert said something, but I didn't catch it. I twisted in the seat slightly so I could see him out of the corner of my eye. "What?"

"Spokane River bridge up ahead. If he catches us on it, we're completely effed."

"Gotcha. Let's see what I can use to slow him down. I'm going to augment our speed again, too, so brace yourself."

I pulled speed from the Spokane River below us and added it to the Pontiac's momentum. Robert let out a wild whoop beside me. He hadn't gotten us killed yet, so if he wanted to yell like some racing fan, I guessed that was all right with me. The Cornuprocyon bounded down the interstate cracking asphalt and concrete behind us with abandon.

That electricity had really juiced him up. His movements reminded me of a destructive, vindictive kid on a sugar high, which for Rick, said something. Last time I try to listen to unknown spirits, let me tell you.

In front of us, I could see taillights at the far end of the bridge. Crap. We had caught up to some actual traffic. The chitinous, spiked hide of the Cornuprocyon looked black in the moonlight. A harpoon to the Cornuprocyon itself might not do anything, but...if I could get it off in time...I might still be able to use one to slow him down. As I started my summons, I double-checked the space we had before the bridge. Not a whole lot. Great. I needed to pull this off in thirty seconds or less, or it wasn't going to work. No pressure, Grace.

The harpoon gun popped out into my hands. Immediately I started drawing the impurities out of the steel barb, strengthening and honing it. I proceeded to do the same super-strengthening on the chain and anchor it attached to. I slapped tags onto the gun itself. Finally, I wrapped a tag around the harpoon's shaft to activate at the last minute, providing extra speed and force from one of the dam's turbines.

I rearranged the runes on my summoning board, ignoring the screaming nerve endings in my shoulder. Balancing the harpoon gun to fire would be...well, tricky.

Rick loped along only about fifteen feet behind our mangled car, and the bridge loomed in front. We would be crossing it in the next five seconds. Now or never. I stuck my whole torso out of the car to aim accurately, perching on the windowsill.

The first summons went off as planned. Boulders snatched from the Spokane River gorge sped toward the Cornuprocyon's face. I brought the harpoon gun up to my shoulder, gritted my teeth, and prepared to fire as soon as Rick deflected the rocks. As I expected, he brought up his telekinesis and fended them off easily. I just needed him to expend the ability, giving me the opening to fire before he could bring it up again. My finger tightened on the trigger just as the car swerved enough to unbalance my precarious position. I felt myself begin to fall.

Time slowed. I re-aimed, and fired. The harpoon soared through the air as planned. It hit the Cornuprocyon while its telekinesis was still recharging, piercing the log already embedded in his back. It can only have taken a fraction of a second. It felt like I had all the time in the world. I slapped the runes into place, anchoring the gun deep into the bedrock under the road. Time sped back up. Now I hung half out of the car, scrabbling with the top of the window to try and get my center of gravity back inside.

The chain caught up with Rick mid-air, wrenching him back, slamming him into the asphalt with a thunderous crack. It reminded me of a fisherman landing a trout. He thrashed at the end of the tether, regaining his feet, biting and clawing at the chain with no success. I had tethered a giant. I gave a fierce grin. Not that I expected it to hold, mind you, but we'd crossed the bloody bridge, making it much less likely that the Cornuprocyon would take it in its head to destroy it or drop us in the Spokane River below.

Safely across the bridge, Robert reached over and reefed on my ankle to get me back inside the car. On my way in, I hit my chin on the top of the car, bit my tongue, banged my shoulder, and saw stars for the third or fourth time that night. My father often joked he'd misnamed me. Tonight, I had to give it to him.

The road followed the river for the next few miles while I continued to pull force from the turbines to apply to the momentum of the car.

"Let me know if we get to the point where you can't steer," I cautioned Robert as my fingers fired up the summons to pop another stunned driver into a different lane.

"What's steering?" Robert quipped. "I've decided this has more in common with tobogganing. Fortunately, I don't think there are any sharp turns anytime soon, or we'll be out taking a swim faster than you can blink."

"Well, if you need to blink," I said drily, "I can at least peel off enough of the momentum for us to turn momentarily."

I didn't see the Cornuprocyon behind us. and harbored a secret little hope whispering *maybe* I'd managed to hold it up long enough for us to give it the slip yet again. I tried not to listen.

We were just passing the weigh station on the Washington side of the border when I saw the street lamps glint off something large, spiky, and approaching fast.

"Our company is back," I told Robert. The sound of chopper blades and a spotlight made me look up. "And we have *new* company." Perfect. I squinted against the glare. The side of the chopper read "Spokane County Sheriff's Department." On second thought, I had no idea how any of us were going to get out of this one.

Fortunately, we flashed past a sign that read "Granite and Rock." That at least gave me an idea how to delay the Cornuprocyon again. As for the police we would invariably be running into, well, my goal was just to stay alive until then. One thing at a time, folks.

Rick caught up faster than I liked by leapfrogging down the interstate using the overpasses as launch pads. I readied my next summons, hoping and praying I had predicted his next landing correctly. Right before he came down, I took a huge chunk out from underneath him. He plummeted into the hole. I slammed the earth down on top of him.

Yeah, that was a favorite trick of mine, but for a reason. This time I capped it with a ten-foot wedge of solid granite. Even in his souped-up state, I figured that should hold him for a minute or two.

It held for about thirty seconds. It got us a *little* farther down the interstate. The Cornuprocyon sent the granite flying with enough force that it hopped the barrier and skidded into oncoming traffic on the other side. I swore, stalled a few cars that were about to hit it, and used their momentum to throw the granite into the ditch on the other side. Rick shook the dirt out of his quills and resumed the chase.

The helicopter decided to activate its loud speaker, instruct us to pull over, call off our summoned beast, and wait for law enforcement.

"Does that look like something we're able to call off?" Robert shouted back. I just shook my head. It's not like they could hear us over their engine anyway.

We passed the turnoff for Liberty Lake: more ambient light and businesses tucked away on the sides of the interstate than before. We needed to stop Rick, and fast, before we entered a really populated area, but my idea tank was already running on empty. I don't like to think of myself as a fatalistic person, but this was starting to look like another bloodbath in the making.

Rick hopped another overpass, inevitably reclaiming his spot behind our vehicle. The Cornuprocyon was back and super pissed by that last stunt. Apparently, it had developed a severe dislike for being repeatedly buried alive.

He galloped down the road, still about sixty feet off our non-existent bumper. With a mighty roar he unleashed a lance of kinetic force at our car. Swearing, I swiped blood across my last bangle and summoned enough counter-force to minimize the impact. The car fishtailed. Robert wrenched it into the outer lane. We skidded on the rumble strip for a few seconds before he could straighten us back out. Inexorably coming closer, Rick blasted outward with another even larger sphere of pure kinetic force. I managed to grab and re-route some of the energy so we weren't smashed to smithereens. The shock wave visibly impacted the chopper above us, though. It started to spin crazily, the spotlight flashing in all directions.

It was going to crash-land in the middle of a Porsche dealership. The helicopter had been hovering low to follow us, enough that even with my lightning fingers I couldn't do much for the crew. It collided with the pavement with deafening finality. The helicopter blades scythed through several vehicles, leaving a ruined parody of luxurious German engineering in their wake. I stared at the scene and the crumpled helicopter cabin helplessly, willing the crew to walk out of the wreckage. At that height I'd hoped they might live.

Our vehicle and its uninvited guest barreled down the highway, almost to the Spokane Valley city limits. I summoned the few cars still on the road out from under Rick's sweeping tail. The Cornoprocyon had obviously decided that if we were evading it, then it wanted to crush as much stuff as possible.

I didn't try to save everything, just things with people in them. Light posts, cement barriers, supports and buildings all were destroyed when the raging demon came up beside them. The nut factory didn't fare much better. Rick specifically took out all the cars sitting in its parking lot from the night shift. I was finishing a summons to redirect Rick's attention with all kinds of flashing lights in the lot when Robert let out a whole string of profanity.

I didn't even have time to look before I heard the tires exploding. The car immediately started sliding sideways, straight for the police barricade and a horrified Detective Allen. Judging from the barricade's proximity to spike strips, they hadn't expected us to come in quite this hot. They managed to take out our tires but not stop us, and we were going to crash right into them.

ROBERT

AS CHILDREN, we are all taught that the police are your friends. If you need help, talk to the nice policeman. We are raised on a steady diet of the cops being the good guys, usually pitted against the robbers (clearly bad guys). The police are there to serve and protect; that's what's written on all of their cars.

So it's a little disillusioning when they do something deeply and profoundly stupid.

I hit the spike strip; no choice in the matter. The Pontiac lurched into a sideways skid. I groped around in my aching skull, trying to bring up some kind of Sense to sap away the momentum, but it eluded me. Grace did not have time to react. We crashed in our side-on skid directly into a green-and-white Spokane County Sheriff's patrol car.

My head cracked against the door frame. I struggled for consciousness as Grace fell into me, adding pressure to my already fractured rib cage. My world burst into a bloom of pain, and as I began to regain my senses my ears filled with the sounds of idiots screaming at me.

"Come out slowly, hands up, no funny stuff! Do it now! Now!" Lovely.

Those lights Grace had thrown into the nut factory parking lot would only hold Rick's attention for a minute or so, and these cops were worried about arresting *us*. That...that was just great. Grace left the car first, hands above her head. I waited for her. My door was firmly embedded into the patrol vehicle next to me. I needed to slide out her side.

"Down! On the ground! Now! Get down *now!*" barked the deputies.

Grace complied, saying, "You know, fellas, this is a really bad idea."

"You have the right to remain silent..." The recitation of rights continued in that no-nonsense, commanding voice as I rolled out of the car. I didn't bother standing with my hands up; it seemed like too much effort. I simply rolled directly onto the ground, hands outstretched, and let the cops cuff me.

It seemed laughable. If I'd been able to muster even a fraction of my Sense, these handcuffs would be meaningless. The problem was, I was barely hanging onto consciousness. In no way could I hold the state of concentration needed for the Sense.

They stripped away Grace's bag of tricks and my bracers and stood us up. I shook my head as I looked into the face of the man arresting me. Deputy Rosen. New, young, and scared as hell; the worst person to have in this position.

"Guys?" Grace said in an altogether too reasonable-sounding tone of voice. "You might want to lose the roll bar lights. You see, Cornuprocyons, much like the raccoons they resemble, are attracted to—"

Too late. Rick came in from a high angle—one of his telekinetic jumps. The SWAT vehicle put a spotlight on him; *that* was a mistake. A blast of his force knocked the large, armored van into the air, smashing it onto the far side of the freeway in a wreck of twisted steel and kevlar-clad bodies. He leapt toward it and began tearing the van open, pursuing its contents.

"Shit!" yelled Rosen. "Call him off! Call him off *right fucking now* or I won't wait for the courts to execute you!" He was screaming as he yanked his pistol clear of his holster, leveling it point-blank at Grace. The deputies still at the barricade of vehicles ducked behind their cars as though they were actual cover and began firing their semi-automatic assault rifles and police-issue shotguns into Rick.

Grace met Rosen's eyes. "Are you even paying attention? We were running *away from* that thing, not *with* it. If I had that kind of control over him, I'd have called him off loooooong ago. If you're going to kill me, then just do it. But as we're the only people here to have fought that thing and lived, you may want to think twice about it."

"That's not exactly true," said a calm, cool voice to my right. I whipped my head around, and there stood our old compatriot, Detective Frank Allen, his arm in a sling. "Most of the deputies in the Valley office lived through that fight. Didn't they, Rosen?"

A faint glimmer of hope arose in me.

"That's true," said Grace. "You did live. I amend my statement. Of course, would you care to explain to this young and trigger-happy deputy *how* exactly it was that you lived?"

Allen chuckled. "Well, the way I figure it's one of two options. One: you two had summoned this beast in order to free you, which worked very well. In that case, I imagine you staged the entire rescue in order to ingratiate yourself with me. Two: this beast just *happened* to show up as soon as I had both of you in custody, just *happened* to take me hostage, and just *happened* to leave as soon as you two did. Problem with that second theory is, there's a lot of coincidence. I'm not a fan of coincidence myself, so I'm inclined to agree with Rosen here. Call off your little pet, and he won't pull the trigger."

"Third option," I gasped. "No control, but it wants to eat us for our power. I lured it there by ringing the dinner bell. Used it. Left with us to follow us."

Allen seemed to consider that. Behind him, the deputies were still fighting, but their ammunition had about as much effect on Rick as I'd expected. Rick, on the other hand, was *fascinated* by the shining lights on the roll bars. He finished rending the SWAT van and slammed one of cars with his giant club of a tail, flinging it backward and crushing the deputy hidden behind it. He then jumped up on one of the cars and began chewing on its light bar.

"That's an interesting idea," said Allen. "Certainly more plausible than simple coincidence." Deputy Rosen's gun trembled; Allen put his hand over it, lowering it for the moment. "Calm down, son," he said. "I know you're scared, but don't do something we might regret."

"Look at him, Detective," said Grace, pointing at me. "That wound on his side? He didn't get that in the car wreck. Look at the bruising pattern. Just lift the shirt."

Allen lifted my shirt, exposing my bruised, cracked ribs. "You're right; it looks like someone hit him with a giant baseball bat. Plus, I didn't see any fire in that car; did the beast burn you as well?"

"Kind of," said Grace. "He countered one of my attacks. But the 'baseball bat?' Compare that tail over there."

"Hmm, interesting. Well, I'm willing to believe you're not fully in control here. Mostly because you'd have tried to negotiate your way out of this by now. Rosen, please escort the prisoners to the van. Hold them there pending transport while we secure this situation. Don't let them out of your sight; they can be tricky."

"What?" Grace was not pleased by that call. "Detective, let me fight alongside you. I'm the only one here who has anything approaching the kind of power it would take to stop that thing. Without us, you're going to have a lot of men die for nothing. With us, maybe you can get these people out of here."

"Ahhhh," sighed Allen. "There's the negotiating. No. You're under arrest for summoning and a whole host of other charges. You will have the opportunity to speak to a judge within twenty-four hours to discuss bail. Before that, you're not getting out of custody. Not again."

I didn't actually think it mattered that much. With or without Grace, it looked like we were all going to die tonight. Grace had barely managed to keep people alive in the running battle on the freeway; now we faced a knock-down drag-out head-to-head cage match with a thirty foot raccoon-thing. We hadn't managed to even come close to beating Rick as yet; the best we could hope for was some form of noble self-sacrifice.

Deputy Rosen ushered us at gunpoint into a van behind the battle lines, ignoring all further protestation. The chatter of weapons fire accompanied more crashing and screaming as Rick continued the not-really-that-slow process of killing deputies. More seemed to be pouring in along the freeway; as the van doors closed behind us I snatched a glimpse of the State Patrol, Spokane City police, and Liberty Lake city cops adding to the fray.

If this sort of backup kept up, the whole county would be depopulated of law enforcement by the end of the night.

Sitting with Grace and Deputy Rosen in the back of the van presented an odd illusion of safety. The van had no windows, and so the horrors we heard outside had no context. Deputy Rosen's face looked pale and sweaty; he was losing friends as we just sat there and he knew it. His eyes flicked between Grace and me, and I got the impression his complexion wasn't being helped by the presence of two known summoners.

"So," said Grace conversationally, "looks like it's time to die." She reclined on the bench as she said it, kicked her legs out in front of her and crossed them, stretching her back. "We had a hell of a run, though. Sorry you got caught up in it, Robby boy, but at least I extended your life span by a couple of weeks."

She had, too. The last couple of weeks had been a gift of Grace's, a little window into life before I lost mine. If not for Grace, I'd have died in front of the arcade back at the mall. With Grace, at least I got to go down fighting. The way she said it, though, was just so *comical.* Here we were, about to die, and she tossed it off like she was ordering a couple of cheeseburgers.

I cracked up. Grace was right. With nothing to be done about it, we may as well have a little fun. I burst into hysterical giggles, pounding my head into the metal walls of the van. "Oh, God," I chortled, "The look on Rick's face when you hit him with that harpoon-thingy. It was like a cartoon dog hitting the end of his leash."

Grace broke down with me, deep belly laughs coming from a small set of lungs. "You should have seen his face when you cracked the dam open on him. He was so close, then you poured an entire river on him. Classic!"

We both sat there with Rosen's gun nervously on us and the

sounds of slaughter and mayhem muffled through the steel walls of the van, riding the wave of laughter merrily towards our graves.

"Stop!" Rosen squeaked. "Just...stop it. I don't know what you're doing, but stop. Don't make me shoot you."

"Deputy," said Grace, still chuckling a little. "Do you think it matters at all? Listen to what's happening outside. We've been in a running battle with the Cornuprocyon for the last half hour, and we're at our wits' end here. Soon he's going to kill the last of the cops fighting him. After that, he'll come and kill us. So shoot if you must, because there's only one way for us all to get out of this, and it's the most suicidal thing I've ever contemplated."

My head whipped up; Grace actually had a thread of hope? What had she held back? I tried to meet her eyes, but she was too busy with the deputy. "And I see that you're not letting the two of us go; you're going to keep us here so that we can all die screaming. We may as well enjoy these, the last moments of our lives. On that note, by the way, you missed the runes tattooed on my wrist. They're really small, so I don't blame you, but still something to watch out for."

There it was. Grace could still summon; we were going to be safe! She leaned over with her cuffed hands, rubbing some of my blood off one of my many flesh wounds into her wrist. I tensed myself, ready for the inevitable last-ditch fight to come. Deputy Rosen drew down on her, gunpoint trembling as he witnessed firsthand the art he no doubt considered an act of supreme evil. Grace's head sagged, the focus of the Sense entering her. The world paused, taking a breath, waiting for the burst of action to follow.

A plate of cubed poultry and chopped vegetables tossed with a sauce over rice popped into existence, steaming hot, filling the van with the aroma of coriander and lemongrass. The plate itself was oblong, with some sort of a china pattern on it. A fork had been plunged into the rice, the silver-plated handle of which jutted out over the plate's lip. It appeared as though it had a bite or two missing. This wasn't her normal take-out, then; she had simply filched the plate from a paying customer. Last resort indeed.

Deputy Rosen stared at it in shock.

"What?" Grace sounded innocent. "Thai-curried duck. My last meal. Could you give me a hand here, Deputy? I could use a little length in these cuffs." The deputy stared at the plate of curry as though the dish had poleaxed him.

"No? Ok, that's fine. I can do it myself." While the deputy stared at the curry, Grace removed her right wrist from the cuffs, then produced her own. She closed hers around her right wrist, attaching the two sets of cuffs together. Then she reached down with her cuffed hands, grabbed the fork on the curry plate, and lowered her head to take a bite.

I'm sure I must have looked as shocked as Rosen, though I don't know why. It made perfect sense, in the end. Of course Grace would have one last meal tattooed onto her wrist. This was, after all, *Grace* we were talking about. As my hopes sagged, the hysterical laughter returned, enhanced exponentially by the absurdity of Grace's final summons.

"You guys want in on this? Robert? Deputy? We'll have to share the fork, I only tattooed one of those into my wrist, but even so...better to go out with the taste of good curry."

Deputy Rosen still acted confused, so I figured I'd add to it. Heck, it was an interesting distraction from the fact that the van might be crushed at any moment. "Sure. I could go for some."

Grace leaned forward, holding the laden fork in her shackled hands. I leaned toward her to take a bite. It did smell good. My mouth wrapped around the succulent piece of duck—holy God, it melted in the mouth—and the door to the van flew open.

We must have made a bizarre tableau. Deputy Rosen's gun was swinging wildly back and forth between Grace and me, the confused deputy not realizing he was simply threatening us with a faster, cleaner death than we would otherwise receive. A plate of duck curry sat beside Grace on her side of the van; I was just sliding back from my bite, and Grace still held the fork out in her shackled hands.

Detective Allen's face was *to die for.* Which, given the circumstances, was just about right.

"Deputy! What are you—get out of there. Go help the wounded. I'll take care of these two."

"Want some curry, Frank?" offered Grace, leaning forward to push the plate and fork toward him. Behind Frank, a patrol car went spinning up the freeway, presumably pushed by one of Rick's force-blasts.

"Not particularly."

I had to hand it to him; the man could keep a steady head. After his moment of shock, he didn't so much as look at the curry. "Were you serious, before? Can you get my men out of this alive?"

Grace leaned forward, resting her head on the back of her wrists, and said in her whip-crack serious tone of voice, "That's not what I said. What I said was 'Without us, you're going to have a lot of men die for nothing. With us, maybe you can get these people out of here.' Emphasis on the *maybe*, Detective. I make no guarantees. In fact, I'm going to risk a great deal for something that may not work."

Allen shook his head. "We're dying out here. That thing—"

"Cornuprocyon." Grace's correction reflex was still working overtime.

"What? Never mind. Whatever it is, it's killing my deputies, and we haven't managed to damage it at all. I'd dearly love to believe you can stop it, but office policy says I have to keep you in custody no matter what." Saying this, he took a key on a ring from his pocket, twirling it about his finger as he spoke. "As much as I may want your help, or think it's the only thing that—"

I'm sure Detective Allen was going to give a clear speech establishing how the key getting into our possession was going to be nothing more than an accident, but it turned out he was right.

Rick blindsided him.

I'd been hit with that tail. I'd had the advantage of not being pinned against a van, though. Rick took Detective Allen low, slamming his knees into the bumper of the van. Allen bellowed a low roar and the key flew out of his hand.

Into Grace's.

Deftly, Grace unhooked her own cuffs, then handed me the key.

She shot out of the van and did something explosive; by the sound of it, she managed to pull Rick's attention away from us. I'm still not sure what she used for a rune, but it was enough. Rubbing my wrists, I limped out of the van and knelt beside the detective. He was alive and conscious, but his kneecaps had been shattered, his legs useless.

"Sit me up," he gritted from between clenched teeth. I nodded and grabbed him under the armpits, sitting him on the floor of the van. Then I grabbed the bag containing our "evidence" and ripped it open, pulling out my bracers.

"Grace!" I called.

Her head appeared in the van's doorway. I threw her the bag, and she began girding herself once again. Once together, she turned to the detective.

"I'm no healer," she said softly. "But I can get you some pain meds if you need them." Detective Allen shook his head and drew his sidearm with his sole functioning limb. He pointed it at the raging Cornuprocyon gleefully pouncing on top of a Liberty Lake police car, slapping that massive tail into the officers hiding behind it. Allen opened fire, unloading his clip to no effect.

Grace met my eyes. All semblance of jesting had left her. "Round Five. We're going to die. You ready for that?"

I was. I'd been expecting it since the moment I summoned that energy drink on the bridge, a very long forty-five minutes ago. I'd been expecting it as I ran along footholds of my own making below the dam. I was amazed we'd lived this long, and I was past caring. My mind couldn't take the hope of living, and the pleasant numbness of fatalism had settled in between my rasping breaths. I nodded to my mentor.

Grace smiled at me. "Good. That means if I have to sacrifice someone for the greater good here, then it's cool if I use you. Good to know; I'll work that into the plan."

"Sure," I said reflexively. Wait...what?

GRACE

I SURVEYED THE SCENE. The wreckage of the sheriff's barricade lay strewn everywhere. Several of the police vehicles had been completely ripped apart; their dismembered lights, doors, seats and engines rested drunkenly in the roadway. The bodies of several deputies lay ominously still.

Deputy Rosen struggled to drag one of the unconscious officers to a more sheltered location away from Rick, who was still tearing into the barricade. Rosen acted with an selfless bravery and quickness of thought that impressed the hell out of me. Despite my flagging strength and pounding head, I quickly summoned sturdy boulders to shield the flat area he was headed to. I hoped it proved far enough away from the action to serve its purpose as an improvised medical drop-off. Captain Carlenos limped his way behind them next. I winced at sight of the giant gash down his right leg and hip. I dropped some summoned blankets and bandages behind the boulders, trusting that Deputy Rosen would know who to use them on first.

The less-injured would have to put them to use on the more-injured, but at least they would have a better chance at doing some rudimentary first aid and warding off shock. I hoped Rick didn't take it into his head to crush that little shelter. The rocks would protect the wounded from flying debris if Rick threw any more kinetic missiles their way, but not from a direct attack.

I summoned a blanket over Detective Allen where he sat and wondered if he was bleeding out on me. Right now, priority one was to get Rick's attention off the deputies with their shiny cars and badges. Rick smashed another light bar to smithereens, crushing most of the police car along with it. I stepped out boldly from behind the van, my fingers blooding the runes, my flagging Sense already powering my next summons.

I supposed, at least if *I* died, I'd go out with the succulent, sweet spiciness of duck curry still on my breath. Cold comfort. Besides, I wouldn't allow Rick to take all these people with me. I took a deep breath and shook my aching head. Saving them meant finding the endurance somewhere for another fight.

"Hey. Ugly!" I yelled. "Get your spiky butt over here."

I used my summons to fry the wiring to the few functional roll bars left. The cop cars went dark. For good measure I popped some fireworks above my head, lighting them off into bright white stars using the fire licking up from a nearby police car's destroyed engine. They went off with a resonant boom, and the Cornuprocyon's head whipped around to give them (and me) a better look.

Swell. I had Rick's attention now, but what to do with it?

That seemed like a question better asked while running away from the injured. I took off, away from the van and the deputies, making sure to summon everything I had left in my bag of tricks that might harass the Cornuprocyon enough to keep its sights on me. I only had a few tags left in my purse, and I'd pretty much already depleted the artillery the Seattle Grove had given me. I was scraping the bottom of the barrel here.

I threw out the last of my mines, a couple of grenades, one pure smoke bomb (it did seem to confuse him for a second) and tossed a couple of the gas tanks from the trashed police cars at him like Molotov cocktails. The splashing gas *did* festoon him in brightly colored flames to match his chitinous hide, but I doubted it did any real damage. I considered napalm for a moment but decided that projectile napalm, telekinesis, and non-mobile wounded folks made a bona fide recipe for disaster.

I dodged behind the husk of a patrol car just as I heard the *woomph* that meant Rick had activated another of his telekinetic jumps. I dove for the open window. The Cornuprocyon came down on the far side of the car with his claws extended in a swipe, just as I managed to wiggle all the way inside. The frame of the cop car squealed and ground around me as Rick started prying at it with his claws. I prayed he didn't sit on it. I'd be toast.

I managed to squirm my way through before he figured out to just crush the damned thing. The plan was to exit on the far side and continue drawing him farther away from the barricade.

In burrowing through the mangled car, I discovered to my horror that an unconscious deputy still lay trapped inside. His legs looked pinned by the twisted metal of the dash, but the engine block hadn't fallen on him. I guessed him unconscious rather than dead. I reached across him to grab a wrist and was rewarded by a finding a pulse.

My own heart thumped in my ears. That was both wonderful and horrible. How the *hell* was I supposed to get us both out of here in one piece?

Out of the corner of my eye, I saw Robert helping Deputy Rosen assist more of the injured deputies behind our crude shelter. Unfortunately, the Cornuprocyon saw it, too. I let out a string of nasty four-letter words as his gaze fixed on Robert. Rick telegraphed his intent, gathering himself to pounce on Robert where he stood, surrounded by injured deputies.

I didn't have time to think; my fingers flew across my rune board. Heavy steel construction chains came into being, wound around one of Rick's hind legs. I fastened the loose end deep into the ground. The Cornuprocyon hadn't had time to re-up its telekinesis field before I summoned the chain. He didn't expect it. He didn't have time to augment his speed to break it either. It brought him up short, crashing into the ground like a giant, barbed tether ball just short of the boulder wall.

It was a ridiculous thing to watch. It made me remember Robert likening some of my moves in the mall to the Saturday morning cartoons, and I had to admit that was grade-A animated hi-jinks right there. I had made the big-bad-all-powerful being kiss the dirt with a length of chain, and I loved it. A demented grin curled my lips. Maybe, just maybe, I could pull a plan out of my ass that might let some of us live through this.

Using my rune board, I summoned the car from around us and sank it in the ground to block off more access to the wounded folks behind the boulders. Of course, that left me and an unconscious deputy in the middle of the roadway with nothing to hide behind. Damn. I should have just put it down in front of us. I quickly dragged the deputy over to the shoulder with strength born from adrenaline. My fingers flew over my rune board. I summoned and threw a blanket over him.

Robert looked up, saw what was happening, and turned his skinny butt to run toward me in a limping, hobbling kind of way. Rick shook his encumbered leg experimentally as he lumbered to his feet. I only had seconds before he realized his quarry had escaped.

Rick swiveled his head to look at me. His beady red eyes glinted in a cruelly crafty way. That's when I knew. Our puppet master had returned, and in just a second he would have taken stock of the whole bloody situation. The cops just to his right would be toast. Robert presented a woefully unprotected back as he limped toward me. They all made prime targets.

Unless, of course, I distracted Rick first.

I ran forward, throwing runes together on my board with frenetic speed, gathering all the kinetic force that I possibly could. "Robert!" I yelled, "Get down!" He dropped flat without even asking. I threw a stream of pure force over his head at the Cornuprocyon to keep his telekinesis busy. Rick countered with a return blast of energy that I redirected into the already demolished nut factory sign. If he got over to any of the wounded deputies, this whole shindig was all for nothing. To keep them safe, I needed to keep Boss Rick too busy to use them as bargaining chips.

Boss Rick had finally managed to free the Cornuprocyon's trapped hind leg, and I had a sinking feeling that whoever held the strings knew exactly how outmatched I was. Regardless, I kept hitting him with all the force I could muster in a desperate onslaught to keep him from targeting the deputies in easy reach of that club-like tail.

Rick gathered himself for a leap. For one crazy second I thought I had managed to lure him back over to my side of the highway away from the wounded cops. He propelled himself high into the air, much higher than necessary to reach Robert or me. By the time I realized he'd set his sights on another target entirely, it was already too late.

Deputy Rosen had run out from behind the barricade in a wide circle around the Cornuprocyon, trying to make it to the deputy I'd pulled out of the wreckage. "Rosen!" I yelled, my fingers frantically outlining a summons to try and knock Rick's pounce off-target. "It sees you. Get away from there!"

The Cornuprocyon hit the ground. His claws and teeth latched onto his new prey as the summons went off. My effort was a fraction too late and much too little.

Rick tore Deputy Rosen asunder and tossed him aside like a broken and disappointing toy. It stood over its gory prize and fixed me with a gloating eye.

"Whuft! Not going to save that one, summoner? Was that human not worth your time? Or were you not *able* to save him?" Boss Rick taunted. "There are many other humans over here to sacrifice to your pride. Admit that you must submit to me so I can let them go. Luck and a cheap shot drove me off last time. It will not be so easy this time. You have a minute to consider your lack of options."

It had killed Rosen for no other reason than to try and make a point with me. It had made a point, all right. A cold rage started to build in my chest.

"The Cornuprocyon is incredibly powerful," I said. "Its raw power is vastly superior to my own." Keeping an eye on it, I stepped over to Robert and helped him to his feet. He wobbled under my hands. "Hold on just a little longer," I whispered. "Do you think you can run?"

"I can try," he told me gamely.

"Ok, then. When Detective Allen gives the signal, run down the highway and put as much distance between Rick and you as you can."

"What's the signal?" "You'll know. Trust me."

"Sure." He grinned. "I trust you to death."

I gave him a light, playful slap on the back and shot him a wry grin to acknowledge the truth in his pun. The small tag I'd placed stayed unnoticed on his back. Then I stepped briskly over to Detective Allen and the detention van.

Boss Rick was still speaking. "I do appreciate you giving the Cornuprocyon a power upgrade at the dam. That was ever so fortunate for me. I never would have been able to give it that kind of immediate power burst on my own. I am gratified you honed this tool for me."

"It was strictly an unforeseen effect. I hoped to electrocute him and turn him into a smoking wreck. As you see, it didn't work out so well for me."

I leaned in toward Allen and pretended to adjust his blood-soaked blanket. Oh, God, he had bled a lot. "I need you to provide cover fire for me," I said.

"Not much I can do with this empty little handgun," he whispered back. "Even if I had ammo, wouldn't even get that thing to flinch."

The muscles in my face instinctively peeled my lips back from my teeth in a feral-feeling grin. "I can fix that part. You just need to be able to point and squeeze the trigger."

Study enough compound rune combinations and eventually you stumble across a few Grove "secrets." The Seattle Grove owned a weapon, one I wasn't even supposed to know about. Probably it represented the capstone of Seattle Grove's arsenal. I hadn't used it yet. I'd always wanted to try, but I'd never had the guts or the opportunity. The one time I'd seen it, I'd summoned it by accident. I'd been so shocked I put it back immediately. I'm still not sure the Grove knew it had been missing for those two or three seconds. They would be livid if they found out I'd taken it and used it. I'd just have to make sure I lived through this, so I could put it back with no one the wiser.

And if I died, well, it's hard to get chewed out, exiled, or executed as a dead person.

If I could use that to keep the Cornuprocyon in one place, I might just have a glimmer of a plan. But for it to actually work, I needed Allen, and I needed the time to summon it without getting anyone else killed.

I must have been muttering with Detective Allen too long, because Boss Rick suddenly barked out, "I don't know what you are plotting over there, but it is futile. Surrender yourself and the boy to me, or I will be forced to feed more of your pet humans to this Cornuprocyon. I have given you time to consider. Make your choice."

"I was just ensuring the detective is taken care of," I said demurely. "Since all of my runes are futile and useless, there's not much else I can do. I think I have some painkillers here in my purse somewhere, though. You don't mind if I find them for him, right? Of course not, since it's not like I'm any threat to you—and by my own admission!"

I dug through my purse to match my words, but really I was was powering one of my last force tags. Rick hadn't been expecting it, but the telekinesis still activated. That was what I had been anticipating. The next force tag went off a second after the first, blasting Rick head over heels back down the highway.

As soon as the second tag activated, I quickly switched to my rune board, pulling out the Grove's biggest, most secret, most going-to-get-me-canned-when-I got-home weapon. It was a GAU-8 Avenger, the culmination of all Gatling guns, modified to sit on a large triangular platform and outfitted with a gunner's chair. The barrel extended over twenty-one feet; the rounds a full foot. I had heard somewhere that its usual payload consisted of three armor piercers followed by an explosive round, repeated for however many thousands of shots. Just seeing it sitting out on the highway kind of gave me the chills.

I turned to Allen and helped lift him into the gunner's chair. His face turned gray with the pain of trying to maneuver up into the firing position. I worried that he might pass out completely, but he gasped, "It's ok. Get me in that chair and I'll keep this S.O.B. off your back for as long as you need."

We got him in the chair with a final push of willpower and stupid stubbornness. I didn't have time to give him more than a second to catch his breath.

"Here's your gun. It's just a little bigger than your old one." I took a second to wink at him and enjoy the stunned look on his face as he surveyed its controls. "I think the aiming and firing mechanisms are here and here. I could only summon the ammo that was already loaded and I have no idea where to get more. What you see is what you've got. It's probably only about thirty seconds' worth. The empty shells will spew out to your left." I pointed them out to him. "Oh, and we'd better deploy these."

I pushed the button that shot big, runed, steel pylons deep into the earth to deal with the gun's massive recoil. "I've always wanted an excuse to fire this," I said conversationally. "And now you definitely have one, because here comes the Cornuprocyon."

I ducked behind the giant gun to do my next summoning.

Detective Allen took a fraction of a second more to line up his shot and started firing at Rick in one-second bursts of total wanton destruction. The armor-piercing rounds ripped into Rick's hide and started punching gaping holes. Then the explosive rounds hit and smoking pieces of quill and hide started peeling off in large chunks.

Robert, as always, proved quick on the uptake. He started down the highway as soon as Detective Allen opened fire. I had maybe thirty seconds to do my final summons before the GAU-8 ran out of ammunition and we were all officially totally outmatched and back at that thing's non-existent mercy.

I took a precious half second to visualize Uncle Herman's crazy notes. I mapped out his formula for portal making and altered it with a little modification of my own, tying it back to the Cornuprocyon's home Weave. It used so many runes that it took every single inch available on the rune board. I had just finished slapping it together when I heard the hollow clacking that signified the giant gun had run out of ammo.

The Cornuprocyon shook itself like a wet dog. Under the glare of the street lights, the missing flesh started visibly mending itself. I smeared blood from my wounded shoulder over the runes and sent my will through them just as the Cornuprocyon smashed his tail down on the GAU-8, cracking my abused left arm, sending Allen tumbling like a rag doll. I skidded across the pavement on my face, but I'd managed to get the summons off. Robert vanished through Uncle Herman's portal. The Cornuprocyon bounded after him.

ROBERT

OOOOOOKAY. I was not in Kansas anymore.

I'd been running down the freeway in the desperate hope that Grace had some brilliant plan to save us all. I hadn't been able to stop and *look* at the portal that burst into existence in front of me; I just found myself careening through the air, landing with a nice, fresh explosion of pain to my cracked ribs. I rolled to lie on my back, gasping for air, taking stock of the world around me. I'd fallen into what appeared, in the dim light of evening, to be grass. It had a wider blade to it than most grass, though, and the color looked much lighter than normal. I felt it, expecting it to crackle in my hand as yellow grass does, and found it strangely supple.

Not. Kansas.

I knew Rick had been hot on my tail when I'd come through the portal, but I didn't see him. Apparently I'd hit Oz without Toto. I looked toward where I'd come from, but nothing visible appeared in the air. I stood and scrambled about, trying to find the portal I'd come from. The pain in my leg and my chest drove me to my knees, and still I found nothing. Panting with the terror of it, I groped for my Sense, but the pain and the exhaustion kept it out of reach. I was stuck in this place, alone.

I was, effectively, out of the fight. I had been prepared to die; I hadn't been prepared to be the sole survivor. I didn't cry. Teenage boys aren't allowed to cry. That moisture on my face was simply sweat from all the exertion.

Shut. Up. Let me have this one.

The night sky here sparkled like the one at home, but the constellations were completely unfamiliar. No Big Dipper, no Cassiopeia. No Orion, though it was still early in the year for him anyway. Uncle Herman and I had spent many nights examining the night sky, and it looked nothing like this.

Definitely not Kansas.

The temperature felt pleasant, not hot, not cold. I lay in a very soft bed of grass. I had just been through what could easily rank as the second most traumatic experience of my life (losing my parents was still worse). The soft grass beckoned my sore, tired body to lie back, close my eyes, and let sleep carry me away from my troubles. I knew I should try to get back into the fight, to find a way out of this world, but my aching body refused to respond.

A low growl to my right got my undivided attention, however. I swung my head that way and saw an extra-large, brilliantly white wolf, roughly twelve, maybe thirteen feet tall. It snarled at me, pacing, getting ready to attack.

Oh good. Looked like I was going to get to die after all.

The wolf jumped—and met a blast of some sort of energy mid-air. A flash of light blinded me for a second. The wolf whimpered, and ran off out of my line of sight.

"Whuft! Close one you had there, lad."

A tan-faced man stepped into my line of sight and lowered his hand down to me. The voice sounded oddly familiar, but in the haze of my pain and exhaustion I couldn't place it. His eyes were dark, peering out past blue paint traced onto his face. As he pulled me up to my feet, I noted that the blue markings were runes—futhark runes, which meant I was dealing with a summoner. His clothing, though, looked rough, mostly animal leathers, with some wooden, hand-carved jewelry.

I extended my hand. "My name's Robert."

"Or at least that's what they call you, eh?" He had an odd accent, something between English and German, but his tone sounded soft and friendly.

"Uhhh...I guess. Thanks for the help."

"First one's free, lad. That Lycaon looked none too happy to see you."

"Lycaon... Is that the Wolf-on-Goofballs thing?"

He sat down and considered a bit as though indexing the language. "Ah, yes. Goofballs. Drugs. Good one, that. Do you fancy a cup of tea?" Tea. I was in some kind of alternate world, and a strange, blue-painted man was offering me tea.

"Look, normally I'd go for a cup of tea, but I really need to get back. My friends are in trouble."

"Trouble, yes. An overfed Cornuprocyon. Normally they're easy to deal with, but that one's had way too much power. You have to keep them on a strict diet or else they go on a rampage."

"Well, this one's rampaging through my friends right now."

"Yes, quite. But we've got time to spare. Come have a cup of tea."

"Time to... What? No, the fight's happening *right now*."

"Yes, but there's time dilation. Didn't you consult your Grove book on this place before you came here?"

"Time dila—what? Look, I'm hurt, I'm exhausted, and I haven't actually read that book yet. Just give it to me straight."

"Haven't read it, eh? Whuft! Another amateur! Look, time is...thinner...in this world. Easier to move through, you see. Helium instead of air, yes? The portal you came from is open for the same amount of time in that world as it is in this one, but time's moving faster in this one. The beginning and the end of the portal need to line up in both worlds, and it'll open and close in that one. So here it's not open all the time. Just flashes, yes?"

I considered what he was telling me. "Kind of like those old movies with the cameras that didn't take the pictures as quickly."

Again the small man paused for a while before answering. "Ah. Yes. Just so. It will stagger itself out for a bit; we have a couple of hours until the next window, I think. We can wait here, or you can come take some tea with me and see what we can do about those injuries."

There was nothing else for it. I followed the weathered summoner as he walked through his foreign world.

~

"WHAT'S YOUR NAME?" I asked as we stepped through the mouth of a cave. Some five feet into the recess a door had been woven together from small branches.

"My name? You're a bold one. You can call me Cythymau, as others from your world have in their time."

Others may have, but I had never heard the name. I tried it on my tongue. "Kithy-moo?"

He chuckled. "Close. Kee-thee-ma-oo," he sounded out for me. "Cythymau."

Beyond the thatched door lay a homely sort of cave with a pallet, a table, and a couple of hand-crafted benches. It reminded me a great deal of Uncle Herman's cabin, but other passages led off this front room deeper into the cave. Cythymau shuffled to a small recess in the wall and summoned a pile of wood into the fireplace using some blood from a hide container at his side. A second summoning ignited the fire. He hooked a length of chain to the top of the recess and hung a small metal pot on it.

"So," Cythymau said conversationally as he sat back on a bench, waiting for the pot to boil, "tell me of your fight with this Cornuprocyon. Where is the Grove, and why do you and your mentor battle it alone?"

I did just that, covering the elimination of the Spokane Grove, the death of Uncle Herman, and the battles Grace and I had been through. I left out some of the more embarrassing bits, and I may have embellished my own role a bit in an effort to impress a fellow summoner, but I gave him the basic gist of it.

"And this mentor of yours, this Grace. She has not requested that aid be sent from her Grove to help in this struggle?" A strange glint came into Cythymau's eyes as he asked this, an eagerness that I could not explain.

"She told me she doesn't want to risk anyone else."

"Whuft! This Grace of yours is a brave one. That's a rare quality, and explains much. But now she fights alone. And you are injured."

True.

"Look," I said, "I'd give almost anything to get back there and help her end this. There's nothing I want more. As soon as that portal opens up, I'm jumping back into the fight even if it kills me."

"*Two* brave ones! Never saw that. Never imagined *two*. You're a wild card, lad, you really are. I find that I like you. You said you would give anything to help her out of this?" His voice quickened, and I saw eagerness in his eyes that set me on edge.

Grace had warned me about spirits from other worlds. And I was *in* another world—Cythymau was one of those spirits. Sure, Cythymau had been polite and hospitable, but that open-ended devil's bargain was a trap. I'd seen enough movies to know that the hero who agreed to do *anything* without knowing what he was agreeing to got screwed every single time.

"*Almost* anything," I said. "If you're proposing a deal, I need to know your terms." I hardened my expression.

"Whuft! So you do, lad, so you do. All in good time. Sit, enjoy your tea. Relax, build your strength for the fight to come, yes?" Cythymau went back to puttering about the hearth, mixing leaves into an earthenware cup, pouring the boiling water onto them. He placed the steaming cup on the table in front of me. "Drink up, lad. You'll need your energy if you're going back to fight that Cornuprocyon. Even if you don't take my help, you at least want to die well, yes?"

Die well. I had known that probability going into this. This strange, otherworldly respite had made me feel safe, but the fight wasn't over. I was hiding, resting in the space between moments here. I leaned my head back against the wall and considered that. The momentum I had felt since I stood at the head of the bridge faded. I didn't want to die at all. I had been resigned to it, but that had been in the heat of the moment. Now, my resolve faltered. What would my death add to the situation?

I looked down at the tea, wondering if it was safe or if it contained some strange herb that posed a threat. Cythymau looked at me expectantly as I raised the cup to my lips, but I let none of the liquid pass into my mouth as I feigned a sip.

"Good, good. Catch your rest, lad. We'll talk of your life, your death, anon."

I leaned my head against the rough stone wall of the cave and closed my eyes. I didn't know what this strange spirit-man would do while I was asleep, but I was finding that I cared less. He had been nothing but kind to me. My head was spinning, I was in pain, and I let sleep take me away from my concerns.

I WOKE to a room with a fire burned low to embers and no sign of my benefactor. I didn't know how much time had passed. My injuries still throbbed with a low pain, but the nap had at least restored my energy.

I closed my eyes, pulling my Sense in around me. The focus came to me, and I extended my awareness out into the world.

The cave wall behind me separated me from another chamber. Cythymau puttered about in there, preparing some sort of an inclined shelf with a number of straps covered in runes. Next to it...

Next to it was a girl who put Jeanelle to shame. My stupid teenage hormones raced into my broken body as I Sensed her; she was strapped naked onto the platform with those same rune-covered straps. Her auburn hair fell past the platform in its wavy lengths. Her eyes were open, but locked into a thousand-yard stare.

My arousal at Sensing her was immediately quenched when I felt the link between her and Cythymau. Power seemed to run through the straps. It drained from her, emanating towards the strange little man with the blue tattoos. A shiver ran down my spine.

Next to her, Cythymau prepared a second platform, and a second set of straps.

Hopeless, I knew, but I had to try. Using my Sense, I relocated a large portion of the rock wall between us above Cythymau's head. He spun, waving his arm above his head, sending the rock crashing harmlessly into the side of the cave wall.

"Whuft! You've got a Sense on you, lad, and no mistake. Why the attack, though? I think I've been kind to you. The rules of hospitality tell us you're to do likewise." Cythymau looked at me with a soft smile on his face, but his eyes were steel behind his lying mouth. We both knew who that second platform was for.

"Who is she, Cythymau? Another summoner from my world?"

His head swiveled as though noticing the redhead for the first time. "Her? She's fulfilling her part of the bargain. I helped her with a Lycaon, she agreed to give me what I needed. All she has to do is lie there. It's not so hard, really. And she saved many by doing it. Would you not do the same? Ah, decision time is upon us, is it not?"

A rumbling shook the earth; I knew it. The portal had opened back up in this world, and Rick was on his way.

He had followed me through the portal. Grace hadn't sent me away from danger; she'd used me to send danger away from everyone else. My survivor's guilt vanished entirely—mostly because it looked like I wasn't going to be the survivor, and she was.

"Very clever. The Cornuprocyon approaches. I will have it consume you when it gets here. Then I will send it back through the portal after your Grace. You can die here in futility, or..."

Or I could agree to his terms. I could lie down on that platform, making a prisoner of myself and giving him my power. His steely gaze didn't flinch away from me as the side of the cave blew in, revealing Rick the Cornuprocyon slavering in the newly made entrance.

My Sense suddenly flared with the power running between the tattoos on Cythymau's body to Rick. *That* was where I'd heard that voice, that peculiar turn of phrase. Cythymau had been controlling Rick this entire time.

"This was a *setup?* To snag *me?*"

"Whuft! You think too much of yourself, boy. *You* are a happy accident. Still, I would keep to my word. This Cornuprocyon would stay in this world, as would you. Your city—Spokane, yes? It would be safe from any of my beasts. I would have no more interest in it. You can take your rest here, with me, and save your city and your mentor." His voice was level, calm. He held the cards here and he knew it. I made no sudden move, Sensing out the power running between him and Rick.

"If it helps," he went on, "you two *did* manage to thwart me a bit. I was expecting more of the Grove from the city called Seattle to respond to Spokane, but they only sent one summoner, and a mid-level one at that. Seattle wasn't nearly as vulnerable as it should have been; the beasts I sent there were handily defeated. Sad, really. My timetable's pushed back a bit."

That seemed cold comfort, given my position.

"So," Cythymau said, keeping those eyes fixed on me. "Decision time is upon you. I wish it had been more pleasant." He gestured toward the redhead under the straps. "Andrea here agreed without getting the full terms. Much more congenial. You, I'm afraid, still must agree. I wish it weren't this painful for you, but there you have it." His tone was still pleasant and warm, but it sent shivers down my spine.

I remained silent, trying to buy time. He wanted me alive; that was my only leverage. He wasn't going to use Rick's full power to kill me instantly; he wanted to strap me in and steal my power to add to his own. His promise was simply to leave Spokane alone, but if I got onto that platform he would use my power to attack my world.

It was a devil's bargain he was offering, and taking it would be worse than suicidal. As my only other option was, in fact, suicidal, that made it the better choice.

I closed my eyes and gathered what I could into my Sense. I tried to focus on the bond between Rick and Cythymau. Then I slammed my own power into it as hard as I could. Cythymau's eyes widened at the raw force of my Sense. His expression hardened.

"Whuft! You're a strong one, lad. No mistake there." The cord of power wavered back and forth as the two of us struggled.

Our focus bore completely on one another, and his slowly began to overcome mine. I may have a potent Sense, but his power was amplified by leeching the girl he called Andrea. Slowly he began to overwhelm my attack on his link to Rick, his face blank with concentration.

Which is why it completely blindsided him when Rick's kinetic force drove him into the wall. I seized the distraction to shatter the link between Cythymau and Rick. The Cornuprocyon looked like he wasn't very happy with Cythymau. The small, weathered summoner stood away from the wall, his own blood flowing over his rune tattoos.

Andrea. In the confusion of Rick's attack, I ran to the girl's side. I jerked the first strap away from her forehead, and her eyes focused on me.

"I'm getting you out of here," I said. Behind me, a crash indicated that the fight between Rick and Cythymau was in full force. I could do this. I reached for the straps securing her wrists and unbound her left. Her hand began to move. That was a good sign. My heartbeat began to race as I reached across her for the right strap.

Suddenly a hook wrapped around my spine and jerked. I fell through the world, the scene with Rick, Andrea, and Cythymau dropping away on all sides. It was strong and it was painful, but I had used up what power I had managed to regain in shattering the link between Cythymau and Rick. Helplessly I went along as it dragged me off to whatever new demon awaited.

And I had left Andrea behind.

I hit the pavement hard and skidded along it, tearing flesh away in bits and chunks. I came to rest and started to scramble up to determine what new opponent awaited me.

"Hey," said Grace. "Turns out your Uncle Herman knew what he was talking about."

GRACE

THE BREATH I'd been holding flew out of me when Robert reappeared. There had been a chance my tag wouldn't work at all, that I had just stranded a defenseless seventeen-year-old alone in the Cornuprocyon's home Weave. Thereby saving the cops, but actually making the menace stronger. Oh, and killing my brand-new apprentice in the process. Now that he had made it back safely, all the bravado completely drained out of me. Immense relief flowed through me that at least Uncle Herman's formula had worked. My information for the dam showdown had gone so sideways.

Robert stood by the side of the road waiting for me, barely alert. I told him to hold on to any news he had until we were away from official eyes. The summons to bring him back had been excruciating, both mentally and physically. I needed to get us both away from here or I wouldn't be able to walk either. The world already looked fuzzy around the edges.

First, we had to get the situation here under wraps.

I peered around at the dead and injured deputies with a horrible knot of guilt forming in my stomach. We still had a lot of wounded. There was no helping poor Deputy Rosen, so I left him where he lay staring sightlessly up at the sky. I sent the bent GAU-8 Avenger back to Seattle Headquarters with a strong premonition of the coming headache from having used, and also essentially destroyed, the Seattle Grove's biggest gun.

Cradling my abused arm, I walked over to Frank Allen to see if he was conscious, but also to have one last talk with him before the ambulances got here, if I could. His eyes were alert, but struggling to remain so. I summoned another blanket and stooped so I didn't loom over him.

"Detective," I said softly, so only he could hear me. "That was some mighty fine shooting. I believe the Spokane County Sheriff's office just managed to defeat a rogue summoner and drive her demon back into its own dimension. It's not every department that could boast that. The paramedics will be here shortly."

"You defeated it," he rasped. "Not me."

"Ah, but the honest truth is, I couldn't have done it without your covering fire. And no one will believe you if your report says the summoner saved the day. That way leads to demotion and a psych evaluation. You and I both know it.

"I'm asking for more medical aid to be sent here to help the child in the hospital and your men. If I succeed, I will have brought one of my most precious allies to help you. I hope that I have your silence, if not your support at that time."

"This medical aid—another summoner?"

"It will be someone who has devoted her entire life to learning how to heal impossible sicknesses and injuries."

I got up. Emergency vehicle lights began to flash on the horizon. "Come on, Robert. It's time to go."

He gave a jerky nod. We limped off into the darkness away from the approaching sirens.

IT HAD BEEN two days since the showdown on I-90. The burn on my shoulder had scabbed over, but moving my left arm proved extremely painful and difficult. The side of my face that had smashed into the pavement when Rick crushed the GAU-8 was also in the process of scabbing over and turning interesting shades of purple and brown. Robert didn't fare much better. His rib cage looked like a painful piece of modern art. We'd wrapped his ribs as soon as we'd summoned his rust bucket and got back to Uncle Herman's the first night, but I desperately wanted to have someone with medical training look at them. While the healer was over here, I'd shove Robert in her direction.

There would be a memorial for the fallen deputies over the weekend. According to official reports, the Spokane County Sheriff's department had defeated the summoner at high cost and forced her summoned monster back to where it came from. Detective Allen had at least done me one good favor. According to the reports, the rogue summoner had died, killed by the monster's last attack before the police drove it away. No one was looking for me.

I wrote my report and sent it back to the Seattle Grove that first night. I impatiently waited for them to dispatch the medical summoner they'd promised, and honestly, I thought they could have been a bit faster about it. Seattle is only two hundred and eighty-nine miles from Spokane, and it had been two days already! I could have walked between the headquarters in that amount of time. I hoped, for Robert's sake, that the antibiotics the hospital gave the other kid had proved to be more potent than expected. At least I hadn't seen Duane's name in the newspaper obits.

I suppose, in Seattle's defense, there had been a rash of flash flood warnings for the areas downstream of the Post Falls dam. But the warnings and road closures had been in effect less than twelve hours. Robert and I hadn't done permanent damage to the dam after all, and the city officials handled it all pretty swiftly. If it didn't end in major property destruction or loss of life, I called it a win.

A note suddenly piffed into being on the table. I picked it up and looked down at Amy's handwriting.

Hey, Grace,

The Seattle Grove is dispatching a contingent to the Spokane Valley Medical Center. We expect to be in Spokane this evening by about five. Please let me know a safe meeting place, as Ms. Miller is coming with the contingent and would like to hold a briefing session before moving to the hospital. Just so you know, the Grove is very upset with you. Something about a last line of defense, and you breaking it or something. I'm not clear on it. Either way, I can't wait to see you this evening, and your apprentice! Congrats on succeeding against the odds. As your friend, I am selfishly pleased, and determined to keep a better eye on you from now on!

See you later. Amy

I jotted a note back to her setting up a meeting place near the hospital. I also let her know Robert and I were both injured, so if Ms. Miller needed us to accompany the contingent to the hospital, we would also need some healing beforehand. Otherwise, we would be swarmed by doctors the moment we walked in the door.

She sent back an acknowledgment. Robert and I piled into his rust bucket to drive to Spokane yet again. My nerves thrummed at the thought. The whole way there, I kept looking in the rearview mirror to confirm the Cornuprocyon wasn't lurking on the horizon.

The trip itself turned out uneventful, but my nerves felt like they'd been stretched too thin by the time we pulled into the parking lot of the Spokane Valley library. Per Robert, it had a conference room in the basement we could use for the meeting. He'd already used his foster parents' library card to reserve it. I worried his foster parents might notice the card being used, but he seemed sure neither of them went to the library anyway.

Robert's injuries were mostly hidden under his shirt, so he went in to talk to the librarians. The real benefit of the conference room was a side door leading directly outside, avoiding the main entrance. It opened and Robert popped his head out, waving me in.

We only had to wait a few minutes before the Seattle Grove contingent started filing in. They had brought ten people, including Ms. Miller, Seattle Grove historian. I dreaded the coming chat, which I expected to focus squarely on my deficiencies and the mall. Amy started to wave cheerily, but froze when she saw my face.

"Grace! Your face—it looks horrible."

"I told you I wasn't fit to be seen in public," I joked feebly. Amy frowned, her brow wrinkling fiercely. She spun around on her heel and stomped up to Ms. Miller, hands on hips.

"Look at her face! You sent one summoner alone to take down something that demolished an entire Grove. And you have the *gall* to be mad about some piece of equipment she took or broke to do it? She didn't put it in the report, but look at her! She almost died. The skin on half her face is missing! And you're going to reprimand her? Really?"

"Amy..." I began.

"You shut up! I can't believe you didn't tell me you needed help. Even if the Grove couldn't send anyone else, I would have come." Amy seemed of the opinion that *she* was the only one allowed to reprimand me.

I walked up and wrapped her in a big hug, ignoring the stab of pain through my shoulder. "I know. I know you would have come. Thank you for being such an awesome friend, but it wouldn't make me feel any better if you'd gotten injured, too. And I'm perfectly fine. Nothing that won't mend with a little time." She actually started *crying* into my good shoulder, putting me at a total loss. I looked at Robert. "I don't look that bad, do I?"

"Only about B-horror-movie grade. You still have a long way to go if you want to be taken for a real zombie."

I frowned at him. Ms. Miller cleared her throat. "Well, Amy is somewhat right. Lesley, if you could come help Grace and her apprentice look a little more...whole." She winced visibly at her choice of wording.

A tall summoner with pale brown hair and light blue eyes stepped forward, introducing herself to Robert as Lesley Anglino. I'd known Lesley since right after I moved to Seattle in 1998. I'd been almost certain that between her and Amy they'd be able to pressure the Council into letting her come. Groves like to keep their healers happy, otherwise the healers have a distressing tendency to move to more hospitable Groves. No Grove turns away a healer.

She smiled at me and told me she'd seen worse. I assured her *I* might look worse, but I believed Robert's injuries were more serious, which she quickly confirmed. Awkwardly he pulled his shirt off over his head so she could get a better look. If anything, the bruising looked worse than before. He turned bright red all the way up to his ears when Lesley placed her hands on either side of his rib cage over the bandages. I snickered. I couldn't help it. Teenage boys have waaaaay too many hormones.

She sat with her head bowed, and I could feel her Sense extending. As she worked, she kept up a light conversation with Robert, telling him what she was doing so he wouldn't freak out. I can only imagine that having one's bones rearranged by someone else feels bizarre, even if the pain is being redirected. Lesley realigned his ribs and started them mending, and coaxed the muscles to repair themselves in his sprained ankle within the space of fifteen minutes. The bruises on his face and arms faded away as I watched. I knew medical summoners were badass, but I'd never watched one work firsthand before. Lesley pulled Robert's bones and muscles back together with an ease that seemed effortless, though I knew it took great skill and focus. He would still be sore, but she took months off his recovery and ensured everything would heal correctly.

Ms. Miller stepped up beside me and said in a low tone, "While you two were over here fighting the Cornuprocyon, Seattle Grove was also inundated by wave after wave of summoned creatures. The little demons you banished the day before you left were only the beginning. We could not have sent backup even had you requested it, because our teams had their hands full banishing creatures and sewing up holes in the Weave every day. As soon as we got one shut, another one opened. We are researching the Cythymau spirit that you and Robert describe in the report. I will let you know if I discover anything useful."

"I am so sorry," I said, my stomach sinking into my feet. "I didn't realize."

"I know." She smiled gently. "But you understand why the

disappearance of the weapon reserved for the Grove's last defense met with such chagrin and outrage. The attacks have stopped since you and Robert defeated the Cornuprocyon, so it did not turn into as big an issue as it might have. And it also lends weight to your apprentice's story of the two events being linked. I have several people trying to discover the identity of the girl Andrea. So far we have not come up with any leads. It would be useful to know how great the time dilation Robert experienced is. Currently we are going through paper records that date all the way back to the turn of the century, so as you can imagine it is a slow process."

"Even if we can't discover who she is, a rescue mission should be attempted." I frowned. "Surely her identity isn't a requisite for sending aid."

"All of our experience with this Visitor indicates he is extremely hostile and very intelligent," Ms. Miller countered. "How do we know the girl Andrea is not another trap, otherwise? Any teenage boy is likely to want to rescue a maiden in distress."

She raised her brows at me. "Even if you'd gone to the other world, you would not be likely to leave another summoner behind. You've already proven that." She glanced significantly at my new apprentice.

I blew a breath out in frustration.

"In any case, it will not do the girl any good if we send in a squad without knowing his true strength and Cythymau captures the whole group. Surely, both you and your apprentice see the wisdom of that, given the last few days."

I didn't totally agree, but we didn't know what Cythymau was capable of by a long shot. The Cornuprocyon could be the tip of the iceberg. Robert and I alone wouldn't be much of a rescue either. That was so far over in the suicidal column that even *I* thought it was a bad idea. Still, I'd keep researching it on my own and see if I could gain us more allies willing to risk a rescue.

I gave a terse nod to Ms. Milller for the time being. She took that as permission to move on to other subjects.

"I am evaluating whether members of the Seattle Grove can be left here for a time to help you stabilize Spokane's Weave and re-establish the Grove here. I'll let you know before I leave. Amy has asked to be transferred here, and I have granted that request. After seeing your condition and that of your apprentice, I admit that the urgency of the situation here has become a little more obvious."

Lesley finished tending Robert's wounds and waved me over. My injuries were taken care of in a matter of minutes, and we got ready to head out to rescue Duane at the Valley Hospital. A thought occurred to me.

"Are we all going into the hospital?" I asked Ms. Miller.

"Yes, why?"

"A smaller group might be better. The hospital will be crawling with deputies because the injured cops were transported there. They also have security cameras."

"If there is the possibility of a large police presence, a bigger group is better. There is no way that a group of ten summoners can be subdued by one or two deputies, or even ten deputies. I have arranged hospital badges and disguises for us all, so the security cameras should not be an issue. You didn't think the whole delay was just because the council dragged its heels, did you?" She shot me a look that clearly communicated we both knew that was exactly what I'd thought.

I frowned.

"Don't worry. The badges will not be linked to anyone at the Grove or cause anyone else harm. *I* don't plan to pull another Spokane Valley Mall incident," Ms Miller said wryly. "Plus, we will leave most of our group outside as guards while Lesley heals the boy."

She had me there. "Fair enough."

The disguises turned out to be scrubs with visitor badges and caps that proclaimed us to be observers from a college nursing program. There was even a blue and white tote to replace my usual cavernous shoulder bag. Lesley, as the instructor, got to keep her lab coat. Ms. Miller finished by handing Robert and me shaggy wigs. Suddenly we were both blonds. With everyone properly disguised, we trouped out of the library and drove over to the hospital.

At the doors we gathered up our contingent and started down to the elevator lobby with Lesley in the lead. The name on one of the hospital rooms caught my eye: Francis Allen.

"Wait." I pointed at the placard. "I believe this is the detective who helped us defeat the Cornuprocyon. Let me check really quick. If Lesley would heal him as well, I believe we can get some goodwill from law enforcement here. He already reported me as killed in the last fight."

"Why would you show yourself to him if he believes you dead? That seems foolish."

"He knows I didn't die; he allowed me to leave."

"It seems a big risk," she said doubtfully.

"He kept Robert and me alive. The demon hurt him even more horribly because of it. He's already put his life on the line for his men and us before. He's a good man. I would feel guilty forever if we don't at least ensure his wounds heal correctly. His legs were shattered, and that's before the GAU-8 got smashed up with him in it." My voice spluttered to a stop as I realized *who* I was talking to about the piece of heavy weaponry I *shouldn't* have had.

"You put the detective in the Avenger?" Ms. Miller asked incredulously. "And he provided cover fire? I knew you had fired it, and that it had been destroyed, but..."

"He was an asset I had available. And we did manage to get rid of the Cornuprocyon."

Ms. Miller sighed. "All right, we will take Lesley straight back to the Seattle Grove from the hospital, but I'll allow her to provide the detective with healing. On one condition. He must agree to be blindfolded first. Then, you and she may go into the room together. I do not want to expose more Grove faces to the detective than we have to. The rest of us will wait out here in the lobby."

I opened the door and stepped in. Allen lay amid the white sheets and blankets in a full body cast. It looked like he was asleep. I pulled a bouquet of flowers "out of my bag" and put them on his night stand.

"Detective," I called tentatively as I walked up to the bed. "Are you awake? I've brought the help I spoke to you about before."

His eyes opened. "Ms. Moore?" he whispered.

He didn't even blink at my altered appearance. I frowned and reached a hand up to double-check. The cap and blond wig were still firmly on.

"Yes, sir. I've brought the medical person I promised before."

"That's nice," he mumbled, making me wonder how many drugs they had him hooked up to.

I paused. "She has agreed to heal you, but I need to blindfold you. It is the only way we could think to shield her identity. Grove healers are very protected."

"Go ahead then and let her do it," he croaked. "If she kills me it can only be a relief."

"Don't say that," I chided as I fished a scarf out of my tote and tied it over his eyes. "You'll be just fine."

"I don't feel just fine. I need to have my brain examined." A flash of pain twisted his mouth, and I patted his shoulder on reflex.

I motioned Lesley in. She lowered her head and began healing him, beginning with his shattered legs, speaking to him in that calm voice the whole time. I admired her voice. It reminded me of a sedative all by itself. She spoke to him the whole fifteen minutes she was realigning his bones and mending his injuries. Her voice didn't crack from dryness once. I'm sure I would have sounded like a frog by the end.

Lesley finished by letting him know she had healed everything she could without bringing undue suspicion on him, that everything should mend well. She started to move away from the bed, but his voice called, stronger than before, "Ms. Moore, can your friend do this for the rest of my deputies? At least the ones that are bad off?" He turned his blindfolded head toward where Lesley had last been speaking. "I really appreciate you doing this."

Lesley smiled down at him. "Of course. If my aid is requested, then I am happy to help."

"Will the Grove let you do that?" I asked doubtfully.

"I am a doctor; they can't stop me." For the first time she gave me a big toothy grin. It looked out of place on her soft face. I must be a bad influence on people.

Briskly she exited the room. I removed the blindfold and started to follow, but Frank called me back. "Thank you," he said.

"You and your men were injured because of me. It is more of an apology," I said simply.

"If your friend can really help my men, then I may have to reevaluate my views."

I realized we'd won a huge concession. "Thanks." I leaned down and kissed his cheek. "I appreciate that. If she says she can do it, then she will."

I gave him a final wave and led our group to Duane's room, my customary bouquet of flowers in hand. I am a firm believer in traditions. They give people something to hold onto in stressful situations.

The scene that greeted us seemed eerily familiar. Robert's ex-girlfriend Jeanelle sat crumpled up against one wall in the hallway as though she had never left. It felt as if Robert and I were taking part in a play and the other actors had already reset the scene and awaited a cue from us.

As the footfalls of our little group echoed down the hallway, the girl lifted her head and leapt to her feet. "Omigod, Robert!" She started toward him. "Are you here to save Duane? I heard you were arrested, and I thought he was going to die for sure."

She tried to throw her arms around him but he stepped to the side, saying gruffly, "I brought someone who can help. Wait here."

Ms. Miller motioned Lesley forward and nodded to me. "You and Robert accompany Lesley. We will keep this girl company out here."

"I'll probably be sending out one more girl," I said as I opened the door.

As predicted, the other girl sat in the chair next to the bed. I put my hands on my hips as I asked, "Do we have to have another showdown?"

The drama queen sniffed and flounced up. "I'll leave, but I'm going to tell the cops you're back. You crazy bitch!" She huffed right out the door and into Ms. Miller's grasp.

"That won't be necessary." Ms. Miller marched her back into the room. "Let her watch."

"What?" I asked.

"We'll see if she wants to get the person who brings her friend back to health arrested. That doesn't seem right, does it?" She pinned the drama queen with her eyes.

"I'll watch," the girl blustered. "But I don't believe you can heal him."

A weak voice came from the doorway. "Can I watch too?" Jeanelle peeked around the door frame, her dark green eyes huge. She was a looker. No wonder Robert got so twisted up over her.

I looked at Ms. Miller and shrugged. I motioned her inside and shut the door so we couldn't be seen from the hallway. Honestly, there really wasn't that much to see. Lesley settled herself on the edge of the kid's bed and placed one hand on his chest just above his sternum and the other lower on his abdomen just above his bellybutton. As she lowered her head, I felt her Sense envelop the boy's form.

Her head whipped up suddenly. She looked straight at Robert. Damn it. I'd been deliberately vague about what Robert had done to Duane in the report. Robert met her eyes for a moment and hung his head. She looked from him to me.

I grimaced. "It was an accident. I've already dealt with it." "What?" asked Ms. Miller. "Dealt with what?"

I waited for Lesley to explain and totally throw me and Robert further into the doghouse. She considered Robert for another moment, shook her head, and lowered it again, concentrating on her Sense. "This boy is in very bad shape. This will take some time."

Lesley worked for the better part of an hour. Duane's color slowly came back. When we'd entered the room, he looked ashen. Gradually, he regained a normal skin tone, and it may have just been me, but it looked like his face became less gaunt.

The teenage girls in the room seem to hang on the sick boy's every breath. I couldn't remember ever being that young. The boy's eyes fluttered, and Lesley leaned back with a big sigh. "The antibiotics should be able to take it from here. He'll still be weak and need to be in the hospital for awhile. He'll get steadily better from now on, though."

Robert looked like he might cry. He tried to put on his teenage-boy-tough-face, and failed. Lesley stood up, stretched, and walked over to ruffle his hair.

"How do you know he's better?" the drama queen asked shrilly. "He still hasn't woken up! You people are all frauds. I should have gotten the cops." She marched toward the door.

A groan came from the bed. "Cindy?" Duane's voice came out a bare croak. "Cindy, where am I? What happened?"

Cindy flew back to the bed and flung herself on Duane in a giant hug. He smiled weakly up at her. She leaned over and kissed him long and hard on the mouth. I could almost touch the flood of teenage hormones in the room.

Jeanelle watched from the back of the room like a deer in headlights. After it became obvious that Duane and Cindy weren't coming up from their lip-lock any time soon, she gave a choked sob. She looked around the room wildly, tears streaking her face, and collapsed toward Robert's arms. I'm not a big fan of teenage drama generally, but I know that what he did next cost him.

He caught her at arm's length and slowly shook his head, a stoic look on his face. He pushed her gently away, then walked out of the room without looking back. Jeanelle sank to the floor, crying into her hands.

Ms. Miller looked perplexed as we left. "Teenage romance drama," I told her. "I'm glad not to be that young anymore." I watched Robert's back as he walked down the hallway in front of me. I didn't follow him. Right now, he needed the space.

THE NEXT WEEKEND, I attended the memorial for the deputies who had been killed, wearing a black sweater, jeans, and sunglasses, complete with the blonde wig Ms. Miller let me keep. Captain Carlenos gave a heartfelt eulogy that brought tears to my eyes. Our gaze met once during the ceremony, but I slipped off before the end. I doubted he'd recognized me, but I didn't want to put more of a strain on the Sheriff's department than I had to. Better if they knew as little about me and my current whereabouts as possible. I still don't know exactly what Detective Allen did, but they declared Robert to be under the "thrall" of an evil summoner (me) when he broke into the Sheriff's office and the prosecutor dropped the charges. Officially, he was never a summoner himself; just controlled by one. Robert went back to school and returned to his fosties. I'm sure they were overjoyed to see him, even though he made it sound like they faked it.

Ms. Miller came to see me and Robert at Uncle Herman's before she left. Her demeanor projected an illusion of business as usual. Robert had resumed school, but he drove the rust bucket down to see me on Fridays and Saturdays. From what he said, the fosties thought he was with Jake.

"About the matter of the GAU-8 Avenger, I am recommending that no disciplinary action be taken at present," she said. "However, in the future, please be sure to obtain permission before taking such an asset out of Grove hands."

"Yes, ma'am." I wanted to get it over with. Robert shuffled his feet.

I didn't do that, at least.

She shot us a disapproving look and rummaged through her handbag. She fished something out, took a deep breath, and paused dramatically. "Grace Anne Moore," she announced. "I have been authorized to appoint you the Spokane Grove's temporary director."

She handed me a golden rune token. I felt weird taking that status symbol. It weighed heavily in my hand. Usually there's a whole ceremony to appoint a new director, but apparently we were doing away with that, though it made me uncomfortable to let it go. Like I said, to me tradition equals something to hold onto in stressful situations. This qualified as stressful.

"I *am* honored, Ms. Miller. But I don't think I'm qualified," I stammered, my stomach doing a flip-flop. I've never, *never* wanted to be in charge. Hadn't they seen how much trouble I got *myself* into?

Having an apprentice to be responsible for was bad enough. "Plus, there's an awful lot of people around here who think I'm dead."

Ms. Miller shook her head at me in a way that I tried not to interpret as condescending. "As the new Spokane Grove director, you don't need to be so formal. You may call me Analisa. And you are qualified *enough*. I have a feeling we will be talking a lot more. You may find being dead to your advantage in some ways. It *does* make it difficult, if not impossible, for you to go back to your apartment in Seattle without causing an even larger mess, I would think. The Spokane Grove needs a director, and you need new living arrangements. It seemed like a perfect interim solution for everyone."

That sounded more ominous than comforting.

"I'm the temporary Grove director. How long is temporary?" I couldn't help asking.

"Until you find someone from Spokane who is able to take over."

I glanced over at Robert, all legs and arms in his frayed T-shirt and scruffy running shoes.

Unless Spokane summoners suddenly started popping out of the woodwork, I had a long wait in front of me.

In the meantime, Robert needed training, more than the on-the-fly crash course he'd gotten from me these last few weeks. *This* time, Cythymau's gambit had failed, but that didn't mean he'd given up. Not by a long shot. I'd eat stale fast food for a month before anyone could convince me differently.

I looked at Robert again. Not enough time. Cythymau would be back way before Robert became a full-fledged summoner in his own right.

The official story from the Sheriff's office had killed me off, but I wasn't sure I was done with law enforcement, either. Too many cops had seen what had happened on the freeway, and not *all* of them believed I wasn't at fault. Allen and Carlenos I could probably trust in a pinch, but the others would jump on Robert or me if given half a chance.

I wondered if Seattle realized all the leeway they'd handed me along with this new problem. But even if they did, they had probably decided it was preferable to being tied too closely to whatever went down when Cythymau came back for a rematch. No matter where you go, you can't get away from politics. Not even if you defeat a real man-eating monster in the ninth inning. Sure, we'd saved the day and the city. Our reward was to go get ready for the next catastrophe.

Don't worry guys. Robert, Amy, and me? We've *got* this.

THE END

ABOUT THE AUTHORS

FROG AND ESTHER JONES are a husband-and-wife writing team who live in the wilds of the Olympic rainforest in Washington State. They can usually be found pursuing one of several geeky pursuits, including board games, video games, anime, rpgs, or firing things out of Frog's catapult (a hand-built Roman onager).

You know, just the common things you might find yourself deciding to do after sitting around the garage on a Saturday.

You can find out more about what they're up to, and forthcoming projects at www.jonestales.com

CPSIA information can be obtained
at www.ICGtesting.com
Printed in the USA
LVHW020756060322
712270LV00001B/4